I0645422

From Laurie Bell:

In *The Stones of Power* Series:
The Butterfly Stone
The Tiger's Eye
The Crow's Heart

More from Wyvern's Peak Publishing

The Secret Watchers Series
by Lauren Lynne
The Recalcitrant Project
by Lauren Lynne

Charlie Sullivan and the Monster Hunters
by D.C. McGannon & C. Michael McGannon

THE CROW'S HEART

THE CROW'S HEART

WYVERN'S PEAK PUBLISHING

An imprint of The McGannon Group, Ltd. Co.

The Crow's Heart

The Stones of Power, Book 3

Written by Laurie Bell – www.solothefirst.wordpress.com

Published by Wyvern's Peak Publishing. 2022
An imprint of The McGannon Group, Ltd. Co.

Cover design by www.FlirtationDesigns.com

The Crow's Heart / by Laurie Bell – 1st Ed.

Summary: Tracey Masters and her friends go undercover and travel to England to track down the next Stone of Power; digging up concealed history, crossing lines with friends and enemies both old and new, and discovering a conspiracy against their very livelihoods

1   2   3   4   5   6   7   8   9

ISBN-13: 978-0-9990212-8-6

www.WyvernsPeak.com

The Crow's Heart is dedicated to Taylah Bell. Thank you for reading!

Also to Skye, Mark, Bree and Amy, Mia and Isabel, Chloe and Bryce, Elsa, Emily and Hannah. Lisa, Jenny and Kathy. Thank you for waiting.

To every child who opens a book and gets lost in another world. You are why I do this. Be brave, be strong, be kind. Help whenever you can and read to whoever will listen. Magic is inside you if you believe it is. Be awesome. Keep trying.

-Laurie Bell

I tried again to warn those whose endings I saw before they came to pass. But when my warning proved true, I was thought a witch. A foul prophet who supped with the devil and did his bidding.

1

It is my greatest wish that they get along. I fear that the distrust between them will cause a rift I cannot repair—

"Sorry, coming through. Sorry." Jonny shuffled past his mom sitting in the aisle seat and stumbled, thrusting out a hand to catch himself before he landed on Tracey in her window seat. The journal she held jolted at the movement. She clutched it to her chest as her friend dropped into his middle seat. As the tingling book pressed hard into the Butterfly Stone necklace hanging around her neck, a jolt ran through the book. It vibrated so much in her hands she had to tighten her grip on it. "Whoa."

"What?" Jonny asked, wriggling around to get comfortable. The plane seats were a tight squeeze for his long, lanky frame.

"The journal. It just went crazy." Tracey pressed her hands to the cover. "The tremors have stopped." She flipped the book open.

> *It is only up here that I feel free.*
>
> *I see forever as I stare into the distance. Here, there is no judgement. My mind is my own, my heartbeat is endless. Gift or curse? No one can see what I see when I peer into the future. I cannot speak of it. I can give no warning for there are none who would believe me. I am dismissed as fanciful, yet I am terrified of the truth.*
>
> *For I see how it ends.*
>
> *And I am alone.*

"Whoa! What?"

"What?" he asked.

"The journal! It just changed. It must have been when I pressed it against—" she lowered her voice to whisper "—when the journal touched the Butterfly Stone. It changed. The handwriting, the ink color, the voice, everything. And it stopped buzzing. It's been buzzing ever since Tony found it."

"Stephanie's journal? What did it change to? Is it still—?"

Tracey checked the cover page. "Oh look, Jonny. It says, *The Private Musings of Millicent Flowers*. This is so weird. It looks like another journal was hidden inside the other one. At least the words on the pages. I wonder why it was spelled?"

"So no one could read it, obviously. Magic and secrets, man. These stones. You know, I still can't believe my moms agreed to this. I can't believe yours did too. This. Is. So. Cool."

Jonny bounced in his seat so energetically Tracey worried it might take off with him in it. "It is super cool," she agreed brushing a hand over her wrinkled, navy-blue superhero shirt. She tucked the Butterfly Stone necklace back underneath it. How Jonny didn't look like he'd just got out of bed she didn't know. She was a sweaty, rumpled mess next to his tight jeans, creaseless red and yellow bowling shirt, and bowler hat.

His grin was enormous, taking up half of his glowing face. "I. Just. Can't. Even."

Tracey put her Prince Henry bookmark between the journal pages and grinned at Jonny's excitement. "When you went for that walk up the aisle, did you see what the others were doing?" Beside Jonny sat his mom, Martha. Cinematic music echoed from her earbuds, allowing her to ignore their excited chatter. Tracey stretched into a half stand to search the forward part of the plane for her friends. *Damian. You're looking for Damian.* Uncle Donny's unruly curls bobbed above the seat cushions in front of her.

"Tony's reading. Laura and Jilly are watching a movie." Jonny bounced some more. "Soooo, what do you think it's going to be like in England? I've never been there. Have you?"

"What's Damian doing?"

Jonny's grin slipped off his lips. "Kinda staring at nothing. His sister's asleep on his shoulder." Jonny lowered his voice. "So how are you going to do it?"

Tracey plopped back down into her seat. "What? Remove the evil Stone of Power his sister is forced to wear because of a deal I made? I have no idea."

"You promised him you would. I'm still thinking that was not smart."

Her skin tingled, thinking back on the moment Damian had asked her to help his sister, Kylie. "He was looking at me all … and his eyes were like … Jonny, I couldn't let him down."

"Girl, you are so gone on him, huh? You can't take your stone off and Jilly doesn't want to remove hers. What are you going to do?"

Tracey moaned. "I don't know."

Jonny grabbed his book out of the seat back pocket in front of him. He didn't open it. He tapped her arm with his elbow. "I don't think Damian's mom likes us. I keep getting squint eye from her, you know?"

It's me she doesn't like. Mrs. Carter had come with Damian and Kylie, and they were sitting all the way up the front half of the plane, just outside the business section. Mrs. Carter had not wanted to sit near Tracey and her friends. Tracey peered through the small oval window beside her shoulder. The fluffy white clouds beneath them and blue, blue sky seemed endless. Memories of the battle over the Stones of Power at school, and the agreement she had made with the stones' guardians, played back in her mind. When Tracey found the Butterfly Stone — the magical necklace her ancestor, Stephanie, once owned — she had no idea how much her life would change. First, her magic had become faulty. Then she became a target of the Shadowman and his evil boss Timothy. But what had really changed her life had been the discovery that the Butterfly Stone was one of a set of six stones created by the Mage-kind members of a secret sect. And Tracey's ancestor — Stephanie — had helped to create them. Timothy's spirit was stuck inside his stone, just as Stephanie was inside the Butterfly Stone. Timothy needed all six stones to recreate his body and return to power. If they were to stop him, Tracey and her friends had to find the stones first.

Kylie only wore Timothy's stone, the Serpent's Kiss, because Tracey had made a bargain with the stones to save Kylie's life, but the deal meant

Kylie couldn't use her magic. At all. Any magic use could allow Timothy to take control again. Tracey had made the right call. Holding Timothy's stone was like being marked for evil. Timothy has already possessed Kylie once. At the slightest slip, he would do so again.

Changing pressure inside the plane muted her hearing. Tracey yawned to make her ears crackle, but it didn't help. She pushed her worries about her friends aside to share in Jonny's excitement. They were on their way to England to find another Stone. If they found it, it was one less chance Timothy had to come back and the best chance Tracey had of freeing Kylie from Timothy's stone.

"Why aren't you sitting next to Jilly?" she asked Jonny.

"Ah." His voice dropped to a whisper. He shot his mom a quick, narrow-eyed glance to check if she was listening. She wasn't. "Mom keeps giving me these *looks*. My mama should have come instead. She wouldn't go on about it." Tracey hid her grin behind her hand. "Aw, stop it." Jonny peered at his mom again. She was absorbed in her movie. They could hear loud explosions coming from her headphones. Jonny scrubbed a hand over his neck. Tracey held up her hands as if to say, *"Me? I said nothing."*

Jonny's massive crush on Jilly was fully returned by the gorgeous Asian girl. Tracey thought it was epic trolling by his mom, Martha, who loved to make really loud observations about them being so cute together. Jonny squirmed every time.

Tracey leaned her head even closer to her friend and whispered. "What did your mom say when she found out about Jilly wearing the Tiger's Eye?"

"She's not happy about it." He sighed. "She's excited about the movie experience for us though. It's that we're all missing out on school to do it that she's flaming over."

"Agent Malden said he cleared the trip with all the parents," she reminded him. Agent Malden was their M-force contact and guardian for this trip, along with Tracey's uncle and Jonny's mom. Mrs. Carter had insisted she come too. The parents knew the real reason they were going to England, but their school had been told they had won a competition to be extras in Prince Henry's new movie. Luckily, Prince Henry—their friend and a secret M-force agent—had followed through and made the ruse a reality. But only after Jonny, Laura, Dave, and Tony raised hell about coming with the three stone protectors. They had threatened to spill the beans about the stones to everyone if they couldn't come. Agent Malden relented and somehow managed to get all of them on a plane within days of the battle at the school.

Tracey nibbled one fingernail, the polish tasted bitter in her mouth. She jammed her hands under her thighs to stop chewing on them further or from grabbing her cell phone. It was hidden away in the seat pocket in front of her. With her phone on airplane mode she couldn't even message her friends. Laura sat on the other side of the aisle. Jilly next to her in the middle and Tony had the far window seat. Tracey wished she knew why Laura had chosen to sit with Jilly and not her.

That little doubt monster still whispered in Tracey's ear about Laura's loyalty. Which was totally stupid. True, their friendship had been rocky lately, but if Tracey could just sit and chat with Laura, like they used to do before Jilly appeared, they would sort out the lingering misunderstandings. Jilly wasn't trying to steal Laura away. It had just been that stupid "hidden one" curse affecting Jilly. Once they had broken the curse, everything should have gone back to normal.

Only it was still weird. Everyone had been excited for Jilly to join their group. Jonny because of his crush, Laura because of their instant friendship. Even Tony had taken to sharing his love of books with the smarter girl. Tracey's instant dislike had come from the curse. She had thought her jealousy would melt away when they broke it. It hadn't. Tracey just wanted her best friend back and she was being forced to share. "Should I message Damian?" *I meant to say Laura, didn't I?*

Jonny shrugged. "You can't anyway. Airplane mode. Besides, what would you say? I think he's still sore about Kylie."

"It's not my fault," Tracey said. It really kinda was though. She sighed. "At least Prince Henry has a lead on one of the stones. Hopefully, when we find it, it'll help us figure out how to take Kylie's off. Still, should I say sorry again?"

"He knows it's not your fault. He was the one who gave her the stone. You were just trying to help."

"Yeah, but he must be mad. He's barely spoken to me." And boy did that smart. Her crush on Damian had not diminished in the slightest by his inattention.

"He's sitting all the way up front with his mom and Kylie. Come on, you haven't really had a chance to talk to him either. He's probably not as mad as you think."

Tracey tugged out her phone, holding it up so Jonny could see the screen. "No messages." Jonny shrugged. On a roll now Tracey added, "and Sarah's sitting up there too."

"She's Kylie's friend."

"Ugh." Tracey scrunched lower in her seat. Agent Malden sat a few rows behind them in a row all to himself. Jonny sensed where her thoughts had gone and rose up to glance over his seat toward the rear of the plane. Tracey yanked him down. "What are you doing?"

"Just checking he's still there. Oh hey, the drinks trolley is coming."

"Where would Agent Malden go?"

"I dunno. He's a Mage-kind agent. Who knows what he can do?" Jonny pulled his bowler hat lower over his forehead. "Always feel like he's judging me."

"Not you," she reminded him. "It's me he has to watch."

"What if he casts an illusion to seem invisible and sneaks up on us?"

"Jonny, he can't turn invisible. I can't either. We can't fly or wield electricity or teleport. You know magic doesn't work like that. Besides," she waved her Mage-kind identification bracelet. The center glowed green. "We're not permitted to use magic outside home and camp."

He squinted at her. "Uh-ha, they tell ya you can't fly."

She snorted. "Okay, it would be super cool if we could, but we can't. We aren't superheroes."

"Trace, you don't know what those stones can do. No one does."

Her hand drifted up to cover the stone. "True." All she knew was that her ancestor, Stephanie, had filled the Butterfly Stone—a gray stone with a painted butterfly on it—with extraordinary amounts of magic. Magic that was still stored inside it. Magic that called to Tracey and tempted her to use it. "When I first put it on, Grandma, Mom and Dad, even Agent

Malden told me not to use it."

"I know. You seem to have more energy now. Getting used to double shielding, yeah?"

"Sure."

A doll-like, perfectly groomed flight attendant stopped her trolley beside Martha. Her lips were so red they almost glowed and her eyelashes seemed razor sharp. "Would you like something to drink?"

"Please," Martha said. "Just water. Kids?"

"OJ?" Jonny asked.

"Same." Tracey said, ignoring the flight attendant's intense stare. The woman's gaze flicked to Tracey's wrist. Tracey pulled her sleeve down over her bracelet and released a soft sigh. The bracelet identified her as Mage-kind and no matter how much she wanted to remove it, it was illegal to take it off. Her parents had protected everyone from Tracey's unintentional power use as a child by manipulating her identification bracelet not to expose her with a red flashing light when she slipped.

Grandma was teaching her how to handle her power. What was more, she had realized the Butterfly Stone did not control her. She could control it. In the last few days—since the battle at school—she had even started experimenting with it. Tracey also neglected to tell anyone what she was doing. Since the battle at school, she had found she had better control over her own magic and had stopped double-shielding. But Jonny didn't know that. None of her friends knew.

Tracey and Jonny drank their juice quickly, nearly spilling them as they pulled open the lids. Tracey stacked her empty cup into Jonny's and raised her tray. The sour expression from the flight attendant still grated.

She had locked her magic away when they boarded the airplane like all Mage-kind had to do. Even Agent Malden. Tracey hadn't deserved that dark look.

Jonny tapped her arm. "You still remember Jilly?"

Tracey rolled her eyes. It was not the first time they'd had this conversation, but unlike when the curse was still active, Tracey remembered each time Jonny had asked. "Yeah. Whatever the stones did when they touched broke the memory curse on Jilly for good." She tilted forward trying to see past Jonny but couldn't see Laura or Jilly. "Are they talking? Can you see?"

"Trace."

"I'm not jealous."

Jonny stared, blinking really slowly.

"I'm not. It's just … why is Laura sitting with Jilly and not me?" Tracey tugged her phone from the seat pocket in front of her again. No messages. She sighed and squeezed the case tightly.

"Everything's still a little messed up, isn't it?" Jonny said, covering her hand with his.

She turned her hand over and squeezed his fingers. "Yeah."

A shorn head and big shoulders rose up from the seat in front of Jonny. Dave Two peered down at Tracey. "Will you shut up! I'm trying to sleep."

Tracey glared back. Dave Betts. The one member of their crazy gang still trying to fit in. The school bully had become a reluctant team member when he discovered he was Mage-kind. Tracey and her friends were teaching him how to use his magic.

"Why are you even here?" she said to him. "You could've stayed home."

"No way. Where you go, I go. Every time you've found a stone you've needed my help. You need me." Dave Two — so named because his best friend at school was also named Dave — loomed over her. Mostly it was just shoulders and attitude. "This is my chance to become a breakout movie star and to learn to control my magic better. No way was I staying at home. Now shut it, so I can sleep."

"Uncle Donny!" Tracey whined.

Her uncle popped up beside Dave Two, all wild curls and tired eyes. "Kids — cut it out." He sat down again.

Dave's grin grew sharper. He winked at Tracey and plonked back down in his seat. Tracey moaned and shoved Jonny's shoulder. "Shift up. I've gotta go to the bathroom."

Jonny squeezed his lanky frame into a ball as Tracey inched past. Martha jerked as she was surprised out of her movie. She held her water up to raise her tray and shifted sideways letting Tracey shuffle past. Tracey stretched, reaching for the ceiling and heard several pops. "Don't cause trouble," Jonny called after her.

Despite Jonny's warning, Tracey could not stop herself from staring at Laura and Jilly as she moved into the aisle. Both girls had their eyes closed, and were snuggled up like best friends sharing an earbud each. Tony's head was buried in his book. Four flight attendants were still handing out drinks down the aisle near Damian and his mom, so Tracey headed toward the back of the plane. *I should message Laura again. Oh, I can't. No phone.* Tracey stopped a few rows away and peered back, hoping Laura would stand up and call out to her. She didn't. Tracey sighed. *Stop it. She's still your best friend. Only Jilly is now your friend too.*

Agent Malden sat a few rows back. The scent of his cinnamon after-shave tickled Tracey's nose before she got anywhere near him. *Mmmmm doughnuts.* He looked up at her approach. His eyes were a little red and his hair seemed grayer, hiding the white streak gained when he had helped them defeat the Shadowman. His blue suit and white shirt had wrinkles all over them, but at least he'd removed his tie. He was staring at a photo. Tracey caught a glimpse of it as he slipped it between the pages of the black leatherbound book he was reading. *Agent Striker?* Agent Malden's partner had died in the fight against the Shadowman. Tracey examined the thick tome as Malden slid it into the seat pocket in front of him. "What's up?" he asked.

"Nothing. Bathroom." Tracey continued past. Malden held up a hand.

"On your way back, stop for a bit. I want a chat."

"Sure," she agreed. When she reached the long, thin toilet door, she found it locked. The red occupied sign glared at her, making her bladder twitch. Bouncing from foot to foot, her thoughts returned to Laura. *Is she pretending to be asleep so she doesn't have to talk to me?* Tracey shook her head, forcing her brain to find a new topic to obsess over. Her thoughts landed on Damian. Now that the flight attendants had moved further along the plane, Tracey could just see Damian's black-jean covered leg poking into the aisle. She could say she needed to stretch her legs and wander up to say "hi." There might even be a spare seat up there. Then she could sit and talk to him about the flight or one of the in-flight movies — or just stare into his gorgeous brown eyes.

A thin-faced man with more stubble than was stylish sat in the final row beside the toilet, reading a book. He glanced up, aware Tracey was hovering. She shrugged as if to say, *"What? You know what I'm waiting for. I'm not reading over your shoulder."* He checked her wrist, and twitched, crossing his legs and leaned away from her.

Tracey held in another sigh. Even thirty thousand feet above the entire world, she was judged for what she was. With Agent Malden within earshot, she bit back her snappy comment and shuffled closer to the toilet door. It clicked as the lock disengaged and popped open. A round woman with a black, bob hairstyle and sharp eyebrows stepped out and stopped, surprised to find Tracey in front of her.

The woman's snooty gaze roamed up and down Tracey's body and froze on her Mage-kind identification bracelet. "You better be careful." The woman's voice was sharp. Her raised chin made her tiny eyes stare down the length of her nose at Tracey.

"What?"

"It's dangerous for your kind to be in the air. There should be a separate plane for you people."

If Tracey let her anger boil over, she might trigger her magic and make this horrible woman's fears come true. She gritted her teeth as the woman shuffled past, her ridiculous looking fluffy pink slippers scuffed against the floor. Tracey hid in the toilet and swiped a lone tear from her eye.

Why can't everyone be like Laura or Jonny and his mom? They've never treated me as if I'm different to a Norm. Slow, deep breaths helped calm Tracey's bubbling fury. The Butterfly Stone throbbed. It always knew when she was angry. Sometimes she wondered if the Butterfly Stone was making her anger worse. *Breathe.* When a soft knock rattled the door, she hurried to use the facilities, flushed and washed her hands all while avoiding her reflection in the mirror. She inhaled deeply and yanked open the door. Kylie stood outside phoofing her blond hair with her fingers, picking apart a large knot. Her eyes widened at Tracey and a giant smile broadened her lips.

"Oh hi, Tracey."

"Hey. How are you doing?" Tracey examined Kylie's pale face. "Is this your first time on a plane?"

Kylie shook her head, jangling her large hoop earrings. Her messy hair was held in place with a thick green metallic headband over her head like a crown. "Nah, I've been on heaps of planes. Goes with having a military dad, you know?"

"Oh yeah, of course. I've never been on one. It's um … "

"Boring? Yeah, once you've seen the movies and played all the games on your phone it's just one big, long boring trip. Try to sleep."

"I can't. I'm too excited." She smiled at Kylie's laugh. "How are *you* doing?" Tracey touched the Butterfly Stone beneath her wrinkled T-shirt. Kylie mirrored the move, pressing her hand to the lump under her shirt collar.

"All quiet. Whatever you did worked. I don't feel anything from it. And with this stupid headband on I can't even feel my own magic, which is weird because I can feel the headband humming and that's super annoying. Especially when I try to sleep. I wish I could take it off."

Tracey lowered her voice hoping Kylie would pick up on the hint and lower hers. "Yeah, that's a stone thing. Once it's locked onto us, it's stuck. So, the new headband Agent Malden gave you—"

"—sucks. The M-force doctor said it's stronger than the one the paramedics gave me. It's got a spell on it so I can't even shield anymore. No magic. Nothing." She held up her wrist. The glowing light that would normally be green and flash red if she used magic was an unnatural bright blue color.

"I'm sorry. It's there to stop Timothy from possessing you again."

Kylie scrunched her nose. "I know. I just don't like it."

"It's to keep you safe."

"You said the stone was going to do that. Why do I need this stupid headband too?"

"I guess the M-force doctor doesn't trust the stone to stop you from using magic. It's a safeguard. You'll say if —"

"—if I hear his voice. I will. I can't even feel the stone's magic anymore. I can't feel anything. Damian said you promised to find a way to take it off. I want everything to go back to normal, the way it used to be. I want my magic back."

Ah, yeah. The Promise. Tracey wished she knew how to do that. "So, um. How is Damian?"

Kylie grinned. "He talks about you *all* the time."

Tracey straightened her spine. "Really? I thought he was still mad at me."

"He's been arguing with Mom about it. He trusts you and he wants her to trust you too. I think it's because he likes you." Tracey squeaked at that information and Kylie laughed out loud. Heads turned in their direction as they giggled. Kylie pulled her hands away from her mouth. "Sarah says you like him too."

"Sarah needs to shut her big mouth," Tracey muttered. She knew Kylie could hear her and Kylie knew she had been meant to hear. *He likes me!* Tracey's cheeks flamed. *He likes me.*

Kylie's grin grew. "She says I talk about you too much. Not my mom. Sarah." Kylie's grin fell away. "Mom's mad. But that's not your fault. She's still dealing with the Mage-kind thing." Kylie scraped her feet against the floor.

"Oh, that sucks. I'm sorry," Tracey said.

"Not your fault like I said. But thanks anyway. I need to go." She pointed at the toilet door.

"Oh, sure. Sorry."

Kylie moved into the cubical and locked the door.

Tracey wandered back along the aisle toward Agent Malden. It was sad Kylie was having to deal with all of that, but letting slip Damian liked her gave Tracey a giddy feeling inside, like that time she'd had gas at the dentist. She stopped beside Agent Malden and slid into the empty seat across the aisle. "Hey."

He shoved his giant black book into the seat back pocket. *He should get that on an e-reader. Must be heavy to carry around.* Tracey caught the word *Magic* in the title.

"How's Kylie?" he asked.

While Tracey was in the bathroom, he had removed his suit jacket and folded his white shirt-sleeves up to his elbows. Now that she was closer, the lines around his eyes and mouth looked like deep craters, the way her mom's skin looked when she had a migraine and couldn't sleep.

Agent Malden must be under a lot of pressure from his office to sort out the stones. Hanging around a bunch of teenagers could not be easy either.

Tracey glanced over her shoulder toward the toilet door. "Kylie's okay."

"And how are you?"

"Yeah, just …" She shook her head. "Nah, it's okay." A little ding drew Tracey's gaze to the roof. The seatbelt light had come on.

"That woman you were speaking to before you went in. What did she say to you?"

"That it's dangerous," Tracey leaned forward and whispered, "to have Mage-kind on a plane. I just—" She released a held breath as if blowing the nasty woman from her mind. It didn't work. "Some people suck."

"Ah, ladies and gentlemen you will find the seatbelt sign has come on. We can see a little turbulence ahead, but there's nothing to worry about folks," the captain's voice drolled over the speakers.

"I understand your anger, Tracey. There is an unsubstantiated fear that Mage-kind and electricity don't mix," Agent Malden said softly.

"I said that to Jonny too. We're not superheroes. We don't fly or wield electricity or anything cool like that."

"Actually, we can wield electricity with a great deal of training."

"Seriously?"

"Magic and electricity are two separate entities. As you know, we can use cellphones and tablets with no problems. We don't destroy electrical items just by walking past them, right?"

"Right."

"Well, electricity *is* a form of energy."

Tracey held up her hands. "Like in science? You need magnets and copper coils to make electricity, or like steam turbines or fossil fuels. Renewables are better though, wind and sun and water. Oh, you mean that's what magic does? Acts like renewable power?"

"Well, I guess you could say spells work along those lines. Think of magic as another form of energy. And like magic, electricity *can* be wielded safely—with a lot of practice."

Tracey spotted Kylie wandering down the plane aisle on the opposite side. She waved, but Kylie didn't see her. "So, Jonny was right? Oh man, he'll never shut up about that. Wait, so then we *are* dangerous on a plane? Should we be flying?"

"It's perfectly safe," Malden said. "Fear has a way of making normally rational people say and do things they wouldn't ordinarily do. Don't pay that woman too much mind."

"Easy to say, hard to do." Tracey fiddled with her seatbelt buckle. It reminded her of the seatbelt sign. *Should I go back to my seat?* She pulled the belt over her lap and clicked it into place. "Do you remember I asked you about a spell to remove the stones? You said you have some contacts."

"Tracey, I don't think the stones should be removed."

Her eyes widened. "What? What about Kylie? I promised Damian I'd find a way to get it off. I know each stone locks onto a protector—like me—but what if it locks onto the wrong person? It's not fair. Kylie can't take it off without suffering horrible pain."

"At the moment the stone is dormant. It is safer around Kylie's neck than if we were to take it off."

"But I promised," Tracey said.

"Right now, we know where three of the stones are."

"But Kylie can't use her magic."

"Our mission is to find the other stones. Kylie is safe with us," Malden said.

Tracey blew out her anger in a long breath, imagining dragon-fire spewing from her nose. "Is that all you wanted to talk about?"

He pulled a briefcase from under the seat in front of him and rested it on his knee. Lifting the lid, he removed a file. "We should chat about what will happen when we land."

She took the file as the plane jerked sharply beneath her feet. It felt as though her stomach rose up between her lungs. Her body went all floaty and her seat dropped away beneath her. "Whoa!" She clenched the file tightly as her other hand slammed against the seat arm.

"Bit of turbulence." Agent Malden smiled and pointed to the file. Tracey flipped it open. The plane jerked again, snapping her teeth together. Trays rattled and a few people exclaimed in surprise. The file fell from Tracey's knees onto the floor.

For a moment they didn't speak as the plane juked and jolted, snapping Tracey hard from side to side. Her knuckles turned white as she gripped the armrests.

"Ladies and gentlemen, as I mentioned earlier we have some turbulence ahead. Seems it's a little stronger than we realized." The captain's voice held a hint of concern. *That can't be good.* "Hold tight, we should be through the worst of it momentar—" The speaker shut off with squeal.

Tracey hoped her sister was okay sitting up the front with Kylie. A strange whistle filled the cabin. "What's that?"

Agent Malden cursed.

Tracey's head snapped toward him. "What?"

"Magic. Someone's trying to bring down the plane."

I can tell no one of what I see, what I alone know.

2

Screams and shouts filled the plane. Tracey clutched the arms of her seat as they bounced violently. "Is it Timothy? Is he back?"

Agent Malden shook his head. "I don't know. We need to check on Kylie." The plane dove, then pulled level again. A pop announced face masks dropping from the ceiling like the flight attendants said would happen in an emergency.

"I'll go," she shouted, but she couldn't get her legs to move. Instead, she threw open her imaginary closet door she kept her magic locked behind and tried speaking to Sarah in her head. She couldn't hold the thought. Her magic slipped through her fingers like water. Fear made it impossible to focus.

"Stay here. We'll create a circuit to keep the plane in the air." Agent Malden unbuckled and pushed to his feet, immediately stumbling from the abrupt up and down jerking of the plane.

"A what?"

He gripped the seatbacks on either side of the aisle, digging his fingers into the padding to pull himself forward. "I'll call you."

"How? We can't use our phones."

"In your head."

"Okay."

He bounced side to side all the way down the aisle. The uneven sharp movement of the plane grew more erratic. Tracey's teeth clattered together. She let out a sharp screech as the plane dropped away beneath her. Somehow Agent Malden held his footing. Two babies screamed behind her. Tracey almost couldn't hear them under all the shouting.

"Your fault."

The accusation was hissed at her by the man with the book who had glared earlier. "Just read your book," she snapped back.

"It's your fault. Mage-freak. We're going to die because of you. What did you do?" His words carried across the rear rows. Heads turned in her direction. A wall of angry and scared eyes locked onto her. Sweat covered Tracey's skin. The stares digging like knives into her body. The plane leveled off again, the pilot was clearly fighting hard for control.

"It's not my fault." Anger pushed Tracey's fear into the dark corners of her mind. Her voice rose. "We're trying to help."

"Freak."

That came from somewhere in front of her. Tracey tried to block out the fear and hatred bombarding her and wished Agent Malden would hurry up and do something. The shouting grew louder as the floor rose up beneath her feet, almost flinging her into the roof. Tracey screamed, echoed by what felt like the entire plane. *We're going to die.* The way the plane jerked was like a dog with a rope, rapidly flicking it up and down. What good was having power if she couldn't use it? She drew warm magic from her core and made her body heavier, imagining her hands as strong clamps, then released her seatbelt and dragged herself over the seats to the window, searching for the cause of the violence. There was nothing in the darkness. Agent Malden said they were under attack.

Wait. Darkness? Only minutes ago she had seen unending blue sky and white fluffy clouds outside.

"Demon!"

"Monster!"

"Mage-bitch."

Tracey's anger spiked with every name shouted her way. These people should be focused on the plane not on Tracey. She gave up trying to convince them she wanted to help. Were these Norms really so stupid that they thought she would risk her own life to make the plane crash? She would die too. Or did they think she was powerful enough to cheat death itself? She glanced around searching for the flight attendants. There was no sign of them.

Agent Malden's voice popped into her mind.

Open up your magic. Go to the back of the plane and anchor the circuit I'm about to create between us. I'll encircle the plane with an energy field and repel the negative forces acting on the plane's electrical systems.

What's happening? Is Sarah okay? she asked.

Tracey, they're fine. Please concentrate.

What do I do?

Are you at the back of the plane?

Tracey dragged herself into the aisle. She lost her footing and was thrown onto the person sitting in the aisle seat. Tracey apologized and pushed back into the aisle clamping her hands onto the seatbacks. She did her best to ignore the panicked, screaming passengers and pulled herself toward the back of the plane. *Okay, I'm here,* she told Agent Malden.

Drop your shielding, Tracey. I need you at full power.

It took less than a blink to open her mind to the Butterfly Stone. It was always ready, always hungry to be used. Her footing became sure, grounded, as solid as a tree with roots dug deep into the earth. *Ready!*

Lock onto my magic. Reach out for your uncle, Sarah, Jilly, Tony, and Dave.

It took no time at all for Tracey to find her friends and family with her mind. Their voices shouted encouragement, and she could almost picture them, scattered throughout the plane in both aisles, creating a network of magic that weaved through and around the plane. Tracey grabbed hold of their magic. In her mind, each person had a different color, like the ribbons of color that came from the Stones of Power during her tracking spell. Jilly was golden like a tiger. Her sister Sarah was her favorite color, pink. Tony was yellow like the sun and Dave as green as freshly cut summer grass. She couldn't sense Kylie at all as her magic was locked away. Agent Malden was gray, like cement, and her uncle was just her Uncle Donny. She knew his magic like a second skin. The sudden power boost that came from Jilly's stone—the Tiger's Eye—filled Tracey's body in an instant—the orange golden light growing twice as bright as the rest. Tracey wrapped her mind around the threads of her friends like wrapping ribbons around her hands.

Agent Malden chanted something but Tracey could not focus on his words. Her attention tugged her toward the rear of the plane—to the outside of the plane. She stretched out her mind searching for what was attacking them and found an oozing blackness and red flames. Her breath caught. *The Shadowman?* But no, it didn't feel icky like Timothy, or his evil henchman—cold and clammy. She tasted ash and smelled barbeque smoke. Something was on fire but there was no smoke coming from inside the plane. The panicked noise around her escalated as the plane dove and leveled off again.

It's outside, something is on top of the plane.

Tracey couldn't exactly go out and check. Magic pulsed inside her core as Agent Malden reversed Tracey's grip on their magic and took over, weaving all the threads into a thick chain that ran the length of the aisle and gathered around the cockpit.

What's happening? Jilly's voice echoed inside Tracey's head.

Something is attacking the plane—I can't see it. What's Agent Malden doing? Tracey asked.

He's focused on the cockpit, hands pressed to the closed door. Magic is everywhere.

Tracey could hear Jilly's anxiety and tried to calm her while hiding her own fear. *We've got this. All of us working together—we're too powerful to stop. Remember. We help each other.*

Tracey! Are you listening? Agent Malden shouted, cutting into their mind conversation.

Yes, sorry. I'm here. She confirmed.

You're the anchor. I need you to push your magic into the vertical and horizontal stabilizer.

The what? she asked.

The tail of the plane. Focus your magic on the tail and the parts that move, the flaps and the rudder. Do you understand? I'm going to push out the field to surround the plane. I need you to get rid of whatever it is that has hold of the tail.

Okay. Tracey pictured the outside of the plane and the tail as she'd seen it through the airport viewing windows before they boarded. A vague impression formed in her mind. It was not a clear image like that on a TV. "Oh." A strange buzz of magic hovered around the rear of the plane. A vibration. The rippling blur shimmering off the road in the distance on a hot day. She could almost see a hand shaking the plane like a baby with a rattle. *There's something there.*

What is it? Agent Malden asked.

What? The echo of her friend's voices inside her head made Tracey dizzy.

One at a time! She mentally shouted. The jerking of the plane grew even more pronounced and the passengers' screams spiked. Tracey wanted to scream too; her brain was splitting in two. Part of her attention was on the tail and the rest was on the connection with Agent Malden and her friends.

Malden's voice boomed. *Inside or outside the plane, Tracey? What can you see?*

Uh. She had to focus on the magic, but the screams and pulses of emotion hammered her from all sides. *I don't know!* she shouted.

Focus on the fin — the tail, Tracey. I'm giving you a boost. Push the force off if you can. I'm shielding the cockpit. I can't come back there and help you. Can you do it?

I'll try. Magic slammed into her chest like a football, hard and fast. Her core overflowed with raw power. The Butterfly Stone turned white hot and sucked Tracey inside. She blinked at the sudden silence of the white place. Stephanie — her ancestor and the woman who looked eerily like Tracey — stood in front of her.

"Hello, Tracey." Stephanie stood proud. Defiant. As if daring Tracey to say something about the last time they spoke. She wore her usual white, short-sleeve dress and lace gloves. It was creepy seeing Tracey's own face forming such unfamiliar expressions. "It's been a while since we last spoke. How are you doing?"

"Stephanie." Tracey didn't know what to say. She was still angry at the spirit for the way she'd hijacked Tracey's body and used her magic to fight Doctor Chan, but Tracey didn't have time to deal with it right now. "Send me back."

"What is happening, Tracey?" A light appeared in Stephanie's chest, growing brighter and brighter until she was glowing from the inside out. White light poured from her mouth, her eyes and her long hands. It was hard to look at. "Where has all this glorious magic come from?"

"Something is attacking the plane."

"Plane?"

"A flying carriage. I'm inside it."

"You are flying? There are carriages that fly?"

"Just listen! We're going to die unless I can stop the thing that grabbed onto us," Tracey shouted.

"Let me into your mind, give me control and I—"

"You're not controlling me ever again!"

Stephanie stumbled back, her hands held up in surrender. White yellow light poured from her body. "Very well. Channel this excess of magic into the Butterfly Stone then through your body and out via your hands. It will allow you to focus the strength of your magic and target it, like an extension of yourself. Moving your hands will move your magic."

"That's impossible. I don't have an Object of Power like a wand or a scepter."

"You have the stone. And of course, I can assist you."

"I don't trust you. You tricked me last time."

"I cannot take control again, if you refuse me. But I can guide you."

Tracey shook her head. "Just tell me what to do."

"There is—"

"I said no!"

Stephanie's lips tightened. "Force the magic into your hands. Will it to become your hands and it will answer to you."

Oh, like the magic slings she had created when she'd caught the Tiger's Eye and the Serpent's Kiss to stop them from touching. "Yeah, but how do I do that exactly?"

Tracey rocked back on her heels as her mind was thrust from the Butterfly Stone and back into reality. She focused on the magic pulsing through her body. It pounded like a drum solo she couldn't turn down. It was too much, too fast. She wasn't drawing it to her, it was being forced upon her and she was collapsing under the weight of it. Her brain shut down.

"Trace, Trace."

Someone shook her by the shoulders. Tracey dragged her eyes open and when she did, Jonny's face was the only thing she saw. He knelt beside her, shirt soaked in sweat, eyes fearful as he held onto her. The plane jerked them both up and down. She stuttered, "It's too much. I can't focus. The noise, the screaming, the bouncing. It's too much. I can't—"

"Tracey, what if you thicken your shield bubble? Block it all out?"

"Won't work. I can't use my magic if I do that." Tears leaked from her eyes, wetting her cheeks.

"Pretend it's a video game?"

"H-how?"

"Imagine you're a character inside a game and you're using a virtual reality helmet. Remember, like last year at the university science demo?"

"A game?" she repeated.

"Yeah, and your … um … magic can be wielded like a sword or something."

Like a superhero! "Thanks, Jonny."

He threw himself into a nearby seat and buckled up, grinning madly — all teeth. She could tell it was to hide his fear. "You got this, girl."

Heck yeah, I do. Tracey closed her eyes. *It's all a game.*

In her head she pictured an avatar — a cartoon superhero version of herself — with a cape, giant muscles and perfect hair. She drew all of the magic into the Butterfly Stone and pushed it around her body like Stephanie had told her to do. She pictured herself standing outside, on the plane's wing, her hair whipping wildly, cape billowing behind her in the gale-like wind. It wasn't really her body. She was still inside the plane. But her superpowered avatar stood on the skin of the fuselage. Tracey turned her avatar around. A giant hand gripped the tail fin clamping the rudder and elevators in place. That was the cause of all the shaking. The plane's skin and frame squealed as it was squeezed out of shape by the ghostly gray fingers pressing hard into the aluminum. *Where is the hand coming from?* She couldn't see an arm. Whoever made the hand could be anywhere.

Tracey stretched her avatar's hands and grew them to monstrous size. She grabbed onto the armless hand with her own glowing fingers and yanked hard. She felt rather than heard a grunt from somewhere and the evil, ghostly hand tightened its grip.

She pulled harder. *Let go!* The ghost hand wouldn't budge. Tracey stretched for its giant gray fingers and one at a time, just like when she and Sarah wrestled over the TV remote, peeled each finger away. As she shifted the third finger, the ghost hand lost its grip and dissolved into magic dust, blowing away in the wind. *I did it!* Her avatar cheered and raised her arms high. "Yeah! That is how you do it!" She let her awareness return to her body in a long wave and realized she still sat slumped in the plane's aisle. Jonny was seated beside her, talking, his voice a familiar drone for her to focus on and find her way home. He urged her to concentrate and told her how brilliant she was. Her vision blurred and her mind snapped fully back inside her body the way an elastic band did after you stretched it.

Did I really just let go of my body and travel outside the plane in ghostly spirit form? Or did I actually create a whole world inside my mind to fight the ghost hand? The plane trembled beneath her butt. Why were they still experiencing turbulence? She had stopped the hand, hadn't she?

Tracey. Don't let go. Grab the stabilizer— the tail, Malden screeched inside her mind.

She slammed her eyes shut and pictured her avatar on top of the plane again. As the skin covering the fuselage became solid under her feet, Tracey ran toward the tail and pressed her hands against the icy cold surface. *What now?*

The elevators and rudder are damaged. We need you to keep us steady, Agent Malden said inside her head.

How? Tracey's thoughts swung to Jonny and his computer game comment. If it was all a game, then she could control the plane—or at least her avatar could—inside the world. Every comic book superhero in a series saved a crashing plane by flying under it. In her computer game world Tracey believed she could fly. She launched her avatar into the air and flew parallel to the plane. "Whooooooo!" She pointed her hands and zoomed into a dive, away from the plane and then under it. "Whooooooo!" *Freaking fruit tingles, this is so awesome!* Tracey could feel the wind in her hair and slapping over her skin. She caught onto the tail and pushed up with both hands. The shaking stopped as the plane steadied and leveled off.

"You're doing it, Trace!" Jonny shouted from somewhere nearby. Tracey imagined she could see him standing at the rear window of the plane waving madly.

The world in her head *was* just like a computer game and Tracey was in total control. It was awesome!

Not even Stephanie knows the full power of my curse. I cannot warn them. I cannot stop it. I can only see their end and ache for their loss.

3

I can't believe you did that!" Jonny shouted, bouncing on the balls of his feet as Tracey blinked back into her body. She stared at his moving white sneakers. The left lace was coming loose.

"We've landed?" Tracey closed her magic off behind the imaginary closet door inside her chest. She sat in the aisle next to the toilet cubical. The plane seats around her emptying as passengers evacuated, throwing wide-eyed glances back her way. Tracey hated being stared at. It made her skin crawl. Agent Malden headed up the aisle toward her. Tony, Sarah and Kylie were with him. Tracey climbed to her feet, grabbing onto Jonny when she wobbled and nearly fell over. "Whoa!"

"Hang on, sit back down. Are you okay?"

"Bit dizzy."

A strong hand pressed her into a seat. "Put your head between your knees, Tracey. Take a deep breath, nice and slow." Agent Malden's steady, comforting voice focused her scattered thoughts.

"Holy crap, that was wild," Jonny said.

"Scary as anything," Sarah told him. "Trace?" Sarah crouched and grabbed Tracey's hands.

"Hey." Tracey stared at her sister until the cartoon tiger on her shirt stopped bouncing. Sarah's messy hair had a giant knot at the back. Tracey wanted to poke at it and see if it was alive.

"You were amazing," Kylie said, kneeling down beside Sarah.

"I was freaking out," Tony said handing her a bottle of water. His face—like Sarah's—was shiny with sweat. His gray NASA shirt had damp marks around the neckline and under his arms. "I was too scared to even focus properly. Agent Malden positioned us along the plane and people were screaming. The plane bounced us all over the place. Then we felt your magic go nuts. What did you do?"

"Pretended I was in a video game. It was Jonny's idea," she said.

"Of course it was." Tony smirked.

Tracey glanced around the almost empty plane. "Where's Laura?"

"With your uncle, the Carters, Dave, and Jilly," Agent Malden said. "They've gone down to the baggage carousel. The airport officials want to chat with you for a minute, and then we'll join them."

A flight attendant appeared behind him. "Sir? Is everyone in your party okay, do you require medical assistance?"

"Not necessary," Agent Malden told him. He gestured to the younger girls. "Off you go. You too, boys," he said pointing to Jonny and Tony.

Jonny bristled, but did not argue. His mom waved at him to hurry up from the end of the aisle. The flight attendant's smile was broad and completely sincere. "Thank you all for your help. You saved us." His gaze drifted over every member of the group and stopped on Tracey. "Whatever you did. Thank you."

Sarah hugged Tracey tightly and followed Kylie, Jonny, and Tony out of the plane.

Tracey wished she could go with them. She guzzled down the bottle of water and wondered how the Norm airport police would react to a bunch of Mage-kind teens fighting a monster on a plane in midair. "Agent Malden, what actually happened?"

"What did you see?"

Why did he always answer everything with a question? Feeling stronger, Tracey pushed to her feet. "I don't remember much. Just the smell of campfire smoke." She thought back to the time Agent Malden and his partner, Agent Striker, talked her through defining a magical signature for identification purposes. "Flames and ash and, uh, a giant gray ghost hand. It played with the plane like it was a toy." Tracey made *vroom-vroom* engine sounds with her mouth and swooped her hand down as if she was holding a toy plane. "No voice or anything. Just, you know, a lot of shaking."

"Could you tell if we were targeted specifically?" He rubbed a hand over his face.

Tracey shook her head. "It didn't feel angry or anything like that. Not like Timothy angry. I dunno."

"When they ask you what happened, I want you to tell them the truth." His nose twitched, making her wonder if he wanted to say something else. Did he or didn't he want her to tell the truth? Was he trying to protect her as a Mage-kind student, someone who should not be using their magic? Or limit what she said, so they could get out of here quicker?

"Is Prince Henry meeting us at the airport?"

"He's sending a car."

Wicked. Tracey did not want to hang around answering questions all day. "I'm ready, I guess."

Agent Malden turned, gesturing to the plump lady with a wide smile who was waiting patiently for them to finish. She held up her badge as she approached. Her blue suit didn't say *police* but it still looked like a uniform. She reminded Tracey of Officer Jameson, but she could not pinpoint why. Perhaps it was just that this woman didn't look at Tracey like she was a monster.

"My name is Officer Bartles." She had a strong accent with long drawls and stretched sounds like she had all the time in the world. It was weird given they were in England. Tracey had expected everyone to sound like the Queen. Officer Bartles shook Agent Malden's hand and then smiled at Tracey. "How are you feeling, dear?"

"Super tired." Well, Agent Malden said to be honest.

"I understand that is to be expected." Officer Bartles glanced at Agent Malden. "I also understand we need to thank you."

"Oh?" Tracey ran her hands over her hair. It felt like it was sticking up everywhere. *Embarrassing.* She pressed the flyaway strands down as best she could.

Officer Bartles smiled broadly. "You saved a plane full of people today, Tracey. That deserves a hearty thank you. So, thank you. On behalf of everyone on board that plane. All three hundred and twenty-three souls."

"Wow," Tracey mumbled. "That's a lot of people." She felt wobbly again. "No problems."

"Shall we exit the plane and sit down somewhere more comfortable to have our little chat?"

Agent Malden nodded, and spoke softly with the officer as she led them down the aisle to the exit hatch and out into the terminal. She led them to a door with *staff only* written on it and down a long cold corridor. Tracey's sweat had dried but her skin was still clammy and she shivered. These corridors were anonymous. No one knew they were in here. At least Agent Malden was with her. She wasn't totally alone.

The heavy door shut behind them with a clunk. It was super tiny inside, barely enough room for a skinny desk and three chairs. As soon as they sat down, Officer Bartles took a small tablet off the desk and typed rapidly on the fold out keyboard. "Okay then. Tracey, what happened up there today?"

Agent Malden opened his mouth, but Bartles held up her index finger. He nodded and gestured for Tracey to start. Tracey swallowed but her mouth was suddenly bone dry.

"The flight was okay. Normal, I guess. It's the first time I've ever been on a plane, so I don't really have anything to compare it to. Um, the turbulence—"

She glanced at Agent Malden, hoping that was the right word. He nodded.

"—turbulence got really bad and um—"

Again she looked to the M-force agent. He waited for her to speak.

"Agent Malden said he felt something was wrong and told me to go to the back of the plane. Then he um … " She tore her gaze from the adults and stared down at her fingers. "We're not supposed to use our magic." Could Officer Bartles tell Tracey was stretching the truth? This felt like an interrogation and she worried that she was in trouble. *But I helped save the plane.* What if the attack had only happened because Tracey and her friends were on board?

Officer Bartles smiled again. Her posture was soft, round and relaxed. "Agent Malden gave you permission to use your magic. Correct?" She received a nod from the M-force agent.

"That's it really," Tracey said. "Agent Malden set up a, um, he called it a circuit. And then a really cool spell happened and we landed."

The smile stayed on Officer Bartles's face, but her eyes narrowed slightly. "That appears consistent with what your agent friend has reported. Is that all that happened, Tracey? Is there anything else you think I should know?" The woman's eyes burned into Tracey's skin.

Tracey swallowed, fidgeting with her fingers. Her shoulders sloped. "That's it."

Bartles clicked off the tablet screen. "Terrific. Well, as I said before, thank you for what you did today. I think those passengers were very lucky to have you on board. The plane has been taken out of service so its electrical systems can be checked. It won't return to service until we are one hundred percent sure it is safe. I have your number." Here she stared directly at Agent Malden. He froze. The move was almost unnoticeable except that Tracey was watching him and not Bartles. He nodded again. Officer Bartles continued. "I will reach out if I have any further questions. You'd best be off now to customs so you can join your friends. Enjoy your stay here."

Tracey stood up and hurried to the door.

"Oh, just one more thing," Bartles said as Tracey opened the door. "What is your reason for traveling here today? It is an interesting group outside of a school event, isn't it? Especially with an M-force agent attached?"

"They won a school drama competition," Agent Malden jumped in. "The prize is a walk-on role in the new Prince Henry film. I'm escorting them to the set."

The officer's eyes widened. "Prince Henry? Well, that *is* exciting. Enjoy your adventure, Tracey. Agent."

Tracey followed Agent Malden from the room. "She was nice," Tracey said as they walked down the long white-walled corridor.

"Hmmmm," he replied.

Tracey stopped him from opening the door into the airport. "Was it our fault the plane was attacked? Because we were on board?"

"I don't know."

That did not allay her fears. "So, what do we do?"

"Stay vigilant. I'll raise everything with my higher ups and there will be an M-force investigation into the attack. For now, just concentrate on why we are here. I'll handle it." He pushed open the door and stepped out into the airport.

"Sure," Tracey said softly and followed. She hoped it was true. If they had put innocent people in danger by coming here, then it meant someone was after them. Again.

They found the rest of their group gathered at the baggage carousel. All had hold of their bags except for Tony and Jilly. Sarah waved as she spied Tracey. "I haven't seen your bag yet," she called.

"Thanks, Sars. Where are the Carters?" Tracey searched the waiting crowd. "Oh, and Martha and Laura?"

"They went to get coffee. We didn't know how long you would be," Jonny said.

Tracey examined the carousel, searching for her emerald green wheelie suitcase. "Is everyone okay?"

"Still shaken," Tony admitted. "I can't concentrate on my phone. My brain is running overtime."

Dave nodded. "I thought we were gonna die."

Sarah held up her hands. "My heart's racing. Even now."

"Naw, I knew Trace would save us," Jonny said.

Tracey shook her head at him. "I didn't."

"How did the interview go?" Tony asked.

Agent Malden and Uncle Donny moved off, chatting quietly, so Tracey shuffled into a circle with her friends and lowered her voice. "It was fine. The airport officer wanted to know what happened on the plane. I kinda put it all on Agent Malden."

"Yeah, we did that too. Handy having an M-force agent around, though we did get a lot of suspicious looks. At least she let us go," Dave said.

Jilly took Jonny's hand, and Tracey nearly snorted at Jonny's goofy grin. Jilly fixed her stare on Tracey. "Now that we have landed, we should perform the stone tracking spell. Perhaps you will pick up the trail now that we are closer."

Did nothing shake the girl's total focus on the mission? Tracey peeked over at Agent Malden. He was in the middle of an intense conversation with Uncle Donny. They had time. "We need supplies. We might have to wait until we get to our accommodation and—"

Jilly held up a piece of chalk. Tony held out his phone and Dave pulled a bag from his pocket. "Dirt," he said. She raised an eyebrow at him. "What? I was a boy scout," he added defensively.

Tracey had her bottle of water. So, she only needed fire.

Sarah handed her a birthday candle. She shrugged at Tracey's surprise.

"Watch out for my bag." Tracey told her sister.

Jilly took Tony's phone, snatched the bag from Dave, and grabbed Tracey's hand. "We're going to the bathroom!" she shouted to Agent Malden. He raised his hand to confirm he had heard. Tracey let Jilly drag her to the toilets.

They pushed inside the six-stall bathroom and the door crashed against the wall behind them, echoing off the grimy tiles. Jilly nudged each door open to ensure they were alone. Nodding all was clear, she thrust Tony's phone at Tracey with the spell highlighted and handed over the supplies, taking up a position near the door to stop anyone from coming inside. "Hurry."

It might have been the quickest spell Tracey had ever cast. She drew a hurried, slightly wonky circle on the tiles, lit the candle with her mind—she had stolen that trick off Prince Henry—and uttered the incantation from Tony's phone. Several faint ribbons of color flickered into view. A thick silver line circled her own body, emerging from the Butterfly Stone. A gold line ran straight to Jilly and an equally thick black line ran out through the bathroom door—no doubt straight to Kylie. Two other lines were so faint they blurred and dissipated into dust particles that blew away when Tracey tried to focus on them. But a thin blue ribbon was left over and stretched off in front of Tracey heading right out though the door. "Oooo, I've got something," she whispered.

The door rattled loudly. Jilly clung to it to stop it from opening and shouted, "Occupado!"

"What?" A woman's voice called. The door rattled once more.

Tracey swiped her hand over the chalk line and blew out the candle. She scuffed the dirt into a corner, capped her water bottle and shoved it and the candle into her cargo pants pockets. The chalk line was still too obvious. Grabbing some paper towels, she wet them and scrubbed at the circle until the white line disappeared. Jilly grunted as the door handle jiggled beneath her grip.

"Done," Tracey said. She quickly washed her hands at the sink. A scowling pink-cheeked woman wearing a long fawn coat stomped inside as Jilly released the door. She ignored Tracey, glaring so hard at Jilly her eyes crossed, and went straight into a cubical. Tracey and Jilly scampered outside.

"Well?" Jilly asked.

"I can see a blue line. It's pretty thin but it's leading outside so yeah, I think there's another stone here somewhere. I don't know how long the spell will last though. Last time it was only an hour, maybe two, before it faded."

"We know the stone is nearby and we know how to find it. This mission will be easy to complete." Jilly grabbed Tracey's arm and tugged her to a halt. "We should keep this knowledge to ourselves."

Tracey nodded. "Agreed." She thought of all the trouble they had with the Tiger's Eye and the Serpent's Kiss, and of Damian's angry eyes when he looked at her. "At least until we know more. Someone attacked our plane with magic. We have to be careful."

They returned to the baggage carousel. Sarah had Tracey's green bag and Agent Malden had collected his black one. "Come on, gang," Uncle Donny said. "Let's go find that coffee place and get out of here."

"Is that a Chrysler?" Dave gushed as they spied the stretch limousine waiting for them at the curb outside the airport. It was long and silver-colored, and Kylie and Sarah squealed when they set eyes on it. Tracey wanted to do the same. A giant grin spread across Laura's face. Jonny's too. They shared an excited giggle with Tony. Tracey glanced around expecting to see London's famous buildings. She was disappointed. There was nothing to see but gray sky and concrete. Agent Malden waved them forward as the driver stepped out to help with the luggage. Even Jonny's mom, Martha, looked impressed with the car.

Tracey's good mood dropped at the sight of Mrs. Carter's grumpy face. And Damian. He stood next to his mother and would not even look in Tracey's direction. Gee, a stretch limousine was going to feel small if they were not going to talk to anyone. The blue line headed off into the distance, fortunately, in the same direction the limousine faced. When she caught Jilly's eye, Tracey pointed. Jilly nodded.

"This is so cool," Kylie said coming up beside Tracey. "I can't believe we're actually here. We're going to be in a Prince Henry movie."

Three black birds squawked and fought over some trash in the curb. To Tracey's eyes, it looked like the biggest one was the boss. It won the battle and ate scraps out of the chip bag while the others pranced around cawing sadly. *Ha!*

"Right, Tracey?" Kylie asked.

"Oh um, what?" She glanced at the bouncing blond girl. The thick black line ran from the Butterfly Stone to Kylie's chest where the Serpent's Kiss was hidden beneath her green polo shirt. Sarah tugged on Kylie's sleeve. Kylie did not look at her, her eyes firmly shining up at Tracey. Kylie had been through a lot of scary stuff lately and the drama on the plane could not have helped. She must have been terrified and couldn't even access her magic. Tracey tapped her own forehead. "How are you doing?"

"With the headband from hell? Yeah, it's okay. Only hurts a little bit." Kylie touched the magical band.

"No voices?" Tracey asked.

"None."

"What about on the plane? When the attack happened and all that magic was flying around? Did you feel anything from Timothy?"

"Nothing. I'm okay," Kylie said. "It was pretty scary though."

"I'm okay too, Tracey," Sarah added. "Agent Malden wouldn't let Kylie help us." Sarah pushed closer. The move forced Kylie to step back. Kylie frowned at Sarah's back as Sarah continued. "She's got no magic. She couldn't help, even if she wanted to." Sarah smiled at Kylie. Tracey had seen that fake smile on her sister's face before and wondered what she was so cranky about.

"That sucks," Tracey said. "Kylie, I'm so sorry you can't feel your magic."

A loud squawk from the ground snapped Tracey's attention back to the three black birds. They hopped toward the gathered teens until Jonny ran at them. They let out several loud squawks in annoyance and flapped away.

"Mom's happy about it. The no magic thing. At least one of us is. I wish I could have helped you earlier. I miss my magic," Kylie continued.

"Must be horrible," Sarah said, patting Kylie's arm.

Tracey peered past the two girls searching for Kylie's brother. "How's Damian?"

"He and Mom are so cranky. I'm sorry they're being horrible to everyone."

Tracey sighed. "I get it."

"No, I'm sorry. They are the worst. I'm so angry with my mom."

"Can we get in the limo now?" Sarah asked.

"Yep. Get in gang," Agent Malden called.

With a lot of noise, they piled into the extra-long car. Tracey heard several shouts of *"whoa!"* and *"cool"* and at least one *"wicked!"* She slid down the long, S-curved side seat and buckled in, peering around to check Sarah had done up her seatbelt. Damian slid in next to Tracey. His mom and Kylie sat on Damian's other side. "Hi."

Fruit tingles. Nervous with the boy of her dreams sitting so close, Tracey forced her gaze around the limo. There was a long wet bar opposite their seats. Tracey focused on the colorful bottles stacked behind the glass, doing everything she could not to look at, touch, or lean against Damian in any way. She was so aware of him. Heat radiated from Damian's clothes, along with his powder fresh deodorant. The scent curled under Tracey's nose. *Limo, focus on the limo.* The interior was all cream and gray colors with a warm redwood bar. Damian's leg bounced, brushing against Tracey's cargo pants. *Oh boy!* Laura sat on the seat behind the driver with Jilly and Tony. She raised her eyebrows at Tracey and knocked Jilly with her elbow. Both girls grinned at Tracey's wide *OMG* gaze.

Sarah sat on the other side of Kylie, while Uncle Donny, Jonny, and Jonny's mom, Martha, squeezed into the back seat. Dave shoved inside and plonked down on the other side of Tracey, forcing her to inch even closer to Damian. She bit back a groan. Great. Between embarrassing and awful. "Where's Agent Malden?" she queried in a strained voice.

"Sitting up front with the driver. Is everyone buckled in?" Uncle Donny asked. When they all called out "*yes*," the door slid shut and the limo pulled smoothly away from the curb.

"Where are we going?" Tracey questioned. "Are we heading into London or going straight to the movie set?"

"All right kids, we will be checking into our accommodation first." Agent Malden's voice echoed up from the speaker near Tracey's elbow. She jumped in her seat. Dave burst out laughing. Tracey scowled at him and leaned over to flick the intercom button on so Agent Malden could hear her question. "Are we going to a hotel?" A little orange light beside the speaker lit up. That must mean the speakers and microphone were on.

"Somewhere else. I think you'll be pleasantly surprised, but it's a bit of a drive so settle in," Agent Malden said.

"What about seeing London?" Tony asked. "I want to walk along Oxford Street."

"I want to see the palace," Laura called.

"Tower of London," Dave added. "And those soldiers with the big hats."

"They're not soldiers. They're guards," Tony said.

"We're heading to Oxfordshire," Agent Malden said to a chorus of moans. "Maybe we'll fit in some sightseeing at the end of our trip."

"Reckon we can score one of these drinks?" Dave asked. His eyebrows jumped up and down and he pointed at the bar with a finger.

"No." Uncle Donny said with a laugh.

Tracey grinned. Excitement over the limo ride had taken her mind off their real mission, which was to find the stones. She peered out through the window and spotted the blue thread stretching off into the distance. At least they were headed in the right direction. Jilly was staring at her when Tracey returned her gaze inside the limo. She raised her eyebrows. Tracey nodded. *Yep, the thread is still there.* She returned to reality with a *thunk* when Damian tapped her on the arm and asked, "So, what really happened on the plane?"

My introduction to the gardeoar was both
a ploosure and a curse, foo as soon as I touched
his hand I koaw how he would die.

4

Tracey had wanted to talk to Damian during their plane trip, but now all she wanted was to avoid talking to him. "Magic?" *I'm such an embarrassment.* Clearly magic had been involved. "I mean, yes, obviously magic. I don't know what it was. Something attacked the plane. At least we stopped it."

When she twisted away from Damian, she found everyone in the limo staring at her, listening in on the conversation.

"We were attacked?" Martha asked. "It wasn't just severe turbulence or a fault with the engine?" Her frown said she was more mad than scared.

Mrs. Carter leaned over her daughter, spearing Tracey with a sharp look. "Attacked? By who?"

Tracey shrugged. *A monster.* She figured Agent Malden wouldn't want her talking about it. She glanced at the speaker again. The light was still on so he was probably listening. "What happened down your end of the plane? I couldn't see what was going on." If you could not answer a question, ask one. That was what Agent Malden always did. It was also Tracey's twin brothers' favorite saying. They insisted it got them out of any teacher's spotlight. Tracey caught Sarah's grin. *Whoops, busted.*

"Agent Malden made Sarah, Tony, Jilly, Dave, and your uncle get out of their seats and scatter throughout the plane," Jonny told her.

Sarah took up the story. "We had to drop our shield bubbles and —"

"He wouldn't let me help." Kylie jumped in, cutting Sarah off. Sarah scowled at her. Kylie didn't notice the look.

"Well you couldn't help, Kylie," Tracey reminded her.

"Let's not talk about that." Mrs. Carter's mouth pinched tight like she tasted a fresh lemon.

Ugh, parents. Norms are the worst. Tracey had promised to look out for the younger girl and yet she barely had been able to talk to her. Mrs. Carter wouldn't let Tracey get close. Perhaps she should put Sarah on the case. There seemed to be some moodiness between the two girls, but they were probably just tired from the flight. Tracey certainly was.

"Breathe, Tracey, Mrs. Carter is just upset. Give her time." Mom's voice popped into Tracey's mind, reminding her of their conversation at the airport. *"You need to help Kylie, but remember her mom is struggling to understand everything that is happening. She just wants to protect her little girl. The way I want to protect you and Sarah. When she behaves a little ... unreasonably ... take a breath. She's upset. Explain everything you can, acknowledge her fears, but don't ever apologize."*

Tracey wished her mom had come with them. She was still recovering from Doctor Chan's poisonous spell, and their dad had to look after Tracey's brothers. It had not stopped her mom from giving Uncle Donny a stern warning when they left. Uncle Donny's expression had been priceless. He was so scared of his big sister.

Feeling eyes on her skin, Tracey raised her head. Mrs. Carter didn't look away. Tracey shifted her gaze to her hands. Still feeling the glare, she bent over to pull Millicent's journal from her carry-on bag. She put it on her knees but did not open it. They were zooming along the M40 motorway, so there was nothing to see except for cars and lorries. Three black birds swooped close to the limo's side, flapping fast to keep up. *Looks like they're following us. Hilarious.*

"Trace?"

She glanced back searching for Tony. "Oh sorry, I must have spaced. What did you say?"

Tony shared a look with Laura and Jonny that Tracey immediately recognized. The one that said, *"Oh typical, Tracey being Tracey."* She rolled her eyes at them. Tony's nose twitched, and his eyes flicked to the speaker box next to Tracey's elbow. He was still uncomfortable around Agent Malden. Tracey didn't know how to change his mind about the M-force agent. Tony was certain there was something fishy going on but the agent had helped them save a planeload of people, including Tracey and all her friends. He was clearly on their side.

"Agent Malden said to drop our shields. He wrapped our magic up and spun a big, um." Tony's voice drifted off.

"Web?" Sarah jumped in.

"Field goal," Dave said.

Everyone stared at him. "What?"

"Network," Uncle Donny said from the back seat. He cleared his throat as every anxious face turned his way. "It was a rather neat spell. I'll have to ask him how he did it. He said Tracey would act as the anchor and then, I don't actually know what happened next."

"Oh. Oh." Laura held up her hand and jiggled it around. "I do, you all went real quiet and Agent Malden did something with his bag. Then he made a glowing ball."

"A ball of magic," Kylie confirmed.

Laura waved her hands again. "A ball of glowing magic rose up and expanded through the plane. It disappeared into the cockpit and then the plane stopped jerking. You all just stood there silently, staring at nothing until we landed."

Jonny, Martha and Kylie nodded. Tracey imagined how she must have looked during the spell—mouth hanging open, drool dripping to the ground around her feet. She wiped a hand over her mouth. *Gross.*

"So, what do you remember?" Dave asked.

Damian was watching her. It made her nervous. What was he think-ing? She twisted her fingers together in her lap over the journal. "It was like … well … I don't know how to explain it. I had a picture in my head of what happened and you know how in all the superhero shows, the hero who can fly, like, lifts a plane's nose when it's diving to stop it from crashing?"

"We were crashing?" Martha gasped.

Jonny grabbed his mom's hand. "We're okay, Mom."

Fruit tingles, I didn't mean to say that out loud. Tracey rubbed her hands over her cheeks.

"You can fly?" Dave demanded. That seemed to be the distraction everyone needed. Tony and Jonny whooped with glee.

"What?" Tracey giggled. "No, dummy. I can't fly. No one can. Jonny told me to imagine a VR game. So, I created an avatar in my head and imagined she could fly. We landed and then Agent Malden told me I had to talk to the airport police."

"Damn, Tracey can totally fly." Jonny saluted her.

"Jonny!"

Laura and Tony laughed loudly. "Cool," Dave muttered.

Tracey shook her head at them. "I can't fly, jeez." Her face felt like it was on fire. Damian didn't even crack a smile.

After a brief silence, her friends returned to their individual conversations. Tony had his phone out and was searching for sights in Oxfordshire to explore. She heard him say, "castle," and what she thought was, "Bodleian Library." Martha expressed an interest in going shopping and invited Mrs. Carter to go with her. Dave piped up at Tony's announcement of Oxford Castle and Prison. "Yes! Let's go there."

"Only if we can leave you there," Laura said.

Every now and then Tracey heard Jonny's voice rise up over everyone else, insisting Tracey could fly and she scrunched lower in her seat, embarrassed at the attention. Damian didn't say anything else. Several times she opened her mouth to talk to him but nothing came out. She stared out through the window again. Everything in England was so same-same and yet so different from home. The trees were different. House styles and shops and signs and clothes were weird looking but the double decker red buses were cool. And the black cabs. As they drove into the countryside there was more and more green to see, more open spaces and more trees.

When Tracey couldn't feel the burn of eyes staring at her anymore, she sat up straighter. "Hey," she said to Damian, keeping her voice low so it wouldn't travel to anyone else. With one finger she flicked the intercom off. The light went out.

His gaze flicked to her face. "Hey."

"Are you mad at me?"

His soft brown eyes widened. "What?"

"You haven't really talked to me. Not since … "

They both glanced at Kylie.

"I'm not mad," he said.

"I think you are."

"I'm not angry with you. I *am* angry, but I dunno who with."

Tracey leaned closer. "If it's not me, then why won't you talk to me?"

"I am talking to you."

She exhaled heavily and shook her head. He didn't trust her enough to be honest with her. "Come on."

"Look, I'm just mad about stuff. Kylie. The stone. My mom. And yes, okay, a little mad with you. I'm mad at me too. Okay?" His words hurt to hear but Tracey could understand. It was hard to talk about yourself sometimes. Tracey's own default was to say she was fine, always, even when she wasn't. He *was* trying. She just wanted him to know she cared about how he felt and that his feelings were valid. As she hoped hers were to him. *I just want him to like me.* "Why are you angry with your mom?"

"Because she's angry with me? I dunno. Because she made me come on this dumb trip."

You didn't want to come? "Why'd she make you?"

"She doesn't know anyone here and thinks I do."

Ouch. Tracey tried to remember what her mom told her. "I don't think she's mad at you. She's just scared."

He turned his head to look out through the window. "It doesn't sound that way to me. She said it's my fault."

Tracey frowned. "What's your fault?"

He turned back and she worried at the despair in his eyes. "The stone. I gave it to Ky. It *is* my fault."

"It's not." Tracey wished she could make it all better for him. Maybe it was time for one of her brothers' favorite go-to distractions. She pressed her arm harder against his and changed the subject. "Hey, we're in England."

"Yeah, so?"

"We got out of school."

That scored a small smile. "Yeah."

"We're gonna be in a movie. A Prince Henry movie."

"Yeah."

Tracey smiled. "Look, I get it. I'm angry at everything too. It's just there's so much stuff in my head. Questions and actions and attention and people judging me and … I get it. Just don't stop talking to me, okay? It's not fair."

He nodded.

"For Kylie?" she said. "She needs you, and me, and it would be easier for all of us if we got along."

"Yeah." He scooched down a little in his seat. It pushed the diagonal seatbelt strap under his chin and looked funny. He pointed to the journal on her lap. "What are you reading?"

"A journal." Should she tell him? "Written by my ancestor Stephanie's best friend. Her name was Millicent and she, well I think she was one of the … that she held a stone like the one Kylie wears. Like me and Jilly." And she had spelled her journal so no one could read it, pretending it was Stephanie's. Jonny was right. *These stones and their secrets!* How could anyone keep track?

Damian's mouth twisted as he absorbed that. "So, she's evil too?"

"No." Is that what Damian thought about all the stone holders? Did he think that about Tracey too? "Millicent was Stephanie's friend. She hated Timothy."

"Why are you reading it?"

"I thought I might find some clues in it about her stone. To help us find it."

"Aren't you supposed to be looking for a way to take the stone off Kylie? Why are you looking for more of them?"

"I am. Honest. It's just the more we know about the stones the easier it will be to take it off." *I hope.*

"If you think so."

Dave poked Damian's arm to ask something football related and he turned away. Their conversation left a bad taste in Tracey's mouth. After shooting another look out through the window at the rolling hills of the English countryside, Tracey opened the journal.

January 4.

To know one's self is to know true heartache. I long for so much. A friend, a confidant, a love, but there is a cost. To be known is to hide one's true self. For that self can never be accepted. There is always a lie in observation and perception.

I am always alone.

March 18.

She is my friend, but I can never tell her the truth. She desires to fix me. To heal my ills. She will never hear me. Never see the true heart of me. I am a mirror to her and she will only see what she wills to see—that she has changed me, fixed me, made me better. I will allow her this lie for it in turn heals her. I see death coming at every turn. I see her fight it. Deny it. Forbid it.

I see how it ends and I cannot halt its steps. It comes for us all.

I will be alone.

April 7.

The glow that fills me disguises the lie I tell to keep the peace. I only wish to help. I cannot help. I cannot stop what is to come. I speak and I scream yet no one can hear my warning cry. How can I warn them, how can I continue to reach out when all I feel is pain? I cannot save them for who would believe what I have seen. Our disagreements have grown sharper. Rather than cut like a knife's blade, her words nick like that of a page. A sting you can feel even when you cannot hear it. A forever reminder of her words. Her tongue is her paper's edge. The blood she spills from me overflows and soon it will fill a lake. All that will be left of me is the shell she has created. I long for the silence of my own thoughts. In the sky there is freedom. In my mind I soar.

I have taken to running the maze, imbuing it with my power. It is mine. I can do with it as I wish. The center is my heart. My special place. A place where I can be at peace.

I sleep.

I Dream.

I cannot tell her for it would break her heart.

For I see how it will all end.

Agent Malden's voice rose up from the speaker and drew Tracey's attention away from the journal. Her skin was cold even though weak sunlight warmed the air inside the limo. "As we go around this bend, look through the windows on the left."

Every head craned to peer through the windows and for a moment they were all silent, waiting but not knowing what to expect. Immaculately tendered gardens came into view—many of them. The green grass was mowed into a checkboard color of emerald green and olive green, and Tracey was sure she spied a lake in the distance.

"Is that a maze?" Sarah asked.

Black wings flapped madly at the window near Tracey's head. She jerked back, startled. "Whoa!" She gasped again— "Whoaaaa!" —as a house came into view. A chorus of gasps and exclamations poured from her friends. It was a luxurious creamy white brick manor house. At three stories high it looked more like a palace than a house. Probably not though. *Probably*. The front was all high walls and stones with large bay windows that overlooked the gardens. The blue ribbon of light Tracey had been watching traveled straight to the manor house's front door and splintered, spreading out over the walls like a giant spider web. Great! Her tracking spell had broken.

"We're staying at a palace!" Sarah shrieked. Kylie and Laura squealed in excitement.

"A palace," Tony whispered. Dave, still trying to play it cool, nodded and smirked. Tracey didn't care. The blue thread leading her to the stone was gone. What were they going to do now?

The room is silent. There is no warmth or cold
to press against my skin. No light to see by,
no sound to carry.

5

Prince Henry stood in front of the massive entrance doors waiting for them as they pulled up. Next to him stood an older black man with graying hair and a cute-as-anything boy about their age.

"Oh yum," Sarah commented, sharing a look with Kylie. The two girls burst into giggles.

Tracey bit back a laugh. Sarah wasn't wrong. The boy wore a gray suit with a black-collared shirt and, like Agent Malden today, no tie. He looked amazing. Tracey pressed the intercom button in the limo to light it up again. "See Agent Malden, no tie *is* a good look."

Tony snorted. "He's probably already put his on again." The comment sent the whole car into a fit of giggles.

"All right, all right," Malden said via the speaker. "Everyone out."

They piled out of the limousine with a burst of excited chatter. Agent Malden pulled them into a group. "Let me introduce you all." He gestured to the older man. "Mr. Elijah Henderson owns this manor house. He rents out part as a hotel." The man wore a blue suit with a lavender shirt. He looked super professional standing next to Prince Henry, who wore faded jeans and a light blue polo shirt. "And this is Elijah's son, Noel. Noel will be your liaison while you are here. Elijah has agreed to let you stay here as his guests, so be respectful and obey all the rules he sets down. Do you understand?"

They chorused back various versions of *"yes."*

"You are representing your town and your country while you are here, so be on your best behavior."

Sarah and Kylie shuffled around until they stood in Tracey's shadow, sneaking peeks past her to stare adoringly at Prince Henry and Noel Henderson.

"It's a pleasure to meet you," Noel said. He looked them all over and his gaze stopped on Tony as he said, "Welcome to Ellisborough House." His pearly white smile was only dimmed by the braces on his teeth.

"OMG," Sarah whispered. "I love his accent."

"Hot," Kylie agreed. Tony's face flushed as he stared back at the British boy. Laura and Jonny walked over to shake Noel's hand.

Dave raced toward the manor house's front door, shouting. "Bathroom!"

Mrs. Carter smiled. It was the first one Tracey had seen on her face. "That's Prince Henry," she said.

"I still can't believe it." Martha muttered to her son.

"Mom, I told you. We're already met him several times. He's cool," Jonny said.

"I'm still not entirely clear on how that happened." Martha frowned and clicked her long, riotously colored nails together.

"Right place, right time," Uncle Donny said turning his head to address Jonny's mom.

Mrs. Carter, Uncle Donny, and Martha assisted the limo driver with their luggage amid a lot of grunting and complaints about bag weight. Tony and Tracey hung back, soaking in all the excitement. A black bird swooped over them, and Tracey's gaze followed it up and over the manor house. White-framed windows covered the entire front side of the building. Tracey spun around to take in the view. "Imagine looking at that all day." When Tony didn't comment, Tracey glanced over. Tony's gaze was glued to Noel. "He's cute, huh?"

"Shhhh. But yes, so cute!"

"Come on," she said. Grabbing Tony's sleeve, she towed him toward Prince Henry. Tony tugged free as if he didn't want anyone—Noel—thinking they were more than friends. Tracey laughed loudly, earning her a push on the shoulder from her friend. His cheeks were fiery bright but he grinned good naturedly.

Prince Henry nodded as they approached. "Hello Tracey, Tony. I heard you had some excitement on the trip over?"

"Oh, you know, all in a day's work." Tracey gestured to Kylie and then pointed to Jilly who was standing off to the side talking quietly with Laura. Her heart only clenched a little. "The two new members of my special club." She pressed her hand over her shirt where the Butterfly Stone lay hidden.

Prince Henry nodded seriously. "Right. So, there's some things I need to —"

"Hey, there. Good to see you again." Uncle Donny appeared beside Tracey and held out his hand for Prince Henry to shake. "When do we get started?"

"I was just telling Tracey that —"

"All right, everyone." Agent Malden interrupted, clapping his hands twice. "I need to chat with Tracey, Hank — erm, Prince Henry — and Don. The rest of you follow Noel inside. He'll show you to your assigned rooms. Second floor, east wing, I believe."

"Yes, sir," Noel confirmed. Tracey's knees wobbled at the wattage of the boy's bright smile. *Whoa!* Suddenly, she knew why Tony looked so stunned. That boy was like the sun. *Hot as!*

"When do we head to the movie set?" Martha asked. She tugged on Jonny's arm and pointed to her bag.

"Mom!"

Tracey laughed at Jonny's put-upon expression. He'd been inching toward Jilly but was forced to back up fast at his mom's call. Dave, who had returned from his hunt for the bathroom, ran over to help. It earned him a clap on the back from Martha. Tracey rolled her eyes. *Kiss-ass.* Kylie, Sarah, Tony, and Jilly grabbed their bags. Tony, still a tad pink in the face, stood next to their beaming liaison. Tracey waved her fingers at Tony, but he didn't see her. *Oooooo, he's got a big crush!* Though Tony might have a fight on his hands if Kylie and Sarah's expressions were anything to go by. Tracey focused on Noel and his side-eye looks at Tony. Nope. Tony had *nothing* to worry about. "Tell me all about your home," she heard Noel ask her friends as they disappeared inside. Tracey pulled her green wheelie bag closer as they left. She stared a little wistfully after Damian. He didn't look back.

Elijah Henderson waited until the noisy teens and guardians were out of earshot before he shook hands with Prince Henry and Agent Malden.

"Give us a sitrep, agent. What is the status of your investigation?"

So, Elijah Henderson knew about their search for the stones? *Mmmm.* Tracey was pretty sure *sitrep* was an abbreviation for situation report. She heard the term a lot in her science fiction streaming shows. She stared suspiciously at Agent Malden. He'd told Tracey not to tell anyone about the stones. So who was this Elijah Henderson guy really? Tracey gathered her magic into a ball and threw it out to brush over Mr. Henderson like an invisible blanket. It sparkled with light, buzzing against Tracey's skin.

Mr. Henderson's shocked stare snapped to Tracey. "Hank was right about you, young lady. That's a strong search spell you have there."

That answered that question. Mr. Henderson *was* Mage-kind. Tracey's magic blanket spell told her the same thing. His body radiated with power. She glanced at his wrist as she pulled her magic back. His suit sleeves covered any sight of an identification bracelet. He unbuttoned his cufflink and displayed his leather bracelet. The small emerald face stone looked a little like an old-style watch.

"Elijah is a member of the council, Tracey." Agent Malden said.

Her eyes popped wide. *The council?* The ones who had sent the Dust Devil to attack Tracey back in Miltern Falls? She quickly stepped back and squinted at Mr. Henderson wondering if she could actually see evil in a person's face. He looked perfectly ordinary.

"At ease, young lady. I'm a good friend of Hank's and I mean you and your friends no harm. Welcome to Ellisborough House."

She couldn't relax. Prince Henry didn't know about the attack by the Dust Devil. He didn't know the council had been checking up on her. Just because this Elijah guy was Prince Henry's friend didn't mean she was going to automatically trust him. He'd have to prove himself first.

All Tracey knew of the council was that they were powerful and sat in judgement over Mage-kind—like a supreme court—making the rules Mage-kind had to live by to safely interact with Norms. Every Mage-kind, including her grandma, seemed afraid of the council.

"Let's go sit in the parlor." Mr. Henderson pointed toward the manor house's entrance doors.

Parlor?

"What actually happened on that plane, Malden?" Mr. Henderson asked as he led them down a short cream and gold wallpapered corridor and into a small red room. *Now this is more like it.* Tracey's mouth dropped open at the rich ruby carpet, velvet red curtains, and the crimson lampshades and sofa — settee, Mr. Henderson called it. Tracey sat and was swamped with disappointment. The settee was majorly uncomfortable. How could a place as fancy as this not have comfy furniture? She tilted her weight from hip to hip, but it was no use — she could not get comfortable.

"Tracey?"

"Sorry, what?" She glanced up, startled at the sudden attention.

"You can tell them about the flight, Tracey. We might need their help to get to the bottom of the attack." Agent Malden seemed to mean it this time. *I guess that means I tell the truth.*

"We were attacked by a spell I've never seen before. A giant ghost-like hand grabbed onto us and shook us around like a dog shaking off water."

Uncle Donny dropped onto the settee next to Tracey and patted her shoulder. She caught his grimace and his sideways shift. Yep, the settee was *super* uncomfortable.

"How did you stop the attack?" Prince Henry asked.

"Agent Malden," she answered.

Prince Henry, shared a look with Elijah Henderson. Agent Malden sat down in a large armchair and ran his hands through his hair. From his stiff body language, the armchair must not have been any more comfortable than the settee. After a moment, he sighed and rested his head back against the chair. "We need to track down the perpetrator."

"I'll look into it," Mr. Henderson said.

The plane had been in midair when the attack happened. How could Mr. Henderson track down who had done it? The council must be really powerful if they could do that.

Agent Malden nodded as if Elijah's offer was to be expected. He leaned forward. "Hank, what word do you have on the missing stone?"

Uncle Donny jumped to his feet. "The investigation! Yes. We need to get to work. I'll go speak to my client."

"Hold on, Don." Malden waved him back to his seat. "Not yet. Hank, what do you know?"

"I think the stone is here. In this manor house," Prince Henry said.

"What?" Tracey launched up off the settee. Excited, but also using it as an excuse to stand up. Her tracking spell *had* worked. The blue line led her right here. But why had it splintered when it reached the door? There must be a spell on the manor. Something powerful enough to block her search spell. Mr. Henderson *was* Mage-kind and he did live here. He might have protection spells in place, and Mage-kind spells were always stronger when they were cast inside your own home. A house soaks up the magic of its owners.

"I *think* it's here. The records and historical first-hand accounts all point to here. This building in particular, but—" Prince Henry held up one finger "—I can't find it. I was hoping Tracey might have an idea on how to track it down further?"

She sank back onto the settee. "What makes you think I know how to find it?"

"You've found three so far," he reminded her.

"Three?" Mr. Henderson's eyes lit up. Though Agent Malden didn't say anything, his pursed lips indicated he was annoyed Prince Henry said that out loud. *Hmmmm.* Did that mean Agent Malden didn't fully trust the council's man? Why not? They were all staying in his home—would Agent Malden really bring them here if he didn't trust the man?

Realization of why her spell may have failed smashed into her mind like a tsunami against a shoreline. "The stones are spelled!" she reminded them. "They only become known if you already know something about them. I don't know anything about the stone. That's why I can't get a lock on it properly."

"Oh, that's right. You wear a stone, don't you?" Mr. Henderson sat forward in his armchair, elbows on his knees. His brown eyes bore into Tracey's head like he was searching her soul. "Can I see it?"

Uncle Donny held up his hand in front of her. "Best not," he said. "It's a tricky object, rather uncontrollable. You understand?"

Why is he lying? What Tracey found really strange was that Agent

Malden didn't correct him. She was missing something. Something about these four men. She didn't volunteer any more information, deciding to wait until she understood the dynamics more.

Though Mr. Henderson's gaze shone with interest, his lips twitched as he sat back, crossing one leg over the other. "Of course, of course. Apologies, Miss Tracey." He cleared his throat. "Your cover, while you are here, is the same as the one we gave your school to explain your absence. You and your friends will appear as extras in Hank's latest movie. We've set up a meeting later today for the producer's assistant to explain your scene and run you through the necessary paperwork. You'll also meet with the Head of Wardrobe in a day or two. In the meantime, you and your friends are to search for the stone Hank believes is hidden here. I must warn you though, my son and I have lived here for many years, and we have never found a hidden necklace. Magic or otherwise." The gleam in Mr. Henderson's eyes caused a river of cold to run down Tracey's spine.

Uncle Donny slapped his thighs and stood up. "We should get to work. I'll take over the investigation now, Hank. You can walk me through your notes."

Prince Henry's gaze dropped to Tracey before returning to her uncle. "Sure. Let's collect my file, and I'll talk you through what I have." He joined Uncle Donny at the door.

"I'll come with you, gentlemen." Mr. Henderson followed them from the room and silence fell over Tracey and Agent Malden like a thick blanket.

Agent Malden released a long breath. He shut his eyes, and squeezed the skin above his nose. "Okay, that's going to complicate matters."

"What is?" Tracey straightened in her seat. "What's going on?"

The agent's tired eyes opened and focused on her face. "What did you make of all of that?"

"Uncle Donny? He's going to need help. He won't ask for it. You'll have to … kind of … guide him."

"Not that, though I understand what you are saying. No, Elijah's behavior."

"Weird, I guess. Shouldn't I have mentioned the stone?"

"I don't know. I didn't expect that reaction from him. We know the council sent a watcher to Miltern Falls. Perhaps for now, we limit what is said about the stones."

Tracey paced to the window. The velvet curtains were drawn. They looked expensive. "You think Mr. Henderson sent the Dust Devil to watch me?"

"I don't know that Elijah had anything to do with that. Still, I would advise care when discussing the stones."

"He's on the council. He must know about the watcher, right?"

"He might be on the council, Tracey, but that doesn't mean he knows everything the council is up to. I'm sure we can trust him. Hank trusts him. We should give Elijah the benefit of doubt until we know more. The Stones of Power—the idea of all that magic is seductive. Let's observe his actions, not pre-judge him based on his words."

"I don't understand."

The agent smiled. "I'll explain the convoluted politics of council matters another time. For now, start your search for the stone. But keep it quiet and report only to me, okay?"

"Sure." Tracey hadn't told Agent Malden about the tracking spell. And she wasn't going to. Everyone was acting so weird, including Agent Malden. For now, she wouldn't say anything to anyone who wasn't one of her school friends. "About Kylie?" she asked.

"Tracey, I know you promised to remove the Serpent's Kiss from Kylie's neck, but I don't think you should take it off. Right now, the three stones have a protector, and they can't be removed. Which means, they can't be taken away."

"Taken away? By who?"

Malden didn't say anything. It was obvious he was thinking about Mr. Henderson and the council.

"But you said you'd help find a way to remove it so Kylie can't be possessed by Timothy again."

"Tracey. We are in unknown territory. Three stones have never been discovered let alone brought into such close proximity before. We don't have a protocol to handle this. You are in contact with the stone's originator, are you not?"

"Yes. My ancestor Stephanie."

"Talk to her. I'm just asking you to hold off on removing the stones until we know more about them. Someone orchestrated the attack on the plane. We must be careful about who we trust."

Tracey wondered if he was thinking what she was thinking. That Mr. Henderson or the council were behind the attack on the plane. Did Prince Henry know they'd be attacked when he sent for them? *Is that why he called us here? What if it wasn't to find the stone but to put us in the path of the council? Does he suspect the council is behind the attack?* Was that really why Agent Malden didn't want her to remove the stones? So the council couldn't get their hands on them?

"Until we know who is working against us, we should keep anything we find to ourselves. Understand? Just keep me in the loop until we know who we can trust."

Tracey blinked slowly. Was Agent Malden suggesting he didn't trust Prince Henry now?

"Tracey?"

"Ah, sure. Yes. That's fine."

Don't trust anyone. Tracey got the message. She stood up. Since the tracking spell hadn't worked properly, she'd need to learn more about the stones to find the one hidden here.

Maybe she should talk to Jilly's ancestor, Jing Cho. If Stephanie's ancestor was hanging around inside the Butterfly Stone, then the Tiger's Eye should contain the spirit of Jilly's ancestor. He might know something about the next stone. *And then there are the stones' guardians themselves.* They seemed to be separate entities to the spirits housed within the stones. Tracey and her friends needed to investigate that aspect of the stones too. Like, how did they get in there and who were they? What about the sect? How did Stephanie, Timothy, and Jing get together in the first place? Tracey realized there was still a lot she didn't know about the Stones of Power.

"I know I'm putting a lot onto you, Tracey. But the Butterfly Stone chose you. You can figure this out if you believe in yourself and your friends. You've got this."

Tracey stopped at the closed door, her hand gripping the silver handle.

"So, I've got to act in a movie, search for the missing stones, and help Kylie remove *her* stone, all without anyone finding out what I'm doing. Sure, okay. Piece of cake." Tracey rolled her eyes and pushed the door open. "So, where's my room?"

It was as if I was both there and not there. Time lost
all meaning. Minutes became days became years.
I fear the experience has turned me quite mad
and, somehow, made my curse stronger.

6

Tracey's mouth dropped open as she stepped inside the girls' bedroom. "Wow." It was all bright gold and white wallpaper, gold skirting boards and ornately decorated cornices that looked delicate and flowery. The four beds were covered in frilly white ruffles and lace. Jilly and Laura had taken the beds closest to the windows and Sarah waited on a bed furthest away from the door. The cream carpet was thick and springy. When Tracey jumped on the only unoccupied bed, she let out a pleased moan as she sank into the super soft mattress.

"Cool, right?" Sarah said, grinning at Tracey's reaction. Jilly just stared, her eyes narrowing.

Tracey almost looked behind herself to see who Jilly was staring at. She shook off the feeling of examination. "It's brilliant," Tracey said in a mock British accent. Jilly and Laura groaned. "Oh, come on, chaps. It's not that bloody awful, is it?"

"It's not good," Laura said with a laugh.

Tracey gave a royal wave and jumped off the bed. She peered through the ceiling to floor windows at the view outside. "Oh, there's the maze." Tall, bright emerald hedges stretched off into the distance. "Wow, it's huge. I can't even see the middle. We are so going out there to find a way through it. Jonny will love it." She thought about what Mr. Henderson and Agent Malden told her and began to wonder at the connection. Millicent had written about a maze, hadn't she? Maybe Millicent had stayed here? Maybe it was *her* stone they were searching for? But why had the tracking spell failed? There had to be a spell on the manor. She just had to figure out how to break it.

Jilly straightened. "What's our plan?"

Tracey shrugged and turned around. "There's not one. Not officially."

"But you spoke to Agent Malden?"

"Yep."

"And unofficially?"

"Uncle Donny's taking over Prince Henry's investigation."

"Oh." Sarah's face soured at that.

Jilly looked from her to Tracey and then back to Laura. "What am I missing?"

Sarah giggled. "Uncle Donny is not the, um, best detective."

Jilly frowned. "Is he not friends with Agent Malden?"

"I think they were school friends or something." Tracey told her. "Uncle Donny means well, but his usual cases involve missing pets and stolen phones. He is surprisingly good at finding people though."

"Oh." After a moment of silence Jilly stood up and began unpacking her bag. Laura slid off her bed to do the same.

Sarah pushed open the door on the right. "Look, Trace. We have our own bathroom! How cool is that? Better than at home, right?"

"Sharing between four girls? It will be worse than at home."

That prompted a dramatic moan from her sister.

"Now who's the bad actor?" Tracey lifted her green suitcase up onto her bed and unzipped it. "I'm calling a team meeting after our induction with the producer's assistant."

"The tracking spell. You have a lead?" Jilly asked.

"That's the thing. The tracking spell didn't work—well it did, but it didn't—the line broke up when we got here. Prince Henry thinks there is a stone here in the manor somewhere. I think he's right but we just need another way to find it. We need to know more about it. Where are the others?"

"Settling into their rooms," Laura said. She pointed to the bedroom door. "Jonny, Tony, and Dave are in the room at the top of the hall. Jonny's mom has her own room. Damian, Kylie, and their mom are in the room next to Martha. Then there's us. Your uncle is in the room on the other side, and then Agent Malden."

"What did Prince Henry say? When do we film our big scene?" Sarah dumped her clothes onto her bed by upending her suitcase.

"Must we take part in this charade? We are not here for a silly movie. We have a mission to complete." Jilly's eyeroll was epic.

Sarah scowled at her. "But we're here to film too. It's our excuse."

Tracey stood between them and waved her hands. "You're both right. Jilly, we have to participate in the movie, but yes, you have a good point. We're here to find the next stone. I have a few ideas about that. We have to search the manor house." Jilly's stare made Tracey's skin prickle. "And I think you and I should talk to your ancestor, Jilly. He might be able to give us a clue."

"Can we start searching while you do that?" Sarah's question came fast on the heels of Tracey's suggestion.

"Maybe wait—"

"Wait? Why? We can look around without you."

"No, Sarah. You can't go—"

"If you say this is a thing only you, Dave, Jilly and Tony can do. I'm gonna scream. I can help. I'm not a baby."

"Sarah—"

"I can help."

Tracey recognized Sarah's scrunched up face all too well. "I guess so. But we should get more organized. Don't go searching all by yourself." Sarah grinned as Jilly's expression grew darker.

Fruit tingles. I just can't win today.

"You said we can speak with my ancestor? How do we do this?" Jilly asked, sitting down on her bed.

"My ancestor, Stephanie, is inside the Butterfly Stone, or a part of her is—her spirit? I don't know, but we know Timothy haunts the Serpent's Kiss, so I figure Jing might be within the Tiger's Eye. Stephanie hasn't exactly been helpful, but maybe Jing will be more open? It's worth a try anyway. Get comfortable," Tracey said.

"While you're doing that, I'm having a shower," Laura announced. She grabbed her washbag and towel out of her bag.

"I'll go find Kylie," Sarah said, and in a blink she had disappeared out through the door.

Jilly moved to the center of her bed and crossed her legs. Tracey shifted her pillow around to lean up against the headboard and used it as a backrest, sitting with her legs outstretched in front of her. "Has the Tiger's Eye ever tried to speak with you? Have you heard any voices?" Tracey asked.

"No, nothing. Should I have heard something?" Jilly pulled the stone out from beneath her top. It was an orange stone with a black shadow through the center that made it look like its namesake.

"I can't get my stone to shut up. What about heat? Does it ever get hot?"

"No."

Strange. Why was the Tiger's Eye being so quiet, and what did that say about the Butterfly Stone? "One thing you should know. The spirit can possess you."

Jilly frowned. "Like Timothy did to Kylie?"

"Yes. But I've found they can only do it if you let them. They need permission to take control."

"That is good to know."

"Close your eyes," Tracey instructed. "And hold the Tiger's Eye in one hand. In your mind, call out your ancestor's name."

"And then?"

"That's it. That's all I do."

Tracey showed Jilly what she meant. She pulled the Butterfly Stone from beneath her shirt collar. It was a gray stone with a painted butterfly on it. As soon as her hand closed around the Butterfly Stone, that odd sensation of being tugged forward pulled on her chest and when she opened her eyes she stood in the white room. She was alone. "Stephanie?"

Her ancestor appeared in a blink. She clasped her gloved hands together. "I was not expecting your summons. How did your flying machine go? Are you well?"

"I'm fine." Tracey spun in place wondering where Jilly had gone.

"What do you search for?"

"My friend. She wears the Tiger's Eye."

Stephanie's eyes brightened and a large grin tilted her lips up, flashing white teeth. "You have another stone."

Tracey squinted. *Why are you so happy about that?* "Where would Jilly have gone if she's not here?"

"The stones are connected."

Right, yes. Of course they are. Tracey closed her eyes. "Jilly?"

The ground fell away beneath Tracey's feet. She gasped as the world wobbled. Where the inside of the Butterfly Stone was white, the Tiger's Eye was deep red, like the manor house parlor. Jilly's eyes widened at Tracey's sudden appearance. "What is this place?" Jilly asked.

"I think we're inside the Tiger's Eye. Did you call for Jing?"

"Yes, but why can I not move?"

"It's the way the stones work. Only our minds are here, so nothing is real. Not for our bodies at least." Tracey looked around and called, "Jing Cho?"

A slender man blurred into being a short distance away. He wore a red suit with a white, high-necked shirt. His loose trousers looked super comfortable and black slip-on shoes covered his feet, though he wore no socks. His long black hair—exactly like Jilly's—was tied back in a ponytail. His head tilted in Jilly's direction. "Descendant of mine?"

"Yes, sir," Jilly said. Her voice was soft, but her smile was enormous. "Ancestor, this is my friend, Tracey. She is the protector of the Butterfly Stone."

"Greetings young one. Though I should have known who you were without my descendant's introduction. You have her face."

"Stephanie is my ancestor."

"As it should be. But why are you here? I would talk to my descendant alone."

"Oh, um. Sure, but I wanted to ask you about the other stones. Can you tell us anything about them?"

"I cannot."

"Why not?" Jilly asked.

"Descendant, you understand not the matters that have taken place before your time."

"I know that for all of my life I have suffered from a curse that has spelled Mage-kind to forget about me. I was punished for what you and the other stone protectors did." Jilly's voice carried all her hurt and anger.

Tracey worried Jing would be upset by her aggressive attitude. "Perhaps you could give us a clue about the other stones? We're searching for one with a blue thread. It fractured into dozens of lines when we reached the manor house and I—"

"I cannot help you. Each of us has suffered an individual fate—our punishment—as you have accused." He gestured to Jilly. "You have broken the curse on the Tiger's Eye?"

Jilly nodded.

"Then you have done what I could not." He flicked his arm at Tracey. "You may go."

Tracey was flung out of the red room and sat up on her bed. "Whoa!" Her head spun like she'd just gotten off a merry-go-round. The shower was still running in the bathroom so not much time had passed. Jilly sat in the middle of her bed, one hand holding the Tiger's Eye, the other rested peacefully on her knee. Her eyes were closed, and she breathed slowly. *So that's what I look like when I do it.* Tracey lay back on her bed and stared up at the ceiling. *What are Jilly and Jing talking about?*

The shower water cut off with a squawk from the pipes. Jilly inhaled deeply and opened her eyes.

"Cool, huh?" Tracey asked.

"Yes." Jilly lay down, mirroring Tracey, and crossed her hands over her belly. "What a strange experience."

"Did he tell you anything about the other stones?"

"Nothing. I do not believe we can rely on his information anyway."

"What do you mean?" Tracey asked. The dizziness had faded so she sat up.

"He said punishment."

"Yeah, so?"

"Punishment implies a crime."

Huh. Tracey climbed off her bed and wandered to the window. She stared down at the maze. "Who punished them?"

"And why were they punished? Interesting questions, are they not?"

"Yeah."

"Memory seems to be a punishment for all of them in one way or another."

Tracey thought about her Nana's dementia, and Stephanie often said she couldn't remember the past. Jilly had a point. "Who is powerful enough to have carried out their sentences? The council?"

Jilly didn't answer.

"Mr. Henderson got all strange when we were talking about the stones. Agent Malden said to be careful around him." The bathroom door popped open and Laura emerged in a burst of steam, dressed in skinny jeans and a unicorn-imaged crop top. A long, sheer black shirt hung over it. "Didn't I give you that unicorn shirt?" Tracey asked.

"Yep." Laura phoofed her hair and checked her reflection in the mirror. A knock rapped loudly on their door.

"Come in," Tracey called.

Jonny poked his head inside. "They want us downstairs to talk to the movie assistant lady."

Sarah appeared behind Jonny. "Come on," she shouted and ran off as Tracey turned to the mirror to check her hair. Laura pulled on her yellow ankle boots. There was a rising sound of chatter coming from the hall.

Jilly moaned. "Acting!"

Tracey grinned at her. "Well, you finally got what you wanted. You should be happy."

"What do you mean?"

"The curse that kept you unremembered. It's definitely broken now. Everyone will see you in the movie. You'll be famous."

Jilly's face twisted and she moaned. "That was not the result I had in mind when I envisioned finding the Tiger's Eye and breaking its curse."

I would scroom foo hours, and soo
life after life end behind my eyes.
Everyooo I ever touched.
Everyooo I ever koaw.

1

Tracey had goosebumps as she headed downstairs to meet the producer's assistant. Angela was an older Asian lady with hair tied up in a messy bun. She wore black jeans and had a headset hanging around her neck, a pen poked out from behind her ear and she carried a tablet in one hand and a cell phone in the other.

"Hey kids—oh, and adults." She glanced at Prince Henry, who stood near the door. "You are all extraordinarily lucky to be joining us and we are very grateful. I understand it's been a long trip for you all to get here. I'm sorry to say the director isn't available to chat to you today, but she asked that I take you through the basics, get the paperwork done and go over the rules for being on set."

Angela spoke fast, as if she was running out of time or had somewhere more important to be. She gestured for them to follow her and powerwalked down the hallway. Tracey pulled a face at her friends as they raced to keep up. Angela led them into a long room. Three round tables had been set up with no chairs. On each table was a large ream of paper.

Tracey caught the series of raised eyebrows traveling between Uncle Donny, Martha, and Mrs. Carter. *That's a lot of paperwork.* She rose up on her toes to see over her friends. There was no sign of Agent Malden or Elijah Henderson. Noel, their liaison, emptied a box of pens out onto the first table. He looked up and smiled broadly. "Hey."

Prince Henry waved his hand at all the paper. "Confidentiality agreements, insurance, safety stuff, and a number of other releases. It's all pretty standard."

"Where's Agent Malden?" Tracey asked him.

"He's around here somewhere."

Angela waved the adults closer. "You can sign as their guardians and then the kids can add their signatures. Now, listen up everyone. Tomorrow morning, you'll be sent to visit our costume manager. Her team will measure you for your outfits and tweak them if they need resizing. After that, I'll collect you and take you to the set. You'll be walk-on extras, which means no spoken lines. You are not to interrupt or talk during filming. You'll be told where to sit and where to walk. When the director calls action you'll move to your mark and then to your next mark. And that's it."

"That's all?" Dave asked. "We just walk from one spot to another? That's our big scene?"

The excitement on the teens' faces fell away as Angela nodded. Tracey had been hoping for more than that, but she reminded herself that they were not really here to star in a movie. Still, it was disappointing. She glanced at Jilly, expecting to see her smile at the news. She was staring again. Tracey raised her eyebrows at her, wondering if she had something on her face. Jilly turned away.

"The director might have time to give you a quick briefing before filming starts. Don't rely on that though. There will be on-site assistants who will guide you with your moves if you get lost. Once the director calls cut, don't leave the set. Return to your first mark. They may need to reshoot the scene several times. It's going be a long, boring day. Welcome to show business, kids. Now, do you have any questions?"

They shook their heads. Tracey stayed near Prince Henry as Angela guided everyone to the first table.

"Prince Henry?" Kylie and Sarah popped up in the celebrity's shadow. "Do you have any acting advice for us?" Sarah asked. Her face was flushed. Tracey leaned closer, anxious to hear what the actor prince had to say.

"Listen to as many people as you can. Do everything they ask you to do, and treat everyone with respect, from the assistants and catering staff, to the lighting and sound technicians, and to the other actors. Most importantly, enjoy yourselves."

"But how do you act? How do you know when you're doing a good job?" Kylie asked.

"Acting allows you to be anyone you want to be. Believe you are the character hard enough and you become them. I can be who I am not. It's a little like hiding in plain sight."

"Like your undercover work with Agent Malden?" Tracey asked.

He nodded.

"Is it hard to keep secrets?" Kylie asked. "Hiding that you're Mage-kind and not using your magic?"

"No, it's freeing," he told them.

How could that be? Tracey loved her magic. How could you not want to show the world who you were? She'd found it so horrible having to suppress her magic with double shields. When she'd stopped shielding and embraced her natural magic, she'd felt so much better—not as angry. And Jilly had been under a curse that stopped Mage-kind from being able to remember her. She'd been hidden in plain sight—and she'd hated it. Prince Henry couldn't be honest with himself or anyone he knew. It was kinda sad. He could never let down his guard. *What a lonely life that must be.*

Agent Malden appeared at the door and called Prince Henry away. Tracey sidled up to her uncle's side as he was asking Angela, "To confirm, the kids have to sign each page?"

She nodded—"Yep!"—and turned to answer a question from Martha.

Tracey eyed the pile of pages in her uncle's hand. *This is going to take all night.*

"Right, let's do this in order." Mrs. Carter took charge. "Everyone get in line."

Tracey ended up with Tony behind her and Laura in front. They were way up the back of the line. Uncle Donny stood at one table, Jonny's mom monitored the next, and Kylie's mom stood at the last table. Tracey and her friends would wind their way along each guardian to sign a stack of papers.

While they waited for their turn, Laura whispered, "What's the plan?"

Tony leaned over Tracey's shoulder. "Yeah, when do we start searching for the stones?"

Tracey shrugged. "I don't have a plan exactly. After we're done here and eat, I figure everyone can come to our room. Don't let Martha and

Mrs. Carter know."

"Should we leave Damian and Kylie out then? Their mom won't let them leave her side," Laura mumbled.

Tracey glanced down the line at the three in question. "Yeah. Maybe we should keep them out of it. I don't want to get them into any more trouble with their mom." The line wriggled up as Dave moved to the second table and Jonny started signing his name at the first table.

"What about Kylie?" Tony asked. "Any idea how we can remove Timothy's stone? I've got alerts set up all over the M-net, but nothing has flagged." They shuffled forward again.

Tracey shook her head. "No idea. Kylie's safe from Timothy at least."

"Yeah, but she can't use her magic," Tony said.

A dreamy voice came from somewhere near Tracey's shoulder. "Hey."

She glanced over to find Noel standing at her side. "Hi."

Noel's gaze drifted to Tony before returning to Tracey. "How are you all settling in?"

Laura gushed. "This place is amazing!"

"Yeah," Tracey said. I can't believe you actually live here."

"It is strange somedays." Noel locked eyes with Tracey "My father has asked that I show you around the manor. Also to take you into town if that is what you would like?"

"Um." Darn. That would make it difficult to search for the stone. Tracey caught Tony's wide gaze and flushed cheeks. "Tony has a list of places — libraries — he wants to see."

"At Oxford? Certainly. I can even arrange for a private showing."

"Th-thanks," Tony said.

Noel turned back to Tracey. "Please do tell me if there is anything you need while you are here? Anything at all. No matter how odd."

Tracey squinted at their host. "Okay. Sure." He didn't move. "Nothing right now," she told him.

After a moment he nodded. "Very well. I'll make some calls and return. Dinner will be in the dining room this evening." Noel paused as if hoping they'd say something else. After an awkward silence he spun on a heel and left.

"Was that weird?" Tracey asked.

Laura wiggled her eyebrows at Tony. "Soooo," she sang. "Noel?"

Tony's face turned from pink to red so fast Tracey wondered if he was about to keel over and die. She bit back a smile. "He's super cute, Tony. A bit weird, but cute."

"Ah, shut up you two. He's nice. I mean, he was nice. He's supposed to be nice. He's our liaison." Tony moaned. Tracey and Laura shared a look and giggled. Tracey grabbed Tony's hand and squeezed it. He squeezed her hand back. "He might not be —"

"He was making eyes at you, Tony."

"He totally was," Laura teased.

Tracey poked her in the side. Laura squealed and wriggled out of reach. "Maybe at dinner you can ask him if he knows the real reason we're here? Don't tell him about the stones though. Not unless he asks first," Tracey said. "Agent Malden wants us to be careful around Mr. Henderson. I guess the same would go for his son too."

"I don't want to lie to him," Tony said quickly.

"You won't have to. Just don't mention the stones."

He scuffed his shoes against the thick carpet. "Yeah, okay."

They jerked as Dave shouted at them. "Keep moving or we'll be here all night. I'm starved."

Laura slid forward several steps. Tracey caught Jonny's eye. He stood near his mom and it looked like he'd just finished signing all his paperwork. Laura bent over to sign her name.

Tracey whispered to Tony. "I need some ideas about breaking old spells."

"What spell?"

Tracey checked the room for the producer's assistant. Angela stood talking to Mrs. Carter. Kylie and Damian were signing pages at their mom's table. Tracey couldn't see Prince Henry. He must have left with Agent Malden. "The one that stops us from taking off the stones."

"I don't know if we can break that. It's really old, and was set by really strong Mage-kind."

"Kylie's stone is like a time bomb counting down, only we don't know how much time is on the clock. Besides, we broke the Tiger's Eye spell and that was probably the same age. We have to find a way to do it before Timothy tries to escape again."

"I'll expand my searches. I was focused on the stones, but I can add that to the algorithm."

"Thanks." Tracey said and turned around to start writing her name.

"Oh, my hand is sooooo sore," Jonny complained, waving his fingers around in the air. It was the eighth time Tracey had heard the complaint.

They'd gone to the dining room straight after signing all their paper-work and scoffed down the fish and chips the kitchen had served them. Tony sat beside Noel and talked softly with him throughout dinner. Tracey was dying to ask what they had talked about. The teens — minus Damian, Kylie, and Noel — were now in the girls' room in their pajamas and dress-ing gowns, plonked down on every available surface. Tracey felt bad about excluding Damian and Kylie, but it would be easier this way. Noel left them at the door to their bedrooms, lingering like he wanted to be invited inside. Tracey had smiled broadly and announced how tired they were before she said "goodnight" and shut the door in his face. "I hope Noel's not angry," she mused.

"Nah, he'll be fine," Dave said from the chest of drawers he sat on.

"What did Prince Henry say? What clues was he following?" Jonny asked. He was sitting on the floor in front of the bathroom door, leaning back against it. He flipped his bowler hat around in his hands.

"Probably the same things that are mentioned in the journal. A large manor house with a maze. I think this might be where Stephanie actually lived," Tracey told them.

"You mean the book Jonny hid after Tony stole it from Doctor Chan? That journal?" Dave asked. He opened the top drawer, pulled out a pencil and put it back, then a paperclip. He even found a stapler. "Isn't it written by the other lady? Not your ancestor. The other one."

"Millicent? Yeah it is," Tracey confirmed.

Laura sat on the end of her bed, plaiting her hair. Sarah sat next to her, waiting patiently for her turn. It was nice of Laura to offer. Sarah always complained Tracey didn't do it right. Tracey pulled the journal out of her carry-on bag and held it up. "Mainly it's about her fears. She dreams of death a lot."

"Ew, creepy," Sarah said.

"Not really. I think they're Visions."

"Oh, well then that's kinda cool." Sarah's head tilted. "Visions of what?"

"It's not clear. She hasn't been specific, but I've only read about half way."

"Where is Agent Malden?" Dave asked. "I feel like he should have suffered through that signature punishment with us."

"No idea. Prince Henry said he'll join us soon. I sent him a text," Tracey said.

"You text a prince." Dave shook his head.

She shrugged. "Anyway, we have three stones."

"And we need three more," Laura said.

"What about your stone tracking spell?" Jonny asked. They all made interested noises asking about it.

Tracey held up her hands. "I saw a blue thread. It followed the limo, or actually we followed it. That's why I think the stone has got to be here somewhere. Prince Henry thinks it's here too."

"So where did the thread go when we got here? Which floor?" Dave asked.

Tracey shook her head. "It shattered into pieces when it hit the manor house. I think the spell failed because the manor house belongs to Mage-kind. Homes tend to soak up the magic of the people who live in them. It's why you never break into a Mage-kind's house. I mean, it's definitely owned by Mage-kind now. Mr. Henderson and Noel are Mage-kind, but if Millicent once lived here, yeah, an old spell designed to protect a house would do something like that to my spell."

"Do you know anything from the journal about the stone that's here? Once we have an idea about the stones it opens up the M-net to my searches," Tony said, swiping his cell to wake it up.

"It was a blue thread. It's not much. Oh wait." Tracey dumped everything out of her backpack, searching for her crinkled poem, blushing as her clean underwear fell out. "Whoops." She shoved everything back into her bag. "Here it is." She held up the crinkled piece of paper. It was the poem Tony found back when he'd first started researching the Butterfly Stone. "I've been rereading this. It's vague, but it's a start." She gave it to Laura to read and pass on. "I think the middle verses are about the stones, or at least the protectors who held them."

"Bleh, I can barely understand your handwriting." Dave held the page up to his nose. "So, you figure this one's yours? *The one who leads, who dreamed of more, lost her mind in the fire, her charge now her curse.*' I don't see anything that fits with Jilly's stone."

"Oh, oh, Tony?" Tracey bounced excitedly.

Tony already had his phone open. "Checking now. Oooooo. Cool, so there's a new verse. *Hidden in life, lost in love, forgotten by hope, emptiness lies in his soul.*' Whoa!"

Sarah yanked the page from Dave's hands. "So this one's about Timothy, yeah? *The last held desire, for power and purpose. His soul, but a shadow, alone in his curse.*' I mean shadow — the Shadowman. That's a connection."

"How can we find out which verse is about which person for sure though?" Jonny asked. Laying back on the carpet, he tilted his feet up so they rested on the bathroom door.

"What does the poem even mean?" Sarah waved the page around. "Listen. *Death, loss, and madness marked.*' What the heck?"

A knock echoed off the door. "Come in," Tracey called. The bedroom door popped open and Uncle Donny peered inside. "Here you are."

Prince Henry and Agent Malden followed Uncle Donny inside. "We have news."

No ooo comes out here.
It is my place. Mioo alooo.
Out here I do not soo the
consequences of my inaction.

8

Tracey and her friends sat up straighter. "What news?" Tracey asked. She slipped Millicent's journal under her pillow. Jonny pulled his feet off the wall and straightened, plopping his hat back on his head. It was a funny look with his purple flannel pajamas.

Uncle Donny waved a thin file around. "A lead on the stone."

Prince Henry frowned at him. "Well, a lead on the sect, not the stone per se."

"What do you mean?" Tracey knew the others were as curious as she was. "Is that what you've been investigating since you got here?"

He sat on the end of Tracey's bed, facing them all. Uncle Donny parked his butt next to Sarah on Laura's bed. Agent Malden stayed standing just inside the door, arms crossed over his chest. Prince Henry scrubbed his hand through his hair. No gray. She wondered if he dyed it for his movies. Uncle Donny had a lot of gray at his temples, as did Agent Malden.

"You remember your uncle's mysterious British client?" Prince Henry asked.

"Yeah," Tracey said. "A collector who was looking for a missing journal. The book was sold from an estate which means the original owner died, doesn't it?" *Millicent's journal. The one I still haven't told Uncle Donny I have.*

"Right, well this manor house is where the book should have been sent. Elijah bought it from a man named Rodney Transcenni, the owner of Millicent's book. Coincidently, he also lived here."

"Wait a minute." Jonny jumped to his feet and began to pace. "So he got the journal from here? Wait." He spun around to face Tracey. "The guy that came to your uncle's office was called Frank Transcenni, wasn't he? So, Rodney is his … what, brother?"

"The journal was sold to Elijah. Let me guess. Frank says it never should have been sold?" Tracey said.

"Correct." Uncle Donny pointed at Tracey and made a *click-click* sound with his tongue.

Tracey hummed. "Was Rodney Transcenni murdered?"

Uncle Donny turned his fingers into a pistol shape. "Bingo." At the door, Agent Malden sighed and shook his head.

"Who murdered him?" Laura asked.

"Oh!" Tracey jumped off her bed and pointed at her uncle. "Frank is a suspect. He wants the book back. Did he kill for it?"

Agent Malden cleared his throat. "Frank Transcenni is a member of the council."

"Ohhhh," Jonny said. He stopped pacing. "Another victim or the killer?"

"Shhhh," Uncle Donny said, his fingers meeting his lips. "We, of course, don't suspect Mr. Transcenni of his brother's murder." He winked. Tracey rolled her eyes.

"The journal was supposed to come here. Frank Transcenni redirected it, but wait … So Doctor Chan redirected it after it had already been redirected?" Tony asked.

"It was redirected twice?" Jilly repeated. She was staring at Tracey again.

Well, three times technically. Tracey thought of the journal hidden under her pillow. She avoided looking at Tony as he was the one to do the third redirection. Dave waved his hands around. "It's like a game of pass the parcel. So, who won?"

"Two questions," Tracey said ignoring Dave's question. "One, where did Rodney Transcenni get the journal from originally, and two, where is Frank Transcenni now?"

"Three," Prince Henry added. "Where is the journal?"

Tracey mashed her lips together and eyed her friends. Should she tell the two men she had the book? Agent Malden said not to trust anyone, but this was her uncle and Prince Henry. Tony and Jilly subtly shook their heads. Tracey nodded. She went in a different direction. "When did Mr.

Henderson buy this manor house? Did he buy it for the council? Do they want the stones?"

The three adults remained silent.

"If Mr. Henderson bought the manor house and everything in it then the council must have already searched the house. If anything was here, they'd have found it," Tracey concluded.

"The journal had been sold," Tony reminded her.

"They must think the location of the other stones are in it," Jonny said.

Prince Henry glanced at Uncle Donny. "Without the journal, we just don't know." Tracey made sure to keep her gaze away from the pillow where she'd hidden the journal. Agent Malden was watching her too closely.

"Was that all the news you had for us?" Sarah asked.

Uncle Donny tapped his nose. "This manor house *is* the answer."

"What do you mean?" Tracey shared a look with her friends. She sank back down on her bed. *Millicent's beloved maze.* "One of the sect lived here way back then, didn't they? That's why you think a stone is here.

"All of them lived here," Prince Henry said. "This was their homebase."

"Wait, what?" Jonny blurted. "We're staying in the same manor house Timothy lived in?"

"Yup," Uncle Donny confirmed.

"Really?" Tracey pulled her knees up and wrapped her arms around them. The bedroom no longer felt like such a safe place. "Then the missing stone can't be here. There's no way Stephanie and her friends would leave their stones where Timothy could get his hands on them."

"Don't be so sure," Uncle Donny said.

"You think they're magically hidden?" Laura asked.

"At least one is here." Prince Henry said. "Maybe more." Everyone looked excited and stood up, ready to start searching. "Wait, hold up. We need a plan before you all go running off."

"What's to plan, we split up and search the place." Dave headed for the door.

"It's not that simple," Agent Malden said stopping Dave in his tracks.

"Remember, we can't find it if we don't know what we're looking for," Tracey said. "Actually, we were just talking about that." She waved a hand and Laura passed over the page with the Stones of Power poem. Agent Malden read it silently and then handed it to Uncle Donny.

"Where did you find this?" Uncle Donny waved the page in the air.

"Tony found it when he was researching the Butterfly Stone," Tracey told him.

Prince Henry plucked the paper from Uncle Donny's hand and read it silently. "It's vague."

"Yeah," Jonny said dragging the sounds out. "We were just saying that."

"I have an idea. Everyone grab your phone and go to the search bar," Tony ordered. The room filled with shuffling noises as everyone located their cell phones. Dave threw himself down at the foot of Jilly's bed looking bored. Typical. He was an action guy, not a research guy. "Go to the M-net if you're Mage-kind. Laura, Jonny, just try an ordinary search, you never know what will come up. Mage-kind often forget what Norms can do," he said, looking at Jilly. The girl tilted her head and smirked. It was only through Jilly's friendship with Laura that they'd been able to discover and break the memory curse. It had only affected Mage-kind.

Tracey jumped in. "Tony discovered there's a secrecy spell on the story of the stones. If you know what to search for, you can find out more about them. So, our guesses will have to be really close. What did you find out about the sect?"

Agent Malden moved away from the door. He was the only one who wasn't on his phone. "We have their names. Stephanie Alders, Timothy Hart, Millicent Flowers, Jing Cho, Charles Smith, and Matthew Williams."

"Matthew is a Norm though, remember, Jilly? You told me," Tracey said.

"Wait a minute. How do we know all these people are members of the Sect of Six?" Laura asked.

"We don't," Uncle Donny said. "But the first step to any investigation is to note down everything we already know."

"I'll take notes on my phone," Laura offered.

Uncle Donny's smile was wide. "Excellent. Thank you."

"Okay. Search for Millicent, Charles, and Matthew and add in the

Stones of Power," Tony ordered.

The only sound was the little key clicks Uncle Donny made when he typed into his phone. All of Tracey's friends had their cell phone keyboards muted.

"Anything?" Tracey asked glaring at *"search not found"* on her phone.

Sarah sighed and flopped back on her bed. "Nope."

Dave tossed his phone on the carpet in front of him. "Nada."

"What about animals?" Jonny asked. "Just type some in, we might get lucky."

"That's a lot of options," Prince Henry said. Dave dragged his phone back and swiped at the screen with one finger.

Uncle Donny waved his hand around. "Suggestions?"

"Lions, meercats? Giraffe?" Sarah listed. "Mice, turtles, toucan?"

"The animal makes sense to the person," Tracey mused. "Stephanie said I had the qualities of a butterfly—like she did. I think we need to know more about each person's personality, likes and dislikes."

"What else do we know?" Uncle Donny asked.

Prince Henry swiped his phone and scrolled down to check his notes. "Millicent and Stephanie were lifelong friends. Stephanie was promised to Matthew Williams but had an affair with Timothy Hart."

"Timothy spelled her," Tracey insisted. "She didn't have a choice."

"Perhaps so." Prince Henry nodded. "I've been looking into why the manor house was sold and I've found some interesting information about their deaths."

"I've not found out anything about how they died," Tony said scowling at his phone.

"The council archive contains a large number of original documents. Old reports and letters. Elijah has been a great help with pulling it all together. That's actually where Agent Malden was earlier. Going through the archive records."

Malden nodded. "There are a few more reports I want to consult about the incident. As it took place a few months after the Mage-kind rebellion there are missing and incomplete entries. While you are at the studio tomorrow, I've booked time to consult the council library."

"How did they die?" Tracey asked, returning to the original question.

"It's not pleasant. There was a fire. It tore through an entire wing of the manor and killed everyone inside."

"Oh," Laura gasped. "That's terrible."

Tracey wondered if her friends were all picturing it in their minds the way she was. It was especially hard for Tracey. Stephanie wore her face, so imagining her twin stuck in a place filled with flame and smoke was terrible. Silence fell over the bedroom, thick with unsaid emotion. After a long moment, Tracey asked, "All of them?"

"No bodies were recovered. The north wing of the manor was rebuilt several years after the fire."

"How tragic," Jilly said and bowed her head.

They sat in silence while they absorbed that information. Tracey imagined she could hear screaming and smell the smoke. She had seen this place in the memories her grandma had shown her. Now that she was here, she recognized the artistic ceiling cornices and the wall colors. She had to find that room—the one with the fireplace where she'd seen Stephanie in the memory. There might be a clue in there somewhere. Unless that room had been the one that burned down.

"North wing?" Dave repeated.

Prince Henry's eyebrow rose, and his lips pursed in thought. "Why do you ask?"

"We don't have to search that, then," Dave said. They looked at him, so he clarified. "They rebuilt it. There'll be nothing to find."

"Good point," Prince Henry said with a smile.

"What do we know about them?" Tracey asked. "The others I mean. Millicent, Charles, and Matthew?"

"I'm still looking into Charles and Matthew, but Millicent—now she's an interesting case. She was orphaned quite young and spent her early years at a local facility. She was taken in by Stephanie's family as a young adult. She and Stephanie grew up together and were reportedly inseparable. It is my belief Millicent was certainly a member of the sect."

"She was," Tracey said. "I've seen her in the memories my grandma shared—Stephanie's memories. I saw Millicent trying to convince

Stephanie to join them in an experiment." Tracey believed it right down to the pit of her stomach. Millicent was Mage-kind and a member of the Sect of Six. "And Matthew was a Norm. Jilly told me Jing worked for a Norm named Matthew."

"Search it!" Jonny cried and they bent over their phones again. Tracey typed in variations of Matthew and Millicent, but nothing came up.

"Search not found," came the chorus of replies.

"This is so annoying," Dave grumbled.

"What about if we —"

The door flew open, freezing Tracey mid-speech. Damian's stormy gaze swept the room, taking in everyone who was there. Behind him stood Kylie, her lips wobbling. "What are you doing in here?" Damian demanded.

Tracey looked to her friends for help. They shrugged. How could Tracey explain? She stood up. "So … "

Kylie's eyes reddened and she sniffed loudly. Biting back a sob, she spun around and ran off.

"Oh crap." Sarah jumped to her feet and rushed out after Kylie, pushing Damian aside. "Kylie!"

Damian's face turned purple. "Really? After everything that's happened, you don't tell us what's going on? Secret meetings? Damn it, Tracey." He hustled down the corridor after his sister.

"Fruit tingles!" Tracey hesitated. "Um."

"Go after him," Prince Henry urged. "We'll keep working."

Tracey sprinted through the door and almost slammed into Noel Henderson coming the other way. She rocked back on her heels. "Oh, sorry!"

He gripped her shoulders, his clothing smelling of roses. "Whoa there. What's the rush? Are there shoes on sale?" His warm brown eyes were dark pools staring into her soul. His gaze dropped to her neck.

"What?" She immediately checked that the Butterfly Stone was not visible and was suddenly conscious of her pajamas and dressing gown. "Sorry, but what?"

"Shoes? Ah, it is bad joke. You were in a hurry. My father sent me to check you were all settled for the evening. There was no answer on your friends' door —"

"Tony's in there. I mean. Prince Henry is in th—who exactly are you looking for?" Tracey tugged her dressing gown closed over her red flannel superhero pajamas and tied the belt tightly.

"Is something wrong? Can I assist you?"

"No, sorry. I gotta go," she said and stepped around him.

"I am sure we will catch up later."

Tracey didn't reply, taking off down the corridor after Damian, Sarah, and Kylie.

Tracey stopped in the middle of a long hallway as a wave of familiarity washed over her. Enough so, that she paused to examine the memory and catch her breath. Her sides ached. *Stupid running.* The walls here were painted white, but in her mind, great oil paintings of men and women hung in large gold-rimmed frames. She blinked and the walls became clear white paint again. *Whoa! That's weird.* Her movements slowed as she wandered the corridor. The Butterfly Stone pulsed a slow, regular beat against her chest.

"Tracey?"

She spun around. Damian sat slumped on a long thin sofa lining the hallway.

"Damian, are you okay? Where's Kylie?"

He pushed to his feet. "I lost sight of her. Then I saw you, but you froze and you've gone really pale. What's wrong?"

"I just … " Her gaze drifted to the walls again. White paint. No marks and no shadows. Nothing to indicate any portraits had ever hung there. And yet, she'd seen them. "I … ah … nothing." She glanced down and with a startled yelp realized she was still in her pajamas. Her red superhero pajamas. In front of Damian. *OMG.* Heat rushed over her skin. *Don't notice, don't notice.*

"Why did you follow me?"

"I wanted to explain what was going on. Where's Kylie gone?"

"I don't know." His face twisted, his anger returning. "You were having a meeting without us. Why did you leave us out?"

"It's not like that."

"What is it then?"

She scuffed her feet in the thick carpet. "Honestly? I didn't think you'd want to be included."

His nose crinkled. "Why not? Were you talking about us? About Kylie?"

"No, honest. Honest," she repeated, at his disbelieving look. "We were trying to figure out what our next step should be in our search for the stones."

"Another stone? You're supposed to be helping Kylie. You promised you'd find a way to take it off."

"It's not … " *It was.* "Um … " His frown deepened as she fumbled for the right words. "Damian, it's complica—"

"Oh don't." He stomped a few steps away. "Don't tell me it's complicated. This is my sister. You can't put her in any more danger."

"I'm not. I'm going to find a way to take it off. It's on my list. It's just that, urgh. It's a really long list. I'm trying, okay? I don't want to hurt Kylie. Removing the stone will cause her pain. I tried to take mine off and it really hurts. Like ripping-your-skin-off hurts."

"My mom is upset."

Tracey approached him with her hand out—whether to touch his arm or pat his shoulder she didn't know. She pulled her hand back. "Should I talk to her?"

"She's mad at you."

That gave her such a bad feeling in her stomach. Kylie was upset. Mrs. Carter was mad. And Tracey was completely helpless. She wished Damian could understand.

He ran his fingers through his hair, making the ends stick up. *He's so adorable.* "You can't exclude us from this stuff. Not when it's about my sister, okay?"

"Okay, bad call. I get it." She glanced around the long hallway again.

"You said Kylie came this way?"

"I was right behind Sarah." He looked around. "But I didn't see where they went. They came this way, I'm sure of it. The door at the end of the hall is locked."

Again, Tracey was overcome with the strangest feeling. "It's so weird. I feel like I've seen this room before. But I've never … I need to talk to Stephanie."

"Who?"

Whoops. She hadn't planned on telling him about her ancestor. *No, Tracey. He wants you to tell him stuff. No secrets, remember?* "My ancestor. You remember I mentioned her on the drive here? Well, her spirit lives inside the Butterfly Stone." Tracey lifted the magical necklace from under her pajama top.

He squinted at the painted butterfly on the smooth gray stone. "Like that evil guy in Kylie's necklace."

"Exactly. My ancestor, Stephanie, was friends with Timothy. Once. They had this club and each member had a stone. I'm sure that if we find all the stones we can remove the Serpent's Kiss from Kylie — that's what Timothy called his stone."

"Okay, so how do you talk to Stephanie?"

"Don't freak out," she said. "I might zone for a bit." Tracey closed her fingers around the Butterfly Stone. "Stephanie?"

I long for the silence of my own thoughts.
In the sky there is freedom.
In my mind I soar.

9

Her ancestor was waiting for her in the white room. "Hello, Tracey."

"Do you remember the fire?" It wasn't what Tracey had intended to ask, and she cringed at how she'd just blurted it out.

Stephanie's eyes bulged. "What?"

"How you … died?"

Her ancestor spun away with a snap-swish of her dress skirt. "Why would you ask me that?" Her voice wobbled.

"I just found out. It sounds horrible."

"It was."

"You were in the manor house."

Stephanie spun around and speared Tracey with a sharp gaze. "Why talk to me about that terrible place?"

"I'm standing in it."

"What?" Stephanie swished closer. "How is that possible? The fire destroyed everything."

"You died." Tracey reminded her. "Only one wing of the manor burned. Not the entire house."

"It still stands?"

"Yes, and it seems really familiar but I don't know why."

"Fascinating. Could my memories and experiences have transferred via bloodlines as much as be passed on through my recorded memories?"

"What does that mean?"

"That you have my memories subconsciously from your mother, given to her by her mother and so on."

"Is that even possible?"

"Perhaps. It is worth further consideration. Tell me, Tracey. Do you Dream?"

"Everybody dreams."

Stephanie's face fell out of her frown. She smiled gently. "Of course, never mind. What is it you wished to ask me?"

The frown formed on Tracey's face instead. Just like Agent Malden, Stephanie never answered questions, only asked them. What did she mean by dreams? Everyone dreamed, didn't they? "We're searching for another stone."

"Oh, I see. I cannot tell you what I do not know, Tracey. I've told you this before."

"I know, but I want to ask about your friends. Millicent, Matthew, and Charles, and what you remember about the manor house. My sister and her friend ran into this hallway on the second floor and now they're gone."

"Gone?"

"Disappeared. I came after them but … poof. Gone."

"The entire manor house is full of secrets. You must tread carefully, Tracey. Timothy and the others had many hidden places spelled to trap the unwary."

Oh no. Sarah and Kylie must be trapped somewhere, scared and stuck. The image in her mind made her queasy. "I've got to find my sister."

"Can you not call to the other child for help? The one who holds Timothy's stone."

"We won't let her use it."

Stephanie's head tilted back. "Why ever not?"

"Because Timothy is a monster. He hurt Kylie and made her do bad things."

"He can only do what she will permit. Surely you have realized this after our adventures together."

Adventures was not how Tracey remembered it. She'd let Stephanie take control for a moment then Stephanie had refused to give Tracey's body back. "Tell me about your friends?"

"My dear sweet Millicent. And Matthew, of course." Stephanie twirled, her face softening as if reliving a pleasant memory. "My intended. My love. Oh, it was so very long ago. Did you think Matthew was one of my special friends? One of the protectors? No, my dear Matthew had no knowledge of the arts we sought to explore. Millicent, however, oh my dearest friend. She was extremely clever. Such an old, old soul. Cheeky too, and protective. How I miss her."

"Can you tell me —" Tracey stumbled as she thumped back into reality and found Damian holding her by both hands. "What happened?" *He's touching me!* She tingled where his warm fingers touched her skin.

"Tracey?"

"Why did you pull me out? I nearly had something."

"To help Kylie?"

"No, about the other st —" She stopped. "Um. Well … "

Damian pointed at the wall beside them. There was a long crack in it. "It just appeared opened. Did you do that?"

"No." Tracey gently pulled away, the press of his fingers left ghostly impressions on her hands. The tingle in her skin spread over her whole body as she thought about taking his hand again. "Let's look."

"Should we get the others?" he asked, following close on her heels.

She peered back at him. "We can if you want. Or we could take a little peek for ourselves. Then we'll have something to tell them." Perhaps she *should* call the others. She thought about waiting, but realized she didn't want to. Her curiosity was at war with her concern for Sarah. Either way, she was staring at something hidden. What if the stone lay behind it? If Damian searched with her then she could spend more time with him. Just him. And helping Tracey find a way to save his sister might help with his feelings of guilt. *Maybe he'll realize he likes me? Wouldn't that be something?* She hid a smile.

There was only one way to find out. "Come on," she coaxed and pressed the wall crack. A door swung open along the disturbed line. *Cool.* Behind the door was a slender hallway. Tracey turned on her cell phone flashlight and found the hallway too tight to walk down freely. She turned sideways and shuffled along inside the wall. Beneath her feet, old wooden boards puffed dust up her nose with every step she took. Her nose twitched as a sneeze built. Damian sneezed a second before Tracey did and his breath puffed across the back of her neck. "Ew, gross."

"You sneezed too," he grumped.

"Yeah, but I didn't sneeze *on* you." They were both whispering. Tracey wasn't sure why, she just felt a desperate need to keep her voice low.

"What can you see?" he asked.

"Not a lot. Mostly dust and cobwebs."

His voice rose. "Spiders?"

"Are you scared of spiders?" Tracey squeezed past a thick wooden beam and looked back at him, right into the light from his cell phone. "Argh, blind!"

"Stop it," he snorted. "And no, not scared exactly. Come on, spiders are creepy. All those legs and fangs. And they're hairy. Why are they hairy?"

A laugh popped from her mouth. She pushed the cobwebs out of her way, waving her hand in a larger arc to make sure none of the webs touched Damian's skin.

"Do you think they came this way?" he asked.

Tracey stopped dead. "The spiderwebs."

"Yeah, they're gross. What ... oh."

"Yep," she mumbled. "If Kylie and Sarah came down here ... "

"The webs would be broken. Should we go back?"

"Who opened the wall then?"

Damian lowered his cell phone so she could look him in the eye. Stephanie's warning played back in her mind. The sect had boobytraps scattered throughout the manor. Time for something a little bit magical. "I'm gonna do something. Magic something. Don't freak out."

"Okay."

Tracey focused on her core and opened the little door she kept her magic behind. She grinned as her power sprang out, flooding her body with warmth. Her bracelet vibrated madly but didn't change color. Tracey formed a ball of glowing strands in the center of her palm and threw it forward. It expanded to fill the corridor. Her sensory blanket settled down without buzzing or tugging on her core. Nothing. No spells. She inched forward and froze as another thought occurred. If a spell had been set a long time ago, she wouldn't find it with her usual search spell. She drew another glob of magic into a ball. This time, she imagined a clock and wound it back in her mind until the glowing ball of magic turned a sickly vomit green. She tossed it up and it spread over the corridor. When it landed, she felt several sharp tugs along her net like fingers tapping low on her spine. "Oh, fruit tingles."

"What?"

"There's a spell up ahead. We'd better go back."

Damian wriggled and shifted his muscular frame. After a moment he stopped.

"Are you stuck?" she asked.

" … no."

"Then what's the hold up?"

"I can't move."

"So, you *are* stuck?"

"There's a wall." He struggled and grunted, pushing hard. Dust cascaded over them from the wooden ceiling. "I can't move."

Tracey sighed. "Hang on." She wriggled her hand and brushed it against his shoulder. "Sorry, I need to just squeeze past you … um, I need to … okay, this is … I have to … " She pressed up close to his side. *I'm in my pajamas! My hair is a mess, and I'm covered in spiderwebs. Total embarrassment.* Damian's sugary aroma filled her nose making her stomach rumble. "Sorry," she whispered. He clamped his eyes shut.

"Just do it."

OMG. Her face flamed hotter as she squished even closer, pressing her face against his hard muscles. She smelled more sugar and a hint of chocolate, as well as plenty of dust and sweat. Her stomach rumbled louder. "OMG," she gasped.

His body shook as he chuckled. "Awkward."

"Yeah, I just need to get my hand past you to chuck some magic down the other side. I'm pretty sure it's the same spell on the other side that's trapping us."

"Okay, hang on." More grunting as he shifted and crouched. "Man, you're tiny."

She pulled her dressing gown and pajama sleeves up to her shoulder and squeezed her hand past his neck. The skin of her inner arm brushed his hair. His whole body moved as he swallowed. She paused, her face and lips close to his neck. *OMG*. If she just pursed her lips, she could kiss him.

"Hurry up, huh?"

"Right, sorry." Sucking in a deep breath, she gathered her magic and flicked her fingers. Out flew the sickly green ball. It hit the ceiling and sprayed out in a wide net. "Oh yeah," she grumbled feeling the same tapping against her spine. "It's the same spell. An old one."

"Can you break it?"

"Dunno. I'll have to pick at it carefully or it will—maybe—probably—explode in my face."

He smacked his forehead against the wooden frame in front of him. "I need to stand up. Can you unpick it from your side?"

She nodded and pulled her arm back. He straightened with a groan.

"This could take a while," she warned.

"Of course it will."

Tracey pushed his scent out of her mind—it took a few goes—and focused on the corners of the ancient spell. The good news was that she could grab hold of it. The threads felt weirdly brittle, like old aged and cracked rubber bands, like the ones you find in a bottom drawer. It would be too easy to snap them if she wasn't careful. She tugged on one thread with the lightest touch. The thread broke off in her imaginary fingers and the spell slipped away from her grip. *Grrr.* She reached for it again, imagining her fingers were like the wings of a butterfly fluttering about in the breeze. This time her grip held. She plucked one strand and unwound it slowly, like unravelling a knitted scarf. Tug, breathe in. Pluck, breath out. At last, the thread came loose from the spell's weave and pooled at her feet. She reached for the next thread. It snapped. "Oh, fruit tingles."

"What?"

"It's gonna take a while, but yeah I can break the spell." *I hope.*

He sighed and rested his head on the wall in front of his face.

"Sorry," she said again.

"Stop apologizing. You didn't make the spell."

"Yeah, but I said we should explore the secret passageway without telling anyone."

"Let it go. Just get us out of here."

Right. She pushed the guilty feeling out of her mind and breathed slowly, deeply, letting her breath fill her body from her hair to her toes. She let go of her physical self and focused wholly on her magic. Closing her eyes, she breathed out and concentrated on unpicking the next thread.

Our disagreements have grown sharper.
Rather than cut like a knife's blade,
her words nick like that of a page. A sting
you can feel, even when you cannot hear it.

10

I t serves me right," Damian said after a while.

"What?" Tracey was so enmeshed in the old magic she'd forgotten Damian was waiting. *I forgot about him? Seriously?* Holding the tiny thread, she let her thoughts bubble to the surface. Shadows flooded the black space in front of her. He must have turned off his phone flashlight to save the battery. "Oh. Hey is there any signal on your phone?" Why hadn't she thought of that? They could call for help.

"No. I said that earlier."

"Sorry. I didn't hear you." He must be bored stuck here waiting for her to finish. *Way to make a great impression!* Hopefully, she didn't look weird or pulled any dumb faces as she worked. "What did you say?"

"Ah, nothing. I was just grumbling. You were totally zoned. I didn't think you could hear me." He sighed. "Do you think anyone is looking for us? We've been in here for hours."

"If they are looking, they won't know where to start. Anyway, I think I'm nearly through."

"What does it look like to you?"

She took the next thread gently between her fingers. "What does what look like?"

"Magic. What do you see when you look at it? I've got nothing to compare it to and Kylie doesn't talk about it."

Tracey smiled. *He wants to know more about me.* "You don't really see anything unless you want to. Spells look different depending on what it's for or who cast it. You have to spell your own vision to *see* magic."

"What's it look like to you?"

"I see colors and um, lines. Like, oh, have you ever seen those drawings, the pencil ones where they build up an image using line upon line? Smaller lines and thicker lines to create light and shadow. Ugh, I'm not explaining it right."

"No, I think I get it."

"Well, yeah it's like that, only in oranges and yellows and pinks. It depends on the spell caster and the magic they use. It's different for everyone."

"What are you seeing now?"

"An older gray-green. It looks like a fishing net. I'm sort of unpicking it."

"Like the hem on a pair of trousers? My mom does that. Unpicks it to lower the legs every time I have a growth spurt."

"Close enough, yeah. I've almost got it though, so I kinda need to concentrate. I'll try not to totally space on you again."

"I'm sorry I distracted you. I'm tired. It's been a long couple of weeks."

Tracey picked at the spell thread again, tugging at it in that really slow way to pull it free but not snap it. "I'm sorry about everything." She had Damian trapped in a small space with her. *I'm such an idiot.* This was the perfect time to talk to him without his mom glaring at her, or his sister blinking up at her with those giant sad eyes. "About Kylie. I'm so—"

"Stop it. I know it's not your fault. I'm a jerk." He huffed. "I get mad at myself and I ... look when I'm being a jerk, just tell me, okay? I don't want to lose our friendship."

Friendship? That was what he wanted? Yeah, that was cool. *Cool cool cool cool cool.* Actually. It *was* cool. She didn't want to lose his friendship either, except she liked him a lot and was hoping he liked her a little more than just as a friend. The tiny knots that twisted her stomach when she saw him sure weren't because she wanted a friend. "Okay." She tugged on the last thread and heard a tiny *bong.* The spell broke in a wave of magic that flowed over her like sinking into a bathtub of warm water. "Yessss. Try moving."

He shuffled and let out a "Whoop!"

Tracey didn't immediately follow. She turned and glanced down the un-walked part of the dusty hallway. That ancient spell had stopped them from moving ahead. *Why? What's hidden down there?*

"Tracey?"

"I'm coming." She inched back along the cramped passageway to catch up with him. Stephanie said there were boobytraps throughout the manor house—why? To hide stuff? Later tonight she would have to sneak back in and find out what the sect were so desperate to keep hidden. Right now, she'd better find out if Sarah and Kylie had returned and go looking for them if they hadn't.

"Where have you been?" Laura demanded as Tracey opened the door to the girls' room.

"Where are Sarah and Kylie?" Tracey asked, attempting to distract Laura from her question. Damian shuffled on his feet behind her. No doubt as anxious as she was to find their siblings.

"They came back hours ago." Laura pointed to the bathroom door. "Sarah's having a bath. Kylie went to her room."

"I'll go find her. Tracey—text me?" Damian said.

She nodded. Before she closed the door. She caught sight of another figure in the hallway. Elijah Henderson. He saw her looking and turned away. Frowning, Tracey shut the door firmly. "Where *have* you been?" Jilly asked. Her glare raised goosebumps on Tracey's skin.

"Looking for Sarah and Kylie. Did Sarah say where they went?"

"I can hear you!" Sarah shouted through the bathroom door.

Tracey poked her tongue out at the closed door. "Where were you?" she asked.

"We went for a walk."

"Where?"

"Upstairs. Now, let me relax!"

"I am glad I am an only child," Jilly said. She tugged on the folded-up sleeves of her crimson silky pajamas, pulling them down to her wrists. Laura's pajama shorts showed off her legs. Tracey loved the golden hearts flying over the gray tank top.

"Listen to this." Tracey jumped onto the bed next to Laura and the mattress bounced them both up and down. "Damian and I discovered the manor house is full of old spells. Boobytraps."

"What?" Jilly and Laura asked in unison.

"That's not all. There are secret passageways. That's why it took us so long to come back. Damian and I were caught in a trap."

"Caught together?" Jilly raised her eyebrows.

Laura smirked. "Sounds rough."

Tracey blew raspberries at her friends, her face flaming. "In a secret passageway. We got caught in a settled spell. We couldn't move. It took forever to break it."

"You broke a spell set over two hundred years ago?" Jilly's face twisted in confusion. She tucked her long black hair behind her ears. "How did you break it?"

"I know some unusual spells from my work with Uncle Donny."

"I would like to learn these spells," Jilly said.

"Sure, but that spell is broken now so I can't show you."

"As you said."

"Yeah, but what I'm trying to say is that we didn't check out what was at the end of the passageway *after* I broke the spell. We came straight back here to check that Kylie and Sarah had returned. I'm gonna sneak in and see what the sect were trying to hide." She eyed both her friends and raised her eyebrows. "Wanna come with?"

"Oh, heck yeah," Laura said, jumping to her feet.

"Absolutely," Jilly agreed. She glanced at her pajamas. "Though perhaps we should get changed first."

Tracey led them down the secret passageway, listening to the *"ooos"* and *"ahhhs"* fill the constricted space behind her. "How did you even know this was here?" Laura asked, their footsteps shuffling over the wooden floorboards.

"It kinda opened up when we walked past."

"Certainly sounds like a trap," Jilly said.

Tracey nodded, knowing Jilly would see her silhouette move. "It was. As I said, we were stuck, trapped by an old spell."

"Hmmmm. It's tight in here, Trace. Must have been cozy," Laura giggled.

Tracey's skin heated. At least Laura couldn't see that in the dark.

Jilly snorted. "So, it is true. You have a crush on Damian?"

"Jilly!" Tracey hissed. It *was* awfully cramped in here, wasn't it? There was nowhere she could go to escape her friends' jibes.

"Massive crush," Laura whispered.

"All right you two, cut it out. Nothing happened. He was worried about Kylie, that's all," Tracey said.

"As am I," Jilly said, her tone turning serious. "Being the protector of Timothy's stone is too large a burden for her to bear."

Sarah remained silent. She was right at the back behind Laura listening to them talk. When Tracey told her through the bathroom door where they were going, Sarah demanded they wait for her to get out of the bath. "Sars, did Kylie say anything about the stone to you?"

It took her sister ages to answer. Eventually her voice drifted up to Tracey. "Not really."

"Helpful, Sars."

Sarah's response was a garbled moan.

"Jilly, how are you doing with the Tiger's Eye?" Tracey asked. Somehow, it was easier to ask about that when she wasn't looking directly at the taller girl. Jilly hummed but didn't answer. Tracey shuffled along in silence. "I see a brighter light."

She pushed on what looked like an outlined door. It swung open and Tracey stepped into a long rectangular room. A skinny wooden table ran through the center with faded green chairs tucked neatly under it. She didn't need her cell phone flashlight because a dull white glow came from the ceiling. There must be a window up there letting in moonlight.

"Whoa!" Laura said as she and Jilly stepped down from the passageway into the room. Sarah spun around in a circle staring up with wide eyes.

Every wall was covered in bookshelves. "A secret library," Jilly said, following Laura closer to examine the thick tomes. The door they had come through was built right into the shelves. As it swung shut behind them, they saw books on the other side.

Tracey's heart pounded. "Cool."

"You are such a nerd, Tracey," Sarah said, standing beside her. "Where's the light coming from?"

"Windows?"

"We're in the middle of the manor house."

Oh yeah. Tracey craned her neck to peer up. "Must be magic."

"These are not ordinary books." Jilly touched the navy-blue spine of a book at shoulder height. "These are forbidden texts."

"What are forbidden texts?" Laura asked, running her fingers over several crimson spines further along the shelf. "There's no dust."

"Magic books. If they are hidden here, they must belong to the sect."

"Why are they forbidden?" Sarah asked, not moving from Tracey's side.

"They contain dark spells. Magic that should not be used. Life and death magic, compelling spells, and mind control," Jilly told her.

"Damn." Laura pulled her hand back. "Do you think we're the first ones to come here since the fire?"

Tracey wandered along the bookshelves. "I wasn't expecting to find the rest of the Stones of Power in display cabinets, but what is this room for?"

"Maybe it's just an office?" Sarah answered. "Maybe they came here to study?"

"We should take some," Jilly said.

"What?" Tracey spun around to face her. She was suddenly aware she didn't really know Jilly all that well. Why would she want forbidden texts? "We're looking for the stones, not dark spells."

Jilly's return look was withering. "The spells could help us find the stones."

"It's forbidden knowledge," Tracey reminded her.

"So are the stones. So was the entire sect for that matter." Jilly's eyes blazed with a fire that reminded Tracey of the Tiger's Eye.

"Remember the curse?" she said in a soft voice. "Your whole family was punished for daring to use dark magic. We shouldn't tempt fate."

Jilly stepped back, shaking her head. "You are right. I don't know why I … "

"Magic," said Laura.

The way she said it made Tracey squint over at her friend. "That's not negative, though."

"Oh, no, of course not," Laura said.

Tracey sniffed, a twitch of anger flaming to life inside her chest. Sarah's cool fingers pressed on Tracey's hand. All of Sarah's residual anger had disappeared. Tracey could only recognize concern. "Check your magic."

Breathing in and counting to four, Tracey checked her inner closet. The little door had cracked open. She tugged it shut. "Thanks, Sars." Laura and Jilly were focused on the bookshelves. Tracey lowered her voice further. "So, um. Earlier? Why were you so angry? At me, I mean?"

"I'm not."

"Then what is it? Why are you so mad?"

"Kylie likes you more than me," Sarah blurted. Even she looked shocked by her complaint. They stared at each other in silence. Sarah shook her head. "She talks about you all the time. Big puppy eyes. She likes you more than me — she's my friend, but you're stealing her away and you don't even know it."

OMG. That was exactly what Tracey had once thought Jilly was doing with Laura. And she hadn't done a thing. It was all perception. Just what Tracey felt. She grabbed Sarah up into a big hug. "I'm sorry. You're right. She's *your* friend first. Maybe it's an older sister thing. I'll be more boring from now on, I promise."

Sarah snorted. "Thanks." She shook her head. "I know it's not your fault. I'm just … jealous. Which is stupid."

"Yep, I get that. Laura and Jilly, you know?"

"Oh yeah." Sarah blew a raspberry.

"Is this all that is here? Books?" Jilly asked. Her grumpy tone captured Tracey's attention.

Laura tugged a red book off the shelf. "What are you doing?" Tracey asked.

"Jilly's right, there might be something here. About the stones. How they made them." Laura said.

"Why would you want to know that?" Tracey moved to Laura's side, desperate to understand.

"To break the stone's hold on Kylie. I thought that's what you wanted?"

The Butterfly Stone pulsed, suddenly scalding hot against her chest. Her gaze snapped to the hidden door in the bookshelf. What was the Butterfly Stone warning her against? She glanced at Jilly, who leaned down to whisper something to Laura. It sent a streak of something through her Tracey refused to name. She turned away and sucked in a deep breath to calm her boiling blood. *Why am I so angry?* Her awareness of the room suddenly fell away. Color dripped like wet paint down the walls. The resulting gray reminded her of the memories Grandma shared with her, the one's Stephanie had passed down through the generations to Tracey's nana. The ones Tracey's grandma now held for safekeeping after Nana's dementia took her mind away. Tracey stretched out to touch the table and her hand went straight through it. "Whoa!"

The door in the bookshelf swung open. A woman stood in the entrance. It was Millicent Flowers. Tracey recognized her from the first memory her grandma had ever shown her. And just like in that memory, Millicent didn't appear to see Tracey at all. She swept into the room, long skirts swishing with each stride. Her blond hair hung loose around her shoulders. She closed the hidden door and moved to the very last bookshelf. She removed three books from the bottom shelf and piled them onto the table. Millicent returned to the bookshelf and stretched her hand into the space she had cleared. With a soft click, the end bookshelf swung inward. Millicent stepped inside and the wall closed tight behind her. Huh? *A secret room inside a secret room?*

Tracey waited for the Vision to end, but nothing happened. What was she supposed to witness? She examined the books Millicent removed. Three green volumes embossed with gold. *The Dreaming Heart,* Volumes 1, 2, and 3 written by P. Smythe-Smith.

Her hand slipped right through them when she tried to open them. The wall gave a soft click and swung open again. Millicent stepped out. She ran a hand over her hair and straightened her skirts. Tracey raced forward and slipped into the dark corridor before the wall could close. It left her in total darkness. The Vision didn't end. *Now what?* Tracey stretched out a hand, searching for the wall. *Oh silly! You can't feel the wall.*

With hesitant steps she moved forward and stepped down into a completely round room. Able to see again, she realized the round dome ceiling and walls were lit with a weird, lime-green glow. Tracey walked forward and stepped into a pool of water. She stumbled back in surprise. *Water?* With the toe of her shoe, she swirled the water around, but no little waves echoed out from her feet or splashed against the rounded walls. *What's the water for?* She lifted her shoe but it didn't drip. *Weird.* The room was not just a round, it was a sphere and the bottom was filled with water.

What is this place? Millicent had come in here, but why? Tracey reached for her magic, but of course there was no sensation from her core and when she touched the Butterfly Stone her hand passed right through it. *Oh, that is so weird.* She stared around the room unsure what she was supposed to be witnessing.

She tried to whistle. There was only silence. Bored, she turned her back on the round room and returned up the corridor to the sealed wall. Of course, she couldn't touch anything, so there was no way to activate the door. *Fruit tingles. How do I get out?* She eyed the door. *I did not want to do this.* Tracey slammed her eyes shut, inhaled sharply, and stepped through the wall. She popped out on the other side and fell to her knees gasping for breath, scrunching her fingers in the thick carpet pile. *I can feel the carpet!*

"Tracey?"

Jilly and Laura leaned over her, their worried expressions indicating she had fallen to her knees right in front of them. Every color was too bright to eyes that had grown accustomed to the gloom. Sarah knelt beside her and grabbed her hand. *I can feel her. This is real. The Vision's over.* Sarah's hand was clammy where her fingers pressed hard into Tracey's skin.

"What's wrong?" Sarah asked.

Tracey's mind blanked. What could she say? Her mouth was dry and her voice crackled. "I don't know what just happened."

Jilly grabbed Tracey under the left arm and Laura lifted from the other side to help her back to her feet. "You just fell over. Are you okay?" Laura asked.

"Is it a migraine, Tracey?" Sarah's bottom lip trembled. She stared up into Tracey's eyes, searching for answers. Jilly's stare was intense, burrowing into the skin of Tracey's face like a laser burning into her skull.

"Let us return to our room," Jilly suggested.

Tracey nodded. A giant yawn ripped right out of her mouth. "I feel like sleeping for a week." They left the library in single file, shuffling back up along the secret passageway to the grand hallway. Tracey yawned again. She didn't mention the secret round room to her friends, or that she had seen Millicent. *They'll think I'm crazy.*

The blood she spills from me overflows
and soon it will fill a lake.
All that will be left of me
is the shell she has created.

11

Tracey opened her eyes on a room filled with shadows. She stood on a stage-like wooden floor and a bright yellow light shone directly into her eyes. She squinted and raised her hands to shade them. There could be a hundred people in the room, unseen, lurking, watching her. Or maybe there was no one out there at all. The crawl of caterpillars on her skin made her suspect someone, somewhere knew she was there.

Chilly air ran through her red sci-fi pajamas. She wrapped her arms around her body and scrunched her toes inside her slipper-socks.

Why am I here? Why is it so bright and everything else so dark? Her breath tasted full of soot. Grains coated her tongue. "Is anybody there?"

A person clapped, or maybe not. It was more like a bird's fluttering wings. Not the light, gentle brush of air that a butterfly would make, this was a harsher sound—fast and brutal.

Her heart rate skyrocketed, matching her gasping breaths. Her body filled with more of the inky powdery blackness. Cold swept over her skin, blowing hair into her face. She ducked as something flew over her head. Goosebumps rose up on her arms and neck as something swooped again. She ducked lower and let out a screech.

Rapid, flapping smacks were suddenly right on top of her. She hit the ground as a shape swooped over her face. It cawed loudly. Tracey screamed and bolted upright in her bed, breathing fast, her heart racing.

It was a dream, nothing more.

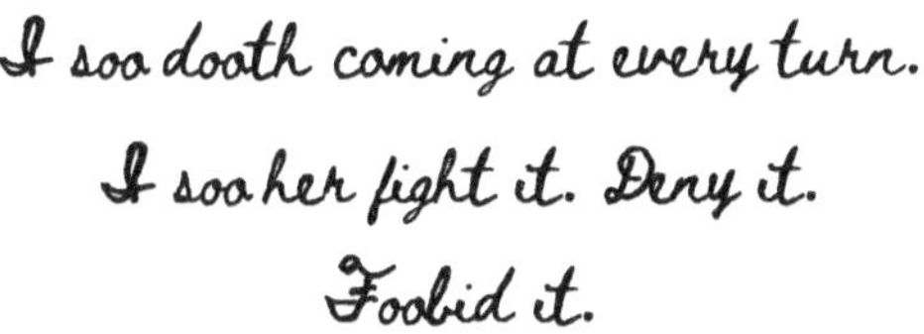
I see death coming at every turn.
I see her fight it. Deny it.
Forbid it.

12

Tracey?" Sarah called.

A snap preceded the lamp bursting to life beside Jilly's head. Laura, Jilly, and Sarah sat up in their beds, staring at Tracey as she panted, eyes blinking and squinting beneath the bright light, trying to dispel the nightmare.

"Tracey, are you okay?" Laura asked.

Swallowing her emotions, and with tears welling in her eyes, Tracey nodded. "I'm okay. Just a bad dream. Sorry I woke you."

"Would you like to tell us about it?" Jilly asked.

"I'm fine. Really."

Sarah rubbed her eyes and yawned. She was a bird's nest of blankets, pajamas, and messy hair. Jilly ran her hands over her hair to straighten the strands and her nose crinkled. Tracey found herself focusing on little details to distract from the pounding of her heart. Laura looked like a fairytale princess just woken from a long nap. Her braided hair was perfect, not a strand had dared come loose, and her eyes were sleepy, cheeks pink. "Want me to come over?" Sarah asked.

"Nah, I'm okay."

Sarah jumped out of bed, cracked open the bathroom door and flicked on the light before she dove back into bed. "There. Now it's not so dark."

Laying down as Jilly snapped off the lamplight, Tracey smiled up at the shadows on the murky ceiling. "Thanks Sars."

Things moved quickly the next morning. Tracey had planned to tell Tony and Jonny all about the secret library over a leisurely breakfast after a long sleep in.

Ha!

They were ripped from sleep by loud banging on their bedroom door. The heavy wood muffled Uncle Donny's voice but they still heard him shout, "Get a wriggle on. We're expected at the movie lot in an hour. Hustle!" His voice grew fainter as he moved up the corridor bashing on the next door along.

"Ugh!" Tracey groaned and forced herself upright.

"What is going on?" Sarah pressed her pillow hard over her head and ears. Only a slither of messy brown hair peeked out. Laura slid from her bed, rubbed her eyes, and yawned before she strode straight into the bathroom. She shut the door.

"Come on, you two. I need coffee. If you're not dressed in five, I'm going without you." Tracey leaned over the side of her bed searching for her bag. She dragged it closer with a grunt and the hunt was on for a clean shirt.

That got Sarah up, bursting from her bed nest. Tracey laughed at her sister's wild-woman-striding-through-a-windstorm look. At least Tracey didn't feel like the only mess today. She had barely gotten back to sleep before Uncle Donny had woken them up. Sarah caught her look. "What do we wear?"

Jilly stretched her hands to the ceiling, then climbed from bed. She ran through a series of yoga poses, exhausting Tracey just watching her. That horrible dream played back in her mind. She ran her hands over her head to flatten the matted mess that was her bed hair and wished the mirror was a magic one. One that would make her look poised and beautiful. She turned her back on her reflection.

"Tracey?"

She blinked, surprised at Jilly's call and found her already dressed. "What?"

"You were sitting there, staring blankly at nothing. Are you awake yet?" Sarah asked.

"You're all just figments of my imagination. It's still the middle of the night, right?" Tracey asked.

Sarah laughed, and stomped over to snatch a shirt out of Tracey's bag. *Ooooo, blue sci-fi, timey-wimey.* One of her favorites. Tracey yanked yesterday's jeans off the chair and stumbled to the bathroom.

"Laura's in there," Jilly reminded her.

Tracey shrugged, her brain still on half power. She got dressed in the middle of the room. Coffee would help her wake up. She tugged open the door.

"Whoa, hair!" Jonny said and joined Tony in laughter as the two boys caught sight of Tracey.

She struck a pose. "You only wish you had this level of cool."

"You are a little loopy in the morning," Jilly said, a grin stretching her lips wide.

Tracey shrugged.

"You know Damian will be downstairs," Tony said, holding onto the doorframe.

Tracey's eyes popped wide and her hands flew to her hair. "Fruit tingles! I forgot. I'll meet you downstairs," she shouted and shut the door on their giggles. Laura stepped from the bathroom in a cloud of steam with a towel wrapped around her head. "That was fast," Tracey told her. She was used to following Sarah in the bathroom. Her sister always took forever to get ready.

"Well, your uncle said to hurry."

Darn, the clock was still ticking. "Right." Tracey raced past her friend and into the bathroom.

"Hey Trace."

Tracey poked her head back out to look at Laura. "Yeah?"

"That was a bad nightmare last night, huh?"

Her grip tightened on the bathroom door. Tracey glanced at her feet. Her toenails were getting long. "Yeah, I get them sometimes."

"Was it about the stone?" Laura sat on her bed and combed through her wet hair. She looked attentive, her expression open and not judgy at all.

"Maybe. I dreamed about tigers when we were looking for Jilly's stone.

Last night was full of shadows and flapping wings."

"Ugh, I hate birds. Pigeons are the worst."

Tracey laughed. She'd seen Laura cross the street to avoid birds. "You would have hated this dream then."

"Shadows too? Was it the Shadowman?"

"I don't think so. But we were attacked on the plane by something, so we know someone's not happy we're here."

"Who knows we're here?"

"Good question. Keep your eyes peeled for anyone watching us too closely. The Hendersons know we're here. Mr. Henderson is on the council and he was acting weird with Agent Malden and me. And then there's the rest of the council. They know we're here too, and we know that Dust Devil was a watcher sent by the council. Oh, and the film people know we're here. The assistant—Angela—and the director, and who knows who else."

"We should write a list. We can do it later. You'd better hurry." Laura said pointing to the bathroom."

Tracey took the fastest shower she had ever taken ever and got redressed in her jeans and blue T-shirt. Her hair was soaking into her shirt as she ran down the hallway toward the dining room.

Noel stood at the top of the stairs waiting for her. "Hey," Tracey said. They headed down together.

"Big morning planned?"

"Probably." Tracey examined the handsome boy. "Any suggestions?"

"The walking tours are full of information."

Oh yeah, sounded fun. Not. Tracey shook her head. After a moment she asked, "Have you ever sensed any weird magic here?"

His eyebrow rose. "What do you mean?"

"Like old spells or residual energy?"

"No."

"What about secret passages?"

"You think there might be secret walkways throughout the house?"

"How long have you lived here?"

"I was born here."

"It must be weird to live in a manor house," Tracey said. "It's huge."

"I don't really know any different," he told her. "Mostly it's okay, but the hotel part is odd. People come and go all the time. All ages. It is hard to make friends."

She could only imagine. "What about animals?"

"What do you mean?"

"Like, I dunno, pictures of animals or carvings in the wood? Knick knacks, weird references or anything? I'm thinking maybe birds."

"Not that I can think of. But I will keep an eye out and let you know if I see anything odd."

She thought that had ended the conversation until he blurted, "Can I see it?"

"See what?"

"The stone."

So he does know about it. Tracey's lips mashed together. "What stone?" she tried.

He tilted his head. "Tracey, my father *is* on the council. He told me."

"What else did he tell you?"

"To be careful around you."

Tracey stopped. "Me?"

Noel halted a step below her and peered back. "The stones are dangerous."

"I'm not dangerous. My friends aren't either."

He nodded. "I like your friends. I want you to trust me. I am not my father."

"I want to trust you but—"

"—you don't know me, right?"

"Right," Tracey said and continued down the stairs past him.

"I cannot help who my father is." Noel called after her.

Tracey joined her friends in the dining room pondering her conversation with Noel. Did she trust him? It wasn't as though he had done anything to make her not trust him. He was just acting a bit weird. His dad was too. Her friends were all scoffing down their breakfasts standing up.

"Right. Grab a pastry, we have to go," Uncle Donny said catching sight of her. Tracey grabbed a fruit scroll and searched the excited group for Agent Malden. He was not there. The boys were chatting quietly with Laura and Jilly. They all seemed happy enough. Uncle Donny was in his worn jeans. She found it so strange to see him dressed casually. Usually, when he worked, he wore a suit.

Laura handed Tracey a travel mug filled with coffee. "Oh, thanks."

"It's even branded," she pointed out. On the outside of the keep cup was an illustration of Ellisborough House.

"Go, go, go." Uncle Donny ushered them down the long hallway to the front door.

Tracey made her way to Damian's side. "Hey."

"Good morning," he said. Mrs. Carter walked faster to draw level with Uncle Donny. She spoke rapidly about going sightseeing and how she wanted to catch up with some friends in London. Kylie whispered excitedly with Sarah. Happily, the two girls seemed more friendly this morning. Tracey hoped her discussion with her sister last night had settled Sarah's anxiety.

Tracey sat down next to Damian in the limousine with Kylie on her other side. Sarah shook her head and let out a laugh. Well, at least she didn't seem angry about Kylie's hero worship any more. Tracey shrugged. She pressed a hand to her necklace. "How are you doing, Kylie?"

The younger girl's hand drifted to her own neck. "I'm okay. It's quiet."

"Good." Tracey said. "If anything changes, please let me know."

"I will," Kylie said.

"Where did you and Sarah go yesterday?" Tracey hadn't got a proper answer out of Sarah last night. "Hey, Sars. Why didn't you answer your phone yesterday?"

"Didn't want to," Sarah grumbled. "I was mad." She locked Tracey in a staring contest, refusing to back down. Tracey wouldn't back down either. Sarah was not the only one who could be stubborn.

"Sarah, from now on, answer your phone, please?" Uncle Donny said from the rear seat where he sat beside Mrs. Carter.

"I would have answered if you'd called, Uncle Donny." Sarah didn't break her eye-lock with Tracey.

"I'm a part of this," Kylie said softly. Tracey broke the glare with her sister to glance at the blond girl. Kylie held up her stone. A jet black, sloped stone with a long bloody-red line like a snake down the center as if the color had forced its way right out of the stone. The shiny side glinted in the weak sunlight sprinkling through the limo's windows. "I have to wear this. Don't leave me out of things anymore, please?"

"Kylie." Mrs. Carter's frown could be felt all the way through the limousine.

"Mom, it's why we're here. Tracey has to find the other stones to help me. We're not just here to do a movie scene. I need her help. Stop trying to keep me out of this."

"But—"

"Mom!"

The whole limousine fell silent at her raised voice. Tracey wished she knew what everyone was thinking. Uncle Donny wore an epic frown. Mrs. Carter stared at Kylie, her lips pursed, her eyes sad. Jilly, Laura, Jonny, Tony, Dave, and Damian all glanced at Tracey as if they expected her to do something. This was an argument between Kylie and her mom, wasn't it? Why should Tracey get involved? She tried a different tact—by returning to her original question. "So, where *did* you and Sarah go yesterday?"

"To the maze," Kylie said, relaxing back into her seat. That seemed to signal a stand down of hostilities.

The maze? Why wouldn't Sarah have mentioned that? "Did you find a way out? Oh, you must have since you came back." Tracey smiled when Kylie laughed. Sarah snorted. Tracey figured the conversation had gone better than it could have. *Huh, not bad, me!*

She flicked a glance through the window at the rapidly moving traffic. Several black birds zoomed up and down, flying in wide circles high up in the sky. It reminded Tracey of her nightmare and she shivered, returning her gaze inside the limo.

"I have a question," Dave said suddenly. "What is the movie about?"

"Does that matter? It's just a bit part, like walking past a cafeteria as the main actors walk and talk, or sit drinking coffee or something as they stand nearby. Right, Tracey?" Jonny said, flipping his hood off his head.

No bowler hat today. His mom must have put her foot down. Martha sat beside him, which pushed Jilly all the way over on the other side. *I bet Martha planned that!*

"Must I do this?" Jilly asked.

"Oh come on. It'll be fun," Jonny said leaning over his mom.

"It's a super cool cover," Tracey said. "And who wouldn't want to be in a movie with Prince Henry?"

All chatter turned to speculation about the movie. Tracey was excited, but her thoughts kept drifting back to her morning discussion with Laura. Someone had known they were coming to England and had attacked their plane. Who and why? Did someone know about their mission to find another stone? Acting in a movie *was* a good cover but Tracey couldn't let it distract her from her real mission. Hunting for the next stone. They'd found one secret room already, there had to be more in the manor house to find. What had Millicent's ghost been doing in that strange round room? Tracey had to wait until they returned to the manor house before she'd be able to investigate more.

"That's all we need, children. We'll alter the costumes this afternoon and they'll be ready for your big scene later this week." Margie smiled at them and flipped her plastic measuring tape around her neck.

The elderly lady with the tightly curled, steel-gray hair had introduced herself as Margie when she had greeted them at the gate. She'd led them through a rabbit warren of buildings and corridors until they reached the jam-packed wardrobe area and then introduced her assistants as Syl and Jan. There were several pins in Margie's hair. Tracey had no idea how she managed not to stick herself with them every time she adjusted her glasses.

The costume department was a wide room filled with clothes racks, boxes and tubs, tables and sewing machines. The three women whipped around the group, taking measurements and shouting sizes to each other.

Tracey and her friends tried on shoes and boots, trousers, dresses, shirts, and hats. At first, it had been like playing dress-up or cosplay. They giggled and laughed at one another in their odd-looking outfits. The clothes were old and ratty looking, too short and too loose. After several hours, they were thoroughly over it. Mrs. Carter and Martha had left to go sightseeing hours ago, and Uncle Donny ran off who knew where. None of them had come back yet and Tracey almost wished she had gone with them.

"Great work, children. We will have your Street Rat costumes ready for when they call you later this week."

"What are Street Rats?" Tracey laughed at the silly name.

"Homeless children. In the script, your characters are referred to as Street Rats. We'll see you back here when you get your call up. That's when they'll ask you to come to set to film your scene." The three ladies waved as Tracey and her friends trooped out the door.

"Is everyone else as bored and tired as I am?" Tracey asked.

Tony itched the back of his neck. "I thought that would be more fun."

"Did you see the jacket they asked me to try on? It stank of dust and bugs," Dave complained.

"I think the trousers had fake blood on them. At least, I hope it was fake," Sarah added.

Kylie pointed to her head. "Margie had pins in her hair, did you see?"

They continued listing off their individual gripes and thoughts as they wandered along the hall outside the dressing rooms. Tracey touched the wall and jumped when it moved. "This whole place is fake. The walls, everything. I can't believe we're just in a giant warehouse."

"Let's sneak past the set while we're here," Dave said.

"We shouldn't," Laura told him.

"Where are we supposed to go to wait for Uncle Donny?" Sarah asked.

Tracey stopped walking. The others quickly surrounded her. "Oh hey, we're alone. That means I can tell you about last night ... come on. Let's find somewhere out of the way." Tracey reversed back down the corridor and pushed on the first door she came across. Inside was a small room with only a desk, wall mirror and a closet full of costumes. A worn, icky-green colored sofa ran the entire length of the wall and took up nearly all the space in the room. Tracey urged them inside. "Come on, before Uncle Donny comes back."

"What do you mean about last night?" Jonny asked. "Is this something to do with the stones?" They each found a place to sit, either on the hard concrete floor or on the uncomfortable sofa.

Tracey squished closer to Damian and he didn't move away. *Squee!* It felt important to keep her voice low. "Yeah, well no. Not really, I mean —"

"—we found a secret passage," Laura blurted. "Oh, it's been so hard not to say anything."

Tony sat up straighter on the sagging cushions. "What?"

"Without us?" Jonny asked, leaning over Tony, pouting epically.

Between Tracey, Jilly, Sarah, and Laura, the group was informed of what they had found.

"Forbidden texts," Jilly confirmed.

"Do you think the books have something to do with the stones?" Jonny asked.

"Wait, you went back last night?" Damian's confused expression made Tracey's stomach twist.

"Um, yeah." She couldn't hold his eye-contact and examined her nails instead. The polish was chipping off her right thumbnail.

"Forget that. What about the stones? What did you find?" Tony asked.

"Well, I ... " Should she tell them about the Vision and seeing Millicent go into that second hidden room? She stayed quiet. Her Vision didn't provide any answers, only more questions. She would tell them about it when she knew more.

"A secret room full of books. That's it?" Dave asked.

Tony clapped his hands. "If we sneak back there tonight, we can check it out."

"There's a lot of books," Laura warned.

"There's a lot of us," Jonny countered.

Dave grumbled. "Yeah, but that will involve reading." They all laughed at him. "Seriously, who hides a room full of books?"

Laura patted Dave's shoulder. "It'll be good practice for school." Dave only groaned louder.

Tracey tapped her fingers on the wall to get their attention. "We have to keep our visit and the room a secret," she said. "There might be other hidden rooms and we know the sect put spells on them to trap the unwary. We have to search the rest of the house, so we'll have to be careful." When she looked up, she found Damian staring at her. "What?"

"Are Kylie and I invited to join this secret investigators' club this time?"

"Of course," she told him. "We need help to search for—"

The door popped open and the producer's assistant stuck her head in. Angela's hair poked up at the back where she had fanned it out and pinned it into a cool spiky pattern. "Here you are. My goodness, we've been searching everywhere for you."

The teens jumped to their feet and followed Angela out into the corridor. "The director wanted to speak to you, but she's gone now. I'll take you past an empty set so you can have a look, then I have to escort you to your parents and out of the studio."

Tracey hung back and whispered to Jonny. "10 p.m. tonight."

"What was that?" Angela spun around. A pen flew out from behind her ear and hit the floor. She bent to pick it up. "You have a question?"

"Oh nothing, sorry." Tracey smiled at the harried-looking woman. Angela's smile was a bit stiff.

"Right well, follow me."

Jonny whispered the time to Tony who whispered it to Dave. Sarah overheard and spread the message to Kylie, Laura, and Jilly. Damian nodded when Tracey caught his eye. She sped up her steps. "So, um, what's the movie about?"

Angela laughed.

Heat flooded Tracey's face and she stopped walking. *Am I not supposed to ask?*

"Sorry," Angela said, holding up her hand to bring the entire group to a halt. "I can't believe no one has told you yet. It's a murder mystery and a period piece set in the Nineteenth Century."

"Mystery? Like a detective film?"

"Yes, but it's family friendly. A group of children have gone missing, stolen right off the streets, and the hero—Prince Henry—is a father searching for his daughter. You are all playing street children. We call them Street Rats in the film."

Tracey and her friends shot each other excited looks. They might be here on a different mission but suddenly their cover story sounded incredibly exciting. Tracey couldn't wait for Thursday.

"Did you have fun?" Agent Malden asked standing up as Tracey and her friends approached his table. An empty coffee cup sat in front of him. There was a crumb filled plate and another mug that was half full. He closed his black book. Tracey's stomach rumbled at the sight of all the cake crumbs.

"We got to see a real movie set. A long street right in the center of London. Well, made to look like London. We also went inside an office and a pub. No one was filming," Sarah told him, her eyes alight with excitement.

"Trying on all those outfits was awful," Dave complained.

"Nah, it was sweet," Jonny argued.

Tracey stood back a little from the bubbly group. She had been to movie studios before and was happy to share in her friends' enthusiasm, but she couldn't forget the real reason she was here. Her gaze landed on Damian. He was laughing at something Jonny said. She felt warm all over looking at his face—the way his eyes crinkled at the corners and how his tongue swiped over his lips to wet them. He talked with his hands. It was so cute. Tracey groaned and shook her head. *Concentrate.* When they got back to the manor house they could split into groups and search the different wings. There had to be more at the manor house to find. Her gaze drifted over her friends again. "Where's Uncle Donny?"

"He was called away," Malden said, drinking the last of his coffee. He stood up.

"By who?" Tracey asked.

"His client. Come on. Our limo is waiting. Martha and Mrs. Carter went ahead. We have time for a little sightseeing before we head back to the manor house."

"Can we see the prison?" Dave asked.

"No, the Bodleian Library," Tony said.

"What about the Radcliffe Camera?" Laura asked.

"That's at Oxford University too, isn't it?" Kylie asked. "I read about it in my guidebook."

Tracey followed behind the large group as they headed off. *Client?* Had her uncle found Frank Transcenni at last? And where was Prince Henry? He said he would meet them here. Against her chest the Butterfly Stone pulsed with warm energy. Tracey brushed her hand across it to soothe it. Hopefully, wherever he and Uncle Donny had gone, they would return soon to help search for the stones.

I am a mirror to her and she
will only see what she wills to see—
that she has changed me, fixed me,
made me better.

13

They got back to the manor house late that afternoon and were given free time to explore before dinner. Dave plopped into one of the armchairs in the parlor. "I'm so exhausted. Walking tour? I would have preferred actually being in the prison," Dave complained.

"You've said that three times," Kylie sniped at him.

"I would have loved to see inside some of the buildings," Laura mused. "I'm sure I've seen them in movies." Jonny threw himself over the settee.

"No time," Tony said. "But I hope we get a chance to go back for an indoor look."

"Oh man, more libraries? There's gotta be a sports ground around here somewhere." Dave said. "Or TV? How about we chill and watch a movie or something?"

"Okay look, I know we're all tired but we've got free time now, let's investigate the manor house," Tracey told them.

"Two hours of walking and you want to do more?"

"We're still on for tonight, right? Everyone meet at 10 p.m. in our room so we can check out the books in the secret room. Until then, let's explore and search for the stone. Maybe we'll get lucky."

"Please, if it were that simple we'd already have it," Dave scoffed.

"Groups with a Mage-kind in each?" Jilly suggested. She had been giving Tracey the willies all afternoon. It seemed every time Tracey turned around Jilly was staring at her. *Is she annoyed Laura's my friend again?* No, that didn't make sense. They were all friends now. Tracey vowed to talk to Jilly about it. Just not in front of Laura.

"I was thinking a Norm each, but sure. There's more of us for a change. Weird, huh? How about Jilly, Jonny, and Dave in Group One,

Sarah, Kylie, and Laura in Group Two. And Tony and Damian with me. We should we take a wing each."

Laura looked resigned. "We'll take the east wing."

"We'll do south," Jilly offered.

Tracey turned to Damian. "I guess we'll start on the ground floor of the west wing?"

"What about online research?" Tony offered.

"Do you want to stay here?" she asked him.

"No, no, I just thought I'd mention it."

"We can do that later. We have two hours before we get called for dinner. Does everyone have their phone?" Tracey asked. They held them up to confirm. "Okay, great. Check in on group chat if you find anything. Oh and, hey, be careful. If the Mage-kinds sense anything, don't touch and don't go forward. Call and wait for help."

They nodded and headed off. Tracey waited until her group were the only ones left in the room, "Should we start in here?"

The two boys shrugged. *Gee, fun group.* Perhaps, she should have pushed for Tony to stay and research the stones on his phone. He'd probably prefer it, and then she could have been alone with Damian.

As they wandered around the room, Tracey cracked open her inner closet door and let out a little magic. "When Damian and I got caught in the boobytrap I broke it by searching for settled spells. Any spell set by the sect will be super old, so keep your guard up."

Tony's face took on the pinched look he got when he smelled something funky — like the stinky alley outside Uncle Donny's office. *Oh, that reminds me.* Tracey unlocked her phone and typed out a quick message to her uncle.

Hey, where are you? Need any help? We're back at the manor house. Call me.

Before she could shove it into her pocket it vibrated in her hand. Expecting a return text from her uncle, she grinned at the "hello" gif from her mom. Tracey's laugh emoji was quickly displaced by another gif from her mom. A pic of a phone not ringing. *Very funny.*

"Tracey?" Damian asked.

"It's just my mom," she said. "Start looking without me. I won't be long." She stepped out of the parlor and wandered down the hallway. Mom answered the phone immediately.

"Tracey, how are you doing? Are you having fun over there?"

"Hi Mom." Tracey cleared her throat. "We're good. We're living in a manor house! Like those palaces on TV."

Her mom let out a jolly laugh. She settled enough to say, "As you said in yesterday's message, and your emails and in your posts. How's Sarah?"

"She's fine." In the distance Tracey caught sight of Elijah Henderson. He noticed Tracey, and rather than nod hello he opened the door next to him and ducked inside. Tracey squinted at the closed door. *Weird.*

"Why hasn't your uncle messaged me?" Mom asked.

"You know Uncle Donny." Tracey mashed her lips together. It was never a good sign when her uncle was actively avoiding her mom.

"He's not there now, is he? Do you know where he is?"

Tracey sighed loudly so her mom could hear.

"When you see him—"

"I'll tell him to call you."

Her mom sighed loudly too. "And how are your friends?"

"All good." She knew what her mom really wanted to know. "Jilly and Kylie are great." What could Tracey say that was vague enough, but that her mom would understand? She glanced toward the door Mr. Henderson had disappeared behind and lowered her voice. Agent Malden had warned Tracey to be quiet about the stone, especially when on the phone. "We're exploring the manor house. It's very cool, but it's so big. I don't think we could see it all no matter how long we search. Anyway, how are you? Are you feeling better?"

"Much better. Your grandma is still staying with us and the boys got into the football final. Oh, hang on, here's your grandma. She wants to say hello." A shuffling sound came through the phone as it changed hands.

"Hello, Tracey dear. How are you?"

"I'm good, Grandma. Our trip over was a bit bouncy though."

"Turbulent?"

"You could say that." Mr. Henderson poked his head out of the room.

He saw Tracey looking and ducked away again. *Super weird.*

"Sounds a little scary," Grandma said.

"It was, but we arrived okay. I made sure Sarah behaved. Kylie was fine—slept right through." In other words, Kylie's stone had remained dormant. She hoped Grandma would understand. "Jilly's good at making everyone feel calm." Jilly's stone had been quiet too.

"That's good dear. Your mother says you're staying in a palace?"

"It's actually a manor house, but I feel so at home here. It's like I've lived here before." *Hint hint.* "We went to the studio for our costume fitting this morning, then went sightseeing. Now we're exploring the manor."

"I see. Sounds like fun. How are the beds? Are you sleeping?"

"Weird dreams," she confirmed. Grandma would know that meant she was having Vision dreams.

"Hmmm, try warm milk before bed. Here's your mom again. Mind your lessons and your elders. Watch out for each other."

"Yes, Grandma." Warm milk? What was that supposed to mean?

"Keep Donald mindful too."

Oh? That was both her mom and her grandma checking up on Uncle Donny. Mom must have sensed something was wrong. She always could tell. It was a mom thing. It was why Doctor Chan—Jilly's evil uncle—had poisoned her a few weeks ago. To stop Tracey's mom from knowing Tracey was in danger. Luckily, Tracey had worked out the plot in time and her mom was okay. They had even caught Doctor Chan and locked him away.

Mom returned so she could say goodbye. "Be careful, honey. Look out for your sister, and keep your shields up. Love you."

"Love you too, Mom."

Tracey shoved her phone into her back pocket and returned to the parlor. Noel was inside talking to Tony and Damian. His pleased expression wavered when he caught sight of Tracey, then returned full force as he beamed at her. "Good afternoon, Tracey."

"Hey, Noel."

Damian was also smiling. He stood relaxed in the middle of the room. Tony was slightly flushed and wouldn't meet Tracey's gaze.

"I was wondering if you would like an official tour of the manor house?" Noel bowed slightly and gestured toward the door with one hand. Tracey's gaze darted to Tony's pink face.

They were supposed to be searching for the stone. A thought occurred to her and she nearly gasped at how perfect it was. Hopefully, Damian would forgive her. "Actually … " She pressed close to Damian's side and slipped her hand around his arm. "I'd love some, uh, time alone with Damian. So many parents hanging around, you know. Would you be awfully annoyed with me if you just show Tony around?"

The look Tony shot her would have melted her sunglasses—if she was wearing any. She smiled brightly in response. Damian's tense arm relaxed. "Oh, yeah dude. Do me a solid? I'm sure Tony would love to have a look around. He has a real thing for you British people, uh, I mean, history, you know British history?"

OMG, Damian was terrible at subterfuge. Tracey bit her lip and buried her laugh in his shoulder.

"Well, yes of course." Noel bestowed his brilliant smile on Tony and stepped closer. "Tony, if you are interested I'd be delighted to point out the manor house's architecture and significance in history." He looked back at Tracey. Behind Noel, Tony shot her a giant smile. "Are you sure you do not wish to come with us, Tracey?" Noel asked.

"I'm fine here," she nodded, smiling up at Damian. Noel led Tony from the room, who threw her a wide-eyed look that was both excited and freaking out. She gave him a double thumbs up before he disappeared.

Her laugh exploded out of her when they were out of sight. Damian joined in, chuckling softly. "Don't let them hear you," he warned.

"Tony's going to kill me," she mumbled.

"Oh I don't know, he might be grateful."

"Thanks for playing along. We couldn't search for the stone if Noel was with us, and this way Tony might get some insight into the building to help us explore."

"The building, huh? You think he'll hear anything Noel says?" Tracey snorted and reluctantly let Damian's arm go. "Before he came in, Tony said he didn't sense anything in this room magic-wise. We tried pressing on the walls and pulled at anything that looked like a handle. Nothing happened. No secret doors in here."

"Okay, let's move to the next room." Tracey headed down the corridor and glanced toward the door Mr. Henderson had shut himself behind. There was no sign of him. She stopped at a cream-colored door.

The handle wouldn't turn. Shooting a look at Damian over her shoulder she held her hand over the handle and with her magically infused senses located the locking mechanism inside. When she found it, she sent a spurt of golden magic into the lock. The handle turned beneath her hand. She pushed it open and sent out her magic sensory blanket. No buzz or vibration of either new or old magic met her search. Damian followed her inside. He hadn't denied her earlier comment about wanting to spend time with her, and was standing awfully close to her now. If she tilted her left hand slightly upward, she could brush against his fingers. Should she do it? She wanted to. Except now her hands were sweating. She scrubbed them against her jeans and Damian moved away. *Drats.*

He pressed his hands to the wall. Tracey examined the room, waiting for her heart to stop racing. Cream-colored sofas, thick gray carpet, and flower-covered wallpaper. She sent out her sensory blanket but got nothing in return. Damian poked at the flowers on the wall.

Tracey started on the other side of the door and knocked softly against the drywall.

"What are you doing?" he asked.

"Uncle Donny told me that if there's a hidden room, the knock will sound hollow." When she met up with Damian near the back wall, she sighed. "Well that didn't work. New plan." She pointed at the bookshelf and the long glass cabinets. There were tiny figurines inside. "Those cabinets could be moved in one piece." She pressed on each whorl and knot in the wood, twisting and tugging but nothing happened. She pushed against one side and then the other to see if it would slide sideways and expose a hidden doorway. It didn't budge. "Any luck?"

Damian tugged at the books on the shelf. "Nothing."

"Let's try the next room."

They found nothing. Damian checked his phone. "It's almost time to meet up with everyone for dinner."

Tracey huffed out a sigh and stopped tugging on the stones around the fireplace. Each room they searched had a large window facing the garden. When she spied the maze, she tried to find the path through it with her finger against the glass, but the angle was wrong. Maybe she would have a better view from upstairs. She flashed back to Millicent's journal. She had loved the maze. Tracey's phone rang with a loud chime of bells.

It wasn't Uncle Donny. She opened the video call.

"Sarah?"

"Help. Level 3. Monster." The video bounced all over the place. Tracey only caught sections of her sister's pale face and flaring nostrils.

"What? What's happening?" Tracey grabbed Damian's hand and dragged him out through the door.

Sarah puffed as if she was running. "A gingerbread giant picked Kylie up and walked off with her. I couldn't stop it."

"What?" Damian snapped.

"Where are you?" Tracey asked.

"Third floor, east wing."

"On our way." Tracey added Jonny to the call.

"'Ello?"

"Something's got Kylie. East wing!" she shouted.

Damian pulled Tracey sideways down another hallway and pointed ahead. "Stairs." They bolted up them, Damian taking two at a time. Tracey had to let go of his hand to make sure she hit each step and didn't fall flat on her face. They burst onto the landing in a sprint. "Where are you, Sarah?"

"Dance hall thingy. The large empty room at the end of the corridor."

A series of thumps rattled the floor beneath Tracey's feet. Ahead of her two large doors sprang open, slamming against the walls on either side. Tracey and Damian froze. "What the … ?" Damian said. Kylie's jeans-clad legs — her boots kicking wildly — hung over the shoulder of a giant, man-shaped thing made of clay, and it was running straight for them.

She is my friend,
but I can oover tell her the truth.
She desires to fix me. To hool my ills.
She will oover hoor me.

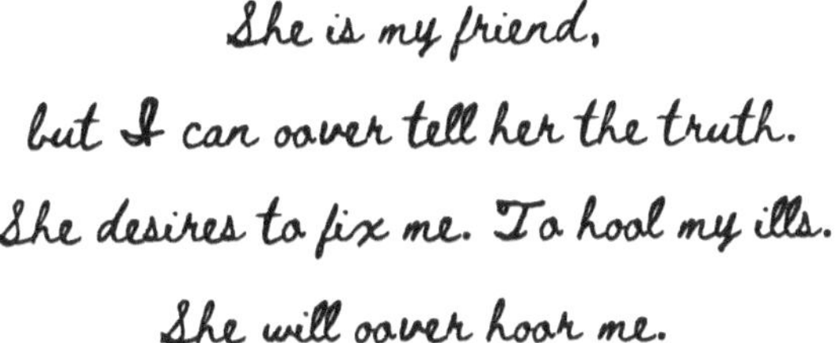

14

The giant caught sight of them and stumbled to a halt. Sarah was right. The clay monster looked just like a gingerbread man, with a sketched face of holes dug into the clay for eyes and a wide cut line for a mouth. "Sarah?!" Tracey shouted, desperate to know where her sister was and if she was safe.

"Behind it," her sister shouted back. "With Laura."

"Kylie?" Tracey called.

"I can't get loose." The blond girl pushed up off the clay shoulder with both hands barely moving an inch.

Jilly, Dave, and Jonny appeared on the stairs behind Tracey. "What the heck?" Jonny said, seeing what had frozen Tracey and Damian halfway down the hall.

"Shields!" Tracey ordered. Dave and Jilly threw up their protective bubbles and stretched them out over Damian and Jonny.

"Tracey, help her," Damian begged.

"That's the plan," Tracey edged forward. Sarah and Laura were out of sight somewhere behind the clay giant. The monster twisted, looking both ways, then stopped moving as if it recognized its escape was now blocked.

"What is it?" Dave asked.

Tracey wished she had an answer. "Create a wall behind me," she told her friends. "Don't let it get past." She raised her voice to address the monster. "Let the girl go."

The monster made no sound. Kylie let out a screech as it shrugged, bouncing her up and down.

Tracey readied a ball of magic three times stronger than the ones she used in training. She hesitated. What if she hurt Kylie? "Let her go!"

Tracey shouted again. "Someone call Agent Malden."

"Shoot it!" Kylie screamed.

Laura's voice came from somewhere behind the creature. "Agent Malden's not answering."

"Sarah. Put up a wall. Don't let it back your way to escape." *What do we do now?* If she hit it and hurt Kylie she'd never forgive herself, but if she didn't strike and the monster got away? Well, that didn't bear thinking about.

"Tracey, help her," Damian said again, his voice thick with emotion.

"Working on it. Jonny, where do I hit it?"

"Low down. Damian and I will catch Kylie when she falls."

Time was ticking while Tracey debated what to do. At the same time, it felt like time had stretched and everyone was moving in slow motion. Any move she chose could hurt Kylie. Indecision froze her solid.

"Tracey!" Kylie's scream jolted her and without thinking Tracey threw the primed ball of magic. Bright orange sparks exploded like fireworks and sparkled along the clay creature like lightning. Kylie screamed again, but her voice was lost under the monster's roar. Tracey readied another blast. "Keep the stairway blocked. I think it's going to try to get past us."

"Tracey, it won't let me go!" Kylie screamed, battering at the clay with her hands and feet.

"Hey, big monster-thing! Hey! Are you listening?" Tracey shouted.

Kylie's body bounced up and down as the monster shuffled on the spot. It hadn't made a move to get past them yet. Hopefully, it could understand her. "We aren't letting you go until you put the girl down. I don't want to hurt you." Where the heck was Agent Malden? "Laura?"

"Still no answer," Laura called back.

"Jilly, I need you up here with me. Dave can you hold the wall?"

"Yeah," he confirmed.

Jilly ran to Tracey's side. "Any ideas?" Tracey asked.

"We move to opposite sides and attack it together."

Tracey tore her gaze from Kylie and found Jilly holding her magic energy spear. "What about Kylie?"

"She will survive the fall."

Tracey could feel Damian's glare on the back of her neck. Yes, she would find a way to save Kylie and somehow not get her hurt. "Fine." She let her hands glow, pushing orange light into her glowing ball. She then pulled magic from the Butterfly Stone and her ball flared brightly. "Put the girl down!" Tracey shouted one more time. "Just do it, then I don't have to attack."

"Pound it!" Dave said.

"I'm trying Agent Malden again," Laura shouted.

"Let me help."

Tracey's sigh of relief nearly buckled her knees. Prince Henry stood beside Dave. He wasn't looking at Tracey, but past her at the monster. He spoke quietly to Dave and passed right through the magical barrier that Dave held.

Prince Henry approached the monster slowly, his hands outstretched like he was trying to calm a spooked horse. "Easy there. Don't move, anyone." His voice was soft, but it projected over all of them. A sense of peace swept over Tracey and her wildly beating heart slowed a little. *Cool spell.* "Kylie, please remain still."

"Okay," Kylie said. Her voice trembled but she seemed calmer.

"What do we do?" Tracey asked.

"Exactly what you did. Keep everyone calm and stall until help arrives." Prince Henry spoke slowly, hypnotically, his voice coming from deep inside his chest. Tracey felt the sudden rise of power as something a little like her own sensory blanket flew out from Prince Henry. Her skin buzzed with the strength of it. His sensory net didn't fade like Tracey's always did. It bounced back from the walls and grew stronger with each wave as it overlapped with the last bounce.

"What is it?" Tracey asked.

"It's a mumble."

"A what?"

He didn't turn, just tightened his lips. "It's a manifested, barely sentient blob of sand, dirt, and water. Magic has molded it into a doll of giant size, and it is programmed with one task. Once that task is complete it crumbles back into dust."

"So it can't talk? Can it understand us?"

"Doubtful. Rather than comprehend what you wanted, it's likely you confused it by preventing it achieving its mission. It doesn't know what to do."

"So how do we get Kylie away from it?" Tracey asked.

"We wait for it to dissipate. It shouldn't be much longer." A burst of magic rolled out from Prince Henry like a wave. The walls her friends were holding strengthened and grew wider until they circled the mumble, constricting around it, trapping it in place.

Tracey released her magic ball and let her power seep back into her body. On the other side of the room, Jilly let her energy spear fade. Kylie squeaked. Her body bounced. "It's letting go!" she shouted.

"Catch her," Prince Henry ordered and dropped the wall around the mumble as it suddenly crumbled like a sand castle falling over. Tracey and Jilly ran forward and joined Sarah under Kylie. She landed on top of them and all four collapsed on the floor in a cloud of dirt and clay.

"I meant for you to catch her with your magic. Still, well done. Kylie, how are you feeling?" Prince Henry knelt beside the pile of bodies. Tracey tugged her arm out from under Jilly's leg and rolled over to climb to her feet. She helped Jilly stand up and together they dusted mumble bits off their clothes.

"Why did it grab me?" Kylie asked. The blond girl held onto Sarah's hand and pulled herself up with it. Damian ran to his sister's side and hugged her tightly showering the ground with clay bits and dust.

Prince Henry shook his head. "I can't imagine. Perhaps, because you were isolated away from everyone? Are you okay?"

"Yeah I'm fine. It scared me though."

Sarah gave Kylie a quick hug when Damian let go. Damian had dust streaks all over his T-shirt.

"What were you doing up here anyway?" Prince Henry asked.

Tracey silently scoffed. *Really, you can't figure out why the mumble grabbed Kylie?* It had to be because of the stone. Probably Jilly or Tracey would have been targeted if they had been up here instead.

"Just exploring," Sarah said and glanced at Tracey.

Prince Henry didn't push for the truth, but judging by his stare he clearly knew Sarah was lying. The whole reason they were in England was to find the stones. He turned to Tracey. "I'm impressed you held off the mumble and kept Kylie safe. Let's get moving, Elijah has called us all downstairs. Well done, everyone."

Tracey passed Tony coming up the stairs. He turned around when he saw them. His face was pale, he was out of breath. "What happened?"

Tracey told him about the attack. "Where's Noel?" she asked.

"He left."

"What happened?"

Tony's lips tightened. "His dad."

"Are you okay?"

He shuffled closer and whispered, "We need to talk later."

"Okay."

Something had happened. Something that involved Mr. Henderson. Tracey's shoulders straightened as she imagined confronting the boy who had dared hurt her friend. They walked into the dining room and found it overflowing with people. Several old men in navy blue suits stood at the far end of the room talking quietly with Mr. Henderson. Agent Malden was missing. Noel stood beside his father. He didn't look up as they entered. The table had not been set for dinner yet and there was a really weird vibe coming from the men, a serious one, full of importance and power. *Oh, oh. Not good.* Tracey's phone buzzed. A quick glance at the screen showed a text from Uncle Donny.

Call me.

"Ah, excuse me." She spun around and her shoe let out a loud squeak on the tiles. Her eyes widened.

Sarah snorted.

"I didn't … it was my shoe," Tracey hissed at her. She ignored her friends' smirks and the stoic, serious expressions on the people she didn't recognize and ducked into the hallway to dial her uncle back. He answered it as a video call. His face was shiny with sweat and his curly hair stuck to his forehead in clumps. "Tracey? Oh good."

"What going on?" she asked.

"I've got a lead on the client." He huffed and the background bounced, blurring as the camera tried to focus on his face.

"Are you running?"

"I'm on my way to meet him. I just wanted you to know I'll be back at the manor late tonight. Very late. Don't stay up."

"Uncle Donny … " She needed to tell him about the mumble. "We were att—"

There was a loud crack and Uncle Donny ducked his head.

"What was that?" Tracey demanded.

The vision blurred as the phone moved quickly up and down. Her uncle reappeared a moment later. He raised his head and peered around, eyes darting wildly. "I gotta go."

"Uncle Donny?" That had sounded like a gunshot. "Uncle Donny?" He hung up on her.

"What? What?" First a clay monster and now this? Tracey glared at her phone. When she got no answer from the silent device, she headed back into the tense dining room.

Everyone was seated and no one spoke. Tracey's sister and her friends sat at one end of the long table, staring at the three unknown men seated at the other end. Every head turned at Tracey's entrance and Tracey felt a shiver dance across her skin — magic testing her. She raised her shield. The lumpy gray-haired man on the right grunted and leaned back in his chair. The three men shared a long look. "What's going on?" Tracey asked.

Noel rubbed his fingers along the pristine creamy tablecloth, refusing to meet anyone's eye. Prince Henry sat in the middle of the table like he was the referee in some silent tennis match and Jonny's mom sat opposite him, glaring daggers at the silent prince. Sarah and Mrs. Carter sat next to Prince Henry. Mrs. Carter had a nasty smile on her face.

Clearly, Tracey had missed something major.

The man in the middle stood up, looking like a long, white, melty candle. Tiny dark button eyes stared down a crooked nose at her. He was about her grandma's age or thereabouts. His lips smacked together as if he was searching for moisture and there was white gunk in the corners of his mouth. He didn't glance at either man beside him. "Miss Tracey

Masters, we have been waiting for you."

Tracey didn't step any closer. Tony peered up at her, eyes wide, eyebrows dancing up and down. When the creepy old guy looked his way, Tony's expression was smooth and innocent.

"Now that you are here, I will continue. My name is Carruthers Stairs. I am the Chairman of the Mage-kind Council of Clans. Your recent unruly behavior has been investigated, and you have all been found guilty of using magic outside of the home. You are therefore Forbidden from the use of magic."

A buzzing sound filled Tracey's ears. Prince Henry stood up so fast his chair flew back and crashed against the tiles. "This is unconscionable. I repeat, you must wait for Agent Malden. He will explain all of this. They have permission—"

Tracey couldn't hear anything else. Mouth open, she gaped at her friends. Dave, Tony, Jilly, and Sarah looked horrified. Kylie's mom sat back in her chair, her smile growing broader.

"Mom, no," Damian muttered.

Tracey heard that, possibly because she was watching for his reaction. He stared at his mother, his mouth a firm line.

What's happening?

Chairman Stairs thrust out a hand and a powerful wind smashed against them. Tracey braced herself, widening her stance and strengthened her shield bubble. Similar bubbles formed around each of her Mage-kind friends. The wind blast reminded Tracey of the Dust Devil. Carruthers Stairs must have been the one who sent it to Miltern Falls to watch her.

Pain hit Tracey a moment later. It felt as though her entire core was being squeezed between the teeth of a vise. Like the ones they used in shop class back home. Tracey grit her teeth against the pain and her hand flew up to press against her chest. She needed magic from the Butterfly Stone. The vise tightened, trapping her breath inside her lungs. She fell to her knees and darkness swept over her, bursting her shield bubble. She cried out. There was no answer from the Butterfly Stone. Black spots flashed in Tracey's eyes. The pain spiked and dug into her ribs. She gasped and blacked out.

I see how it ends
and I cannot halt its steps.
I will be alone.
She will never hear me.

15

Tracey forced her eyes open. Her chest hurt and her friends' faces—the ones she could see—were scrunched up with pain. Each Mage-kind clutched their wrist as if it burned. Tracey cradled her arm to her chest, fingers wrapped around her Mage-kind identification bracelet. She moaned as the burning intensified.

The light blinking on her bracelet was blue. Forcing her trembling body upright, Tracey checked on her Mage-kind friends. Their bracelets displayed the same blue light. Just like Kylie's bracelet. Jonny was on his feet, his mouth hanging open. Beside him, Martha looked horrified. Laura knelt next to Jilly, tears welling in her eyes. Tracey's breath stuttered as she inhaled. *What the heck just happened?* She clenched her fist around the Butterfly Stone, but there was no answer. Nothing. No magic. She searched her core, flinging open her inner closet door. Nothing. A chill filled her body. Her magic was gone. The Butterfly Stone lay completely dormant against her chest.

Prince Henry radiated anger. His face was a bluish purple, boiling over.

The chairman clapped his hands once. "The bracelets that monitor your magic have been locked, preventing access to your core. The sentence has now been passed."

Angry voices filled the dining hall. Tony's clenched hands shook as he stared daggers at Noel. Dave clutched his arm to his chest, his eyes red and wet. Kylie and Sarah sobbed softly. Jilly stood still, silent murder in the intense stare she fixed on Carruthers Stairs.

"How long?" Tracey demanded. The room became silent, waiting for the answer.

"Your case will be reviewed in two years."

A collective gasp sucked all the air from the room.

Suddenly dizzy, Tracey searched for something, anything to focus on, but everything was too bright, too blurred. Nothing made sense. Eventually her vision cleared and she found Carruthers Stairs coming right at her. His slow lumbering steps sounded like the padded drumstick on a bass drum. *Boom, boom, boom, boom.* He swept past her and out of the room, taking the dust smell with him. The minute he and his lackeys disappeared everyone spoke, turning on Prince Henry, complaining about the loss of their magic.

All Tracey could make out over the din was Kylie's voice. "Is this my fault?" she asked removing her headband. She ruffled her blond tresses. "It's dead," she said at Damian's worried look, waving her wrist and pointing at the blue light in her bracelet. "I don't have any magic for the headband to contain, I guess. It loosened up as soon as that guy spelled us."

"It's not your fault, Kylie. It's mine." Tracey silenced the complaints. "This is my fault," she said. "It started with the Butterfly Stone. I wanted to be an investigator … I pushed to find the necklace. All of this is on me." Her gaze darted to the door in case the creepy old man suddenly returned. "Prince Henry? Who is that guy?"

"The chairman of the Mage-kind council. And I can't go against him. His decision is Mage-kind law."

"Couldn't Agent Malden or Mr. Henderson do something? Speak on our behalf." Sarah asked.

Tony's face was a stone mask.

Tracey was worried what that meant. "We need to get our magic back and we need to remove the stones. From all of us."

"No," Jilly whispered, her hand clenched tight around the Tiger's Eye.

"If we have no magic, can we finally remove these stupid identification bracelets?" Dave asked.

"How can we fight the monsters, Tracey?" Sarah said. She held her wrist across her chest, the blue light in her bracelet capturing all of Tracey's attention. "What's mom going to say?"

"What do we do now?" Tony asked.

Tracey shrugged. She had no answers for anyone.

"I'm with Tracey. We have to get *everyone's* magic back," Jilly said.

Mrs. Carter stood. "Kylie, don't you see how wonderful this it? You won't be bothered by magic anymore. You'll be just like us again."

"Mom." Kylie turned on her with tears in her eyes.

"Mrs. Carter—" Prince Henry began, but Kylie continued over him, drowning him out.

"It's who I am, Mom. I'm Mage-kind. You're denying what makes me, me. Don't you like who I am?"

Mrs. Carter stepped back, shocked at the venom in her daughter's voice. Sarah took Kylie's hand and held on tight, standing beside her, creating a united front.

"Did you speak to the chairman, Mrs. Carter? Did you ask for this?" Tracey's voice was as soft and non-confrontational as she could make it. It was really hard to do. How could a woman do that to her own child? Tracey's gaze flicked to Damian. He wouldn't look at her.

Mrs. Carter huffed like a dragon ready to breathe fire. "Don't you dare speak to me that way. This is between me and my daughter. This is *my* family!" Spit flew from her white lips. She grabbed Kylie's arm.

"Ouch!" Kylie yelped.

Enough with trying to be the bigger person. "Let her go!" Tracey ordered. Her voice blended in with Sarah's as they demanded Mrs. Carter release Kylie.

"Mom!" Damian stepped between Tracey and his mother. He put his hand over his mom's fingers where they clenched around Kylie's arm. "Stop, Mom. Tracey is trying to help."

"Help? Don't make me laugh. She's a monster! All of you are. Kylie is under her thrall and so are you."

"Mrs. Carter. That is enough!" Prince Henry turned to Tracey. "I think we all need to calm down. I'll ask the kitchen to prepare some pizzas and bring them to your room. Head upstairs now." He was working hard to keep his face emotionless. He wasn't quite succeeding. Mrs. Carter spun around and stormed out through the door.

"Damian, Kylie. Now!" she ordered.

Kylie didn't move. "No," she mumbled.

Damian stared at his feet and then held his palm out to Kylie. "I'll go calm her down." Tracey's heart clenched as Damian slunk out of the door after his furious mother. Tracey and her friends just stared at the doorway in shocked silence.

"Mom!" Jonny begged.

"JJ, what can I do?"

"Please, Mom?"

Martha sighed. "All right, baby. I'll see if I can help. Off to bed now, all of you."

Tracey's hand drifted to the Butterfly Stone. Still nothing. For once, it was behaving like an ordinary necklace and she didn't like it. A shiver ran over Tracey's skin. She tried her core again, but it was like a brick wall had been raised against her.

"Come on," Laura said.

Tracey followed her friends from the dining room. She glanced at her phone, knowing she should call her uncle, but he had sounded like he was in trouble. She hoped he was okay and settled on sending him a text message to call her when he could.

This was a nightmare. A total disaster. Laura appeared next to Tracey as they climbed the stairs. "Are you okay?"

"I feel empty," Tracey told her. The teens entered the girls' room and as soon as the door closed Laura pulled Tracey into a hug. Jonny and Tony joined in, turning it into a group embrace with Tracey in the center. Dave patted Tracey's head as his way of sharing in the moment. Tracey had tears in her eyes but wiped them away to search for her sister.

Sarah and Kylie stood just inside the door, holding hands. "Get in here," Tracey ordered and they jumped in, joining the hug, making it a ball of empathetic energy.

"All right," Jilly announced a moment later. "We must decide what we are to do next."

The teens scattered and sat down around the room.

"What do we do now?" Jonny asked. He slumped against the bathroom door and slid down to sit on the floor.

"Stick to the plan," Tracey told him. Everyone spoke at once.

"What about the stones?"

"Our magic is blocked."

"Sent to our rooms?"

"Not fair."

"Does this mean the investigation is off?"

"Are they sending us home too?"

Tracey held up a hand for quiet. "What we do now is investigate that secret library and check out those books."

"But we have no magic," Dave said. He fiddled with his bracelet, twisting it around and around his wrist.

"Maybe we'll find a way to break the curse and get your magic back in one of the forbidden texts," Laura suggested.

Tracey grinned at the tiny flash of hope in everyone's eyes. "After the pizza gets here, we'll sneak off."

"Tracey?"

She swung around to face, Tony. "Yeah?"

"Noel knew about the chairman."

"What?" The whole room blurted, sounding an awful like a school concert rehearsal.

Tony's chin pressed hard into his chest, his gaze locked on his fingers, clenching and unclenching his hands. "It might be my fault the chairman is here. Noel kept asking all these questions about the Shadowman, and Timothy, and the stones, and I … he's just … I liked him. I … I told him."

"Maybe it's not as bad as you think," Dave suggested. They looked up at him in surprise. He drilled his feet against the chest of drawers he was sitting on. "What? I just mean … you saw Mrs. Carter's reaction. I don't think you should assume Noel did this. He might have been asking questions because … well curiosity, and as a way to show he's interested in you."

Tony lifted his head. "You think?"

Dave shrugged. "Look, I don't know, man. You could just ask him?"

"His dad is on the council. Noel knew he was coming. He must have known about our sentence. He didn't even warn me." Tony said. "He wouldn't look at me in the dining room."

"Maybe he knew the chairman was coming but not what he was going to do," Laura tried. "He might have been as shocked as us and now he's afraid to talk to you."

"We can't know what he was thinking," Jonny said. "You gotta ask him, man."

Tracey shook her head. "Until we know for sure, no one should volunteer anything about the stones. To anyone. His dad is on the council. Tony, I'm sorry. I know you like him."

"Not anymore. What a slug."

"Tony, you need to talk to him. People's parents can be horrible." She was sure they were all thinking of Kylie's mom. "He might not agree with what his dad let happen."

"I don't know," Tony's voice was low, as if carrying all of his hurt was exhausting. "I'm sorry, Tracey."

She wished she had a way to make him feel better. She was furious with the chairman. And Mrs. Carter too. Tracey glanced at Kylie who sat by the window staring out at the maze. Poor Kylie. Sarah sat near her friend, watching her closely, no doubt wishing she could make it all better. Without her magic, Tracey couldn't even offer a magical embrace to Tony or Kylie. There was a gaping hole inside her body.

Jilly paced the room and huffed loudly. "I thought nothing could be worse than the memory curse on my family. But not having my magic? It is horrible. Like a part of me has died."

"I didn't even want it, but now that it's gone, I want it back," Dave said.

"Does everyone feel cold?" Sarah asked. The Mage-kind nodded sympathetically.

"This sucks," Jonny said.

A soft tap on the door announced the pizza's arrival and Damian's return. Tracey sat up straighter at the sight of him.

"Hey," she said.

"Hey." He went straight to Kylie and took her hand. Kylie yanked away from his grip and stormed across the room to sit on the floor with her back to her brother. Sarah sat down beside her and spoke quietly.

Jonny ignored the awkward silence and put the pizza trays on the floor. He flopped down and pulled a slice from the first silver tray. One by one they joined him. Tracey's phone beeped. It was a text message from Uncle Donny.

Hank just told me what happened. I'm so sorry, kiddo. I'm on my way back to you. How's Sarah?

She typed quickly. *We're okay.*

You were attacked by a rumble?

It's called a mumble. Yeah, but it's fine. Prince Henry was here. The mumble is nothing but dust now.

I'm supposed to be looking out for you kids. Your mom's going to kill me.

Don't tell her. The phone rang in her hand a split second after she hit send. She stood and walked to the window to answer it. "Uncle Donny, it's fine. We're all okay. Are *you* okay? You were shot at."

"Goes with the job, kiddo. Don't worry about me."

But she did. Constantly.

"Tracey, I'm coming back. Without your magic, if you're attacked again, I need to be there to protect you."

"We're fine. Keep searching for the client. There's nothing you can do here anyway."

"But the mumble attack."

"Prince Henry is here and Agent Malden's around somewhere. The mumble is gone. Total dust. We're just eating dinner then we're going to bed. You need to find the client."

"Well, if you're sure you're all okay."

She crossed her fingers. "Food and then bed. Promise." She ended the call and sank down onto the floor next to the pizza trays. Tracey wriggled her butt around until she sat a little closer to Damian. "Hey."

"I'm sorry about my mom." He stared across the room at his sister who ignored his very existence. "She's mad. I'm sorry you were caught in the middle."

"Kylie's the one caught in the middle," Tracey said. The younger girl didn't even look up.

"Yeah, I know."

"Well, I've got a lot of experience fighting with my sister. Give her some space. She'll talk to you when she's ready."

"But my mom."

"I know, just tell Kylie you're on her side. You are on Kylie's side, aren't you?"

He picked at the onion on his pizza and didn't answer.

Tracey's heart clenched at his silence. She had to say it. She was tired of guessing, tired of the uncertainty. Jonny and Dave were right when they told Tony to ask Noel for the truth. "Do you agree with your mom?"

Damian looked up and their eyes locked. She felt the sizzle all the way down to her toes. "I love my sister. Being Mage-kind has hurt her so much, but I don't agree with my mom. Cutting out what makes Kylie who she is, is wrong. I want to help you get your magic back. But, Tracey, she's our mom."

"If she wants to take you and Kylie home, I can't stop her. But it's really important that we help Kylie with the stone. I promised you I'd find a way to remove it and I will." Tracey scoffed down her pizza. "Hurry up, team. Let's go check out the secret room and those books. We need to get our magic back."

"It's a room with books. I mean, who hides a library?" Dave asked. The boys and Kylie walked around with a variety of stunned expressions. Jonny and Tony's wide-eyed awe. Dave, nose stuck firmly in the air. Damian and Kylie quiet and contemplative.

"As I have said, these books are forbidden texts," Jilly said again, her tiredness at repeating herself clear. Tracey wandered along past the bookshelf. Huh. The spacing between the books seemed off, like one had been moved, but maybe she was remembering wrong. She poked her fingers between two green-covered books. *Volumes 1 and 3. Where's 2?* Hadn't that been here yesterday?

"So, what now?" Sarah asked, coming to a stop near the table.

"Everyone grab a book and start reading." Tracey pulled out a blue volume. *Mage-kind Anatomy – Safe Medical Practices.* She plonked herself down at the table intending to open the book but her gaze drifted to the wall that hid the round room. The latch was right there, hidden by these texts. Her fingers flexed. With no access to her magic, it would be too dangerous. What if the strange round room was spelled? She could put her friends in danger. She stayed mute as her friends grabbed a book each and sat down on the floor or at the table. Tracey's gaze drifted back to the wall. *Ugh, I can't concentrate.*

She focused inward, searching for her core, wanting the slightest sliver of magic to brush against her mental fingertips. There was just emptiness. A hollow echo. She blinked. The words beneath her fingers blurred. *"Stephanie?"* Tracey wrapped her hand around the Butterfly Stone. Nothing happened. No white room, no dancing shapes, no annoyingly unhelpful ancestor. It was just a boring stone necklace.

Nausea twitched her belly. Perhaps she had eaten her pizza too fast, or perhaps it was just her body rebelling to the changes forced upon her. Her eyes popped wide and she scooted her chair closer to her sister. "Hey, do you think Mom felt it? When our magic got blocked?"

"I don't know." Sarah checked her phone. "No message," she confirmed. Tracey's phone was quiet too. "Should we call her?" Sarah asked.

Tracey shrugged and put her phone on the table. "Do you think the council had to tell our parents about the sentence?" she asked everyone.

Dave angrily flipped the pages in his book. "Mine wouldn't care."

"Don't tear it," Laura told him.

Tony held up his cell phone. "Mom would have called me."

"Yeah, so would ours," Tracey said. "If they don't know, we should hold off on telling them. Maybe we'll find a spell to unlock our magic and then we won't have to."

"She must know, Tracey," Sarah said. "She always knows."

Tracey clunked her forehead onto the table. "I know."

"Did she say anything when you spoke to her before?" Damian asked.

"No, nothing," Tracey said into the table. "I spoke with my grandma too. She would have known something was up, but she didn't say anything at all. No warning. They both sounded completely normal."

"Maybe we're too far away?" Jonny mused.

"Moms know everything," Tony told him. "Mage-kind ones do at any rate."

Dave shook his head. "Like I said, my mom wouldn't care even if she did know. She hates me being Mage-kind." He flipped another page and looked up. "Stop worrying about it. Just read."

Tracey nodded. "Dave's right. We can stress about what our families know later. Let's start looking for a spell to get our magic back. Keep an eye out for any mention of the stones."

Tracey was on her third book. Laura on her fifth, as was Tony. Tracey yawned and raised her eyes from the boring text. Dave held his book almost to his nose. She grinned at him. He must have sensed her look and lowered the book. "What?" he snapped.

"I don't think I've ever seen you read before," she said, her grin getting bigger.

"Oh har, har. I read. It's just gotta be interesting. And this … is not." He dropped the book and pushed it across the table. Tony put his book down too and rubbed his eyes.

"He's right. We haven't found anything useful," Laura said.

Jonny had taken off his glasses and put his feet up on the table. He was sound asleep. Jilly sat beside him, chin in her hand—eyes closed—asleep as well. Sarah, Kylie, and Damian were on the floor, their backs against the wall, a thick leather-bound book on every knee.

"There's nothing here," Damian agreed.

Tracey sighed. "I guess it was a long shot. I just thought a hidden library must mean the books inside it were important."

"I'm falling asleep," Sarah grumbled. She stood up and stretched her arms wide, moaning at the cracks echoing from her back.

"Ewww," Kylie grinned, holding a thick leather-bound book. "This one is about medical procedures. Like CPR but with magic instead of a defibrillator. I guess they didn't have those back then anyway. It's super boring. All medical jargon and speculation."

"I think I read that one already," Tracey said. Kylie put the book on the table and lay her head on top of it, sighing dramatically.

Laura spoke over Kylie's loud reaction. "Mine's about sewing with magic."

Dave held out his book. "Sheep and farming techniques. Wanna swap?"

"No way," Laura said, pulling her book to her chest.

"I guess we should go back and get some sleep if we can," Tracey suggested.

"Too late," Tony checked his phone. "It's 5 a.m." A chorus of moans followed that pronouncement.

They left the secret library and headed to their rooms. While Jilly showered, Tracey lay down on her bed and rested her eyes. In seconds, she was asleep.

Sarah shook Tracey awake. "What?" she grumped. She was so cold she was shivering. Ugh, she wanted her warm magic back. Tracey pulled the edge of the duvet over her head, but Sarah pushed it off. Tracey swatted at Sarah's arm.

"We have to go down for breakfast and you need a shower. You stink."

"Gee, thanks." Tracey plodded into the bathroom and shut the door behind her. She turned the water full hot until steam filled the tiled room. Her next yawn cracked her jaw. Inside her core it was as silent as a cemetery. Without her magic, she felt like she was walking dead. What if this was what she would feel for the rest of her life? She'd be a zombie, a dead body given enough life to function but not enough to feel. Just like a Norm.

It was horrible.

To be known is to hide one's true self.
For that self can never be accepted.

16

There was no sign of Agent Malden, Martha, or Mrs. Carter when they walked into the dining room. No Uncle Donny or Prince Henry either.

"What do we do today?" Laura asked, pulling a flakey pastry off the pile on the side table. "Go sightseeing? If no one has magic —"

"I vote we go into the castle and prison," Dave jumped in. Everyone laughed.

"Yea, you're all kinda like us now," Jonny said. "For two years anyway."

"Oh my ugh," Sarah moaned and dropped her head to the table. "Two years?"

"I'm going to find Noel," Tony announced.

They looked at him in shock. "Are you sure?" Tracey asked.

"Dave was right," Tony said.

"I was?"

"He is?" Tracey, Laura, and Jonny repeated.

"I'll only know the truth about what he knew if I ask him."

Tracey stood up. "Do you want me to come with you?"

"Nah, I need to go alone."

"Okay," she said. She examined the rest of the table. "We're not filming until later in the week. I guess we should keep exploring."

"I'm going upstairs for a nap," Jonny said.

Tracey groaned. "That's a great idea. But how about — since we're all sort of awake now — we go check out the maze and then sneak a sleep after lunch. Maybe Martha will be back by then and we can go sightseeing. We go back to the secret library tonight."

"Great plan," Sarah said.

They nodded and dug into their breakfast.

The morning was spent running around the maze. Jonny and Dave challenged each other to find the center, but no matter how hard they searched, no one found it. Kylie, understandably, did not want to go off on her own, worried another mumble might attack. Not having magic made the prospect terrifying for all of them.

"Does everyone feel cold?" Sarah asked again when they met up outside the maze.

The Mage-kind teens moaned a collective *yes*.

"What do you mean? It's really nice out here," Laura said. "The sun is out and it's not windy."

"Our magic heats us from the inside," Tracey told her. "I guess we sorta run hot normally."

"Without our magic it feels like winter," Jilly said. She made a fist. "My fingers ache."

"I keep shivering," Sarah added.

"It'll pass after a while," Kylie told them.

Oh, that's right. Kylie had been without her magic for a lot longer than the rest of them. Tracey's face heated, making her warm for the first time since their magic had been taken from them. "I'm really sorry, Kylie."

"I'm still cold, but I only really notice it when I think about it," Kylie said.

Ouch, point taken. They should stop complaining about the loss of their magic. Physically exhausted, they all trooped inside for lunch. Tony met them in the dining room.

"How'd it go?" Tracey asked, looking around for Noel. Martha was back from her family visit and was chatting with Jonny about where they wanted to go that afternoon. Tony nodded toward Martha. "Tell you later."

Jonny's mom happily accepted the task to plan a sightseeing trip for mid-afternoon. "A nap? Really?" Martha pressed her hand to Jonny's forehead. "You feeling okay, JJ?"

"It's my fault," Tracey said. "We stayed up chatting last night, well, playing charades and didn't end up sleeping much."

There were nods of agreement all around.

"Well, an afternoon nap sounds absolutely fine." Martha grinned at them. "I'll wake you in a couple of hours." She eyed Tracey and Jilly. "How are you doing?" She pointed to her own wrist. Tracey glanced at the blue light.

"It's weird," Sarah said.

Tracey nodded. "So blah." She was super glad when they returned to their bedroom after lunch. She collapsed onto her bed and moaned. "I am *so* tired."

Sarah flopped onto her bed face first. Laura ducked into the bathroom while Jilly changed into her pajamas and drew the curtains.

Tracey thought she would fall asleep instantly. She didn't. She tried sleeping on her side and then on her back. She tried all of the blankets on and then tossed them aside. Nothing. Sarah, Jilly, and Laura fell asleep really quickly, their breathing gentling with an occasional snort. After a time spent staring at the ceiling, Tracey tried counting sheep. Then dogs, then birds. *Ugh!* She rolled out of bed, grabbed her phone and Millicent's journal, and snuck into the hallway where the afternoon sunlight lit the carpet with a warm yellow glow. A glance at her phone confirmed Uncle Donny had not called back yet. She texted Tony. He didn't reply. *Must have already fallen asleep.* She really wanted to know how his talk with Noel had gone. She sat on the carpet with her back against the wall and opened Millicent's journal.

November 12

She has gifted me a maze. I can scarcely believe her generosity. There is peace out here among the hedges. I can run and run and never find the end if that is how I choose. Out here I am wild, free. I am not constrained by my existence.

No one comes out here. It is my place. Mine alone. Out here I do not see the consequences of my inaction.

I can tell no one of what I see, what I alone know. My introduction to the gardener was both a pleasure and a curse, for as soon as I touched his hand, I knew how he would die. Not even Stephanie knows the full power of my curse. I cannot warn them. I cannot stop it. I can only see their end and ache for their loss.

As a child I tried to warn anyone who would listen, and I was punished for my temerity. Locked away in a round room where the master believed I would be saved. The room is silent. There is no warmth or cold to press against my skin. No light to see by, no sound to carry.

It was as if I was both there and not there. Time lost all meaning. Minutes became days became years. I fear the experience has turned me quite mad and, somehow, made my curse stronger. I would scream, for hours, and see life after life end behind my eyes. Everyone I ever touched. Everyone I ever knew. I began to fear it was my touch that caused each death. I tried again to warn those whose endings I saw before they came to pass. But when my warning proved true, I was thought a witch. A foul prophet who supped with the devil and did his bidding. Stephanie granted me my freedom and told me what I was. I did not tell her everything for fear she would realize I was truly damned and leave me too. She granted me my strange quirks. That I do not seek out friendships and that I am unsuited to physical attachments. Without her, I fear what I might have become. I am afraid to make connections, afraid to try, afraid to truly live. She has brought me a little peace. I have even created a magnifier here and taught her how to strengthen our focus. The room that once tormented me is now my salvation.

For I am not mad.

I am magic …

"Tracey?"

Sarah shook Tracey out of her deep sleep. "Whaaat?"

"You fell asleep reading." She pointed to the journal on the carpet beside Tracey's hand.

"Oh. Whoops."

Sarah examined the hallway. "Why are you out here?"

"I couldn't sleep."

"Seems like you did."

"Yeah. I'd better get dressed." Tracey pushed to her feet.

"Jonny's mom called Laura, she's organized the limo and a tour. We'll meet you downstairs."

Tracey nodded and dragged her still tired body into their room as Jilly and Laura joined Sarah in the hallway.

She took a super quick shower and raced downstairs to meet her friends. Damian didn't join them sightseeing. Neither did Kylie. Mrs. Carter must have made them stay behind. Martha didn't say much about it except to announce that they weren't coming.

The whole group spent a fabulous afternoon being Norms, sightseeing around Oxford Castle and Prison. Dave had been right. It was fascinating. And creepy. The cells were cramped and cold. Tracey couldn't stop imagining Millicent trapped in the round room at the orphanage, all alone and terrified of her own power.

"Hey. Creepy in here, huh?" Tony asked, coming into the cell with her.

"Yeah. It's so tiny. And it's freezing."

"Quiet too."

Tracey examined his big sad eyes. "So, Noel?"

"Found him. Accused him of lying. He denied it."

"Well, he would if he did lie. Do you believe him?"

"I don't know. He admitted his dad told him to stay close, but he said he didn't know the chairman was coming. He did say the chairman appears without warning all the time and that his dad and the chairman have" —Tony used his fingers to air quote— "a history."

"What does that mean?"

Tony shrugged.

Dave joined them in the cell and Tony and Tracey shifted apart. "Do ya think there's ghosts here?" he asked.

Tracey smirked. "Are you scared?"

"Ha! No." But Dave didn't meet her eyes when he said it. "Do you think there's a Mage-kind prison?"

Tracey and Tony glanced at each other. "I suppose there must be," Tracey said. "That's probably where they put Doctor Chan."

"I bet they lock their power away too. Like us now," Dave said staring at the blue light on his wristband.

Tracey's mouth dried. "Probably."

"Awful," Tony muttered. "Let's get out of here."

They arrived back to the manor house quite late. There was no sign of Uncle Donny or Prince Henry. Agent Malden sat at one end of the table, eating dinner. A green book lay open beside his napkin. It looked strangely familiar. Mrs. Carter, with Kylie and Damian on either side, sat at the other end of the table. After a pause, Tracey and her friends found a seat and shoveled food into their mouths as quickly as they could manage. It was some sort of roast meat in a thick gravy. *Ooooo, hopefully it's chicken.* Tracey plonked down in the only empty seat—the one next to Agent Malden—and pushed his book to the side to put her plate down. She caught sight of a gold-embossed title before he moved it to the floor out of the way. *Mage-kind Practical Illusions and Control. Volume 2.* Oh! Agent Malden must know about the secret library. She'd seen this book there the other night. She squinted at him. "Where have you been?"

He smiled and moved the book to the floor. "At the Council of Clans arguing your case before the chairman. Or I would have, if he'd seen me."

Tracey sighed and started eating, glancing up occasionally to examine the silently eating teens and Mrs. Carter's pursed lips.

No one seemed game to start a topic. Tracey had a dozen questions for Agent Malden but didn't feel comfortable asking any of them in front of Mrs. Carter.

"Are you filming tomorrow?" Mrs. Carter asked. "You must all be excited."

No one answered. Kylie shrugged. Damian shoved a bread roll into his mouth.

"How are you feeling?" Agent Malden asked. He tapped his watch and the green bar across the face. "Any ill effects from the curse?"

"We're okay," Tracey mumbled. "Just cold. I hate not feeling my magic."

"I must officially protest," Jilly said. That seemed to break the dam on the silence and everyone spoke at once. Everyone but Damian, Kylie, and Mrs. Carter.

"I'm working on it, kids. I promise you," Agent Malden said.

The dinner was so weirdly uncomfortable they skipped desert and quickly excused themselves from the table.

"Back to the secret library?" Jonny asked when they were alone in the corridor.

"We'd better wait until the guardians have gone to bed," Tracey said.

"Mom will be angry if we come to your room," Kylie told Tracey.

"We'll go for a walk then," Sarah said.

Tracey nodded. "Okay. Meet upstairs in the long hallway at 10 p.m."

"Fruit tingles." Tracey's head thumped onto the table. They had been reading for hours. "This is so dull."

"I don't think we're going to find anything," Laura said.

Tracey nodded. "I love books, but this is really —" Her vision blurred and a sucking sensation yanked her suddenly forward. Tracey stumbled and found herself standing in the white room. The red square and blue diamond greeted her.

"Something is wrong," the Butterfly Stone's guardian said.

"The Mage-kind council sentenced us for using too much magic. They cursed us — blocked my magic."

"They have bound you?"

"I don't know what that is?"

"Death. It is unnatural. Do you wish to end this curse?"

"Yes. You can do that? Yes definitely."

"We require you to hear us."

"What does *that* mean?"

"You are the protector."

"If you can give me back my magic then do it. Please help me."

Tracey couldn't protect any one like this. She felt so empty and cold. So lifeless. If anything attacked her sister she wouldn't be able to save her. No, she wouldn't let it happen. She wanted her magic back. Not just for her sister or for her friends but for herself. "What do I have to do?"

In an instant the shapes were right beside her.

"Put your hand on us."

Tracey assumed her fingers would go right through the shapes, but the shapes were solid and warm to her touch. It reminded her so much of the Butterfly Stone she was heartsick to realize how much she missed it. This was the Butterfly Stone itself. Not Stephanie. Not Tracey's own magic. It was the Butterfly Stone's magic and it was glorious.

"This will hurt."

"What?" Pain slammed into her mind like a football to her gut. Everything inside her shriveled into a ball and then sucked inside itself like a cartoon black hole.

Tracey gasped as she was flung back into reality. She doubled over the table. Jonny snapped upright, waking with a snort. Jilly fell off her hand and smacked her face against the table. Sarah, Laura, and Damian jumped to their feet and gathered around Tracey, asking her what had happened. When the burning stopped, Tracey dragged her head up and stared at her friends. A wide grin spread slowly across her face as golden, magnificent warmth filled her chest. It was the like the sun had come out after a storm. She exalted in the return of her power.

"Tracey. Your bracelet!" Sarah said. The blue light now a steady, beautiful green.

"My magic's back." Tracey flipped her hand over and let a ball of light appear in the middle of her palm.

"How?" Dave demanded.

Tony beat her to the answer. "The Butterfly Stone."

"Yup. It gave me back my magic."

"What about me?" Jilly demanded. "Can the Tiger's Eye do the same for me?"

"I don't know, but probably yeah."

Jonny let out a whoop. They all stared at him. "What? It's good. Tracey has her magic back. It's the start of everything getting back to normal."

"Wait … wait." Kylie's shout silenced them all. "I found something." They turned to look at her. Kylie flushed under the intense scrutiny.

"What did you find?" Jilly asked.

"This book. It's got a handwritten name on it. Says it belongs to Millicent Flowers. She's one of the six, right? There's a folded note in the same handwriting."

Everyone sat up straighter. "Read it," Jonny urged.

Kylie cleared her throat. "*I'm not sure if we should do this. The danger is immense and so many will be hurt as a consequence. It is unlike me to second guess a decision after the path ahead has been decided yet something stays my hand. Stephanie and Timothy have grown close. I have seen the way he watches her. I have seen the bruises on her wrists and the wildness in her eyes. There is darkness surrounding us. This is not a game. Stephanie told me my abilities are a gift and make me special. I see now that they are anything but a gift and what I was accused of as a child is true. We walk alongside the monster.*

"*While my friends spend their time on the focus stones, I have acted against them in secret, looking for an unending spell. My Dreams foretell a terrible end and my winged guardians hound my steps. I hope this spell will not be required, but I am alone in this. I cannot tell the others for they would try to stop me. I fear Jing has an inclination of my plan, but he has secrets of his own that he keeps. I do not think he will speak against me. I am the only one who can remember the past and see what is to come.*" Kylie took a deep breath and looked up. "That's all it says."

"Wow," Laura said. "Millicent tried to stop them."

"And then they all died in a fire," Tony said.

Tracey pursed her lips. "Do you think Millicent did it? Set the fire?"

"Wait. But Tracey, Stephanie must have escaped," Laura said.

"What do you mean?" Tracey asked.

"She *must* have had children, otherwise you wouldn't exist."

Laura was right. "Huh."

"Did they stop Millicent?" Jonny asked.

"We need to learn more about the fire," Jilly said.

"Yeah," Tracey agreed. "Are there any other notes in the book?"

Kylie shook her head. "I flicked through every page."

"Maybe there are notes in the other books?" Tony's words prompted them to glance at the bookshelves. Only a third had been examined during their search.

"We must return again tomorrow night," Jilly said.

Tracey held out her hand. "Can I have the note?"

As soon as her fingers touched the paper Tracey's mind was thrown into the past.

To know ooa's self is to know true hoartache.
I long foo so much. A friend, a confidant,
a love, but there is a cost.

17

Tracey now knew what a Vision looked and felt like, so she didn't panic when her world grayed out and she lost touch with her body. She knew she was still in the secret library — at least, her body was — however in this space with a view to the past, she was completely alone. It was her job to be a witness. She waited in silence and for a moment nothing happened.

Huffing out an imaginary breath, Tracey spun in a circle and then twirled again. "Come on."

A loud crack signaled the secret door swinging open. Millicent stormed in.

She stomped her feet and threw books off the shelves and onto the table. One skidded across the surface and landed on the floor with a loud smack. "Argh!" Her face, shiny with sweat, darkened further, though Tracey wasn't sure how that could be possible. Millicent's hands clenched. She paced back and forth in front of the table, taking short fast steps. Every now and then she stopped and stamped her foot.

The door popped open and Stephanie swept inside. "Are you okay?"

"I'll kill him. I will, Stephanie. Did you hear what he said?" Millicent's skirts hissed as she twisted sharply.

Tracey's ancestor held up her hands. A gentle smile graced her lips. "I did. My dear, you must—"

"Don't you *my dear* me, Stephanie. I have a very long memory. I will not forget what he said. Or what he did. You'd best remember that too."

"I know. We are family, Millie. Not by blood perhaps, but by soul and friendship too. I see your anger and I hear you."

"Oh!" Millicent huffed and spun away, pacing to the wall and back.

She stopped right in front of Stephanie and released a heavy breath. Her shoulders sagged. "Why do you listen to him?"

"Millie … "

"We're moving too fast. My winged friends tell me the omens are against us. We haven't tested all of the spells fully. You know it. I need your support with this. We must stop — before this becomes something we cannot stop." The woman's lips quirked as a thought suddenly occurred. "Perhaps I should … "

"Millie?"

The Vision faded and Tracey blinked herself back into awareness, her body thrumming with magic. "Whoa!" Tracey stopped as her friends glanced up. "Um." Should she mention the Vision? Something inside her clenched at the thought. Unsure why she was feeling so squinchy, she chose to stay silent.

Sarah yelped, staring at her phone. "It's 6 a.m.!"

"We should go downstairs before the adults realize we're missing. Jilly, after breakfast we'll try and get your magic back." Tracey said.

Jilly nodded. "Very well."

"Are we coming back here tonight?" Sarah asked. Her yawn confirmed how they all felt, and their heavy-lidded, half-asleep looks proved it.

"Maybe we should take it in shifts. We need sleep too," Tracey suggested.

"Great idea," Jonny said. He yawned as he spoke.

"I think I'm going to fall asleep in my cereal," Laura said. They left the secret room and trooped toward the dining room. Tracey caught movement of the corner of her eye. She spun around, sure she'd seen a figure standing in the shadows watching them. There was no one there. She rubbed her eyes and stifled her own yawn.

"I'll meet you downstairs," Jilly said, turning left when the rest of them turned right. "I need to get something for a headache."

"Are you okay?" Tracey asked, letting the others move past. The skin around Jilly's mouth was tight and there were lines around her eyes. Between her eyebrows too, and she was paler than usual. All classic signs of a migraine.

"Just tired."

"My mom gets migraines. Take your time." Jilly's pain and exhaustion could be the result of the Tiger's Eye fighting the curse blocking Jilly's magic. Then again, it could just be all the reading they had been doing and staying up all night.

"Thanks. I'll be fine. You go ahead."

Tracey nodded and followed her friends down the corridor. Her stomach rumbled and she squeaked, getting a laugh from Dave and Tony. Even Damian cracked a smile. Then all of their cell phones beeped at once.

"Oh crud. I didn't notice we weren't getting a signal in there," Tony said.

Tracey had voice messages from Uncle Donny and Agent Malden. One from her mom too — as well as a few missed calls. She listened to the first one.

"Tracey, I need your help with the client — stuff is happening. Call me back." Uncle Donny sounded super stressed.

The next voice message was from Prince Henry. "Tracey, you'll get your call up today. Your scene is filming this afternoon."

The third message sank her stomach into her feet. "Tracey, I've just spent a few hours with Mrs. Carter. You need to pop in and chat with her. Call me back." Agent Malden's words were soft but crisp. Tracey sighed. She *really* didn't want to talk to Mrs. Carter.

"Trace, honey. Call me." Mom's voice quivered. She must have sensed the block on their magic. Grandma's message indicated the same. Tracey figured she would call them all back after breakfast. Uncle Donny's message sounded urgent, but she figured she'd see him in the dining room, so he could brief her about the client there.

They trickled into the dining room with their eyes glued to their phones. It meant Tracey didn't immediately see who was waiting for them. The room was empty except for a table heavily laden with breakfast. And Noel Henderson. The teen stood at the far end of the table waiting for them. His suit — black today — gave him the look of a funeral director. *Quite fitting actually.*

He stood up. "I was hoping for a chance to speak with you before you go out today."

Tracey tucked her hand behind her back to hide her green bracelet.

Tony stepped forward, shoulders back, feet braced. "I told Tracey what you said. About not knowing the chairman was coming. I also said I didn't know if I believed you."

Noel bowed his head. "I can assure you—"

Jonny pushed ahead, his hand held up, finger pointed directly at their host. "Dude, you need to check yourself."

Laura did one better. She stomped right up to their liaison, got in his space and forced him back a step. The heat in her eyes cooked him.

"It wasn't my—"

"If the next word out of your mouth is 'fault' we are going to have a serious problem," Laura said.

"You pretended to be our friend," Tracey accused on Tony's behalf. "Your dad wanted you to get close to us."

"Yes, and I've come to apologize for that. I am sorry. To all of you, but especially you, Tony. I am caught between two worlds. My father." Noel sighed. "My father may not agree with the council's orders, but he must follow them."

"He's *on* the council. Doesn't he make the orders?" Sarah asked. She and Kylie stood side by side glaring at the British boy.

"You're right. My father should, only he didn't decide this one. He didn't know the chairman was coming until he showed up. My father has been looking for the stones for years. It's like a fabled lost treasure, only you don't know where the X is, let alone which island it's on." He shook his head. "My father, Agent Malden, and Mr. Masters have spoken to the chairman to argue your case. There has been no response as yet."

"We can't use our magic." Tony waved his hand around in the air. His Mage-kind identification bracelet bright blue. "You asked me all those questions about the stone and what powers Tracey has. You told them everything, didn't you? Apologies are only words. Don't make them unless you mean them. Prove we can trust you."

Noel snapped his mouth shut.

Laura, Sarah, and Kylie widened their eyes at Tracey. Jonny made a "go on" gesture with his hands. *Gah, oh fine.* "Listen, Noel. I get that you're sorry, but our magic has been blocked. Maybe you can't understand what that feels like, but let me tell you, it's awful. It's like part of you has died. I don't think you can make it up to us, up to Tony, unless you help us break the curse."

"I … I can't … " Noel looked straight at Tony. "I'm not … " He nodded sharply. "Sod it. All right. I'll look around my father's office. The council shouldn't have taken your magic away. It was wrong. I didn't say anything, which makes me complicit. I'm not their pawn and I won't be used."

Tracey stepped forward still keeping her hand behind her back. "Where is your dad's office?"

A scream pierced the air, echoing down from the floors above.

Jilly!

Without hesitation, Tracey bolted for the bedroom floor. Thundering footsteps sounded behind her as her friends followed.

They found Jilly trapped in a corner of the hallway holding a chair and thrusting it at a mumble to keep it away. Its big hand made grabby moves as if it were trying to pick her up.

Without her magic, Jilly was unable to hold it in one place. She had done well just to stay out of its grip.

"Jilly!" Jonny yelled. He tried to get past Tracey but she pushed him back.

"Wait!" Tracey threw out her shield bubble, flattening it into a wide wall between Jilly and the mumble. The mumble clenched a fist and thumped it down against Tracey's shield. *Whoa! Strong.* Tracey strengthened the wall.

"I can't help you," Tony said standing at her side, his fists clenched unable to do anything magical.

"Hold Jonny and Laura back." Tracey couldn't protect Jilly and block the mumble from escaping. Fortunately, the mumble ignored her. It kept trying to get its clay hand around Jilly. When it realized it couldn't get to her, it froze.

A giant electrified fist punched the mumble in the side of the head and then on the nose as it turned around, knocking it onto its butt sending blue lightning over its clay body. The ground trembled as the mumble landed.

Where did that come from? Tracey glanced over her shoulder and found Noel standing beside Tony. Noel shot her a brief smile. "I won't say anything about your magic."

"Don't let the mumble move. We have to confuse it. Stop it from reaching its goal and it will crumble into dust."

The mumble held its nose, looking sad, like it didn't know why it was in pain. When it took its hand away its clay nose was twisted sideways.

Tracey dropped one hand and bent the bottom of her wall up to form a tunnel. Jonny slipped Tony's hold, scooted past Tracey and pulled Jilly out of the mumble's path. Tracey flipped her wall around so that it was now between the mumble and the teens.

"I'm okay," Jilly whispered. Tracey wondered how long she had been shouting for help for before they heard her. Tracey inched backward, her stare locked on the mumble. Noel's magic hand reminded her of something. *What is it?* The thought burst and the more she tried to focus on it the quicker it drifted away. Tracey flicked a quick glance at Jonny and Laura. "Get Jilly out of here."

"What about you?" Laura asked.

"I'll stay with Tracey," Noel said. "You should go to somewhere safe."

"He's right," Tracey told them. "You can't help without magic. Find Agent Malden or Prince Henry."

"Be careful," Sarah said, helping Jonny and Laura get Jilly out of the hallway.

Jilly called back over her shoulder. "Keep the barrier up. If he moves—"

"I got it," Tracey said.

Dave didn't leave. "I might not have magic, but I have muscle. I'm not leaving you here by yourself." His glare focused on Noel.

Tony stood tall beside Dave. "Me either."

Tracey's chest was strangely warm and, weirdly, she had tears in her eyes. She cleared her throat and focused on the mumble. "It's fine you guys. I just have to hold it in place. Prince Henry said it will fall apart if it can't get what it wants." Noel had jumped straight into help them without question. Maybe Tracey had judged him too harshly. She pondered the mumble's attack on Jilly. It must have attacked her because she had been alone. The mumble first tried to grab Kylie and now Jilly. Both were Mage-kind and both had been alone, or nearly alone in Kylie's case. There was one glaring similarity. Both Jilly and Kylie were stone protectors. Tracey hadn't been attacked, but she also hadn't explored the manor house by herself. She needed to test this hypothesis and sneak out on her own. Where had the mumble planned to take Kylie and Jilly when it got hold of them? Who was the mastermind behind all of this, Timothy, or someone else? Ugh, something kept pinging her mental radar. As soon as the mumble was dealt with, she would try to work out what it was her brain was telling her.

"Tony, I am truly sorry," Noel whispered.

"You lied to me," Tony said.

"That was not my intention. I just wanted to get to know you better. I'll make it up to you. I promise."

"Do I really have to listen to you two lovebirds making up? Because there are more important things happening at the moment," Dave said sharply.

Tracey laughed. She couldn't help it. "Sorry," she whispered when Tony pushed on her shoulder. She mashed her lips together, but a snort burst out of her nose. "Sorry!" When she got control of herself silence fell over them.

All right. Tracey would give Noel a shot. "How did you made that electrical fist? I've done a sling spell that acts like a hand once, for like, a few seconds, to catch something. But you electrified a hand shape and punched with it. How did you do that?" Something tickled the back of her mind again. Something she should remember. *What is that?*

Noel smiled. "Of course. My father taught me this spell. Make a fist."

She held up her hand forming a fist. Her other hand was splayed out, facing the mumble, holding her wall in place. She was used to doing two things at once with her magic so the split in her focus didn't bother her.

Noel's gaze darted to the mumble. When Tracey's wall didn't so much as flicker he whistled. "You are rather strong, aren't you? Focus on your fist and imagine an echo of your hand hovering over your actual hand."

She did as he described. Nothing happened. Maybe two spells at once *was* too hard.

"Try again, Tracey," Tony urged.

Tracey focused on her fist and imagined her magic filling her hand and then duplicated it, like when you copy and paste a shape in a computer program. A golden copy of her fist flickered into being.

"Well done," Noel said. "Now imagine your core is like a motor, um, a generator." At her blank look he tried again. "Think of the way your brain talks to your body. It creates electrical pulses to send messages to other parts of the brain and to your nerve cells. You already have electrical impulses jumping throughout your body. Call on those electrical pulses like you do with your magic. Use your magic to grab hold of the electricity and carry it through your body, gathering more and more along the way until you reach your magical hand. Don't force the electricity into your actual hand though, it's electricity and the stronger it is the more dangerous it is."

Tracey thought of her science classes at school. She knew the brain was made of two hemispheres. Electrical sparks or impulses traveled from one part of her brain to the other. Her biology teacher called them synapsis and neurons. There was a lot of math too. That was when Tracey had lost track in class, but she remembered the bit about the electrical sparks. There was something called an action potential. She pictured all the sparks lighting up her brain and brought her magic in so they blended together to make orange sparkly lightning in her mind. Magic and electricity. Then she drew it out of her brain—using her magic to contain it so it didn't shock her—and pushed it all the way down to her hand. Her magic fist sparked and hummed. She cheered. Without her focus the hand disappeared with a pop. "Darn."

"Keep practicing," Noel said.

"I wish I could do that," Dave grumbled.

"Me too," Tony said wistfully.

"I'll show you when you get your magic back," Tracey told them.

The mumble shuffled from one giant clay foot to the other, snapping their attention back to where it should be. The mumble let out a long moan and popped, sprinkling clay dust all over the floor. When it was gone Tracey relaxed her magic fist by drawing all of the electricity inside her core — the way she did with her magic. She could store the electricity in there too it seemed. It didn't even occur to her whether it should work or not. She wasn't electrified so it must have worked.

"Come on," she told the three boys. "Let's go find Jilly and make sure she's okay."

Noel shuffled and for a second Tracey was reminded of the mumble. "I'm not sure your friends will want me to join you."

"You should come," Tony told him. "Explain again that you're sorry."

That's when Tracey's brain finally connected the dots and worked out what her feelings were trying to tell her. "Noel." She stopped dead in the center for the hallway. "Where did you learn that spell again? The magic hand one."

"From my father, why?"

Noel's father had attacked their plane? Tracey locked eyes with Tony. "Noel, do you know where your father was the day we arrived?"

"Here. At the manor house. There was an issue with a busted pipe in the residential area. He wanted it fixed before you arrived. Why?"

"Our plane was attacked mid-flight by a giant magic hand."

"You think my father … ? No, no he would not … it is a council spell though."

"The chairman." Dave grumbled. "I knew it."

"Why would the chairman attack us? He sentenced us for using our magic illegally. Why would he make us use it in the first place?" Tracey asked.

"To ensure the sentence was legal," Tony mumbled. "Think about it. We all had to use magic on the plane. That way, he didn't just sentence you, Trace. He could sentence all of us."

That made her steaming mad. The chairman had set them up! "Let's go find the others. Come on, Noel. You're coming with us," Tracey said.

He nodded and fell into step beside them as they walked down the corridor.

Tracey checked her phone again and her missed call list reminded her of all the things she had to do. Before she called everyone back, she wanted something to eat. She was starving.

204

There is always a lie
in observation and perception.
I am always alooo.

18

Tracey pondered her friends' reactions to Noel's presence as he entered the dining room. They stayed quiet but speared him with dark looks sharp enough to draw blood. She was impressed he withstood the non-verbal accusations and carried on.

"Tony's right. It makes sense that the chairman would attack our plane." Jilly's clenched fists cracked.

"But how can we prove it?" Jonny asked.

Noel raised a hand. "I'll search my father's office. If the chairman had council approval it will be minuted."

"What like a clock?" Dave asked.

Noel smiled. "Minutes are the notes taken at the council meeting."

"What if he didn't have approval?" Laura asked.

"He must have. Magic that strong—cast from earth to reach a plane in the sky—for that much magic the whole council must have been involved," Noel said.

"The question is if your dad's a part of it or not?"

"I don't know, but I'll find out."

Tracey's phone buzzed. She glanced at her notifications and bit back a swear. Grabbing a few pastries, she wrapped them in napkins for later and stuffed them in her pockets.

"What are you doing?" Sarah asked.

"Uncle Donny wants me to meet him outside. He found the client. He thinks I can, I dunno, talk to him or something."

"Oh," Sarah stood. "I'll come—"

"Actually no, you have to stay and film the movie scene today."

Sarah's eyes narrowed. "You're not coming?"

"Depends on what Uncle Donny needs. Noel—"

"I'll let you know what I find."

"Be careful," Tracey said.

"I will."

Her sister sighed. "I wish you were coming with us."

"I'll get there as soon as I can. Jilly, can I talk to you for a sec?" Tracey motioned toward the door. Jilly followed after her. Tracey munched on her pastry and when the door sealed shut behind them, she said. "Are you okay?" Jilly's skin was still sweaty and she was awfully pale.

"Yeah, the mumble surprised me. Without my magic, I was helpless against it."

"You did a good job staying out of its grip until we found you."

"My training helped. Tracey, it came straight at me. It wasn't a mistake. I was its target. It wasn't after my magic—I can't feel it. It must be after the stones."

"Yeah, that's what I figured." Tracey's shoulders straightened. She pushed open the door to the parlor. "Let's get your magic back. We need you at full strength. I have to help Uncle Donny, so it will be up to you to watch over Kylie."

"I understand."

Tracey shoved her pastry into her mouth. Around her mouthful of food she said, "Do what we did before, grab the Tiger's Eye and call for the stone's guardian." Tracey watched Jilly, waiting for that odd freezing of movement and blank stare that indicated travel inside the stone had worked.

It didn't come. Jilly said, "Nothing. I can't sense it."

"Okay. Let me try." Tracey gripped the Butterfly Stone and stepped toward Jilly. She touched the Butterfly Stone to the Tiger's Eye and a familiar yanking sensation pulled her forward. Tracey blinked her eyes open on the white room. The Butterfly Stone's guardian was waiting for her. The red square and blue diamond rotated and wobbled in its strange amoeba dance—the movements similar to those she had seen in jellyfish specials over the streaming networks. Tracey was alone. She'd hoped Jilly would get sucked inside with her. "Hi," she said to the guardian.

"We cannot find the other."

"The Tiger's Eye?" Tracey clarified.

"Yes."

The guardian said no more.

Tracey waited.

Silence reigned.

"Oh, for crying out loud. You helped me get my magic back. Can you help Jilly too and release her magic? She can't speak to the Tiger's Eye because, well, obviously her magic has been blocked, maybe you can talk to the Tiger's Eye or Jing Cho—and find a way for it to connect with Jilly?" The shapes shifted in sharp movements. Tracey wondered if her request had upset them.

"Jing Cho?"

"Yes, he's in the Tiger's Eye. You know like Stephanie is with you?

The shapes squished and expanded, rotating around themselves for a moment.

"Stephanie?"

Tracey's mouth dropped open. She forced her mouth closed but it popped open again. "Stephanie. The original creator of the Butterfly Stone. You must know who I'm talking about."

"We know her. How do you?"

"She's here. *In* the stone. Seriously, do you not talk to her? Ever?

The shapes danced some more.

"We do not sense her."

"But ... but she's trapped *in* here. Do you really not know that?

"We are ... unaware."

Tracey was lost for words. Okay, that was a thing. She had no idea what it meant for the other stones. "But ... " She shook her head. "But you knew about Timothy inside the Serpent's Kiss. You helped Kylie by locking the stone and blocking her magic."

"Yes. It is his punishment."

"Right. It's the same with Stephanie."

"Incorrect."

"No ... no, correct. She's here. I've spoken to her. You need to clean up your house, seriously." Tracey pointed with a lecturing index finger. Then she remembered, she didn't have the time for this. "We'll discuss this further later. Right now, I need to know if you are connected to the Tiger's Eye?"

"We are."

"Can you link me to the stone?"

"Yes."

The world around Tracey wobbled and bled red, dripping down around her until everything she could see was crimson. The Tiger's Eye guardian wobbled in front of her. A purple circle and a gray octagon.

"Hi." Tracey waved and felt completely stupid for waving at rotating shapes.

"Why are you here?"

"Can you sense Jilly? The current protector of the Tiger's Eye?"

"Yes."

"Great, okay, well she can't feel you. I mean, she can't connect with you. Her magic has been blocked." Tracey quickly explained what had happened. "Can you rebuild your connection and return her magic to her the way the Butterfly Stone did for me?"

The shapes flashed and spun so rapidly Tracey's vision swam from the motion. Dizziness made her sway and she stumbled, widening her stance to stop from falling. Jilly popped into the red room.

"Whoa!" Jilly said, wobbling on her feet.

Tracey pointed to the shapes. "This is the Tiger Eye's guardian."

Jilly pushed her hands together. "Hello, Guardian."

"We can restore your connection to your power, if it is your wish."

"Yes," Jilly blurted. It had never been in question.

A familiar sucking sensation pulled Tracey from the red room and she landed on her butt in front of Jilly's frozen form. Tracey scrambled to her feet. "Jilly?"

There was no response from the girl, but Tracey did have four new text messages from her uncle. He was waiting outside, at the end of the long, long driveway. Tracey bounced on her toes. She couldn't just leave Jilly here like this. Moving her fingers quickly over the alphanumeric touch pad on her phone, Tracey sent a text message to Laura. Her phone buzzed.

Her best friend poked her head inside the parlor a minute later. "Hey, what's up?"

"Can you stay with Jilly until she wakes up? She's talking to the Tiger's Eye to get her magic back, but I have no idea how long it's going to take."

Laura's gaze sprang to Jilly and she tiptoed closer. "Sure."

"I don't think you can disturb her," Tracey said. "Just be here for her, in case?"

"Okay," Laura said. "Thanks for getting me."

"Hey, I know I was weird a few weeks ago, but that was the memory curse affecting me. Jilly is my friend now too. I worry about all of you."

Laura grinned and pulled Tracey into a quick hug. "I know. I wondered if you were a bit jealous though."

Eeeep. She picked up on that? "Nah," Tracey said brushing off the concern. Her skin prickled from embarrassment.

"Good. Because we're best friends. Always. No matter what."

"Always," Tracey agreed. She waved and moved toward the door. "Uncle Donny's waiting for me outside."

"Text me later?" Laura asked. "I can't believe you're going to miss the filming."

"Hopefully I'll be back in time," Tracey told her. "Uncle Donny—"

"Needs help, yeah I know." Both girls laughed. Tracey waved and ran toward the front door.

It was a long run to the bottom of the driveway. The air was quite crisp, and her nose dripped from the cold, forcing her to yank a handful of tissues from her pocket as she ran up to the tiny black car. She bit back a smirk when Uncle Donny unfolded his body from the driver's side. "Come on, quick." He ducked back inside and revved the engine.

Tracey tugged open the door, wincing at a squeal that sent jagged fingernails into her ears and buckled up, kicking something in the footwell. She reached down and her fingers closed around a thin flat object. She lifted it up. "Uncle Donny! Another one?"

"What?" He glanced over and then lifted his wrist. Sure enough, the button had torn off his green shirt cuff. "Whoops."

Tracey shoved the button into her pocket with a snort. Uncle Donny pulled away from the manor house with a screech of tires. The little car roared, but didn't move very fast.

"Are you okay?"

"Yeah, the mumble didn't get Jilly."

"Jilly? Wait, what? I thought the mumble tried to get Kylie. Are you saying you were attacked again?"

"Um, yes. Wasn't that what you asked about?"

"I was talking about your magic, the council. Are you sure you're okay? Was anyone hurt?"

"We're fine."

"I've spoken to your mom. She said she's been trying to call you."

"What? Oh, Uncle Donny, no. I didn't want to worry her."

"I had to, Tracey. This affects you and Sarah. Besides, she called me. I'm sorry I wasn't there to support you and Sarah in front of the council."

"Of course she called you." *I really need to call her back.* Tracey stared out of the car's side window. "What did she say?"

"She's upset obviously, but she can't go against a council edict. She has petitioned them."

"And?"

"We wait. I know you—"

Her head snapped around to stare at her uncle when his words cut off. He was rapidly glancing from the road to Tracey's wrist and back again. Tracey looked down at her green bracelet. *Oh.* "Um."

"I'm not going to ask. No wait, I am. Tracey, how did you get your magic back? Does the council know? Did they give it back?"

She shrugged.

"Let me guess, the Butterfly Stone had something to do with it?"

"Yep."

"And the others? Your sister?"

"Only me. And maybe Jilly. The council doesn't know."

"What do I tell your mom?"

Tracey shrugged again.

Uncle Donny sighed loudly. Then he grinned. "Actually, that's great. I feel better asking you to come with me now that I know you can protect yourself."

"Why? Where are we going?"

"Right. Listen. The client—Frank Transcenni—is in hospital. In a coma." Uncle Donny's flyaway hair was wilder than usual and his face was all shiny. Sweat stains blotted his armpits.

"Explain."

"Let me go back to the beginning. Prince Henry came here to investigate Mr. Rodney Transcenni. The man who sent the journal to Doctor Chan, which then went missing. Didn't it, Tracey?" For a brief second his stare stabbed into her and she knew that he knew she had the book. The book Doctor Chan bought from the Transcenni estate sale and shipped to Miltern Falls. The one Tony redirected so Tracey could get her hands on it. Millicent's journal.

Uncle Donny faced the road again. Tracey turned her head and stared out the window, her skin burning. Her uncle didn't ask, and she didn't tell him the truth. He cleared his throat. "Prince Henry surveilled Frank Transcenni and managed to sneak into his house."

"Why did he think Frank Transcenni knew about the stones?"

"There was a wall of photos in his house."

"Like the whiteboards on police shows?"

"Exactly. Like the one we made to find Mrs. Bellings's son."

Oh yeah, she remembered that. Uncle Donny had put together a board of clues when he was investigating the disappearance of nine-year-old Bobby Bellings. It turned out to be a waste of their time because Bobby had simply snuck over to his best friend's house and fallen asleep in his closet. "What was on the board Prince Henry found?"

Uncle Donny's silence sent a shiver over Tracey's skin, as if the car had plunged into an icy lake. "Uncle Donny?"

"You and your friends."

That's super creepy. Tracey rubbed her hands together. "Oh."

"Yeah."

The creepy feeling spread to her gut. "So. Frank Transcenni is in a coma?"

"Yes, a magically induced one. That's why I need your help."

"Why didn't you ask Agent Malden or Prince Henry to help?"

"I did. They've already tried to wake him."

"What makes you think I can do something?" she asked.

He turned his head to stare at her then glanced back at the road. "Honestly. It can't hurt, can it? I thought it was a long shot after Agent Malden told me about the council's sentence. But now that you have your magic back, well, you might think of something. Besides, Frank Transcenni knows about the stones. And someone made sure he couldn't tell anyone about them."

"That's creepy."

Uncle Donny glanced at her again. "It is. You still want to come?"

"Absolutely." Through the windows Tracey watched the green and gray landscape give way to red brick homes. Rows and rows of them. "Where are we going?"

"Saint Josephine's. It's now a private hospital for Mage-kind."

"Now?"

"It used to be an orphanage. In fact, the old church and the orphanage are still attached to the rear of the new building. This whole area used to be something else. It's all been repurposed over time. I think you'll be impressed with the adjoining buildings. They're over two hundred years old."

"Kinda of like the manor house, huh? Everything is really old here."

"It is."

"So, what else did you find in Mr. Transcenni's home? Any clues about what he knows, uh, knew?"

"No. Well, maybe?"

"Uncle Donny?"

"Ah well before the orphanage was turned into a hospital, it ah … "

"What?"

"It housed patients who were, um."

"Uncle Donny?"

He wouldn't look at her. "People like my mom, your nana, Tracey."

"A mental health facility?"

"Back then it was called an asylum."

"Oh." Tracey stared at the road again.

"You know people thought differently back then."

Tracey twisted her hands together on her lap. "I know. Patients weren't really insane, it's just what the doctors called them. They were just sick and needed help. Dementia and Alzheimer's and depression, things like that. Like at Tavel House."

"Exactly," he said.

"It's sad they were locked up for being sick."

"There is a strong magical imprint on the hospital, Tracey. You will need to keep your shields up."

That worried her. Tracey nodded. "Okay."

She felt like a mouse trapped in a maze as she walked through the dimly lit hospital corridors. They were long and snaky without any logic to them, weaving back and forth with rooms sprouting off in every direction. Tracey's shield bubble was up and as strong as she could make it, still, it didn't completely block out the sick feeling pressing against her skin. All the doors had bars over the windows. And this was the *new* building. She wasn't even in the church or the old hospital part.

Shadows moved as they walked along the cold corridor. Tracey flinched at lunging shapes caught out of the corner of her eye. In her head, she heard the Shadowman screeching and her palms started to sweat. How could anyone get better in a place like this?

Uncle Donny opened a solid white door with the number seven

painted on it. A man lay on the bed underneath a tightly tucked, faded blue blanket. It seemed too thin to keep him warm in this cold room. The machine at his bedside offered a steady beep. It was attached to the man with long cables that snaked under his white hospital gown. He didn't wear a breathing mask or have a ventilator tube sticking out of his mouth, so his face was clear to see. It was the same man she remembered walking out of Uncle Donny's office a few weeks ago. The one that had given her such an odd look and hadn't said a word before he left.

"What am I supposed to do?" Tracey whispered. It seemed wrong to speak any louder in here. Like someone could be listening and she didn't want to disturb them. Perhaps the man on the bed? *Should I try talking to him?*

"I don't know. Drop your shield?" Uncle Donny said as he shut the door. It clanged loudly and the sound reverberated inside her tummy. Her uncle stayed near the door and peered out through the bars. "I'll keep a watchful eye."

His behavior was giving her the willies. "Are we allowed to be in here?"

Her uncle's eyes flicked side to side. "Oh yeah, sure we're allowed, but um" — he rolled his right wrist — "you should hurry."

Tracey huffed and shuffled closer to the bed. "Mr. Transcenni?" She nudged his shoulder. "Mr. Transcenni, can you hear me?" Her fingers brushed his cold skin. She half expected him to bolt upright from her touch. Nothing happened.

She let out a slow laughing breath. *I'm scaring myself!* Tracey thinned her magic bubble. Nothing attacked or put pressure on her shield, and Uncle Donny's magic was a comforting familiar cloud behind her. Tracey latched onto his magic and lowered her bubble completely, letting her power out to fill the room. It swelled, filling every crack in the ancient walls. Darkness crowded in on her, pressing down on her skin like an oily stain that quickly spread out over her body. *Ewwwwwwww.* Sadness. Like a murky cold winter night. Her shoes squeaked on the linoleum as she crept closer to the bed. The sad feeling wasn't coming from the patient. The cloying sadness came from the walls, a faint, faraway sound of voices; crying, singing, gasping and screaming, wailing and moaning in pain. Tracey slammed her eyes shut as tears leaked from the corners and dripped onto her cheeks.

"Tracey?"

Uncle Donny's voice boomed in her ears. Her eyes widened. Uncle Donny hadn't moved. "Try to block it out. Focus on the here and now. Be present. Breathe. Listen to your heartbeat."

Right.

She pressed her hand to her chest and focused, listening to her heartbeat thumping madly inside her chest. As her breathing slowed, the crying sounds faded. She could still hear them, but concentrating on the room helped lessen the effects on her mind. Uncle Donny's feet shuffled over the linoleum-covered floor. Tracey focused on the beeping of the heart monitor and the cool skin of the man lying so still beneath her fingertips. She let her eyes close and tugged magic from her inner closet, imagining the strands covering her body bringing warmth and safety. In her mind she called out *Mr. Transcenni?*

Frank Transcenni's eyes sprang open and he sat up.

"Hello, Tracey."

Gift or curse? No one can see what
I see when I peer into the future.
I cannot speak of it. I can give no warning
for there are none who would believe me.

19

She let out a squeak and jumped back. Mr. Transcenni turned his head to follow her and she realized he was actually a transparent figure sitting up out of the body lying on the bed. She could see hospital equipment on the other side of the room through his skin. She checked Uncle Donny to see if he was seeing what she could see. He stood still as a statue, his mouth half open as if he had frozen just as he was about to speak. The spirit climbed out of his own body and Tracey stepped back again, realizing she was also in spirit form. Her actual body hadn't moved and she was still holding the man's hand, but her spirit form was all the way on the other side of the room.

"What's going on?" she screeched, flinging her hands up. She could see right through them. "I'm a ghost?"

Mr. Transcenni's spirit wore the same hospital gown as his body. "It appears as though I am a tad indisposed at present. A rather unflattering look, I admit," he said examining his body on the bed.

He had said her name earlier. "How do you know my name? How am I like this? Am I dead?"

"You are not dead. Please don't panic. It is merely a spell I cast many years ago, as a—I guess you could say—insurance policy. And I know who you are, Tracey, because I am your third cousin twice removed. We are family. Stephanie is my ancestor and you look just like her. You may call me Frank."

"Whoa!"

"Indeed."

"How do I wake you up?" She walked, or floated, closer. "And how do I get back into my body?"

"I am afraid you can't wake me. No one can. I was hit by a powerful spell, an old one. There is no one alive who can unweave it."

"I'm so sorry," Tracey said. How sad. And worse, his spirit was awake and aware even as his body lay dying in the hospital bed.

"Nevertheless, you are here, and I am able to pass on to you what I have learned. If you would please accompany me?"

"Where are we going?" She followed the spirit past her frozen uncle and right out through the door. An icy shiver of prickles ran over her body as she passed through the solid wood. *Oh, I hate that feeling.* Immediately she told herself not to walk through any people.

"Do you know the history of where we are currently standing?" Frank asked.

They walked past hospital staff and visitors. All were frozen in the middle of what they had been doing. "It's a new hospital. Built beside or maybe over an insane asylum." The words were bitter in her mouth. They passed a cleaner holding a mop and a nurse with a cup of coffee—a steam curl had frozen above the liquid.

"Yes, and what was it before that?"

"An orphanage."

"Precisely. How would that be connected to the Stones of Power?"

"Oh … Millicent! She was an orphan, wasn't she?"

"Very good, Tracey. Yes. It is not exactly how I intended to come here, nevertheless, it is most fortuitous." He disappeared through a white door. Tracey followed and floated down a long corridor to another door. A heavy door. When she passed through it the prickles were sharper, digging into her ghostly form. *Why do I feel pain when I don't feel anything else?* The corridor beyond was lined with red bricks. Tracey didn't feel cold or hot, she could taste nothing in the air and smelled nothing either. She floated, insubstantial and neutral, both here but not here. It was so strange. And like in a Vision or a memory, she couldn't feel her magic.

Tracey followed Frank down another corridor, through a red-painted door and into an old building. The windows were covered with thick wooden boards and the walls had long cracks in them. The empty room contained several large holes in the floor. *I'm a ghost. Can I fall down a hole?*

She figured it didn't pay to experiment and she edged around them, following Frank through another door and up a flight of stairs. "I planned to petition the hospital to allow a search through their ancient records. I had hoped for free reign over the upper levels of the building. Did you notice the bell tower attached to the church outside?" he asked.

"No, I didn't see it."

"The bell tower is part of the original building. This monstrous block of bricks was built directly over the previous site—a church, I believe. Millicent spent her younger years here. There was a journal you see, the one that was stolen from me, I'm sure it would have told me where all their secrets were hidden."

Tracey would have flushed from embarrassment but as a floating spirit she couldn't. "I have the book."

"What?"

"The journal you were looking for in Miltern Falls? I have it."

He clapped once. "Oh, that is fantastic. Have you discovered its secret yet?"

"Secret?" Tracey shook her head. "I haven't finished reading it." She had read nothing about a bell tower.

Frank would've grabbed her hands if he could touch her. Tracey was sure of it. His fingers shook. "Secret writing. A spell, dear girl. Millicent spelled her journals to hide her true words."

Tracey nodded. "The Butterfly Stone unlocked it."

"It did? Marvelous. Did she write anything about this place?"

"Not that I've found," she said.

"Well, it doesn't matter. We no longer need the journal. I believe Millicent's hiding place is here."

"You think her stone is hidden here?"

"Yes." They climbed higher and higher until they crossed a barrier of steel. The concrete steps became uneven bricks and traveled up in a spiral. "Aha. We must be close now." They moved in silence and finally walked through a closed wooden door into a hexagonal room lined with chipped and peeling wood. There was a giant hole in the floor and above it hung an enormous brass bell. Tracey could see the clanger inside. *It's as big as my head!* A wooden fence surrounded the hole, but it didn't feel very safe. She pinned her transparent body against the wall.

Frank laughed. "You are in spirit form, Tracey. You are perfectly safe. See?"

To Tracey's horror, he floated out over the hole. He didn't fall. He just hovered there, smiling at her. Tracey straightened and attempted a smile — it felt kinda wobbly. Whether it was safe or not she still avoided getting near the hole. No need to take unnecessary risks. She focused on the walls to take her mind off the speedy way down. Each of the six walls had a large square window, only there was no glass. *That can't be safe.* If she had been in her physical body, she imagined she would have felt the wind in her hair and the uneven floor boards beneath her feet.

Why did Millicent like this place? Tracey stood next to the window and stared outside. *Oh, that's why.* The view went on forever. Green grassy hills, trees and parks and tiny people, cars and trains and rooftops. "The people are all moving. But your spell … "

"Is breaking down. I do not have long. We must hurry." A number of black birds flew in super slow-motion circles close by. Tracey found herself mesmerized by their slow flight. She imagined that if you were feeling trapped, a view like this would be very freeing. "Wow."

"What did you find?" Frank appeared at her side so fast she wondered if he had simply imagined himself there. She stumbled back, catching herself at the edge of the Hole of Doom.

"Don't do that!" she scolded. He tilted his head, waiting for her reply. She thought back over what he asked. "Oh, nothing. I was just appreciating the view. It's nice."

He made a *"guh"* sound in his throat. "Start looking."

What a grump. Tracey returned her gaze to the inside of the bell room. *Where would Millicent hide her secrets in here?*

There was nothing to see. It was just a wide, six-sided room with a giant hole in the center like a doughnut. She glanced up at the bell. You couldn't hide anything up there. It would fall out when the bell rang. At the base of one wall was a group of wooden and steel cogs. That must be how they rang the bell back in the old days. She examined the peeling wood. She couldn't use her magic in her ghostly form, so she couldn't tell if anything up here had been spelled. She should go get her body. Return and try—*oh, what's that?* A shadow in the corner of her eye looked like a word. Tracey stepped back. The wood and shadows blended together and what she had thought was a word disappeared.

"Oh, this is maddening. There is nothing here." Frank swept around the room, circling faster and faster.

Tracey wasn't so sure. Remembering books she'd had as a little kid, the ones her grandma had given her, Tracey stepped close again, crossed her eyes, and slowly stepped back.

There was an invisible word in the wall. *Alone.* "Oh, that's cool."

"What? What is it?"

Tracey didn't answer. She moved to the next wall and repeated her movements.

Quiet.

She did the same thing at each of the six walls. The words were: *Alone. Quiet. Lost. Love. Anger. Death.* It reminded her of the poem about the Stones of Power.

"What did you find?"

"Words. Alone, anger, lost, love, death, and quiet."

Frank gazed at the walls, trying to see them. "What does that mean?"

"I don't know."

"There should be something here. A hidden cavity, a secret wall. There must be." He was growing angrier, his circles faster and his hands waving in wider arcs. "All my study. All my work. I thought I must be close, but no, there is nothing here!" His body flickered, disappearing and reappearing like a phone's cell tower signal in the country.

"Do you know who attacked you and put you in a coma?" Tracey asked. He couldn't be wrong about being close to finding the stone. Someone *had* attacked him.

He ignored her. "There is nothing here. My life's work. A failure." He faded.

"Sir? Mr. Transcenni? Frank?"

He disappeared completely. And this time he didn't come back. "Hey!"

Tracey checked every corner. "Sir?" He didn't reappear. "Mr. Transcenni? Frank?" *Now what?* Would she fade too? She held up her ghostly hands. Nope. Still here.

This was Millicent's place. Frank had been so sure something was hidden up here. Tracey had found words, but what if there *was* something else? She glanced around again. The light was poor and the words had appeared out of the shadows. If Tracey had her magic, she could search for settled spells.

She glanced at the bell. On the opposite side of the room was an odd shaped brick. It was chipped and the mortar looked a different shade. "Aha."

"Caw!"

Tracey's head snapped up. A black bird hopped along the window ledge closest to her and stared right at her. He could *see* her. "Caw!" The sound went straight to her chest. *Jeez creepy.* She glanced back at that odd brick and her body flickered. She was sucked forward at such a speed it felt like she was on a rollercoaster. Tracey hated rollercoasters. When she stopped moving and the dizziness faded, she opened her eyes. Uncle Donny was speaking about trying her magic. *I'm back in my body.* Tracey flailed her hands in the air, enjoying the physical movement. She let her inner closet door spring open and gloried in the magic that spread through her body. Other than the noise her uncle was making the room was completely silent. *Oh.* Tracey glanced at the bed. The heart monitor had stopped beeping.

Oh no.

Her back met the wall as the door smacked open and several nurses and a doctor raced in.

"Tracey." Uncle Donny motioned her to his side.

"Is he ... ?"

"Dead? I fear so. We were too late."

Tracey and her uncle snuck out of hospital room during the medical commotion. "Uncle Donny, I have to tell you something."

A nurse approached. Her shoes click clacked sharply upon the linoleum floor. Her red face glowed and her breathing was heavy. "What were you doing in that room?"

Uncle Donny turned to answer and flicked his fingers behind his back, gesturing down the corridor. Tracey tiptoed away, but rather than exit the hospital she crept behind the columns littering the reception area and headed back to the church's bell tower. Feeling only slightly guilty, she used her magic to unlock each door. Halfway up the spiraling staircase, her leg muscles—the ones she never really used—complained bitterly, sending sharp pain into her calves. It forced her to slow down. *It was so much easier doing this as a spirit.* She panted, grabbing the railing and forced her legs to continue climbing.

A thump sounded on the stairs behind her. Darkness flooded the stairwell below her feet and rose like flood water. Tracey created a ball of light with her magic to brighten the stairs and push back the shadows, staring straight into the eyes of a mumble. "Oh rats."

The glow that fills me disguises
the lie I tell to keep the peace.
I only wish to help. I cannot help.
I cannot stop what is to come.

20

The mumble's head tilted, staring at her as if curious. She gripped the Butterfly Stone and called on its magic. Immense power bloomed beneath her fingertips as the stone grew scalding hot. Tracey thrust her hand at the mumble, raising a wall between them. The mumble's clay lips pouted. She fumbled for her cell phone one-handed, found Uncle Donny's name, and dialed.

"Tracey, where are you?"

"Bell tower stairs. Southside. I need a hand." She hung up and glared at the mumble.

"What are your orders?" she demanded without really expecting an answer. Its high-pitched voice took her by surprise.

"Take the protector of the stone."

"Take me where?"

"Back."

"Back to where?"

"Back."

It sounded like a replay button had been pressed. "No," she told it.

The mumble blinked at her and its head flopped in the other direction.

"Tracey!" Uncle Donny appeared behind the mumble. She could just see him between its legs. "Is this one of those mumble things?"

"Yeah. Prince Henry said it's like a clay doll. You give it a task and it goes and does it."

"Are you okay?"

"I'm good," she said. "It's not moving."

"What does it want?"

"Me."

"Right. Well, that's not going to happen." His weaker magic flared behind the mumble.

"Make a wall. Prince Henry said we have to stall it and it will crumble into pieces," she called out. Her uncle's magic solidified into an uneven brick wall behind the mumble. Tracey smiled at the sight of individual bricks glowing yellowish-orange. He was such an old-school mage. The mumble had no way forward and now no way back. Tracey sat down on the stairs.

"Did it chase you up here?" Uncle Donny asked.

"No, I was coming up here anyway," she called back. "Frank, uh, Mr. Transcenni was a ghost. He brought me up here. The bell tower is a secret haunt where Stephanie's best friend Millicent used to hang out."

"When did Frank bring you here?"

"Before he died. When I touched him I activated a spell. He recognized me because I look like Stephanie. He said he's my third cousin twice removed."

"Oh."

"Hey, Uncle Donny?"

"Yeah?"

"You know the council's curse, the one that stops my friends from using their magic? Do you know how we can break it and get their magic back?"

"Tracey, it's a punishment set by the council, of course I don't know how to break it. I wouldn't even if I could. That invites trouble. If the council finds out you have your magic back, we'll *all* be in serious trouble."

"So there's no way to do it officially, what about unofficially?"

"Well … No, I shouldn't. Forget I said anything."

"Uncle Donny?"

He sighed so loudly it echoed up the staircase. "Tracey, don't ask me —"

"Come on, it's not fair. Sarah, Tony, and Dave are all blocked from using their magic. It's dangerous. What if a mumble attacks Sarah next time?"

"The mumble only wants the stones, right?"

Her eyes itched. She rubbed them gently. "Who knows? It's Sarah. Mom will kill us if something happens to her."

"Tracey."

She could hear him wavering. The mumble twitched. "Hey! Don't even think about moving," she warned. The mumble rocked back on its heels. "Please, Uncle Donny?" she begged.

"Well look, thinking about it, there might be a way around it. It's Mage-kind science so it's a bit complicated. But think about this. How does the identification bracelet work?"

"It knows when we use magic and changes color."

"Right. So you are taught at camp to imagine your magic behind a door."

"Yes."

"To use your core magic you imagine opening and closing that door. Well, the bracelets monitor that door."

"Okay, but what's your idea?"

"Well, if the chairman shut the door and locked it to stop you from accessing your magic, you need to unlock the door to get at your magic again. In your case, the Butterfly Stone busted open the door."

"And if the bracelet was spelled as a lock, we need to pick it?"

"Right. I'm thinking your mom and grandma might have a better idea about it, and I'm just spit-balling here, but what if we alter the bracelets? It would allow your friends to use their magic without alerting the council, a little like what your mom and dad did when they raised the threshold of your bracelet when you were a baby. It won't break the spell you see — so the council won't know. Rather than unlock the door, we're cracking open a window. Hopefully. I'm just not sure how we can do it." He was quiet for a moment. "You said Frank's spirit brought you here? What did you find?"

"Some hidden words but no magic stone."

"Bugger."

Tracey snorted.

"Hidden words?"

"Six words. I think they're connected to the sect. Alone, lost, quiet, anger, death, and love."

"I take it each word belongs to one Mage-kind? Which belongs to which?"

"I don't know. *Lost* is probably Jilly's ancestor Jing. That leaves *alone, quiet, anger, death,* and *love.*"

"Stephanie?"

"I'm not sure. I've been thinking about it and Millicent was an orphan. I think *alone* would match her, don't you think?"

"Sounds right."

The mumble groaned and turned to sandy dirt, forming a large pile in the middle of the stairs. Tracey sighed and stood up, dropping her wall. Uncle Donny dropped his brick barrier and raced up the steps to hug her. "You okay?"

Tracey nodded and pointed up the stairs. "Wanna see the bell tower?"

He grinned at her. "Naturally."

Uncle Donny's attention fixed on the giant bell.

"Pretty cool, huh?" Tracey said.

He nodded. "The secret hiding place?"

Tracey brushed her fingers over the odd shaped brick. "Here." She tugged at the corners, scratching her skin on the sharp edges. "Ouch." She smacked the offending brick for hurting her.

A wooden floorboard popped up. *Aha!* She pulled it loose, her breath catching as she peeked inside. The cavity was empty. While Uncle Donny examined the empty hole, Tracey let loose her magic. He cocked his eyebrow. "Tracey?"

"I couldn't use magic in my ghost form. I just wanted to see if I can feel anything."

"Go ahead."

She threw up her sensory blanket and let it settle over the six-sided doughnut shaped room. When that achieved nothing, she altered the spell to search for settled spells and tossed it up again. The brass bell vibrated, giving off a low deep sound that rumbled in her belly.

"Caw!"

The black bird was back. It tilted its head as if to get a better look at her and squawked loudly.

"That's not good," Uncle Donny said.

"What's not good?"

"Seeing a crow. It's a bad omen."

Tracey swallowed and shooed it away. It didn't move. She turned back to the bell and ignored it, hoping it would fly away. "Did you hear it ring?"

"Yup."

"It's a settled spell," she said. "A really old one."

"Right. I've got this." Uncle Donny bounced with excitement and pulled a soft bag from his pocket. He removed a vial of pink powder.

"What's that?" Tracey asked.

"A little something I've been working on."

Oh no. Tracey hid her frown beneath the hand she rubbed over her face. He caught her expression and scowled at her. "Come on, Tracey. This is my job."

"Sorry. What's your spell supposed to do?"

"Give us an imprint. An image of who set it." He shook a small amount of the hot pink powder into the palm of his hand and blew it out over the bell. As it sprayed across the room, he sent a burst of magic into the powder.

Tracey could hear the muttered words of his spell and recognized the mix of her blanket spell to Search for settled spells with a Find spell like her button spell as well as hints of Grandma's memory spell that she used on Nana that time she went with Tracey to get a tarot reading. Tracey repeated the words in her mind. If she could remember it, she imagined it was a spell that would be handy for an investigator to have.

Uncle Donny whispered. "Show us your final moments." The powder settled over the figure of a woman.

Tracey gasped. "That's Millicent." The figure stood staring out of the window near the word *alone* then turned to face the bell. She raised her finger and drew something in the air. The bell rang once, a low, loud clang that brought Tracey's hands to her ears. Uncle Donny did the same. The pink dust woman crouched at the hiding place and removed a dark stone.

Oh. Tracey tiptoed closer and stretched up over the crouched figure to peek at what she held. "Can you see it?"

Uncle Donny ran around to stand in front of Millicent. She stood and walked right through him. Uncle Donny was left with pink powder all over his clothes. He shuddered, his face turning pale and sweaty. Millicent had disappeared.

"Uncle Donny?"

"Remind me never to do that again."

"Could you see it? The stone she held? Was there an animal on it?"

"I couldn't see, but it was shaped like a heart."

"A heart?" Tracey turned until she stood in front of the word *love*. "Who did she love?"

"Perhaps, that's what we need to find out."

Tracey spun back to the bell. "Look!" Illuminated with pink powder and fading by the second was a giant bird. "Oh."

"Oh." Uncle Donny echoed. "I think that's your answer."

The crow on the window frame flew away with a slapping sound of its wings. "The Crow's Heart. That's Millicent's stone. It's called the Crow's Heart," Tracey whispered.

"Try your tracking spell."

Tracey examined the floor. "I need a circle." Uncle Donny held up a piece of chalk. "And Tony's phone. He has the words."

Uncle Donny deflated. "You don't know them?"

" ... Tony did that bit of the assignment and um. I don't always remember the words in the right order."

"Tracey."

"I know, I know." She waved her hand. "I should do my own camp homework. Come on, we have to find Tony."

"They'll be at the movie studio. Let's go. We might be able to wrap this case up today."

"But who attacked Frank? And who keeps sending the mumble? If we don't stop them someone else could get hurt."

"Good questions. We might not be able to fully close the case today, but we'll have the stone. Your mission will be over at any rate. We can leave Agent Malden and Prince Henry to catch the mumble mastermind."

"What, we don't get a holiday while we're here?"

"Priorities, Tracey. Come on, let's get out of here."

She followed her uncle from the bell tower. The Crow's Heart. She had the stone's name now. All she had to do was find it and avoid any more mumble attacks and it would be — as Uncle Donny said — mission over.

I speak and I scream yet no one can hear my warning cry. How can I warn them, how can I continue to reach out when all I feel is pain? I cannot save them, for who would believe what I have seen.

21

ngela greeted them at the security gate and escorted Tracey and her uncle through the seething movie studio. Her pink cheeks indicated her walk over to collect them had been more of a run. Angela's long hair swung across her face as she shook her head at Tracey's question. "Unfortunately, you can't be in the scene today. I'm sorry, but you've arrived too late. They've already filmed several angles."

The excitement bubbling in Tracey's chest faded. "Oh, that's okay. We're still allowed to watch though, aren't we?"

"Yes, but you must be very quiet from this point on. I'll take you to the viewing area where you can watch a monitor. You'll see what the camera sees—what the director sees. Don't say a word."

The walk from security took them past several sound stages. Tracey and her uncle followed Angela into one with a large letter D on it. "This is where the internal sets for this particular movie were built."

"Like the inside of cafes and houses? Like on TV?" Tracey asked.

"Exactly. This scene is a partial street, part internal pub. 1852. Oxford Street. Though of course it all looked very different back then. Quite a dark place. You may not recognize it."

"We haven't seen all that much of London yet," Tracey said.

"A green screen is being used to pop the Marble Arch into shot in the far background. We have a hand truck rather than the fixed cameras you would see used by sitcoms. It's a fluid, moving set so you will see one camera on a rail and another called a wheeled dolly, though it's really just a large trolley. It means the camera operator can sit down. We also have a steadicam—a camera operator who follows the actors around for their close-up shots." They reached the end of a short corridor. Angela put her finger to her lips. Tracey leaned forward, heart racing, and caught sight of Tony and Laura dressed in their torn and dirty costumes. Dirt stained their cheeks and their hair was a mess. Tracey had never seen Laura looking so imperfect and a giant grin spread across her face. Tony had a piece of green cloth tied around his wrist, covering his Mage-kind identification bracelet. The two were crouched on the edge of what looked like a cobblestone street. Kylie, also dressed as a Street Rat including the green cloth, ran up and crouched beside them.

Tracey's gaze traveled the length of the fake historical English street, seeing horses—real horses—and other actors and actresses dressed as regular "common" townspeople. Dotted here and there were fancy, wealthy looking women in long-sleeved dresses and men in suits and tall hats. Lesser dressed street characters moved back and forth in the shadowy corners. The background was a giant green screen. She'd seen pictures of modern-day Oxford Street but here every building was only built to the first floor, as though someone had taken a pair of massive scissors and sliced the tops off.

A big, entirely black camera on wheels traveled the length of the street. As it moved, Tracey could see who it was focused on. Prince Henry—dressed as a soldier in a red coat—strode across the road. He was talking to a beautiful woman in a purple dress. Tracey couldn't hear what he was saying. In the distance, past Prince Henry, Tracey spied Jonny standing with several unknown boys and girls. Her gaze flipped back to the woman Prince Henry was talking to. Long black hair, plum colored dress, and gleaming brown skin made her a standout—even from across the stage. Tracey didn't immediately recognize the actress but something about her pinged her celebrity radar. *I'll kick myself when I know who she is.*

Sarah popped up close to Prince Henry and reached out as if to touch him. Dave yanked her back and they both ducked. Prince Henry swung around as if he'd sensed them. He shook his head at the beautiful woman and pushed open the doors of a creepy, stained, and shadowed building. The camera stopped moving and everything froze until a loud female voice called. "Cut!"

Each person then sprang back to where they had started from as if on a string.

"Okay, come on." Angela walked straight toward a large white canopy. Beneath it, shielded from the bright lights was a TV and several chairs. They drew closer and Tracey's eyes bugged out of her head as she recognized the black woman in the director's chair. Justine Prentice-Croft. Tracey's mouth dropped open. She was going to be sitting with the director of Prince Henry's most successful franchise.

Justine Prentice-Croft turned her head, her long dreads looped up in a messy pile on top of her head, and squinted at Tracey through crimson-rimmed glasses. "Yes?"

"The missing girl," Angela said.

Tracey's face flamed and she stared at the ground wishing it would open up beneath her. Justine Prentice-Croft wore the coolest looking silver ankle boots and tight gray leggings. The unimpressed director sighed loudly and stood up. "Sorry, hon. I can't put you in now, you understand? You should have been here with the others."

"It's okay," Tracey whispered. "I don't mind watching. I'll be real quiet, I promise."

Justine Prentice-Croft eyeballed Tracey's bracelet and smiled broadly, "Come on then, let me show you my world." The knot in Tracey's chest loosened. Uncle Donny strode forward and held out his hand for an introduction.

"I'm Donald Masters—one of the guardians—and this is my niece, Tracey. I'm afraid she was rather unwell earlier."

"Nice to meet you." Justine Prentice-Croft's smile lit up her whole face. Her lips were painted violet. "Take a seat, Tracey." She pulled a chair closer to the screen beside her and Tracey nearly exploded with joy as she plonked herself down next to her idol. *Justine Prentice-Croft is so nice!* Tracey listened intently as the director named the equipment in front of her and explained what everything did.

She couldn't contain her excitement. "You are the best director ever. I've seen *Walk* and *Jump Up* and *Run* and every episode of *Trap Michaels, Pirate Lord.* Oh, and *Share the Spotlight* was awesome."

Justine Prentice-Croft grinned. "Well, thank you."

"Is it true they want you for the latest super—"

"Shhhhh. I can't tell you about that." Justine Prentice-Croft winked. Tracey jumped up and cheered. Everyone spun around to stare at her. She sank back into her chair embarrassed.

"I won't tell anyone," she whispered.

Justine Prentice-Croft laughed loudly.

"They're ready, ma'am." A man called from the set. Tracey stood up and waved to her sister and Dave. Sarah grinned, shocking Tracey with several missing teeth. Hopefully, they were just colored in black, otherwise Mom would lose her mind.

"Silence please," called a woman's voice and the set instantly hushed. Tracey sat down and watched the TV monitor. There was a white box around the camera viewing edge and lots of numbers scrolled past counting up as time passed. A clap board appeared on the screen with the scene number on it. The *clack!* echoed in the silence.

Justine Prentice-Croft leaned forward and called, "Action."

Tracey watched, mesmerized, as the scene played out again right in front of her. The camera view stayed tight on the woman talking to Prince Henry. *OMG, OMG, it's Alicia Barrow! The woman in the plum dress is Alicia Barrow.* Tracey's gaze kept flicking above the television to the scene playing live right in front of her, but she couldn't see much. The cameras were in the way. Peering back at the screen Tracey spied her sister and a fire sparked low in her belly. *I'm actually jealous.* She was also super proud and excited for her sister. Being in a Prince Henry movie was a dream come true.

A low rumble rose up from the ground beneath Tracey's feet. The sound boom guy grimaced and lifted his head to stare at the camera operator. They both turned to glance at Justine Prentice-Croft. The vibration grew more violent as the table shuddered beneath Tracey's hands. "Cut!" Justine Prentice-Croft shouted. She turned to Angela. "What the hell is that? Earthquake?"

The word "*Cut!*" echoed across the set. Everyone froze as the rumbling grew louder. The camera dolly and the props on set rattled in time with it.

Uncle Donny sprang forward. "Ah, Tracey and I should go, uh, look for what is, uh, making that—"

Tracey ran to his side. "Where's Jilly?"

"Who? What is going on?" Justine Prentice-Croft called after them.

"Tracey?" Sarah and the other Street Rats were gathered in a group in the middle of the set, their hands splayed out from their bodies to help them maintain balance.

Kylie and Damian stared toward two half-built buildings at the end of the set. "Jilly was with me in the alley. She was supposed to run out when I did," Kylie called.

Tracey and her uncle raced across the set—the temporary and very fake stone paved road beneath their feet trembled. "The others don't have their magic," Tracey reminded her uncle.

"Rigggght, we'll manage," he told her. Jilly appeared at Tracey's elbow.

"Well, except for me and Jilly," Tracey added. "Glad you're here. Is your magic—"

Jilly tore the green cloth from around her wrist. Her bracelet shone brightly red as she readied her magic. "Have it back? Yes."

"Where were you?" Tracey asked. The rumbling sound grew louder. Jilly and Uncle Donny were right beside her as she ran toward the sound.

"Acting is a waste of time. I snuck off to call my mother." Jilly flashed her cell phone.

"You can't just run off."

"Where were you?" Jilly countered.

"Tracey, now is not the time for this," Uncle Donny hollered. They ran off the set, down the short corridor and burst out of Building D into bright sunshine. Half a dozen scared individuals ran straight for them, screaming "*Run!*" Behind them was the biggest mumble Tracey had ever seen. It was almost as tall as Building D itself.

"Oh, heck," Uncle Donny muttered as they skidded to a halt.

"Something is different," Jilly said. Tracey saw it too. The mumble had red eyes.

"What do you think it means?" Tracey asked.

Jilly fell into her warrior stance, her spear appeared in her right hand.

The energy weapon glowed and sparked with orange magic. "Whatever it is, it can't be good."

Tracey peered over her shoulder. "I wish the others were here."

"They have no magic. It is too dangerous for them to assist us," Jilly said.

The mumble stepped forward and lowered its head like a bull about to charge. Tracey raised her shield bubble over herself and Jilly. Running footsteps snapped Tracey's head around. Prince Henry raced out of Building D, heading their way. They needed his help but the studio security guards were right behind him. The guards wouldn't know he was Mage-kind. He couldn't drop his cover.

The mumble thundered forward and Tracey couldn't spare Prince Henry any more attention. She snapped out her hands and spread her bubble into a wide wall to stop the mumble's forward movement. It hit Tracey's wall and bounced back, stumbling to regain its footing. Tracey cheered, but victory was short lived when the mumble braced its feet, lowered its head and pushed against her wall.

"Whoa!" Tracey slid backward across the concrete.

Jilly dropped her spear. It dissolved before it hit the ground. She threw up her magic to reinforce Tracey's wall. Uncle Donny joined in from Tracey's other side. The mumble grunted and pushed harder. For a moment, Tracey thought they had stopped it, until the mumble lowered its hands to the ground, grunted and forced itself forward. All three Mage-kind slid back several feet.

"Argh!" Tracey groaned, the strain on her magic growing by the moment. "It's too strong!" Uncle Donny's additional magic wavered. "Don't let go!" she shouted at him.

"I can't hold it!" His voice wobbled from the extra power he forced into his arms. They needed Prince Henry's magic—or help from Tracey's friends. They were out of options.

"We have to get everyone out of here!" Tracey shouted.

"No, we can hold it."

Pressure built, buzzing the air and raising the hairs on Tracey's arms. Jilly had called on help from the Tiger's Eye. It was still not enough magic.

The mumble kept pushing. Uncle Donny's arms trembled and their wall wobbled.

Golden magic sprang up, strengthening their wall and created a curved arch around the mumble. Tracey's head twisted to see Prince Henry stop beside her. "What are you doing? No one knows you're Mage-kind. They'll see!"

"The guards are evacuating the studio. No one's watching," he said.

"But you—"

"This is a little more serious, Tracey."

"They don't know—"

"Then we'd better work fast." He flashed her a brief smile.

"This one is way stronger than the others. I think it's … thinking."

The mumble pushed and all four Mage-kind slid backward. Prince Henry's eyes sprang wide and he dropped one foot behind the other to brace his body. The magic flowing from him grew suddenly stronger.

"We have to attack it," Jilly said.

Prince Henry grunted. "I believe Jilly is correct."

The mumble's eyes flared brightly, and it grew larger still. Their wall had a perceptible vibration running through it now and back up their arms. Tracey gritted her teeth. "Uncle Donny?" Sweat dripped down his face, plastering his hair to his skin. "You have to go get help."

"I'm not leaving you."

"You must," Prince Henry insisted. Tracey had never heard him sound so strained. "We cannot hold it. Summon Agent Malden."

"I … "

"Please, Uncle Donny?" Tracey begged.

"Yeah. Okay. Get ready."

The buzz and warmth of his golden strands of magic withdrew in stages, allowing her and Prince Henry to strengthen their magic to compensate. For a moment it worked. Tracey braced her feet and imagined digging them into the concrete. She pictured the magic pouring from her core in a gust of golden light, thickening and burning brighter. Uncle Donny shifted away and then let go completely. The mumble's eyes flashed like a traffic stop sign, and the three remaining Mage-kind slipped back faster than before. Uncle Donny ran to catch up—not wanting to be caught too close to the mumble. His power snapped on, rejoining them. "Okay, so that was a bad plan."

"Girls? Ideas?" Uncle Donny begged.

"We attack," Jilly said.

They had no other option. Tracey nodded. "Uncle Donny and I will create obstacles in its path. Jilly. You and Prince Henry attack it." They really needed more Mage-kind for this. "Prince Henry, are there any others in the cast or crew who are like us?"

"Yes, but they will have been evacuated by now. Besides, they're not trained to fight," he said.

Darn. There went that idea.

"I'll go left. Jilly, you go right," Prince Henry ordered.

Tracey caught her uncle's attention. "When I say go, drop the wall and run toward the entrance to building D. Stay low."

"I'll be right on your coat tails, kiddo."

"What?" She shook her head. "Never mind." Tracey had to keep them both covered. As far as she knew the mumble had no magic of its own. At least she didn't have to worry about oncoming fire. It was just brute strength and unrelenting stubbornness she had to defeat.

"Ready?" Upon hearing three confirmations, Tracey counted down. "Three, two, one, go!"

The magic wall dropped, and the mumble thundered forward—its momentum unchecked—and overbalanced, tripping over its own feet. It hit the ground hard landing on its hands and knees. As it climbed back to its feet, Tracey, Uncle Donny, Prince Henry, and Jilly ran in opposite directions. Jilly let loose her energy spear. It tore right through the mumble's chest. Clay turned to liquid and flowed back in to fill up the hole the spear left behind.

Tracey raised a barrier wall stopping the mumble briefly before it forced its way through with both arms outstretched. Uncle Donny put a wall up barely an inch in behind Tracey's. The mumble pushed through with only a flinch to show it noticed.

Prince Henry shot a spiked ball of sparkling magic at the mumble, confusing it. It blinked, swiping at its face. Tracey threw out a knee-high wall. The mumble smacked into it and toppled over it a second before Prince Henry's next spiky ball hit. The ball sailed over the mumble's head and hit the ground, disintegrating on impact. "Sorry," Tracey shouted in response to Prince Henry's swear.

Uncle Donny captured the mumble's left hand in a gooey magic net of his own design, and it actually worked. The mumble tried to get up, but Uncle Donny pulled its hand out from underneath it. Jilly fired a spear at the mumble's stomach but it got its other hand in the way and the spear impaled its wrist. The mumble raised its hand, looking at it as if surprised. It didn't appear to be in any pain. Prince Henry launched another spiked ball. This time it connected and blew a hole in the mumble's chest. Tracey used her magic fist to grab hold of the mumble's left ankle.

Uncle Donny pulled the mumble further off balance by tugging hard on its trapped hand. Prince Henry's spiked balls continued to hit the mumble's chest, blowing off clay in large chunks. Jilly sent another spear through the mumble's head. It re-formed around the spear, leaving it sticking out of its forehead. They were winning — slowly, but it felt as though the battle had turned.

Tracey created a ball of glowing magic and powered it with her storehouse of internal electricity. "Everybody get down!" she shouted. She threw her ball. It exploded as it hit and blew the mumble in half.

"Yeah!" she shouted, standing up and pumping her hands over her head.

Uncle Donny brushed bits of clay off his shirt. He stared at Tracey, his eyebrows climbing into his hair. "How did you do that?"

"Look!" Jilly screeched.

Tracey swore softly, her stomach churning in horror as the two clay halves grew tentacles and dragged themselves back together.

"Again," Prince Henry shouted.

The ground beneath them rumbled and shook. Tracey's head snapped around and she let out a long loud groan. Coming from the opposite direction was a second red-eyed mumble.

"New plan," Prince Henry shouted. "Run!"

I am dismissed as fanciful,
yet I am terrified of the truth.
For I see how it ends.
And I am alone.

22

"Where did Prince Henry and your uncle go?" Jilly whispered, glancing cautiously around the wall of the water tank they had quickly hidden behind.

In the distance, Tracey could make out the mumbles' mad path of distraction. Metallic screeches and echoing cracks came from the concrete, brick, and steel as it tore apart beneath the mumbles' hands. They seemed intent on destroying everything in their path.

"I don't know." Tracey slumped to the ground. Sweat coated her face and her hands trembled. All this magic use was exhausting.

"What do we do now?"

"No idea. We have to find Sarah, Jonny, and the others."

"The mumbles are after us, aren't they? Because of the stones?"

"Someone wants the stones' power, yeah."

"We must discover who has sent the mumbles after us," Jilly said. There was a sharp gleam in her eyes. "We have been on the defensive for too long. We must attack the source. Go after the mastermind who has created them."

"Are you crazy?"

"The mumbles will keep coming, Tracey. These ones are stronger. We cannot destroy them alone. We need a new plan." Jilly stood up, her spear forming in her hand.

Tracey yanked Jilly back down. "If the two of us attack that mumble, we'll get squashed." There were more screams. Dust billowed into the air above the water tank and blew over them.

"If we allow the mumbles to take one of us, then we will discover who is behind this madness and finally stop them."

"You *are* crazy!" Tracey said, coughing dust out of her throat.

"Then what do you propose we do?"

Tracey threw up her hands. "I don't know, I just thought … look Jilly. I don't know what I'm doing. Everyone keeps looking at me, expecting me to have all the answers, but I'm just making it up as I go along."

"Does it feel right?"

"What?"

"When you make the choice to do something. Does it feel right? Do you feel better once you have decided?"

Tracey stared as her mind exploded. "Yeah. Yes, I do."

"Then it is the right choice. Tracey, we are all scared. We do not want to make a mistake, so we can be afraid to try."

"You're not afraid of anything."

Jilly snorted. "Are you kidding? Of course I am. You remembered me after we broke the curse on the Tiger's Eye, but every day I am afraid I will leave the room and no one will know who I am upon my return. Every morning I wake up and for a split second, it's all gone. I keep checking your face when we talk, searching for recognition that you know who I am."

So that was why Jilly kept staring at her? Not because she was angry or doubted Tracey's magic or wanted to steal Laura away. She was afraid? "I didn't know."

"Fear stops us from taking risks. My mother always says that. And do you know what? If you do not try, then you have already failed."

"But what if I do try, and make a mistake?"

"It is what you do next that means something. Own the mistake and try again, or change it by doing something differently." Jilly's eyes blazed with belief, passion, and an intense power. *She's amazing.*

"What if someone gets hurt because of something I did?"

"Someone might. But what if you do nothing and they get hurt anyway?"

Tracey remembered Millicent's journal. Her gift. Knowing when someone would die. She'd thought it a terrible curse. And so had Tracey. Wouldn't that knowledge stop you from making friends, from getting close to anyone because you knew how it would end? It was a bit like Jilly's fear, wasn't it? Afraid to make friends in case they forget you? Living that way, full of fear and regret, sounded terrible.

Going the other way though, being like Stephanie and taking too many risks, that was dangerous too. Perhaps being fully one way or the other was the problem. It was okay to be a little bit of both.

She peered around the tank and slipped her hands into her pockets. In the left one she found something hard and round. Uncle Donny's shirt button. Jilly was nuts about letting the mumbles take them, but she wasn't wrong about the attacks continuing while the mastermind was still out there.

"You've decided," Jilly said.

"We came here to find the stones. That's the job. Someone is after the ones we hold. We have to find out who and why. I don't like the idea, but before we let a mumble take one of us, we have to put a tracker on it. Whoever it takes, the other follows and tells Agent Malden so he can rescue us and capture the mastermind." Tracey had the exact spell to use. The one she'd used to track down the gunmen who broke into Uncle Donny's office. The spell that led her to the Shadowman's secret hideout at the top of Mount Hawthy. She held up the button. "I have a tracking spell." Tracey wrapped her fingers around the button and spelled it into an Object of Power. It warmed in her hands. "Now, we just have to get it inside the mumble."

"What if the mumble disintegrates?" Jilly asked.

"If it has one of us, it won't crumble because it will be achieving its mission. It will take us back to its creator. So we create a hole. The clay will fill it in quickly, but if we can get a tracker inside it, it might stay there … "

Jilly stood up again. This time Tracey let her. "Which way did they go? I cannot see them."

Tracey climbed to her feet. "Hang on. Listen." Smashing sounds echoed off the buildings around them. Tracey's own magic was weak, her body exhausted. She drew magic from inside the Butterfly Stone and straightened at the burst of energy and heat that rushed through her. She exploded a sensory blanket up into the air searching for the two giant monsters. "Oh no."

"What?"

"They're inside the sound stage."

Tracey's heart pounded as she and Jilly raced back into Building D. The side wall had two mumble sized holes in it. Her chest tightened. Hopefully, her friends and Sarah had been evacuated and were waiting for them somewhere safe. She checked her phone. No messages. Why would the mumbles go into Building D? Tracey and Jilly were out here. "Oh crud, they're going after Kylie again."

The London street set had been completely demolished under giant clay feet. The two mumbles seemed almost gleeful as they stomped and waved their arms around, slamming into the fake walls and shopfront facades. The movie set was quickly turning into matchsticks beneath their play. Several security guards dressed in black and gray with shining red bracelets were doing their best to stop the mumbles. But the Mage-kind guards weren't going to achieve anything against these monsters. "Hey! Hey!" Tracey jumped up and down, and waved her arms around.

"What are you doing?" Jilly demanded.

"Getting their attention. Wasn't that the plan?"

"And what do we do when we've got their attention?"

"Um."

Jilly formed her magical spear, the tip glowing orangey-red. "I stab it. You tag it."

The first mumble thundered straight for them. Jilly didn't throw her spear. She thrust with it instead. Tracey stayed in Jilly's shadow, holding her shield bubble like a flat round shield above her head, ready to snap it down to cover them if the mumble lashed out.

One of the Mage-kind security guards ran toward them. "You kids, get away from here! What are you doing?" Tracey paid him no mind. Jilly jerked her spear tip forward and dug a hole in the mumble's side. As clay flowed back in, Tracey threw her powered button, using magic to redirect her terrible aim. The button flew into the hole and the clay closed over it, sealing it inside and leaving a long crease right through its chest.

"Yay!" Tracey shouted. She squeaked and snapped her shield up as the mumble's fist slammed into her. She shrieked as the blow threw her away from Jilly. Prince Henry ran into the arena of set rubble and wooden splinters and thrust out his hand. A wall snapped up between Jilly and the mumble. The monster slammed into it and stumbled back, grunting unhappily. It punched both hands into the barrier. "Move!" Prince Henry shouted. Tracey's brain was fuzzy and her body ached from her hard landing. She rolled and pushed up onto her feet. Prince Henry was fighting the mumble. She had to let him know they needed it to grab one of them.

Jilly bolted toward Tracey.

"Over here!" Jonny's head appeared out of the broken shell of the bar. "Hey!"

Tracey and Jilly ran toward him. "Why are you still here?" Jilly demanded. She hugged him quickly, and he pulled her inside. Tracey followed. The thin wooden doors swung shut behind her.

"We couldn't get out," Tony said. He popped up from behind a makeshift wall of tables, chairs and, by the look of it, parts of the set.

"It's not safe in here," Tracey said. "Those things are smashing everything." She spied Sarah and Kylie huddled near the wall with Laura. "Where's Dave and Damian?"

"In the back room searching for a way out," Jonny said.

Tony stood in front of Tracey. "We need our magic back."

"Yeah." Tracey couldn't believe what she was about to suggest. She pointed at Jilly. "We have a tracker on one of the mumbles — the one with the chest crease — but they won't go back to wherever they came from without grabbing one of us. They'll stay and keep fighting. They'll destroy everything."

Jilly nodded. "I will let it catch me."

"I was — no, not you. I was going to say I'll go," Tracey argued.

"Why?" Tony and Sarah asked in unison.

"I mean — its obvious isn't it? This all started with me," Tracey said.

"It should be me," Jilly countered. "You put the tracking spell on the mumble. You are the one who can find it."

Ugh, that's true.

Kylie stood up. "It should be me."

"No!" Damian appeared in the doorway from the back room and

stared, horrified, at his sister. Dave awkwardly slid past him. A thundering cascade of bricks sounded somewhere right outside, and one of the mumbles roared.

Kylie nodded. "My stone is locked. The bad guy can't access it like they can with yours. It makes sense. You can track the mumble and rescue me."

"No Kylie." Damian grabbed his sister's arm and glared at Tracey. "Don't you dare let her do this."

Kylie stopped Tracey before she could utter a single word. "You need Jilly. She can fight. No one else has access to their magic. Tracey, you can find me. It makes sense. Stop it, Damian." She cut off his urgent noises. "It makes sense. I'm the only one who can go."

"What about Mom?" Damian pleaded.

Kylie shrugged. "Don't tell her."

"I've changed my mind." Tracey said, shaking her head. "This is not a good idea at all. We'll think of something else. I'm not letting you—"

"Letting me? I don't get a choice about anything. Not the stone. Not Timothy. Not even coming here. Mom, Damian, yes even you, Tracey. You decide everything. I can't even *use* my magic. I want to do this. It's *my* choice. Please. Please, let me do something. I need to do something."

They all fell silent. Damian stared Tracey down, daring her to agree with his sister and she felt the weight of his expectations fall on her shoulders like a ten-kilogram camping backpack. "You can't let her go."

Tracey turned away. "Tony? What do you think?"

"Don't I get a say?" Laura demanded. Her face was dirty from stage makeup and her hair was an artful bird's nest of threads. It looked like a style choice rather than a mess. "We don't have time to argue. We should vote on it."

"No," Damian argued.

"Well, I don't care what you want," Kylie shouted at him. "Vote."

"Yeah, alright." Dave held up his hand. "I say go." Jilly and Jonny raised their hands too. Sarah kept her hand down and glared at Tracey. Kylie put up her hand. Damian kept his down, as did Tony. It left Laura and Tracey. Laura shook her head and crossed her arms.

Oh, fruit tingles. That was four on each side. "Ah."

The floor trembled. Dust peppered them from the insubstantial wooden roof. Before Tracey could speak, Kylie darted past her and out through the door.

"Kylie, no!" Damian cried.

Tracey ran after her but it was too late. Kylie had run straight into the mumble standing outside the door. Its chest had a long crease line through the center. Kylie screamed as the mumble snatched her up and ran off. To Tracey's horror, she let it leave.

The remaining mumble thundered toward Tracey and froze mid step — halted by a large ball of magic that appeared at its feet forming a huge bubble like a ball of chewing gum. The mumble lifted its foot, or tried to. The gum kept it locked in place, stretching upward with the movement before dragging the foot back down to the ground. Prince Henry stood behind the mumble, his hands outstretched, completely focusing on the gum bubble.

Jilly halted beside Tracey and formed her spear. Tracey raised her shield. They waited for the mumble to break free.

The clay monster struggled hard, grunting with the force of its jerking foot. The ground trembled and the gumball grew, stretching out to capture the other foot. The mumble lowered its head and huffed out a large breath that blew Tracey's hair away from her face and stank of mud. It dropped its hands to the ground and tried to pry its feet out of the gumball. The gum stretched capturing first one hand and then the other.

After struggling another moment, the mumble gave up and flopped unhappily to the ground. Its red eyes flared and turned black. The mumble's body crumbled into dust and blew away.

Uncle Donny stood beside Prince Henry. Of course, the gumball was one of his mad spells. Fortunately, Prince Henry's magic had been strong enough to make it work. "Are you all okay?" Prince Henry called. He dropped his hands and the gumball sizzled and melted away.

"Yes," Tracey shouted. She gazed at Damian. He glared back as if Kylie's sacrifice had been all her fault.

"You let her go," he said. Tracey's stomach cramped with guilt. She *had* let Kylie go. The horrid sensation swarmed over her, bringing cold clamminess in its wake. She swallowed hard. Uncle Donny raced over and did a quick head count. Tracey waited for him to notice.

"Tracey, where's Kylie?"

"The mumble took her." Tracey wasn't looking at her uncle, or at any of her friends. She was watching the studio crew members climbing from the rubble. Some held their cell phones out, filming what had happened. Shocked voices began to chatter. It was then that Tracey realized the cameras were not pointed at her or at any of her friends. They were aimed at Prince Henry.

"Oh no," she muttered.

Prince Henry's shoulders slumped. The actor prince — and the man no one knew was Mage-kind — had just been outed to the entire world.

Stephanie granted me my freedom and
told me what I was. I did not tell her
everything foo foor she would roolize
I was truly damood and loave me too.

23

Prince Henry was gone. "Dealing with the fallout," he called it. Hopefully, things wouldn't go too badly for him, but his pale face said he was in damage control. Uncle Donny told her he would wait for Agent Malden to arrive to explain what had happened so that he could deal with the authorities. He shoved some money into Tracey's hands and herded the teens into three black boxy taxis ordering them to return the manor house.

Damian refused to get into the car with Tracey, choosing instead to join Dave and Jilly in the car behind them. Laura and Tony sat in the pulldown seat behind the driver facing Tracey and Sarah. The driver gave them an odd look as they all piled in. They were still in their costumes and looked like filthy street kids. Uncle Donny's flash of cash kept the driver's mouth closed, though his eyebrows reacted to the address Uncle Donny gave. "You kids are actors?" he asked.

"Yeah, we're famous — you really don't recognize us?" Laura's snotty voice silenced him. "Please focus on the road."

Tracey's mind was stuck on Damian's furious expression and the anger in his voice. She had let his sister get kidnapped — again — and after she'd promised to help her. Kylie's scared face popped into Tracey's mind and wouldn't leave. Whoever had snatched Kylie had better not hurt her. Tracey imagined what she would do to the mastermind behind all of this when they caught him. It had to be that creep, Chairman Stairs, or maybe it was Mr. Henderson. Both wanted the stones. Tracey would only be able to prove it if she caught one of them with Kylie. She imagined creating a magic fire or using her store of electricity to fry the mystery man into ash right in front of her. Anger swelled inside her chest and the Butterfly Strone heated into a burning coal. She pressed her hand to it. *Not yet. We have to find him first.*

Damian must hate her. And when Mrs. Carter found out … oh fruit tingles. She would go berserk! Stressing about how everyone must think of her sent the fire in Tracey's chest through her entire body.

The four teens watched the scenery pass by through the cab's windows in silence.

Tracey nudged her sister. "Are you hurt?"

"What? No."

"You're quiet."

"You let her go." Sarah's whisper contained a sliver of hurt and a lot of anger. Just like Damian.

"I didn't. I—"

"We have to go after her."

"We will." Tracey raised her voice so Tony and Laura could hear. "You remember …" She caught the driver's glance in the rear-view mirror and realized he was listening in to their conversation. She spoke in code and hoped her friends would understand. "In the movie, remember the spell? From the flashback scene when they spelled the monster so they could chase it up the mountain. The spell with the sugar and the map?"

"Oh." Tony caught her look at the driver. "That map. Yeah, I remember that scene."

"You kids are in a Mage-kind movie? How did you get into that?" the driver asked.

"School competition," she told him.

Laura strained against her seatbelt, leaning forward to whisper. "So the spell?"

"Yeah, I'm all over it. Um, I mean they were. In the scene."

"What about the other Mage-kind characters. How do, uh, how did they get their magic unblocked?" Tony asked. "I must have missed that bit."

Tracey shrugged.

"We have to hurry," Sarah said.

"We are. I promise." Tracey held her sister's gaze. "I promise." She glanced through the window to find they were driving back over the bridge through London. "Hey there's Big Ben," she pointed. The big clock towered over the street. As they drove away from it, Tracey glanced back at the iconic landmark through the rear window.

"And the London Eye." Laura pointed to the large Ferris wheel on the other side of the river.

Tony tapped on his phone. Tracey wondered if he was still searching for a spell to restore their magic, or looking for the stones? Tracey's head jerked. She hadn't told her friends what she had found out about the fourth stone at the hospital. Heck, now that she knew what it was called, she could perform her stone tracking spell and they could find the stone! Glancing at Sarah she realized, no. Kylie was their number one priority.

"She must be so scared," Sarah mumbled.

"We'll find her," Tracey promised. Only she wasn't sure how. Sure, she had the button tracker spell, but they didn't even have a car. Once Tracey cast the spell to track the mumble how would they go after it? In another taxi? Would Mr. Henderson lend them his limo if he was the one behind it? None of Tracey's friends had access to their magic, so Tracey would have to rescue Kylie with just Jilly for backup. And what if Chairman Stairs or Mr. Henderson managed to unlock the magic that kept Kylie safe from Timothy's possession?

Sarah was right, Tracey should never have let Kylie go. It just happened so fast. One minute they were all arguing and the next thing she knew Kylie had gone. If the bad guy had a way to remove the stone, all their troubles would suddenly become a hundred times worse.

"Whoa, what?" Laura yelped and turned up the volume on her phone. She held it out so they could all see the video playing.

"*— Henry is Mage-kind. In leaked footage released on social media this afternoon, the actor prince has revealed himself to be Mage-kind on the set of his latest movie —*"

"Well, what do you know," the driver said. He shook his head. "Royalty. How was he allowed to hide something like that?"

Tracey bit her lip. *This is not good!*

"Is that the same movie you kids are in? The Prince Henry one? Did you see —"

"He's not Mage-kind. It's a movie. All special effects, you know?" Tracey blurted.

Tony raised his phone. "The feeds are going nuts."

"Sir, just drive," Laura ordered. Their phones buzzed as Laura sent out a group text. *We have to stop talking. The driver is too suspicious.*

Tracey sat quietly with her phone in her lap reading the world-wide response to Prince Henry's revealed secret. There were both positive and negative posts and it was hard to say which side was winning. Some of it was pretty nasty too. Prince Henry's fans wanted to believe the viral videos had been doctored, sowing confusion through the feeds. More and more articles appeared insisting Prince Henry couldn't possibly be Mage-kind.

"Oh my God, it's mom!" Sarah shouted as the cab pulled to a stop outside the manor house.

"You kids are seriously famous," The driver muttered staring up at the great house. "What have you been in again?"

They jumped out of the cab without answering. Tracey launched into her mom's arms and Sarah joined them in a three-way hug. Mom's perfume tickled Tracey's nose. "What are you doing here?" she asked.

"I came to help. And not just me." Their mom pulled away and pointed toward the front door. Tracey let out a screech. "Grandma!"

"When I felt what happened, I spoke to Donald. Tracey, why didn't you call us? At least Sarah texted to tell us about the mumble attacks and that you were all okay. We came to help." Pink hair, knitted purple cardigan, and wearing her best slacks, Tracey's grandmother didn't look like she had been sitting on a plane for hours. She looked wonderful.

"Perfect timing," Tracey said and gave her grandmother a big hug.

They sat in the parlor and explained everything that had happened. Tracey and her friends fell silent as tea was served. Martha and Mrs. Carter didn't appear, much to Tracey's relief. They must still be out. It was good that Mrs. Carter wasn't there because Tracey could only imagine how she would have reacted to hearing the news about Kylie's abduction.

Noel sat down beside Tony and rested his teacup on his knee. "I have searched my father's office. I could not find anything that said he is acting on word from the chairman." Tracey scratched her neck and sighed. Should she tell Noel she suspected his dad was behind Kylie's kidnapping? He caught her look and winced. "You still think my father did this?"

Tracey sighed again. "No, well, no but he might know if it's the chairman was behind it. He could be under orders," Tracey said.

Noel jumped to his feet and stomped to the window. They watched him silently. Tony stood up and walked toward the young man. "Is it possible he knows something?"

"I don't want to think." Noel started to say and then stopped. He nodded slowly. "If the chairma … my father might suspect something is going on. He's been acting a little odd lately, sneaking out at night without telling me where he is going."

"Is he here?" Tracey's mom asked.

"No. I haven't seen him."

Two waiters came in with a trolley of tea and biscuits. Damian jumped to his feet and paced back and forth. "I should call my mom."

"Please wait," Tracey asked. She had to turn away from his glare. A hole opened up inside her chest telling her Damian had just broken up with her, and they had barely got together. *Are we even together?* She shook her head. They certainly weren't now. Tracey couldn't even blame him. If anything had happened to Sarah when Timothy had kidnapped her, she would have lost her mind.

"Where's Donald?" Mom asked.

Tracey glanced at Sarah. "He stayed at the studio to brief Agent Malden on the mumble attack. Prince Henry is, um, indisposed."

Mom pursed her lips and leaned back in her chair.

Tracey examined Noel. Could they speak freely in front of him? He had tried to help and he knew Tracey had her magic back and hadn't told anyone. She raised an eyebrow at Tony. He nodded. As soon as the waiters left the room, Tracey blurted out everything that had happened, including tagging the mumble.

"That was very clever, dear," Grandma said.

Tracey sighed. "I couldn't stop Kylie, and now she's—"

"Tracey, if Kylie is anything like you and your friends, you wouldn't have been able to stop her," Mom said.

Sarah sat forward. "But Mom—"

"Sarah." Mom shook her head. Sarah slumped back on the sofa next to Grandma and let out a huge sigh. Mom rubbed her forehead.

"Are you well enough to be here?" Tracey asked. Her mom had only just recovered from being poisoned. Should she have really traveled halfway across the world just to check they were all okay?

"Absolutely. I'm just a little tired from the flight."

Tony pointed a finger in the air. "Grandma Masters, how do we get our magic back? We can't help Tracey and Jilly until—"

"It was a council decision, sweetie," Grandma said.

Jonny cut her off. "So you can break it?" He leaped off the other sofa, but before he could step too far away Jilly pulled him back down. He let out a *"ooof"* as he landed on the cushions. Tracey shared a laugh with her friends.

Damian sat stone-faced. "Why are you all laughing? We have to go rescue Kylie."

"I can track the mumble." Tracey said. "I've done the spell before. I just need some sugar and a map and—"

"But what about our magic?" Dave lifted his arm, the blue light on his Mage-kind identification bracelet in full view. "We can't help you without our magic."

Mom stood and brushed off her jeans. "The rest of you children will remain here." Voices rose across the room in objection, but she waved them down. "It is far too dangerous."

"Mrs. Masters, we've helped Tracey before," Jonny said. "Laura and I don't even have magic and we've always been able to help."

"I know, dear boy but—"

"Mom, Kylie is my friend. I'm going," Sarah said. Usually her magic would snap around her like a live wire given how angry she was. It was weird to feel nothing coming from her sister at all.

"Uncle Donny had an idea about the bracelets," Tracey offered.

Mom raised her eyebrows. "Oh?"

Tracey explained about the bracelets and the possibility of picking the lock, not on the door but like creating a window inside the door and cracking it open using the spell her mom had done on Tracey's bracelet when she was little. By raising the threshold on her bracelet, Tracey's parents had tricked the bracelet into thinking she was not using magic when she was. They could trick the council curse the same way.

"Hmm. I could alter the words of my spell. It might work. Not a bad idea from your uncle."

"Mom, do you think the council knows we broke the curse on me and Jilly?"

"Honestly sweetheart, I don't know. Given the magic of the Butterfly Stone and the Tiger's Eye, who knows. The chairman hasn't come looking for you yet. Hopefully that's a good sign. I would say the stones are protecting you both as much as you are protecting them."

Damian stared at his clenched fists while Tracey's stomach churned. *I'll save Kylie. Then he'll like me again.* Jonny leaned over and flashed Tracey his cell phone screen. "I just texted my mom, she's keeping Mrs. Carter busy."

"Okay. Tracey, you activate your tracking spell and find the mumble. While you're doing that, the rest of us will spell the bracelets and see if we can trick them into unlocking their magic," her mom said.

Noel held up his hand like he was at school. "I think I can help with that."

"How?" Tony asked.

Noel held up a small black book. "This is my dad's spell book." He cleared his throat. "I am sincerely sorry for everything that has happened. I want you to know I did not lie to Tony. I was truly interested in getting to know you all better. My father does not control me. Nor did he order me to question you. I would like to help you rescue your friend."

Tony smiled broadly at the handsome boy. Tracey thought it was super cute how Noel couldn't hold Tony's gaze. "Won't you get in trouble?" Tony asked. "If he finds out you helped us break the council curse?"

Noel shrugged. "Only if he finds out."

Noise broke the sound barrier as everyone cheered the brave boy. Tracey shuffled over to Damian. "We'll find her," she said.

"I trusted you to keep her safe," he said softly.

"I'm sorry. It should have been me the mumble took."

He took her hand, holding her fingers gently and stared into her eyes. "If it had been you, we'd have no way to rescue you. I'm upset, but I know you'll do everything you can to get her back. I just feel so helpless. I want to go racing after her, but I don't know where to go or who to fight. If I was Mage-kind I could help you."

Tracey clenched Damian's hand tighter and a weight lifted off her chest. "If you were Mage-kind you'd be stuck like all the others."

"Can you talk to her? In your head? I've seen you do it before. Can you make sure she's safe?"

"I need to be closer, I think. Besides she's blocked from accessing her magic. It's a good thing. It will keep her safe until we get there." Tracey smiled softly at him. *I never should have doubted him. He still likes me.*

Grandma tapped Tracey's arm, breaking up the intimate moment. "Come with me."

Tracey examined her grandma's face and recognized the look in her eyes. *A memory? Now?* "Ah, okay." She squeezed Damian's fingers again and let go. "Why now?" she asked as they left the dining room. "We have so much to do. Kylie must be terrified. We have to hurry and I can't take time to —"

"I can't control when, Tracey. Is there a private room where we can go?"

Tracey led her grandma to the girls' bedroom. They sat on Tracey's bed and Tracey held onto her grandma's cold, bumpy hands. She peered up into Grandma's soft eyes and her head spun like she was in a clothes dryer. She clamped her eyes shut and the swirl of the shared memory carried her away.

She granted me my strange quirks.
That I do not seek out friendships and
that I am unsuited to physical attachments.
Without her, I fear what I might have become.

24

It took a moment to figure out where she stood. Tracey was outside on what would be thick grass. As it had been in the last guided-memory, everything around her was black and white. A wide, thick hedge blocked her path, creating a long wall in front of her. Two women stood at a door-width break in the hedge. Tracey recognized Stephanie's slender frame. She wore a bonnet with a ribbon tied in a bow under her chin and in her gloved hands she held the handle of a sun umbrella. Though Tracey couldn't feel the warmth of the glaringly bright sun overhead, the feeling of a stinking hot day was impossible to ignore.

Millicent was shorter and her shoulders a tad broader than Stephanie's. She was dressed in a similar fashion though her clothes didn't seem quite as fancy, and were stained with grass and dirt. Tracey focused on Millicent's round face. A giant smile exposed crooked teeth but Tracey didn't think she was self-conscious of it. She laughed brightly, whisps of blond hair drifting around her elaborate, plaited hairstyle. Tracey liked Millicent. She found herself smiling at Millicent's infectious laugh.

"Come on, we need a break," Stephanie said twirling her umbrella.

"We should return. We are at a delicate stage."

"Oh, Millie, work work work. Come on, we can race through the maze and get some exercise. I bet I can reach the other side before you."

"How very unladylike," Millicent said. The women stared at each other and then burst into raucous laughter. "I'll win," Millicent challenged and took off running.

"Oh, you cheat." Stephanie dropped her umbrella and ran after her friend through the gap in the hedge and into the maze.

Tracey ran after them. Here was one difference between Tracey and her ancestor. Tracey hated running. It didn't take long to lose the two women in the maze. Tracey stopped at a dead end. *Why am I even here if I can't witness anything? Shouldn't I automatically zoom to wherever Stephanie is?* The maze wall should be prickly, but in her memory state, Tracey's ghostly hand slid through the thick branches without any feeling. *Sooooo freaky.* She turned, searching the black and white world for what she was supposed to see. She had to get back. There was too much to do. Her friends needed their magic back and they had to find and rescue Kylie. Tracey returned to the last crossroad. *Where are you, Stephanie?*

A loud caw snapped Tracey's head up. Three crows perched on top of the hedge wall and stared down at her. The eyes of the closest crow glittered in the non-sunlight.

"What?" she asked.

The crow tilted its head. Its knowing stare sent chills creeping down Tracey's spine.

A scream burst through the air, startling the crows into flight. "Millie! No!"

Tracey ran toward the sobbing voice. Several turns in the maze brought her to a shocking scene. Millicent lay on the ground, convulsing. Stephanie leaned over her, holding her down by the shoulders. "Millie, no. Don't do this to me." Stephanie slid her knees under her friend and cradled Millicent's head to stop her from injuring her skull on the hard ground. "Millie, I've got you."

Racing to the end of the maze row, Tracey yelled for help and then froze, realizing no one could hear her. This was just a memory and all of these events had happened long ago. Tracey couldn't help anyone, only watch. She walked back slowly, her heart in her throat as Millicent's body stilled. Stephanie lay her friend gently on the ground and whipped off her gloves to touch her hand to Millicent's neck.

Stephanie cried out again. "No!" and pressed a hand to Millicent's chest. A white flare of light spread over Millicent's body from Stephanie's hand. Tracey didn't want to see the woman die, but the memory didn't stop playing. Stephanie loosened the neckline of Millicent's dress. A dark heart-shaped stone fell from her neck, landing gently in the grass.

Fluttering wings announced the arrival of the crows. Two landed on top of the hedge. The third landed at Tracey's feet. It didn't stare at Stephanie or Millicent, but at Tracey, as if it could see her, and was willing her to do something to help. Perhaps the crow was just aware that Tracey too was only a witness to the unfolding tragedy.

Stephanie looked over. "Not yet, you don't," she hissed and turned back to Millicent's body. Stephanie's hands filled with magic until they glowed white hot. She thrust her hands onto Millicent's chest and pressed her magic into the limp body in a sharp short pulse. Millicent jerked up and then lay still. Stephanie did it again and again. Tracey recognized the movements as similar to CPR heart compressions. She crept closer and Stephanie's muttered words became clearer. "I need you. Don't leave me. Come back, please. I was wrong, I'm so sorry. Please come back."

Tracey couldn't watch the emotional scene. She turned away and examined the location. They were in a small clearing in the heart of the maze. The two women were on the ground at the base of a statue. Tracey peered up at the gray stone shape. It was a baby angel holding a bow and arrow. The arrow pointed at the ground, weirdly, right at where Millicent lay dying. The plinth the cherub stood on contained a fresco of pleading faces. Or maybe they were screaming.

Tears filled Tracey's eyes. The heart stone lay on the grass beside Millicent's motionless hand. Tracey inched closer, knowing now what she would see on it. A white crow outline was etched into the stone. Tracey tried to pick it up but her fingers slipped right through it. Stephanie's head rose. She squinted as if she could sense Tracey standing there.

Millicent moaned. Stephanie yanked her hands back as Millicent's eyes fluttered. She took one of Millicent's hands in both of her own. "Hold on, my love. Please."

"Stephanie." Millicent's voice was so weak Tracey could barely hear her.

"You gave me quite a scare." Stephanie's stiff frame sagged with relief, she tucked her feet beneath her. "Just lie still. I'll fetch help in a minute."

Millicent touched her neck, searching for her stone. Stephanie scooped it up off the ground. "You will have to refocus it in the amplifier. It fell off when you … when your heart stopped." Millicent clutched the stone and both of Stephanie's hands.

Tracey blinked out of the memory as her grandmother slumped sideways on the bed. "Grandma?"

The old woman's trembling hand clutched at Tracey the same way Stephanie had held onto Millicent. "Let me rest here for a while. You'd best return downstairs. Your mother will need your assistance with her spell."

Tracey helped her grandmother lay further up on the bed so she could rest her head on Tracey's pillow. "Mom will be grumpy. You were supposed to help her."

"You'd better get moving then."

Tracey examined her grandma's pale papery face. "Are you sure you're okay?"

"Of course, I just need a moment to rest then I'll join you."

She should stay and look after the older woman, but she needed to cast her tracking spell and help her mom with the bracelet spell. "I'll tell Mom you're up here."

"Nag, nag. Now let me rest."

"Okay." Tracey lingered at the doorway, but a gust of magic shut the bedroom door in her face. Tracey huffed and headed downstairs. As she walked, she thought about what she had seen in the memory. Stephanie had been distraught over losing her friend. Millicent died and Stephanie had brought her back to life with magic.

Tracey hadn't even known that was possible, and the stone necklace had fallen from Millicent's neck. Stephanie had said Millicent would have to refocus it. *The stones* can *be removed!*

Mom caught sight of her as she wandered past the parlor. "Good, you're here." Tracey barely heard her. There was something important in that shared memory. *What does "refocus" mean?*

A hand tapped her shoulder. "Tracey?"

She looked up, startled to find her sister at her side. "Sorry, Sars. What do you need?"

"Where did you go?"

"Grandma had a memory for me."

Sarah glanced behind Tracey, searching for the older lady. "Where is she?"

"Resting."

"Oh." Sarah's eyes opened wide. "Oh! Another memory. What did you see?"

"Stephanie and Millicent and—"

"Girls? Come and join us," Mom ordered. "Tracey, where is your grandma?"

"Upstairs. She's resting."

Mom didn't look overly surprised. "I wish she'd waited until after we did this," she muttered. "Right, Tracey, you'll have to stand in for her. Over here." She pointed to the top of what looked like a five-pointed star drawn on the carpet with chalk.

"Mom, the floor! It's not our house."

"I'll clean it up later."

Tracey shot an apologetic look to Noel. He shook his head, a soft smile on his lips. "It's fine."

Standing at the top of the star, Tracey watched her mom organize Sarah, Dave, and Tony to stand at three points of the star. It left one point empty. The one to Tracey's left. "Mom?" Tracey asked, pointing to it.

"It would have been for Kylie," Sarah said.

"Okay, Tracey. I'll stand right behind you to anchor the spell. I've asked Jilly and Noel to hold the outside triangle along with me."

A quick glance at the floor showed a green chalk triangle drawn on the outside of the five-point star. Jilly and Noel stood at the base corners of the equilateral triangle right in Tracey's eyeline. Tracey's mom moved to stand behind Tracey. "Light the candles," she ordered.

Jilly and Noel lit a candle at their feet and straightened. Behind Tracey, she sensed her mom do the same, the buzz of the triangle's magic closed around them. "Oh." She'd never seen a power circle done as a triangle before.

"Open up to your core and clamp down on the Butterfly Stone's power if you can. We really don't need it interfering with this. Jilly, please do the same with the Tiger's Eye."

Tracey pressed her hand over the stone and in her mind created a tiny shield bubble to wrap around it. She flung open her inner closet door where she kept her natural magic. All of her practice keeping two shield bubbles in place made this exercise easy. Her magic zoomed out to fill her body and her thoughts became suddenly crisper, her senses sharper. "Now what?"

"Sarah, Tony, Dave, hold your bracelet arms out and point toward the center of the star."

They did and waited.

"Tracey, focus your magic and wrap a magical thread around each wrist over their bracelets. What we plan to do here is to raise the threshold on their bracelets to allow them to use their magic below that threshold. So, we're not technically breaking the curse, more undermining it. For a good cause."

Tracey nodded and sent a slender hand of magic floating toward her sister. She closed her ghostly fingers around Sarah's wrist.

"Oooo, cold," Sarah said.

Tracey sent a similar hand toward Dave and Tony. "Done." Magic bobbed like ocean waves inside the triangle, making Tracey's skin tingle and her jaw ache. *Weird.* She glanced at the wall where Laura, Damian and Jonny sat quietly watching what was going on. Damian locked eyes with Tracey. She felt the warmth of his gaze all the way down to her toes as he smiled encouragingly.

"Jilly, please clap slowly in a regular beat. Noel, if you would do the same but in counter point to Jilly's claps," Tracey's mom ordered.

The beat created by Jilly and Noel grew louder. The triangle's magic steadied as Tracey's mom's magic swelled around them. The hairs on Tracey's arms and neck quivered. Mom cleared her throat. "In life there is no lie, no wall, no barrier. Though the core in this chi—these children is young, they grow still. Each strength is not yet known, not yet fully formed, so should not be contained. A river cannot be stopped with your fingers. See their core, see their power, feel their strength, and allow it to flow free."

The buzz of the magic tickling Tracey's skin vibrated faster, rising up into a rolling wave that crashed over her, growing stronger with every roll. Her magic grew too much to be kept inside the triangle. The pressure was immense. Her ears popped. Sarah gasped.

"Whoa," Dave muttered.

Tony grinned at Tracey and mouthed, "*Wow.*"

It was so different from her own magic, which was clean and warm. It was nothing like the Butterfly Stone's magic either, uncontrollable and oh-so-angry. This was family magic. Like being wrapped up in her mom's perfume and her dad's warmth and her grandmother's hugs. It was like coming home.

Mom's voice softened. "Do not prevent. Do not contain. Allow them the freedom to soar and discover their true potential. Rise up the barrier. Rise up the block. Your threshold shall not punish them. Your threshold shall not hurt them. Your threshold shall act as a moving shield, a hovering lid upon a bubbling pot."

Tracey's magic zoomed along her arms and down the strands flowing over her sister, Dave, and Tony. Then it turned cold. Like the water in a shower when the hot ran out. It started at the top of Tracey's head and traveled over her body, following the flow of magic as if her blood was draining out through the strands. Tracey's eyes closed as nausea swiftly followed. She shivered and swayed, suddenly dizzy, and feared she would fall over, but Mom grabbed her arms to hold her still. Was this the spell her parents had used on her as a child? Had they felt this bad back then?

"I've got you, hun. Nearly done." Mom cleared her throat again and this time her voice was louder as she came to the crux of the spell. "Only a babe, uh, young ones, growing sparks of light and love. Lift their curse higher. Air cannot be constrained—it gives us life. Water runs deeper than time—forming its own path. Flames consume and renew growth. Earth breaks to allow roots to anchor the whole. Control not this, uh, their power. Conceal not their cores. Return to them what has been taken. Rise up their threshold. Open their lock. Restore their souls. Give back their power."

Magic tugged on Tracey's body. Her eyes snapped open following the flow of magic to Sarah, Tony, and Dave. Was this what it was like to have someone suck out your magic? Was this what she did to her friends?

She didn't like it.

"Whoa!" Tony said, a smile growing on his face. Dave's eyes sprang wide, his hair dancing as if in a mosh pit.

Sarah, used to Tracey's pull, let out a "whoop!" She laughed. "This is so cool."

The wild magic settled around their wrists and flowed into their bodies until each Mage-kind glowed sparkly orange. The blue light in their bracelets flared brightly white — flashlight bright. The three beams of light met in the center of the star. When the light faded, Sarah, Tony, and Dave looked as they had always looked, only with messier hair. All three grinned and giggled as if they had just gotten off a theme park rollercoaster. The Mage-kind identification bracelets around their wrists glowed emerald.

We did it.

They had their magic back.

I am afraid to make connections,
afraid to try, afraid to truly live.
She has brought me a little peace.

25

"Try something." Tracey said.

A ball of light formed in Tony's left palm. His bracelet remained green. Sarah cheered and flicked her fingers toward the light switch. Above them, the warm orange-white light popped on and off. Sarah bounced up and down on her toes. Dave zapped Tracey in the arm. "Hey!" she cried.

He laughed loudly. Tracey scowled at him but couldn't stay angry. They had their magic back.

"Success," Tracey's mom said, swiping a hand across the air. The chalk lines dissolved into a powder that rose up off the carpet fibers and blew away with a puff of her breath.

"Now we must go after Kylie," Jilly said.

Tracey eyed her celebrating friends and family. Everything had returned to normal. Well almost normal. Someone was missing. "Where's Damian?"

"He left during the spell," Jonny said, joining her in the middle of the room.

Oh. She had thought Damian wasn't mad at her, but maybe he still was? It made sense. He was worried about Kylie. "There's an Object of Power inside the mumble. I need to cast my tracking spell."

"I'll search the kitchen for stuff. Sarah, come with me?" Laura said. The two girls went off to find the manor house's kitchen. Tracey pointed at Noel. "I need a map of London, well of the whole country."

He nodded and left the room with Tony. Tracey glanced at her mom. "When we know where we're going, I think you should stay here."

"Not a chance."

"It's going to be dangerous," Tracey said. Her mother pressed her chin to her chest and stared her mom stare. Tracey snorted. "Okay, Mom. Fine. You can come."

"Thank you, dear."

"What did I miss?" Grandma asked, entering the room wheeling two suitcases. Sarah and Laura ran back in with a tub of kitchen supplies.

Sarah held up her arm, her bracelet was a bright emerald color. "We got our magic back."

"Very good, dear. Now we must find your friend," Grandma said.

"Tracey?" Laura held out the sugar. Tracey took it from her hand.

"Laura, can you draw a small circle for me?" Tracey asked. Laura spread the salt around in a perfect circle. Tony and Noel returned with the map and Tracey sat down in the middle of the circle spreading the map out in front of her and poured the sugar into a large pile on the map where the manor house was located. In moments they watched the pile of sugar rise up into a mini tornado and then collapse forming a long line to a familiar spot.

"The hospital?" Tracey stared at the map, her mouth dropping open in surprise.

"You know it?" Jilly asked.

"I went there with Uncle Donny." Tracey thought of the hospital and the attached church and bell tower. It couldn't be a coincidence. If that was where the mumble took Kylie then that was where they had to go. The mumble only existed until it achieved its mission. Its mission was to bring Kylie to the mastermind. If the mumble then crumbled, having successfully completed its mission then the spelled button would be left behind. That must be where Kylie was.

"There's an old building behind the hospital." Tracey told them. "It's part of the orphanage that still stands. Uncle Donny wanted to talk to his client, Frank Transcenni, but he was in a coma. He, um, he died, but a mumble did try to trap me in the bell tower of the old church next door. Its base could be nearby. The mastermind must be holding Kylie there."

"We should message Agent Malden," Laura said. "He can go rescue Kylie."

"He hasn't answered any of our calls," Tracey said shaking her head.

"Kylie is in danger. We can't wait."

"Tracey," Mom started to say.

"Mom, I promised Damian I'd rescue Kylie. It's our fault she got taken. Please, we have to go. We'll keep trying Agent Malden but who knows what will happen to Kylie in the meantime? We can't wait, we have to save her." Tracey's voice rose as she got more and more emotional. Tears welled in her eyes. She scrubbed them away angrily.

"Do you think we can take the limo?" Dave blurted. "Those taxis are too cramped."

Noel waved a hand. "I'll tell the driver to meet us out front."

"What about us?" Laura asked, pointing to herself and Jonny.

Jilly took Jonny's hand. "Of course you must come."

It didn't even cross Tracey's mind to leave Jonny and Laura behind after everything they'd been through together. "No way are you staying here. We need you."

Laura grinned.

Jonny punched the air. "Hel—" His celebration cut off as his gaze landed on Tracey's mom. "Heck, yeah."

Mom shook her head at his enthusiasm. "I don't think—"

Grandma held up her hand. "Beth, they have done this a few times now. We need to trust that they're ready. Besides, I brought a few things along that might help."

"What things?" Tracey asked. Sarah dropped to her knees and unzipped the first suitcase.

"Whoa!" Sarah pulled out a pile of purple straps covered in colorful round balls. "What are these?"

"Adele! I had no idea what was in those suitcases, I certainly didn't suspect you'd brought weapons!" Tracey's mom sounded horrified. Grandma picked up the top strap, pulled open the Velcro and wrapped the strap over one shoulder and across her chest, pressing the strap together like a sash on a beauty competition winner. The colored balls were stuck all over it. A cloth pocket hung down from the part of the sash closest to Grandma's hip.

"The water pistol, dear?" Grandma said, pointing Sarah to the other suitcase. Sarah unzipped the bag and yanked out a fluorescent pink water pistol. Grandma spun it around her finger and slid it into the pocket on the sash like she was holstering a gun.

"Cool look, Grandma Masters," Dave said and whistled.

"Inside the water pistol is a spelled liquid that will dissolve clay. In case you run into any more mumbles," Grandma told them. "When Sarah messaged about the mumbles, I decided to come prepared."

"Awesome," Sarah said grinning brightly.

"Nice, Grandma Masters." Jonny's eyes shone from all the mischief he could cause. "And the colored balls?"

"Magic dust. To cause a distraction. Jonny. Laura. I have enough for you too. And you don't need magic to use them."

Jonny's mouth hung open. Laura punched the air. "Yessss."

Tracey's mom sighed. "Well, message Agent Malden with the details. Tell him what we are doing and that he must join us as soon as he is able to. We will only scout the area and see if Kylie is indeed being held there. Perimeter only. Then we wait for Agent Malden. Do you all understand."

"Yes Mrs. Masters." They all answered.

"Lock and load, kids," Tracey's mom said.

Sarah and Tracey shared a giggle. Their mom sounded so badass. The teens grabbed a sash and a water pistol each. Tracey edged closer to her grandmother as her friends chatted excitedly. "Did you know this was going to happen? That we would need your help to rescue Kylie?"

Grandma smiled and touched the side of her nose. Tracey wasn't entirely sure what that meant, but she nodded anyway.

Suddenly, she was very glad her mom and grandma had flown here to help. For the first time in a long time, Tracey breathed easier. She settled the sash over her head, and slid a hot-green water pistol into her holster. "Just wearing this makes me feel more powerful."

Mom's hand landed on Tracey's shoulder. "Remember, these are defensive extras only. You, Sarah, Tony, Jilly, and Dave need to watch over your friends. Your grandmother will stay here to wait for your uncle and Agent Malden if they return here first. Our job is to find Kylie and wait for the professionals. That's all."

"The car is ready, Mrs. Masters," Jonny said, poking his head around the doorway. Behind him, Dave pulled his water pistol out of his holster like a cowboy from an old movie. In, out, in, out. Quick draw practice.

Laura ambled closer to Sarah. They looked like paintballers or laser tag heroes. "Come on, Trace."

There was one sash and pistol left. Tracey glanced toward the door, hoping Damian would appear. She grabbed the extra sash and water pistol to give to Kylie when they found her.

"I'm glad you're here," Tracey said and following her mom down the corridor through the manor house toward the front door.

"Are you kidding. A chance to stay in a manor house? You know I love my old English dramas. This looks like a palace, Tracey. How could I miss that?"

Tracey stopped walking. "I'm sorry you got sick, Mom."

"Oh, honey." Strong arms wrapped around Tracey and pulled her into a big hug. "That wasn't your fault."

"But it was, Mom. Doctor Chan only came after you because of me."

"Stephanie started this, remember? You just happened to be the one to find the Butterfly Stone. We're all in this together."

Grandma appeared in the doorway behind them. "What are you dawdling for?"

Tracey gave her grandmother another hug. "Thanks for the weapons. Have you got any last words of wisdom?" Tracey breathed in the scent of cold cream, baby powder, and warm bread.

"Don't get hurt."

"That's it?" Tracey laughed.

Mom hugged them both. Tracey was surrounded by the strongest women in her life and it gave her body tingles. "Trust your gut and keep your friends safe," Grandma added.

"I will."

Mr. Henderson stood at the front door watching them. *When did he appear?* He cleared his throat. Tracey quickly stepped back from her mom. "I understand my son is going with you on your adventure?"

Grandma pointed at the man. "Elijah. You and I are going to have a little talk."

Ouch. Poor Mr. Henderson. Even though Tracey didn't like the man she still felt sorry for him. He straightened, giving Tracey's grandmother a tight nod of his head and moved toward the window to give them privacy.

Mom patted Tracey on the back and headed out through the door. "I'll meet you out front."

Grandma moved closer to Tracey. "I feel … Be careful. Someone is not being entirely truthful."

Who could her grandma mean? Tracey squinted at Mr. Henderson. *Him?* Maybe she meant Noel. He was the only new person in their group. Tracey nodded. "I will. Thanks."

"Good luck."

Tracey ran after her mom and scrambled into the limo. It moved smoothly off down the driveway. Her eyes popped wide open when she realized Damian was sitting right next to her. "Hey."

"I'm coming," he said.

She handed him Kylie's sash and pistol. He could use them instead. "I'm glad you came back. I was a bit worried when you disappeared. Are you mad at me?"

"I was talking to my mom on the phone, trying to convince her not to come back early from visiting her friends and shopping with Jonny's mom. She couldn't reach Kylie and was getting worried."

"What did you tell her?"

"I lied, Tracey." He huffed out a breath. "We'll find her, won't we?"

"Absolutely."

His eyes narrowed. "Why do you always think I've run off or that I'm mad at you?"

Tracey stared at the end of her sash and tugged at a few loose threads. "I don't know. I guess because I'm worried you blame me for what happened to Kylie and that you won't like me anymore."

"That's not your fault," he insisted. His face pinked. "And I still like you. Just because, well, I'm grumpy, doesn't mean I've stopped liking you."

"You like me like me?"

He took her hand and squeezed it. "I do."

She squeezed his hand back. "I ... "

"And I know you'll find my sister."

"All good?" Tracey's mom called out.

"Yep." And Tracey suddenly was. Her mom was right here. Damian *did* like her, and all her friends had their magic back. Rescuing Kylie would be a piece of cake—hopefully, gooey chocolate cake.

All of Tracey's friends were buzzing about the upcoming mission. Dave and Jonny were even comparing expected water pistol hit numbers.

"—you think, Tracey?" Tony asked.

"What?"

"The plan. Do you think it will work?"

"Um ... "

"You weren't listening, were you?" Jonny barked out a laugh. The rest of the chatter in the limo died away as everyone looked at her. Tracey checked the light on the limo's intercom speaker. It was dark. The driver couldn't hear.

Tracey's gaze flicked to Noel. "I wonder who the mastermind is?"

"You think it is still my father?" Noel asked. "Or that he knows who the mastermind is?"

She didn't answer.

"It's probably that chairman dude. The boss guy," Dave said.

"What makes you think that?"

"Cause he's creepy as," Dave said. "He locked up our magic so we couldn't use it to defend ourselves. Why? So he can get the stones off you and Jilly and Kylie. And so he could order Mr. Henderson to spy on us. I mean it makes sense. All creepy Mage-kind want the stones once they know you've found them."

"But he knows they can't be taken off." Tracey recalled the stone falling from Millicent's body as she received magical CPR. Maybe there *was* a way to take them off. But to do so might mean dying first. Totally not an option. They'd have to find another way.

"He's the boss of the council. I bet he knows how to make mumbles," Jonny said.

"We will have to split up when we get there," Tracey's mom said.

"All of you must be very careful. If this is a trap to get Tracey and Jilly here, then we must ensure nothing happens to them. Which is why we are setting up a perimeter only. No going inside. Girls, I suggest you split up. Jilly's team—Jonny, I presume that's you? Take Sarah with you." They nodded. "Tracey, you and Tony with Laura?" Tracey nodded, she avoided Damian's gaze though his fingers brushed against hers on the seat. She grabbed his hand and squeezed. "Good. We form a perimeter and wait for Agent Malden to arrive." Tracey's mom said, her voice firm.

Tracey didn't like it. Kylie could already be hurt. The mastermind might even be experimenting with the stone. She didn't voice her objection. Instead she said, "Have you all looked at Noel's map?"

"Tony sent us the street view link from his phone," Jonny reminded her.

They nodded. "Three buildings—three groups. We wait outside one building each?" Dave asked.

"Damian, Dave, and I will take the hospital entrance. We need to be careful not to provoke any action near the hospital," Tracey's mom said.

"Mrs. Masters?" Noel called, raising his hand. "What about me?" He was staring at Tony. Tony nodded at him and Noel smiled at Tracey's mom. "I guess that's me, Dave, and Damian with you, ma'am."

"Put your cell phones on silent," Tracey ordered. She glanced out through the window. "We're nearly there."

"The last mumbles we faced were smart and strong. If we find any here you won't be able to hold them in one place and wait for them to fall apart. If you see one, avoid it. If you can't, then hide and call for help," Tracey said.

"Do not attack unless you have no other option. We are here to locate Kylie. Am I understood?" Mom ordered.

They all answered together. "Yes, Mrs. Masters" and "Yes Mom."

Where are Uncle Donny, Agent Malden, and Prince Henry? Tracey peered through the window and spotted a crow flying alongside the limo. She frowned at it. Hopefully seeing the black bird didn't mean something bad was about to happen.

She has gifted me a maze.
I can scarcely believe her generosity.

26

The limo driver let Tracey's group out a street away from the church. They were buzzing with energy and fear, and loaded for bear with water pistols and powder bombs full of magic.

Grandma's warning played in a loop inside Tracey's mind. *"Someone is not being truthful."* They still didn't know Noel all that well. His dad might be the one behind the kidnapping. But Tracey's mom was the strongest and most experienced Mage-kind in the group. She could handle Noel if she needed to. Hopefully, she wouldn't need to.

There was no visible sign that a mumble had headed this way. Tracey examined the grass and concrete as they walked, searching for flattened foot prints in the grass or crack patterns in the pavement.

"Let's head that way," Tracey said, pointing toward a faded sign that read 'Church Entrance.' A less welcoming sign beneath it warned 'Do Not Enter.' *Yeah, so that's not creepy at all.* It was weird. The vibe from the sign clashed with the bright sunny day around them. It wasn't hot enough for Tracey to push her jumper sleeves up to her elbows though. The scent of roses drifted by on the slight breeze, reminding Tracey of Noel. She skipped to Tony's side. "So, Noel."

"I—he's cute. And nice."

Tracey stopped walking. When Tony turned back, she told him about Grandma's warning. "Just be careful. He's already betrayed us once."

"She can't have meant Noel," Tony argued. "He apologized. He didn't really do anything except ask questions. He said he didn't tell his dad anything and I believe him. And he's helped us. He didn't know what his dad was planning."

"His dad is *on* the council," Tracey reminded him. Laura looked on silently. They walked toward the bell tower in the distance. Tracey adjusted the water pistol on her hip.

"There are other people your grandma could have meant."

Tracey moaned. "Not this again."

"Agent Malden is—"

"Really, Tony?" Laura asked. "He's never done anything to hurt any of us. The opposite even."

"Laura, you were there when Agent Striker died. You saw what happened."

She nodded. "Yes. I saw two agents doing their jobs, fighting the Shadowman and Timothy's goons."

"You didn't see what I saw," Tony insisted, his voice strained.

"I know he looked devastated when Agent Striker died," Laura said.

"They were arguing. And when she died, he froze. Like completely. Dave got thrown halfway across the clearing and into that tree. He just stood there."

"Of course Agent Malden was shocked. Agent Striker was his partner and she died right in front of him," Laura said.

Tracey didn't want to talk about death and pointed over the trees that lined the street. "You can see the bell tower of the church from here. Do you think the mumble brought Kylie here? I can't see any hints it came this way, do you?"

"Nothing obvious." Laura peered up at the bell tower. "Has it ever rung, do you think?"

"Probably. It was Millicent's secret place." Tracey wondered if she should tell them about the Visions or that she knew the name of the next stone.

"Whoa, look at that," Laura said. The top of the fence ahead was lined with big black birds. "Crows."

Tony pursed his lips. "That's supposed to be a bad sign."

"Uncle Donny said that."

"Crows are harbingers," Tony continued.

"Of what?" Tracey asked.

"Death."

Tracey halted. "Oh, come on. That's not … are they really? I've seen a few of them lately. Three actually."

"Wait, you keep seeing crows? Tracey, do you think it has something to do with the stone? Didn't you dream of tigers before we found the Tiger's Eye?"

"Um, that's the thing. I already know what the stone is."

"What?" Laura and Tony shouted together. The crows squawked loudly.

"How long have you known? How did you find out? What does it—"

"Tony, breathe. It's called the Crow's Heart. I think. It's a heart-shaped stone with a bird on it."

"Then we can find it with your stone tracking spell," Tony said.

"Finally, something has gone right," Laura added.

They turned the corner and the old red brick wall of the church was right in front of them. "I didn't see it from this angle before, only from the inside. It looks creepy," Tracey whispered. She peered around, searching for signs of life. "It's all boarded up like it's been abandoned."

"That warning sign we saw earlier—do you think this is a condemned building? It might be dangerous to get too close," Tony said. "The mumble can't have come this way."

"Imagine living here as a kid," Laura added with a shiver. "Brrr, what a horrid place. It gives me the willies."

Laura had it right. The building was clearly older than everything around it, the roof was chipped and stained with age. Bricks had cracks in them and some were missing. Overgrown bushes, grass, and vines climbed the walls and buried the entrance, which was sealed with three boards almost as wide as Tracey. One board, the middle one, had a split right through the center. The bottom part was bent. The bell tower loomed above them, casting a long shadow over the chipped path.

"How do we get in?" Laura asked.

"In? We can't go in," Tony said. "Tracey's mom said perimeter only and to look for clues the mumble had passed this way."

Tracey eyed her friends. "But what if Kylie is just inside the doorway? We can rescue her before anyone catches us."

"Or maybe the mastermind is just inside and when we go in, he'll catch us." Tony countered.

The three friends stared at each other in silence. After a moment Tracey spoke. "If she's not here then we've ruled out the possibility and shrunk the search area. Come on, let's go look." Tracey tested the cracked board with her hands. The solid wood barely moved as she tugged and pushed. The crack was wide but not enough to squeeze through. Not even by Tony. Jonny might have been able to slither through with his skinny, long-limbed body, but he was with Jilly's team searching around the old orphanage.

"Look for a basement, or a cellar door?" Tracey called. Tony raised his eyebrows. "What, I've streamed my mom's TV shows. Old buildings have weird entrances — for servants and such. And for, like, storing firewood."

"I didn't say anything."

Tracey raised her nose and sniffed at him, feeling judged.

"Over here." Laura pushed aside the overhanging branches from a thick scrubby bush. "A door."

"Whoa." Tracey was surprised to be right. "Cool."

Laura tugged on the handle. "Urgh, it's locked."

"Or stuck." Tony pressed in beside her and helped her pull but there was no movement.

Laura's cell phone screen lit up. "Jilly just messaged me. They can't get into the orphanage. They're walking around the grounds searching for mumble signs. Should I tell them to come here and help us?"

"Let's see if we can get in first," Tracey said and checked her phone to find the same message from Jilly. Her phone flashed with a new message. "Damian says the hospital is quiet. My mom is speaking to the head nurse," Tracey shoved her phone into her pocket and she shook out her fingers. "Okay, move aside. It's time for something a little more magical." Tony and Laura backed up. Tracey filled her right hand with magic and grabbed the handle, searching for the lock innards with her mind. Despite her lockpicking experience there was no click. *Huh?* She tried again.

"Need a hand?" Tony asked.

"Hand? Oh." Tracey focused on her right hand again filling it with golden magic until her fingers glowed. Then she created that echo hand like Noel had taught her. She tugged on the handle with the super strong magic hand. The door sprang open with a crack of wood and bent hinges.

The three teens froze, eyes darting back and forth searching for anyone nearby who might have heard the forced entry. No one shouted or came running.

"Now what?" Laura asked.

"Let's find Kylie," Tracey said.

The dark basement led to a short murky corridor. Tracey scrunched up her nose at the smell of rodent poop and other dead things. Tony and Tracey created a glowing ball of magic that floated above their hands to light the way. Laura held up her cell phone — the flashlight bobbed as she swung her phone from side to side lighting up the dirt and dried mud. They were forced to step around piles of goop as they walked.

"What is this stuff?" Laura mumbled.

"I don't think you want to know," Tony told her.

Tracey held her glowing ball closer. "Ewwww."

"Then I won't mention the funky smell," Laura said.

"I think we all smell that. This corridor is way too small for a mumble to get inside, even a mumble crouched over. It can't have bought Kylie in here. We must be in the wrong place." Tony raised his hand and shone his magic across the ceiling.

Laura's phone light flickered as she received another message. "That's Jonny. They've found a way in."

"The magic that made the mumbles is strong, maybe the boss — the creator — found the button you spelled and tricked us into coming here," Tony continued.

Laura stopped, her flashlight swinging up to light Tony's face. "Do you think that's possible?"

In the white light, Tony's face was a horror show, all shadows and darkness and glowing yellow eyes. *Oh, wait.* That was the reflection coming from the glowing magic ball he held.

"It doesn't look like anyone has been down this way for years," Tracey said. "No footprints in the dust." Her phone flashed with a new notification. "Damian says they're going to the hospital basement."

"Why?" Tony asked.

Tracey flicked back the question. No answer came. "Come on," she said and they crept forward until they hit a crossroad of corridors. "Um. Are we still under the church do you think?"

Tony shrugged. "Three of us. Three paths."

"Don't even suggest splitting up," Laura said. "That's what they always do."

"Who does?" Tracey asked.

"The ones in the movies. The ones that die when they split up. We have to stay together."

Tracey raised her magic ball to light Laura's face. "Well, yeah, but we're Mage-kind. We should be fine."

"I'm not."

Tracey couldn't believe she had forgotten that. "Yeah, but … "

Laura's eyes widened. "Seriously, Tracey?"

"You're magic to me," Tracey admitted.

"Awww," Laura hugged her. "Fine, we split up. But if I die, I'm blaming you."

"Totally fair," Tracey agreed.

"Scream if we find something?" Tony suggested. Tracey and Laura giggled.

"The mumble might have handed Kylie over to the mastermind outside and then turned to dust. The mastermind probably brought her inside. She could be locked up in a room really close by. If you find anything other than Kylie, make a heap of noise and we'll come running."

"Scream," Tony added.

They each picked a hallway. "Be careful," Tracey whispered and they walked away from each other into the darkness.

Out here I am wild, free.
I am not constrained by my existence.

27

The hallway Tracey chose seemed to stretch on forever. After a few minutes her spine tingled and she stopped walking. *How can a hallway be this long?* Maybe Laura was right. They shouldn't have split up. Tracey spun on her heels and hustled back to find her friends.

Plink.

She spun around again. *What was that?* She waited, holding her breath. There was nothing. It had been a noise though, she was sure of it. A metal noise, high-pitched and deliberate. And a hiss. But *what* was it? More importantly, what had made it? Tracey raised her glowing ball higher, but it only moved the shadows around. She grabbed her cell phone to message Tony. When she hit send, no little tick appeared to confirm the message had been successfully sent. She checked her signal strength and groaned. *Fruit tingles. We should have checked that earlier.* There was no signal this far underground. Tracey pulled the water pistol from her holster and held it out in front of her. Above her other hand floated her glowing ball. She felt braver holding the water pistol. Tracey popped open her inner closet door and raised her shield bubble. As protected as she could make herself, she continued forward.

Plink.

What is *that?*

She spun on the spot. "Tony?" she whispered. "Laura?" She turned again. A figure in blue holding a lit lantern crossed the hallway in front of Tracey and disappeared.

What the … ?

Tracey's glowing ball vanished. Surrounded by endless darkness, her stomach clenched. She waited for a screech and the sudden movement of air telling her something swooped over her head. *The Shadowman?* It couldn't be. She had fought it twice and won. Besides, Kylie was blocked from the power of the Serpent's Kiss.

Unless ... unless whoever had taken her had figured out how to remove the stone. Timothy could be back and readying for an attack. Sweat beaded across Tracey's skin. She recreated her glowing ball and the figure in blue swept past again. The woman stopped and peered over her shoulder.

"Millicent?" Tracey muttered.

The woman's gaze was eerily blank as she looked right through Tracey. She turned and disappeared down a crossroad in the hallway. Tracey raced after her. "Millicent?"

The woman in blue was gone.

"Where did you go?" Worried she was inside a Vision again, Tracey pinched herself. "Ouch." She stared at her magic ball. *I can't use magic in a Vision. This must be real.* Tracey ran through the next hallway and found concrete stairs heading down into more blackness.

She checked her phone. Still no signal and the battery was half full. *Best not use it.* She slipped the phone into her pocket and stepped down the stairs carefully, flicking her magic ball around and poured more magic into her hand to make the light brighter. The shadow coating the stairs was like a pool of ink. No light penetrated. "This is stupid. Just go back and find Laura and Tony."

Yet her feet continued to take her down.

A flash of lantern light and blue skirts in the distance brought speed to her steps. Tracey pulled magic into her free hand and launched it up in front of her, searching for the other Mage-kind. Millicent couldn't possibly be alive. This person had to be a ghost, like Frank Transcenni. Tracey's magic settled over the ground detecting nothing. No magic. No settled spells.

Millicent's ghost reappeared right in front of her. This time she looked directly at Tracey and pointed at a closed door. *Is that where Kylie is?* As Tracey reached Millicent, the woman smiled and disappeared. Tracey twisted the handle, pushed the door open and stepped into an impossibly round room. *The same round room as the one in the manor house!*

Tracey walked forward and her shoes slapped into water. *Argh.* She backed up and groaned at the icky cold wet feeling soaking into her trainers and socks. Her sounds echoed strangely in the room and the air was the same temperature as her skin. She couldn't feel any movement—cold or hot. *How strange.*

She tossed her magic blanket up and instantly it exploded out of her, filling the room and electrifying her skin. She released her magic immediately and blinked into the bright echo staining her vision. *What the heck?* Her magic had reacted so fast, so strong. It had never done that before. She tried again. As soon as she called her magic it rushed out of her body, whipping around her head like live wires. She extinguished it again. *It's this room!* It acted like a giant charger, increasing her strength a dozen times or more. *This room is awesome!*

A loud hissing came from just outside the door. It sounded so much like a snake Tracey started searching for a long scaly body. White gas poured into the round room from the corridor outside. Tracey coughed at the cold metallic taste. Her mouth dried and her throat closed. She gasped for air. The gas seeped through the hand she pressed over her mouth and traveled up her nose. Her vision swam. She moved to slam the door shut to keep the gas out but swayed and fell to her knees instead. "H-h-help … " She fumbled for her cell phone. The black plastic slipped from her fingers and plopped into the pool. She slumped sideways, water soaking her clothes. Her fingers touched the Butterfly Stone. *Stephanie?* Her eyes fluttered shut.

Tracey woke, her face pressed to damp grass. The light was odd. Neither daylight nor nighttime, it was a rather a weird hazy orange. A Vision? She couldn't touch her magic so she figured it must be. Only she could see color. *What's happening?* She sat up. Dark green hedges surrounded her. *I'm in the maze?*

"*Caw!*"

A familiar black crow hopped along the top of the hedge wall. There was an open path to Tracey's right. It seemed to be the only way to go. The crow landed on the grass in front of her feet and hopped around until she looked at it, then swooped off along the path in front of her.

Tracey followed. At each twist and turn she moved deeper into the maze, and further away from freedom. *Where are we going?* The crow stopped and perched on a dead-end wall. Tracey stared at the three hedges trapping her. *What do I do now?* She pressed her hands to the hedge wall. Maybe there was a hidden door?

Something grabbed her hands and sucked her inside the hedge. She let out an unheard yelp and tried to pull free, but the grip tightened on her wrists. As her shoulders and head disappeared into the bush, she feared she was being swallowed alive until she popped free on the other side. In front of her was a familiar white marble, baby angel statue. The crow landed on the angel's shoulder. The serene look of happiness on the angel's face helped slow Tracey's racing heart. *I'm okay.* A blue clad figure stepped out from behind the angel.

Millicent.

She looked right at Tracey. Expecting the Vision to show her something important, Tracey was gob-smacked when Millicent came forward and took Tracey's hand. "Hello Tracey."

It is only up here that I feel free.
I see forever as I stare into the distance.
Here, there is no judgement.
My mind is my own, my heartbeat is endless.

28

ow ... ? Why ... ? I don't ... ? How are you even talking to me?"

"I am not entirely sure. Perhaps it is because you need me to."

"How do you know who I am?" Tracey asked.

"You look just like her. My Stephanie. My friend."

"Yeah, but hang on, that doesn't make sense. You can't know who I am. I wasn't even born when you were alive. This has to be a memory. You're a memory. Right? One of Stephanie's memories?"

Millicent shrugged. "Sometimes it is best not to question good fortune."

"Why are we here?"

The woman in blue closed her eyes. When she smiled she was beautiful, so at peace Tracey was afraid to disturb her. "This is one of my favorite places in the whole world."

"Inside a maze?"

"Of course. We are outside surrounded by the earth, sky, and the natural world. In here, I can be myself. I am inside a world only I can see."

It made sense. The orphanage must have been so dark and small and horrible, but out here, Millicent would be free. "It's so cramped in here though, the walls of the maze are so high I feel trapped, don't you?"

"Safety and freedom, Tracey. No one can find me here. It is a spelled maze. My spell. No one knows the path to the center."

"What about Stephanie?"

"Not even my friend knows the true path. It changes with my will. I control the way in and the way out. But we play here together and it is so much fun."

"I saw you in a Vision and I saw you ... you're sick, aren't you? I saw you having a seizure and … you died."

"I did?"

"Stephanie brought you back. She saved you."

Millicent's hand rose to her chest. She clutched a deep bluey-violet, heart-shaped stone hanging on a thin silver chain around her neck. "My life force would be lost if I died. But no, it's here. I still have it. Stephanie must have saved it and me."

"I saw the stone fall. How did it come off?"

"If I died, my stone would lose connection with my spirit."

"So, it *can* be taken off?"

"Of course. Once we lose connection to the stone it cannot speak to us. Oh, but I must have refocused it inside the amplifier."

"The what?"

"It's a special Mage-kind room, Tracey. The walls are round and smooth. You can surround yourself with your magic and let it swim in and out, and float around you, filling your senses and your mind. There is no distraction. No sound, no thought, nothing but you and your magic."

"Sounds lovely. Like family magic."

Millicent's smile fell away.

"Oh, I'm so sorry." Tracey realized her blunder immediately. Millicent had no family. She wouldn't know the glorious feeling of her grandmother's magic, or that of her mom and dad, or siblings. She would never have felt that. Until she met Stephanie. "Your friends *are* your family."

Millicent nodded.

"So you reattached the heart stone to your life force."

"Yes."

"In a round room? I found your amplifier at the manor house. And another. An amplifier in the basement of a church. That's where I am right now."

Millicent's eyes narrowed. "You are at the orphanage? You must leave."

"Why?"

"There is danger. I see death." Millicent released Tracey's hand.

My death? Tracey stared at her hand. *Oh no.*

"You must go — leave this place."

Tracey gulped. A gift or a curse? *Now that I know, I can be more careful.* "I can't leave. Not yet. I have to save my friend. Her name is Kylie. She's been kidnapped." Tracey swallowed hard. "Millicent, we have Timothy's stone."

"What? Then you are all in danger."

"It's okay — it's locked. No one can use it."

Millicent shook her head. "He is stronger than you know."

"How do we stop Timothy? How did you?"

"I … " Millicent spun back. "I made a terrible choice. You must run while you can."

"I have to rescue Kylie and then I'll go." Tracey peered at the prickly looking maze walls. "The best way to stop Timothy is to find Kylie."

Millicent's gorgeous face turned dark and she scowled. Above her head, the clouds grew stormy and lightning flashed in the distance. "He must not get the stones." Her fingers opened. The heart-shaped stone she held was so dark blue it was almost black, with tiny flashes of pink inside. A crow was etched on the slick stone in white lines, like someone had taken a sharp blade to the stone to dig out the bird from within.

"It's beautiful," Tracey told her.

"Find it, Tracey."

"How do you know my name?"

"I Dreamed that you would find my heart."

Millicent fell silent. Tracey had hundreds of questions and could find no voice for any of them. But time was passing in the real world while Tracey was stuck in here. Kylie was in danger. *Millicent saw death.* Tracey couldn't just leave Kylie out there alone. *I promised I'd save her. I'll just be extra careful.* "I have to go."

"I Dreamed of you."

"You said that already," Tracey said.

"It is a unique gift, Tracey. To Dream of another."

This again? Tracey had heard the term Dreamer so many times now. Old ancient legends. It was nothing more than a myth. Dreamers were not real. "What do you mean?"

"You Dream, don't you, Tracey?"

"What?"

"You see the truth in your sleep."

"I guess. I've dreamed of the stones."

Millicent smiled. "It is a gift. You must learn to use it. It will help you. Tracey, do not listen to Timothy. He has darkness in his heart. He will do anything to collect all of the stones."

"I won't listen to him." She had no intention of ever talking to Timothy.

Millicent pressed her chin to her chest and stared deeply into Tracey's eyes. "Stay true to yourself, Tracey," she said and turned away.

"No wait, don't leave. You said the stone falls off when you die. The kidnapper can kill Kylie and take it off. I have to find her. You have to send me back."

Millicent's hands clasped together. "Tracey. I did not bring you here."

"Then how am I here?" she demanded, throwing up her hands.

"You came to me. Where are you right now?"

"The orphanage remember, where you—" she stopped as Millicent backed away.

"Where in the orphanage?"

"In the basement. I got lost."

"Of course. You are in the amplifier."

"The what?"

"The round room. As I have said, it is a Mage-kind room designed to amplify our magic. It is how we first attuned the stones to our life force."

"Someone knocked me out. There was gas."

"You are inside the amplifier. That is how you are here, Tracey. Your magic is stronger inside the amplifier, but without your conscious thought it is undirected, wild, dangerous. You must wake up."

"I don't know how."

"Simply tell yourself to wake—it is but a thought. You cannot stay in this form for long, Tracey, or you will lose yourself."

"I have to find Kylie."

"Your magic will help you."

"I promise I'll find your stone."

Millicent smiled. "Be careful. Timothy is dangerous. He will do anything to amass more power, including hurting your friends."

"I will."

"Farewell, Tracey."

With a final wave, Tracey closed her eyes and gripped the Butterfly Stone tightly. "Wake up."

Her chest ached something terrible. Tracey's eyes fluttered open.

The smell of cinnamon curled under her nose like freshly made doughnuts. There was the pop-hiss of a candle igniting behind her head. She tried to look, but her head was stuck in place. There was another sound. Humming.

Someone was humming.

It was a sad sound, full of low notes and broken fragments. And yet something in it was familiar. Tracey stared up at the ceiling. It was too low for a mumble to safely move around in without tearing up the walls or leaving dents in the roof. She opened her mouth to call out, but stopped. A lit candle meant a spell was being cast. A man leaned over her. Before she could shut her eyes and pretend she was still asleep her shocked stare locked onto a pale face, wrinkled suit, and graying hair. "Agent Malden?"

His eyes sprang wide. "Tracey?"

"Agent Malden, you found us! Untie me, quick. We have to find Kylie and … " Her voice died as he continued to stare at her.

"You're awake."

She tugged on her bonds and tried to move her head. "Can you untie me?"

"Ah, yes." He fiddled with something beside her forehead and Tracey was able to twist her head to look around. On her left, Jilly lay asleep on a table. Thick straps tied her wrists and ankles to the table. There was another strap over her forehead. Twisting to the other side, Tracey saw Kylie in the same position on a different table. There was a circle drawn on the floor and their three tables formed a triangle inside it. A lit candle fluttered and smoked behind Kylie's head. Jilly's too. Tracey assumed there was one behind her own and that the popping hiss had been the magic that lit it. "Someone's casting a spell. You got here just in time, Agent Malden." Tracey twisted her arm. "Hurry, before they come back."

"Tracey."

She glanced around again. *Circle. Candles. Jilly, Kylie … and me.* There was no one else in the room. No sign of the bad guy. "Did … did you stop … the bad guy from completing … ? A-a-agent Malden?" Her question was slow to form and seeped from her mouth as realization dawned.

There was no one else in the room.

No bad guy.

No mumbles.

Just Agent Malden.

There is peace out here among the hedges.
I can run and run and never find the end
if that is how I choose.

29

How are you awake?" he asked.

That one sentence told her everything. "Agent Malden, you did this?" A hole opened up inside Tracey's chest. How could he be the one behind the mumbles? Her face lost all expression and her skin felt numb. The betrayal hurt like nothing she had ever experienced before.

His hands rose like a man surrendering to the police. "Tracey, I can explain."

She struggled against the ropes and called on her magic. The strap around her left wrist snapped as a sharp, bitterly cold wind blew around her head from her anger. Malden backed up, putting distance between them. Tracey's wild stare flew to Kylie and then to Jilly. How could she rescue her friends from Agent Malden? He was a level three M-force agent. He was *way* more powerful than her. She couldn't leave her friends here and run, but she had no hope of overpowering him, let alone outsmarting him. She had to stall, think of something, anything, that could get herself, Jilly, and Kylie out of here alive.

Tracey relaxed her limbs. From the corner of her eye, she spied the sashes and water pistols piled in the corner. "I don't understand. Why are you doing this?"

His face contorted in confusion. "How did you break the sleep spell?"

"You saved us, helped us fight Timothy, helped search for the stones. You trained us." Tracey rubbed her forehead with her free hand. "Why are you doing this this?"

Agent Malden turned to face Kylie. "It's not what you think. I am trying to help. You asked me to find a way to remove the stone. You know it will end up destroying her. I'm only trying to help."

Tracey's breath exploded out of her mouth. "Then why didn't you tell me what you were planning? Why cast a sleep spell on us or send the mumbles after us? We could have helped."

"It's a dangerous spell, Tracey. I didn't want to put any of you at risk."

"You knocked us out."

"It's also a delicate spell. I couldn't be interrupted. I sent the sleep gas through the vents and ordered the mumbles to bring you here. I won't hurt anyone."

Tracey shook her head, unsure anything he was saying was true. "If the mumbles are under your control, then why did they attack us?"

"No one was hurt. They were spelled not to cause harm, just to collect Kylie. That's all. I could remove the stone and they would put her back. No harm done."

Her mind raced with questions. His explanations didn't make sense. "Why keep it a secret?"

"I wasn't sure the spell would work."

Tracey leaned up onto her elbow and pointed at Jilly. "Wake them up. We can help. You didn't need to hide this from us."

"Your uncle didn't approve and I—"

"Uncle Donny?" She searched the shadows for her uncle. "Where is he? Is he here?"

"Asleep in the other room. I promise you, Tracey. No one was in any danger."

"What about the council?"

His mouth twisted. "That was a complication."

"They didn't approve of your plan, did they?"

"Tracey, you must understand. I'm doing this to help you. If the spell works, then we can use it on you and Jilly and remove this terrible burden on you all."

She slapped her hand over the Butterfly Stone. "I ... I don't want to take it off."

He stepped closer. When she twitched, his hands lit up as he prepared to fire. Tracey froze. Tony had been right. He had warned her Agent Malden couldn't be trusted, and she hadn't believed him. But ... but

Agent Malden *was* trying to help Kylie. That wasn't bad, was it? Tracey had promised Damian she would remove the stone. Using a sleep spell on them wasn't right, but Malden *was* trying to help. Right? "C … can I … do you need help?"

His eyes narrowed, then widened and he nodded, moving swiftly to her feet to release the straps. "If the spell works on Kylie then we can use it on the Butterfly Stone and the Tiger's Eye." He untied Tracey's remaining wrist and spun around to relight the candle behind her head with a flick of his finger. She must have extinguished it in her earlier anger burst. Agent Malden's shoulders were tense and there were long shadows under his sad eyes, deep lines fanning out from the corners. "This is a spell I discovered in the archives. It's untested, but I am positive it will work." He moved to the wall and picked up a familiar green leather-bound book.

Archives? Liar! That book is from the hidden library. Thoughts tickled her brain as she put the clues together and she didn't like the answer. "Untested?" Tracey slid from the table and checked on Kylie. The younger girl's chest rose and fell as if she was in a deep sleep. She looked exactly like Frank Transcenni in his hospital bed.

"There are a collection of texts stored in the council's private archives—"

"No. That book is from the sect's hidden library. You found it. Or did you follow us?" She answered her own question. "You traced our phones."

He didn't even flinch at her accusation. None of this felt right. Hiding in an unused orphanage basement wasn't the behavior of someone permitted to do what he was doing. He was casting spells in secret, he had created the mumbles, and he'd sent a wide-reaching sleep spell through the old building to knock them all out. But did he get everyone? Hopefully her mom and Sarah had been outside the spell's reach and were okay. Maybe they would come looking for her. No. Agent Malden had known Tracey and her friends were all coming here. He'd had time to prepare. They had texted him all the details in the limo ride over! She felt so foolish. They had trusted the agent, and he'd betrayed them all.

"Tracey, my job entitles me to access all sorts of things." His shoulders hunched further. "You asked me to help you with the stones. The research I've been doing on your behalf —"

"The council doesn't know you're doing this," she accused.

"Do you want the stone removed from Kylie safely, or don't you?"

Not if you're doing it the wrong way. "What will you do with it when you take it off?"

His skin reddened around his sweat-damp collar. "I'll lock it away somewhere safe. Now, I need you to come over here. With two of us, the spell will be much easier to cast."

This was wrong. She didn't want to help him. But if he *had* discovered how to remove the stone from Kylie in a way that wouldn't harm her, should Tracey really stop him? "What do I have to do?"

He beckoned her closer. "Stand here at Kylie's head. You'll be inside the spell, so you'll feel a buzz and the push of power as the spell fights with Kylie's stone. When you feel the stone's grip on her weaken, you must remove it. Make sure you only touch it by the chain."

The bad feeling in Tracey's chest swelled up into her throat. She gritted her teeth and nodded.

"Brace yourself. I'm sealing the circle now."

She widened her stance. Every hair stood on end and her fingertips and nose tingled in the electrified air as the circle closed around her. Agent Malden opened the green book again. The sight of it made Tracey's skin crawl, overriding the tingles from the magic. It was as if knowing the book was one of the sect's hidden texts allowed her to sense the evil inside it. *I promised Damian I'd get the stone off Kylie. If this works, I'll have kept that promise.* What Agent Malden was doing might be good, but he was doing it the wrong way. He shouldn't have kept this a secret from her. It made it difficult to trust him now.

"Tracey, open your inner closet. Allow your magic out to fill the circle."

She did as ordered. Sparkling magic blurred her sight of Agent Malden. Her heart sang with the beautiful music of the raw energy swirling around her body. She called to Kylie in her mind. There was no answer. When Tracey's power fell on the girl Tracey could sense the sleep spell. It was dark and oily. Like bad magic. Like Timothy's magic.

Malden held the open green book with both hands and his body stilled as he read from it. "Through flame and shadow, ice and light, innocence and evil, thought and deed, you have remained strong and silent." Magic beat against Tracey's skin. Her hair flew as she was buffeted by the strong wind that sprang up inside the circle.

A howl filled Tracey's mind, echoing a loud scream. She jammed her fingers into her ears to block out the sound and slammed her eyes shut. She lost Agent Malden's voice and stumbled, grabbing onto Kylie's table. The scream dug into Tracey's mind, her throat was raw. *It's me. I'm screaming.* Clenching her jaw, she peeled her eyes open. The black stone tied around Kylie's neck by a silver chain floated in the air above her, bobbing on an unnatural wind. *I have to get the stone.*

Tracey's grandmother taught her that external forces could bombard the senses and weaken her magic. It was the same feeling she had now. She pushed against the wind, but it was like pushing over a brick wall. The roar of power in the circle grew louder. She couldn't hear a thing over it. Couldn't see anything around her. *What's happening to me?*

A pulse from the Serpent's Kiss rocked Tracey back onto her heels. *The stone is fighting the spell!* Tracey let all of the noise and light inside her body to become a part of her, so she could find her peaceful center and regain control. She breathed in the wind and the noise and the light, letting it settle right inside her bones. She opened her eyes and stretched for the Serpent's Kiss hovering above Kylie. The stone repelled her fingers, like pressing two magnets together. The Butterfly Stone floated up from Tracey's chest. She tried to shove it back under her shirt, but as her fingers brushed against it, the Butterfly Stone pushed her away.

Just like the Serpent's Kiss.

Tracey's wild stare darted to Jilly. The Tiger's Eye floated above her like a helium balloon attached to a child's wrist.

Malden wasn't trying to break the spell just on Kylie. He was targeting Tracey and Jilly as well. He was trying to steal the Butterfly Stone and the Tiger's Eye!

"No," Tracey whispered.

"Life is contained within the cell of your being. Break free of your prison. Return the life you have stolen, and your freedom will be found."

Agent Malden's body shone with sweat, his voice sounded thick and heavy in her ears as he poured power into his words.

The wind grew wilder, colder, sharper, like a hurricane, and Tracey was right in the center. She focused her anger on the man who had lied to her and took a trembling step toward him. "No!"

Her voice went unheard above the scream that filled her head.

The Butterfly Stone burst into silver flames—burning Tracey's skin. She gasped and tugged on the chain, her hands shaking violently. The stone would not yield. She couldn't take it off. She was going to die, burned up inside a living flame. *Kylie.* Tracey turned agonizingly slowly toward the unconscious girl. The black stone pulsed and glowed like a galaxy of stars. Kylie's entire body danced with tiny black flames. Jilly's fire burned blood red and crept over her skin like millions of tiny ants.

"No!" Tracey fell to her knees and then to the ground as the silver flames surrounded her body. "No."

"The ties that bind you must sever. The connection ends. Life begins anew!" Malden's voice became a scream. "Return her to me. Restore my heart. Give me back the life that was stolen."

A shadowy shape formed at Agent Malden's feet. The shape grew darker as oxygen was sucked from Tracey's lungs. The silver fire grew brighter, hotter on Tracey's skin. "No." Her voice was nothing more than a whisper now. "Help!" In her mind, Tracey formed her shield bubble around her body. *Fire needs fuel to burn. Needs oxygen to live.* She fought to extinguish the flames by exhaling all of the air from under her shield. Spots danced in her blurry vision. The fire disappeared. Tracey dropped her protective bubble and sucked in cold glorious air.

The shadowy form at Agent Malden's feet solidified into a desiccated husk of a woman.

A woman Tracey recognized.

"Give her back to me!" Agent Malden screamed.

Fruit tingles! The body was Agent Striker. Malden's dead partner. He was bringing her back using the combined power from Tracey, Kylie, and Jilly's stones.

She had to stop this. Millicent's voice thundered inside her head, ordering Tracey to stand up, to save her friends. *"Believe."*

Tracey pushed to her knees, grabbed the still burning Butterfly Stone in one hand and called for her magic. Called for everyone's magic.

Tracey screamed, pressing all of her horror and anger out of her body in one explosive blast.

I sleep. I Dream.
I cannot tell her
for it would break her heart.
For I see how it will all end.

30

The world shattered.

The Butterfly Stone in Tracey's hand turned to ice. Her breath misted and the concrete floor splintered beneath her body. Magic, swollen and silver, hung inside the circle, freezing time. Unmoving. Silent. Tracey glanced at Kylie and Jilly. Not a single burn or singe marred their skin. The flames were gone. *Oh, thank God.* Agent Malden knelt beside the remade body of Agent Striker. He held her tucked close to his chest. As time restarted, Agent Striker crumbled into dust. In a blink she was gone, caught up in a slight breeze and scattered across the room.

"Nooooooo!" Agent Malden wailed.

As the dust settled over the chalk circle, the containment field broke apart and the barrier keeping Tracey stuck inside it collapsed.

Malden launched up like a demon, his eyes wild, teeth bared. "You! How could you? You killed her."

Tracey climbed to her feet. "Agent Striker is dead. I didn't kill her. The Shadowman did."

"I brought her back. She was back."

"She wasn't real. You can't bring back someone who has died." Tracey had a flash of memory, Stephanie's desperate voice begging Millicent to come back as she pounded on Millicent's chest, pouring magic into her body, determined to save her. The devastation on Stephanie's face was the same expression as on Agent Malden right now.

Kylie and Jilly lay helpless, unprotected. They had been unable to fight back. How could he have done this to them? All for a woman who died months ago. Tracey clenched her fingers around the Butterfly Stone. "That wasn't a spell to remove the stones. You weren't helping us at all. Why did you lie to me?"

His cheeks were wet from tears. "Tracey, I didn't lie. I just—"

"You lied!" she roared. Her anger exploded and magic poured from her body in a whirlwind of silver sparkles. "You lied! You wanted the stones all for yourself. You said you were helping us and I believed you! I trusted you!"

Agent Malden raised his shield against her. "Tracey, you don't understand."

Fury smothered her reasoning. "You lied! You hurt Kylie and Jilly." *And me.* "You don't care at all. This is just about you and your horrible partner. You were using us. Using me."

He stepped forward.

Tracey raised her shield against him, spreading it out over Kylie and Jilly. "Get away from me, from all of us. I hate you!" Her magic burst forth in a wave of pure force throwing him backward into the wall. She pinned him in place with a furious magic infused hand. He let out a pained groan. "How dare you. We trusted you. I trusted you. Why!" Her skin glowed white hot with magic. Streamers of power ran from Jilly and Kylie, charging Tracey further as she stalked forward, growing larger with every step, becoming more powerful, a being of pure magic. She stared at the pitiful man stuck against the wall. "Why. Did. You. Lie?"

"Because I loved her."

Tracey's fury popped like a balloon. Confusion flooded her mind and her hands lowered a fraction. "What?"

"Agent Striker. Brigit. I loved her."

The pain on his face drained more of Tracey's anger. "But ... she was your work partner."

"It wasn't a permitted relationship. We couldn't help it. After years spent working together, years of living in each others' pockets, we grew close. I—we—fought it as long as we could but ... and then she was killed. Right in front of me. I couldn't save her. But the magic in the stones. There is so much power. Enough to restore life. If Timothy could restore his body, then I could save Brigit. I could bring her back. I had to try. Don't you understand? I had to try." He hung against the wall, staring at Tracey, begging her to understand.

"But Timothy is *in* the Serpent's Kiss. Stephanie is *in* the Butter-fly Stone. Jing is *in* the Tiger's Eye. A part of them is still here. Agent Striker—your Brigit—is gone."

"I had to try. Don't you see? I had to."

He was stuck on repeat, uttering the same declaration over and over again. Trapped inside his head, replaying the moment Agent Striker had been killed.

"You were willing to hurt us just to bring her back?"

"I had to try."

Tracey's anger turned to pity. She extinguished her magic hand and Agent Malden fell to the floor. The distraught M-force agent was nothing like the man she had come to know, the man she'd thought of as a friend. He lay curled on his side, rocking slightly, his eyes focused on some far-away spot, lost inside his memories. Tracey didn't know how to help him. She needed her mother, but her mother wasn't here. *What would Mom do?* Tracey knelt beside the rambling man. He looked smaller. A sad skinny shape of a man broken by his own heart. A tear ran down her face. "I'm so sorry." She didn't touch him. He was still an M-force agent, still a level three Mage-kind. His magic was dangerous, especially as he wasn't in his right mind. "Agent Malden, what sleep spell did you use on Kylie and Jilly? Can you wake them up now?"

"What?"

"The sleeping spell." She was afraid to get any closer, fearful of triggering him into lashing out again.

He squinted and shook his head. "Not a sleep spell."

"What do you mean?"

"Forbidden texts. Life for life. There must be an exchange. I needed power from the stones. I'm not strong enough on my own, it needs a coven—five Mage-kind of Significant status, or a Dreamer. Of course Dreamers don't exist. But the power from the stones could take the place of a Mage-kind."

His rambling didn't make sense. "We only have three stones. With you as a Significant that's only four."

"Didn't find the next stone in time. Full moon is today. Had to do the spell. I thought it would be enough. You, me, and three stones."

Oh. He thought Tracey would end up rating as Significant like her grandma? Like Agent Malden himself? "I'm not ... " Her voice faded at his knowing look. Perhaps she was — or would be. She shook her head. It wasn't something she could think about now. Her mind replayed his words. "Life for a life?" Her head snapped to Kylie and Jilly. "Oh no, no, no, no."

Leaving Agent Malden on the floor, Tracey ran to Jilly's side. "Jilly? Jilly wake up." She remembered Stephanie touching her fingers to Millicent's face. Tracey felt around for Jilly's pulse. It was faint, but it was there. *Oh, thank goodness.* She ran to Kylie and pressed her trembling fingers to the pale girl's neck. Nothing. Maybe she wasn't pressing in the right place. She moved her fingers against Kylie's cold skin and held her breath.

Kylie's lips were turning blue.

Tracey put her hand under the pale girl's nostrils. No breath. "Agent Malden! Kylie's not breathing."

He didn't get up. "I'm so sorry, Tracey."

"Help me!"

"It's all my fault," he said softly.

Tracey had drawn magic from Kylie and Jilly in her anger. Maybe it was her fault too? Still, it wasn't too late, not yet. It couldn't be. She turned, hands on hips and glared at the broken man. "Help me. We can still save her."

"It's too late. There's no saving anyone, no saving me."

Stomping to his side, she yanked on his shirt collar, forcing him to look up at her. "We are not losing Kylie. Get up and help me. You are an M-force agent. This is your damned job. If you want forgiveness, if you have even a smidgeon of a heart left, you will get off your butt and HELP ME!"

His eyes widened. She held his stare for long, wasted seconds. At last, he nodded and scrambled to his feet. Tracey ran to Kylie's side. "What do we do?"

He touched his fingers to Kylie's wrist. "Start resuscitation. Tilt Kylie's head back, pinch her nose and breathe two breaths into her mouth. I'll start chest compressions."

Tracey had done these classes at school but her mind was now totally blank. She hesitated. *What if I do it wrong?*

"Don't think, just do."

Tracey tilted Kylie's head back. The Serpent's Kiss fell against the girl's throat and Tracey quickly brushed it out of the way. The chain broke and it fell off the table onto Tracey's shoe. Tracey pinched Kylie's nose shut and breathed once into her mouth. Kylie's chest rose and fell.

"Again!" Agent Malden ordered.

She puffed more air into Kylie and watched as he pumped Kylie's chest rapidly, counting as he did so. When he reached thirty, he stopped and nodded. Tracey breathed into Kylie's mouth again, expanding her lungs. They worked solidly, Tracey's mind completely blank, counting, pumping, breathing.

After what felt like forever, she said, "We have to go get help."

"There's no phone signal down here."

"Should I run outside?" she asked. What had Stephanie done to resuscitate Millicent? She'd used magic.

Oh!

"Agent Malden?" The man kept counting, but his eyes swung to Tracey. "I have an idea."

"Eighteen, nineteen. Tracey, we must keep going, twenty-three, twenty-four."

"Stephanie used her magic to shock Millicent's heart."

"Twenty-seven, twenty-eight. Did you see how she —"

"Yes."

"Can you —"

"Yes."

He counted thirty and pulled his hands back. Tracey puffed two more times into Kylie's mouth and swung to the side, building power into her hands to make them glow. She pulled on her electricity storage until her hands buzzed and sparked, and sent her magic in a sharp pulse through Kylie's chest. Kylie jolted up and flopped back against the table.

Agent Malden held two fingers against Kylie's wrist. "Again," he ordered and pulled his hands away.

Tracey rebuilt her magic, stronger this time. She pushed it superfast into Kylie's chest. Kylie jolted up, gasping for breath, her eyes wide.

"Kylie?"

"Kylie!" Agent Malden's shout echoed Tracey's. He looked over and smiled. "Well done, Tracey. Go check on Jilly."

She spun around and the black stone sprang off the toe of her shoe. She ran to Jilly's side, leaning down to scoop up the Serpent's Kiss on her way. Her fingers sparked as she touched the black stone. She slipped it into her pocket and shook Jilly's shoulders.

Jilly moaned. Her head twisted side to side and her forehead scrunched like she was in a lot of pain. She didn't open her eyes. "I think she's waking up," Tracey called out.

Agent Malden spoke softly to Kylie and didn't appear to hear her. Tracey slumped on the table beside Jilly and scrubbed her trembling hands over her face, wiping beneath her eyes and sniffed snot up her nose. "What about everyone else?"

"What?" Agent Malden asked.

"Are they all asleep?"

He nodded.

"Can you break the sleep spell on everyone? Wake them all up."

"The spell will wear off in a day or so."

"A day? What about the people in the hospital?"

"The hospital is perfectly safe. My spell only traveled the pathways beneath and around the buildings."

"It was in the air vents! You don't know where it went. You weren't thinking of anyone but yourself. What about my mom? We can't wait a whole day for them to wake up." Tracey jumped to her feet.

Malden held up a hand. "Tracey, you just have to wait. There's no way to forcibly break it."

She wrapped her hands around the Butterfly Stone. She'd shocked Kylie's heart awake with her magic, what if she could do the same to everyone else? When she voiced the option, Agent Malden shook his head. "They're asleep. Shocking them might stop their hearts. It's far too dangerous."

She thought about how her magic worked. "I take magic from people. But I gave it back to Sarah and everyone when we were in the woods fighting the Shadowman."

"What?"

"If I boost everyone's magic, won't that overcome the sleep spell?"

"No. Tracey. Just wait."

Her glare should have frozen him solid. He had caused all of this, why was she even listening to him? The Butterfly Stone pulsed hot against Tracey's chest. "I am so tired of being told what I shouldn't do. Don't use my magic. Don't use the Butterfly Stone. Don't get angry. Don't cause trouble. I can't trust anything you say." Slamming her eyes shut, Tracey opened herself to her magic and grabbed the Butterfly Stone. Her pocket vibrated. She slapped a hand down to quiet it. *Not now.* She let her magic swell inside her body, building and growing hotter, stronger, louder, until her skin was almost bursting with it.

"What are you doing?" Agent Malden grabbed her arm.

Tracey threw him off. "Don't." She thrust her arms into the air — pouring her magic out of her body in a wide arc of explosive energy. *Wake up!* It flew through the walls and disappeared, leaving the room suddenly dark and silent.

"What did you do?" he asked.

In her mind Tracey heard her friends calling her name. And her mom. *Tracey?*

She answered them. *In the basement of the church. I'm with Kylie and Jilly.*

"What did you do?" Agent Malden said again.

"I woke everyone up." Tracey raised her shield bubble against the M-force agent. "Don't move. No wait. Get on your knees. I don't trust you. My mom is coming and she'll sort you out. Don't even think of using your magic."

He nodded. Face somber, he sank to his knees.

Jilly moaned and her eyes popped open. "What happened?"

Beneath Tracey's feet, the ground trembled. "Whoa!"

"What was that?" Jilly asked.

The ground trembled again. Or was it the building? *An earthquake?*

"Tracey, what did you do?" Agent Malden demanded from the floor.

"I woke everyone up," she told him. In her mind her mother shouted that they were on their way and to hang on.

The floor rocked and the walls shook. A long crack tore up the wall beside her. Ceiling plaster began to crumble. Agent Malden stared up at the roof, "That's not all you woke up."

As a child I tried to warn anyooo who
would listen, and I was punished foo my
temerity. Locked away in a round room where
the master believed I would be saved.

31

W hat do you mean?" Tracey demanded. Plaster and bricks flaked away from the walls and ceiling raining down over her head. Tracey stared at the damage in shock. "Woke what up?"

"The mumbles."

Tracey groaned. "Well, tell them to stand down, or shut them down."

Agent Malden shook his head. "You woke them up. I can't hear them anymore. The connection I had to them is gone. They're rogue."

"Oh great."

"Tracey?" Jilly's tired voice pulled Tracey to her side.

"Hey. How are you feeling?"

"Super tired. Like training for months on top of school exams and family parties kind of tired. "What happened? Why is Agent Malden on his knees?"

The M-force agent looked away as Tracey told Jilly and Kylie what happened. Jilly glared furiously at Agent Malden. "He did this?"

Kylie rubbed her cheeks. "I don't understand."

Tracey?

"Mom's almost here. Then we can figure out what to do with him."

"You're going to need my help," Agent Malden said.

Tracey scowled. "Yeah, that's not going to happen. When my mom gets here—"

"When I get here what?" Tracey's mom led her other friends into the room. They were all covered in grime and dust. Jonny, Dave, Noel, Tony, Sarah, and Laura stopped just inside the door, their chatter dying as they spotted Agent Malden.

Damian ran to his sister's side and yanked her into a tight hug. "Kylie!"

Tracey launched into her mom's arms. Her mother leaned back to stare at Malden without letting go. "Tracey?"

She could have gone into a lengthy explanation about lost love, heartache, and betrayal, and how Agent Malden had lied to them all, completely disregarding the danger to Kylie, Jilly, and herself, but all she said was, "He's the bad guy."

"What?" Tony and Laura shouted. Dave stomped toward the fallen agent, Tony and Noel hot on his heels. Tracey pulled from her mom's embrace and grabbed Tony's hand, tugging him back.

"You were right about Agent Malden. I'm so sorry I didn't believe you."

"I didn't expect … I didn't think it would be this bad."

"Wait a minute." Jonny held up his hand in the air like he was at school. "Are you saying Agent Malden did it all? The mumbles, the attack on the plane, everything? Why?"

"First things first. Is everyone safe? Anyone hurt?" Tracey's mom asked. The ground trembled again.

Jonny stared up. "Ah, we should probably get out of here, yeah?"

Tracey couldn't tear her gaze away from Damian and Kylie. Everything Damian had feared—that his mom had feared—had come true. Tracey brushed her fingers over her pocket. When would they realize Kylie was free of the Serpent's Kiss and its influence?

Sarah noticed something else first. "Kylie, your bracelet. Your magic is back!" Sarah ran to her friend's side and held up her arm. Kylie's bracelet glowed emerald. It no longer pulsed that horrible blue.

"Yay!" Kylie lifted her other arm so both were raised and cheered. "I can feel it! It's back."

"Oh, Kylie, the stone! Where's the stone?" Sarah pointed at Kylie's neck. Kylie's hands flailed around her shirt.

"It's gone!"

"You're not sick," Sarah said.

" … I'm not." Kylie's knees buckled as she fell back against the table. "Whoa! I'm a bit dizzy though."

"Where did it go?" Agent Malden stared at Tracey. "She was wearing it. I checked. Did my spell work?" The floor trembled as a massive bang rattled everything. The walls shook so hard Tracey feared the building might collapse on top of them.

"What the heck *was* that?" Dave asked.

The floor shuddered once more. Tracey's footing shifted and she widened her stance, her hand slipping inside her pocket. Her friends wobbled from side to side, like bad sci-fi spaceship acting.

"What the — ?" Jonny grumbled.

"Mumbles." Tracey reminded them. "Mom, stop. Don't go near Agent Malden." She warned as her mom approached the kneeling M-force agent.

Dave punched a fist into his other hand. "What do we do with him?"

"Stop!" Uncle Donny ran into the room. His hair was wild, sticking up in all directions and his clothing torn and stained. "Agent Malden betrayed … oh … " His voice died as he caught sight of the kneeling M-force agent.

"We already know, Uncle Donny," Tracey told him.

"Where have you been?" Sarah asked.

"He met me at the studio. Must have knocked me out and dragged me here. He lied to me!"

"We know," Tracey reminded him.

Uncle Donny stomped over to stand right in front of Agent Malden as the ground rumbled again. "We were friends, Trent. You put my nieces in danger."

"Don, I'm sorry."

"Honestly, I don't want to hear it. Wait — did you attack Frank Transcenni? He's dead, Trent, and someone shot at me!"

Agent Malden examined the floor as if it held all the answers. Tracey almost felt sorry for him and then was cross with herself. He was the bad guy. The ground trembled again, reminding her he had started all of this. "How do we stop the mumbles?" she demanded.

His head rose. "You'll need my help."

"Like we can trust you now," she hissed.

"The mumbles are my creation. I have put all of you in danger. Let me make it right."

Laura came up to Tracey's side. "He's been caught. We should trust him."

Tracey glanced at Tony. "You knew. Before all of us. What do you think? Can we trust him?" The floor trembled and chunks of ceiling fell away, hitting the floor in loud clumps.

"We don't have time for this," Dave said.

"Agreed." Tracey's mom helped Agent Malden to his feet. Uncle Donny moved closer. He probably thought he looked threatening. If Agent Malden knew what was good for him, he would be more afraid of Tracey's mom.

As if she'd heard Tracey's thoughts, her mom leaned close to Malden's ear and whispered something as she tightened her grip around his forearm. He gritted his teeth and nodded. Ohhh, her mom was scary. Tracey shared a look with her sister and hid her smile behind her hand.

"How do we defeat the mumbles?" Jilly repeated Tracey's unanswered question. She pulled her sash of powder bombs and her water pistol off the floor.

"What are they?" Kylie asked, pointing to Tracey's sash as she pulled it on. Kylie still sat on the table that had been her bed. Damian sat beside her, holding her hand.

"Weapons that Tracey's gran gave us," Jonny said, spinning his water pistol around his finger like a cowboy.

"Didn't work on Agent Malden though—we all fell asleep. How easy was it to defeat us, huh?" Dave said, snorting.

"The mumbles should have disintegrated when you put us to sleep. They'd succeeded in their mission, hadn't they?" Jilly asked.

Agent Malden shook his head. "I needed them to take you all back after … I put them in hibernation."

"Then do it again," Noel said. He stood close to Tony's side. "Put them back to sleep. Or just crumble them. Break the spell.

"I don't have the required ingredients." The trembling stopped. They all stared at the roof in concern. Somehow the silence was more disconcerting than the shaking.

"Do you think they've gone?" Sarah asked.

"No, they're still out there," Agent Malden said. "Waiting."

"Then we go kick clay butt," Dave said, brandishing his water pistol. "Remember. Dissolves clay. Couple of shots and boom. Dead mumbles."

"They're not alive," Agent Malden said. "You cannot kill what is not alive."

"Answer them, Trent." Uncle Donny stood in Agent Malden's way and stared him down.

"The mumbles are stronger, faster, and can problem solve. They will do everything they can to achieve their mission."

"So, what's their mission now?" Laura asked.

Agent Malden shrugged. "My connection with them has been broken. I don't know what they want now."

"How do we destroy them?" Jilly's voice had become hard and sharp.

"You need to trap them. Rather than crumble, they will wait you out, and when you grow tired of caging them, they will attack. You need to get in first. Get them on the ground and concentrate all your firepower in one spot. The mumble's stomach. That is where the Object of Power that gives it animation is located. Destroy that and the mumble disintegrates."

"How many mumbles are out there?" Dave demanded.

"Three."

"Right. So, we go in three groups and take one mumble each. You," Tracey's mom grabbed onto Agent Malden, "will stay with me."

Jilly, Jonny, Dave, Noel, and Sarah ran out through the door. "Come on, Tracey." Laura said. She and Tony waited for her in the doorway.

"What about me?" Kylie hopped off the table. "Do I get a gun?"

"Kylie, you need to rest. You're staying with me," Damian said.

Tracey's mom nodded. "Donald?"

"Ah, of course. I'll stay with them." Uncle Donny sat down on Jilly's table bed and clicked his fingers at Tracey's mom like guns. "Be careful with him." He lifted his chin in Agent Malden's direction.

"Actually, Mom. Uncle Donny should come with us. We might need his magic," Tracey said. Uncle Donny jumped to his feet so fast she thought his shoes would fly off. His wide grin took up almost his entire face. Mom's eyes widened in Tracey's direction.

"Fine. Damian, dear. Take Kylie outside. It's not safe to remain down here." Tracey's mom herded Uncle Donny and Agent Malden out through the door. Damian stood up.

Tracey turned to face him, wanting to explain. "Damian … "

"Go. Destroy the mumbles," he said. "We'll wait for you where the limo dropped us off. You saved her, Tracey. I don't know how you did it, but you got the stone off just like you promised."

She smiled up at him and didn't mention that for the stone to come off, his sister had died.

He pulled her into a quick hug. "Thank you."

"Oh, I … " His embrace was gentle and he smelled like sweat. She looked at his lips and wondered what it would be like to kiss him.

He looked down at her. "Can I, um, can I —"

"Will you kiss already?" Kylie snapped.

Damian groaned and Tracey laughed. "So, can I?" he asked.

"Sure," she said. *OMG, OMG.* His breath was a little sour, but his lips were soft. *My first kiss!* Laura cleared her throat. Tracey turned her head to see her friends waiting for her, grinning like two clowns. Tracey's fingers tightened around Damian's sleeves and her face burned with embarrassment.

"You'd better hurry," he said, letting her go. "Be careful."

Tracey led them out of the basement. Damian and Kylie turned left, heading toward the street while Tracey, Tony and Laura turned right, off to hunt the renegade mumbles. Laura poked Tracey in the arm as they walked. Tracey didn't say anything, but she was unable to wipe the smile from her face. *He kissed me!*

I have even crooted a magnifier here
and taught her how to strengthen our focus.
The room that once toomented me
is now my salvation.

32

Tracey was walking on air, and felt as if she could take on all three mumbles by herself. Her magic popped into her hands—glowing ping-pong sized balls that appeared and disappeared over and over again in the darkness. Tracey's mom, Agent Malden, Uncle Donny, and the rest of Tracey's friends were waiting for them in the overgrown courtyard outside the basement doors. "Where were you?" Dave complained.

Tracey forced the giant smile off her face. "We're here now."

The bell tower loomed over them. Only a few gray clouds marred the late afternoon sky. Out here, the garden was quiet. No thumping, no shaking, and no trembling. Jilly's back was covered in dust. Actually, they were all filthy, their clothes and hair streaked with muck and grime. The only bright color came from the sashes tied around their chests and from their fluro water pistols.

Jonny ran to Tracey's side. "I have an idea how to stop the mumbles. I mean they probably won't stand still for us to shoot them until they fall apart, right?"

"Good point. What's your idea?"

He held up his water pistol. "Remember how you got your button inside the mumble? Jilly stabbed a hole in it, and you threw it in. We do that. We spray a hole and then drop in these magic powder bombs and boom! Big explosion and lots of mumble bits everywhere."

Tracey skidded to a halt. "That's a pretty good plan."

"Course it is, it's mine."

"But how do we explode the powder bombs once the clay closes back over it?" Sarah asked.

"Hit it really, really hard," Uncle Donny said. "Let's make it an even bigger bang, shall we?" He called them all into a circle. "Put the sashes here."

When there was a giant pile on the grass, he pulled out his soft, squishy spell bag.

"Where'd you hide that?" Agent Malden exclaimed. "I searched you."

"Disguise spell. Hank gave it to me. I'm sick of being captured with no way to escape. I can't wait around for Tracey to save me every time," he said, nodding in her direction. He removed a vial of blue liquid and sprinkled the powder bombs with it. "They'll make a much bigger bang now. Once the bombs are in place, trip the mumble over. The fall should set them off. If not, hit 'em really hard with something."

They snatched back their sashes of magic balls and strapped them on. Malden pointed to the large double doors set into the side of the red brick wall stretching off behind the church. "They were in there." Dave and Jonny grabbed a handle each and tugged.

"It's locked," Dave said. Tracey ran between them and pressed her palm to the middle of the doors. In less than a second, everyone heard a loud clanking sound.

"Tracey?" Her mom squinted at her. "What has Donald been teaching you?"

She smiled innocently at her mom and shrugged. Uncle Donny avoided eye contact as the boys tugged open the doors.

A wide hall took them into an open rectangle of space. Any partitions and internal walls had long ago been torn out leaving just the four outer brick walls. It was a totally empty space and there were three mumble-shaped holes in the back wall. "Aw, fruit tingles," Tracey exclaimed. "They got out."

"Split up. Separate the mumbles so they can't cause too much damage," Uncle Donny said.

"And keep them away from the hospital," Tracey's mom ordered. "M-force will be here soon given all that earth shaking and three giant mumbles walking around wrecking things. Someone will have reported them. We'll have help and —"

"Ah," Agent Malden interrupted. "About that."

"What?" Uncle Donny turned on his old friend. He grabbed Malden's jacket collar and pushed him into the brick wall beside the doors. "Damn it, Trent, what did you do?"

"I informed headquarters there would be an emergency drill on site and that they should disregard any report of magic coming from this area."

"Oh, for crying out loud," Uncle Donny growled.

"I know, Don. As I said, I'm trying to make it right. There's a cell phone signal jammer at the perimeter."

"Where?"

"The junction box, outside the ambulance bay."

Uncle Donny addressed Tracey's mom. "I'll go. Much as I hate to admit it, you need this jerk with you." He spun back to face Agent Malden. "As soon as it's down—call your damned boss."

Agent Malden nodded. Uncle Donny ran off toward the hospital.

"Right. Draw the mumbles away from any people. Block it, confuse it, tag it, and then hit it hard, all right?" Tracey's mom ordered.

"Right," they agreed.

Tracey pulled on her magic and threw up a large sensory blanket. It sprayed out over the entire area. "I can't sense anyone. They must have run when they saw the mumbles."

"That will help."

"Hey, check it." Jonny pointed to the broken pavement. There was another dent outside the church heading away from the adjoining orphanage. He gestured to a third crumbling sidewalk. "This way."

"I'm not sure how smart it is to be running after these things," Laura said.

"There's a footprint over there." Jilly pointed, peeling off to the right with Jonny and Sarah. Screaming rose up from the hospital. Tracey's mom, Dave, and Noel ran in that direction, Agent Malden was tucked securely between them.

"Let's go this way," Laura suggested, waving at the path behind the church. It was a good choice. They immediately found the grass had been trampled by a giant foot. The bell tower cast a long shadow across Tracey and her friends.

"I can't believe it's so late," Laura said with surprise.

"Time moves weirdly when you're stuck underground," Tony told her. There was no telling how long they had been under the sleep spell. It was totally discombobulating. They found a courtyard nestled between all three buildings. The bell tower was behind them. The hospital on their right and the old orphanage on the left. An ancient tree with branches that stretched out like long fingers created a large leafy green canopy over a hexagon of bench seats that had been built around the base. The trunk was wider than Tracey could stretch her arms. Hospital windows peered down on the greenery and ordinarily she imagined it would be a nice place to sit and eat lunch. It was empty now. Anxious faces peered down at them, gesturing and silently shouting.

"There it is!" Laura said pointing to the tree. A mumble head poked up above the topmost branches then ducked away out of sight. There was a loud bang and the hospital wall shuddered.

What is it doing? "How do we get its attention?" Tracey asked.

"WWJD. What would Jonny do?" Laura grinned at her.

"Blow something up," they answered in unison.

Tracey pulled a powder bomb off her sash. "Tony and I will distract it and—"

A shout and several squeals erupted from behind the orphanage. "Sarah!" Tracey spun on a heel. Laura grabbed her arm, pulling her back around. "This mumble is right here."

"Tracey, your sister is doing her part. We have to do ours," Tony said.

"Right, right. Yeah, she'll be fine." Tracey closed her eyes and sucked in a quick breath. She opened her eyes and nodded. "You go left, Tony."

"Yep."

Tracey ran in the opposite direction around the tree. As soon as she caught sight of the mumble, she threw her first powder bomb. It exploded against the mumble's left leg, spraying powder and clay everywhere. The mumble wobbled as its leg buckled. It bellowed and bent over, squinting at Tracey and grumbling unhappily.

"Hey there," Tony shouted, popping up on the mumble's other side. He launched a dust bomb of his own. Pink powder and wooden fragments from the picnic seats sprayed out all over the mumble as the bomb hit the ground at its feet. The mumble bellowed and thudded toward Tony.

"Over here!" Tracey shouted, getting its attention back. She ran toward the mumble and then twisted, running away from it as it turned and came lumbering after her.

The next powder bomb she threw landed at the same time as Tony's, spraying red and green powder over the mumble's eyes.

While it was blinded, Tracey ran up behind its feet, squatted, and raised her shield bubble over her head, thickening the walls into a dome.

Tony's next powder bomb sent the mumble stumbling backward. It tripped over Tracey's rock-like form and hit the ground hard, throwing them all onto their butts. Tony blinded the mumble with another explosion of magic powder as Tracey wriggled out from under the mumble's leg. Laura climbed up the mumble's back, letting out a sharp squeal when it shook like a dog, trying to throw her off. Tracey grabbed hold of the mumble's left arm with her magical giant hand and pinned it to the ground. Tony held the mumble's right hand, stretching the monster out between them. Laura balanced precariously on the mumble's chest and sprayed her water pistol in a single spot on the mumble's belly, opening a large deep hole.

The mumble shouted and squirmed. Tracey and Tony held it down. Tracey even stretched out another magic hand to catch one giant clay foot to stop it from kicking them.

Laura dropped her entire sash of powder bombs into the clay hole. Softened clay flowed back over it, trapping the sash inside its belly. Laura looked down to find Tracey. "How do we trigger it?" she called, leaping safely off the mumble's chest. She landed on the ground in a stumbling run and fell to her knees, jumping back up to run off as Tracey and Tony released the mumble's limbs. It climbed to its feet, pushing up off the ground with its enormous hands. A violent crash came from somewhere off to the right. Dave and Noel cheered loudly, whooping and hollering. One mumble down.

The ground shuddered and a long crack formed in the brickwork of the bell tower, traveling swiftly upward with a popping, tearing sound.

Mortar, ground into dust by the moving bricks, sprayed out from the tower in a cloud of particles. Above their heads a crow circled and cawed loudly. Tracey's head snapped up, searching the sky for the black bird and caught the wobble in the tower. *Oh oh.* With another ripping sound the crack in the tower spread. Another smack of the mumble's stamping foot hit the ground sending a rumble through the wall. The top half of the tower slipped a fraction sideways. "Ah, team?" Tracey called.

"How do we explode the bombs?" Tony shouted. Laura ran to his side. Tracey quickly joined them.

"Look." The bell tower cracked right through the middle in a long, jagged diagonal. The top half slid again. Popping noises echoed deep inside the brickwork.

"We should run," Laura said.

"Yep," Tracey agreed.

They bolted away from the church. The mumble shook its head and thundered after them. *We have to stop it moving.* She spun around and fired her water pistol at the mumble's legs. Laura and Tony jerked to a halt and ran back to spray its feet too. "Hope you know what you're doing," Laura said.

The mumble fell, swiping out with its giant arms on the way down. "Tracey, what are we doing?" Tony shouted as they jumped side to side to avoid the wild blows.

"Listen!" Tracey shouted. A rhythmic thumping was coming closer. Jonny, Jilly, and Sarah ran around the corner at full speed, their mumble right behind them.

"Tracey!" Jonny shouted and pointed.

From the other direction, Tracey's mom, Noel, Dave, and Agent Malden appeared. "Ha! We got ours!" Dave shouted.

An ear-splitting crack shot through the air. "Get clear," Tracey bellowed. The bell tower broke off completely and landed straight on Tracey's injured mumble. Its chest was instantly crushed, setting off the powder bombs inside.

Boom!

Bricks and clay went flying. The bell clanged once as it flew through the air and landed right on top of Jonny's mumble, squashing it flat. A second boom sprayed debris across the courtyard and all over the gathered teens. When silence fell and the ground stopped rumbling, Tracey straightened out of her crouch. She stared at the disaster area. Clay, bricks, mortar, and dust coated everything, but the hospital was undamaged. She shook clay bits off her clothing. Laura did the same. Jonny took off his hat and slapped the dust off it before plonking it back on his head. Tony checked his phone was undamaged as Noel and Dave whooped in delight. Sarah ran over and hugged Tracey tightly.

"Not bad, Tracey," Agent Malden called. "Not bad at all."

The center is my heart.

My special place.

A place where I can be at peace.

33

They sat outside the hospital in the children's playground as they waited for Uncle Donny to return. He ran up, followed by an M-force team. Malden stood and placed his hands on his head. He was calmly cuffed while the M-force officers spoke to him softly. Before he was led away, he asked to speak to Tracey. The officers stepped away as she approached.

"You stopped me from making a big mistake, Tracey. I'm sorry for everything that has happened here. My grief blinded me to what was right. I just wanted her back." His skin was shiny with sweat and streaked with dust. It was like looking at a thin china shell of the real Agent Malden. His hair still had that white patch, but there was a lot more gray to hide it now.

"What will happen to you?"

"I'll be fired. I may go to prison. It will depend on the investigation report and the presiding judge. I need to see a professional and deal with my grief in a better way. I'm sorry, Tracey. I put all of you in danger."

"You orchestrated the attack on our plane, didn't you?"

"I needed to test the strength of the stones."

"I still don't understand.

"When you located both the Tiger's Eye and the Serpent's Kiss, I realized you might hold the power I needed to bring Brigit back. I had to be sure."

"I'm sorry you were hurting so much. I wish you'd told me."

"So do I. Our training teaches us to hide our emotions. It's unhealthy and it leads to secrets, lies, and bad habits. I should have talked to someone about how I was feeling. So I will tell you now, I fear for you and your friends."

"Why?"

He was tugged away by the agents but resisted long enough to say.

"Timothy's stone has disappeared. I fear for whoever finds it. You must track it down, Tracey. I don't understand where it went. I know it was around Kylie's neck. I checked several times. It was necessary for my spell to work."

Tracey's hand slipped into her pocket, and she shrugged. "The stones seem to get found when they're supposed to be found. I'm just glad Kylie is okay."

"Be careful, Tracey." Agent Malden was led toward the waiting M-force SUVs. Mom and Uncle Donny stopped Malden before he was put into the car.

"What do you think they're talking about?" Sarah asked coming up to stand beside Tracey.

Tracey shrugged, keeping her hand inside her pocket. "He was Uncle Donny's friend and he'd promised to look after us."

"Yeah, Uncle Donny's angrier than I think I've ever seen him."

The limo pulled up to the curb and the teens piled inside. The ride back to the manor house was quiet, each lost in their own thoughts. They climbed from the limo and watched it depart down the long, long driveway. Dave poked Tracey in the arm. "What happens now?"

She shrugged and stared up at the manor house. Uncle Donny's client was dead, Agent Malden had been arrested, and Prince Henry was in hiding. "They'll probably send us home."

Off to the side, she spotted Noel speaking quietly with Tony. Should Tracey tell him about the secret library hidden inside his home? She was sure Agent Malden had found that spell book there. The other texts were probably dangerous too. But if Noel and his father didn't know about the room, then the council wouldn't find out about it. Perhaps one day soon Tracey would get to come back and investigate further. She decided not to mention it. Her gaze drifted to the maze as Jonny and Jilly walked up, holding hands. Laura tagged along behind them.

Tracey rubbed her arm. "Mom said she's going to talk to Noel's dad about the curse they put on our magic. Hopefully, the council won't renew it. We did stop Agent Malden after all." Tracey turned. "Where's Damian and Kylie?" Her lips tingled a little at the memory of kissing the handsome boy.

Jonny pointed into the distance at a black cab driving away. "My mom is going with Mrs. Carter and Kylie to a local Mage-kind doctor. They want to check she's okay. Damian went with them. He waved at you, but you were talking to Agent Malden."

Darn. She'd hoped to talk to him before his mom arrived. She checked her phone. No messages. She typed out a quick text. Damian's reply was almost instantaneous.

I didn't want to interrupt. Kylie keeps saying she's fine but Mom wants proof. She's happy the stone is gone but not about Kylie's magic coming back. Jonny's mom is talking to her so fingers crossed.

Tracey grinned. Damian had ended his text with a kissy face emoji. "Kylie is safe now. And she has her magic back."

Sarah nodded. "She thinks her mom is going to change their flights to make them leave tomorrow."

Tracey hugged her sister and then let her go, slipping her hands back inside her pockets. "They'll send us all home I think. It feels like everything is over. I'm sorry about that film scene. I don't know what will happen to Prince Henry's movie now that he's been outed. The set was destroyed so it'll probably be massively delayed. They might not even keep the scene you guys filmed."

"They can't send us back yet. We have to find the other stone, right Tracey?" Dave asked.

A crow caw snapped her head up. Tracey's gaze followed the sleek black body as it swooped over the entrance to the maze.

"Should we go inside and keep searching for it?" Laura asked.

Jilly was staring at Tracey. Her head cocked to one side. "You know where it is, don't you?"

The friends quickly surrounded her, peppering her with questions, but Tracey ignored them. She leaned around Jonny's body. "Hey Tony, wanna come with us?"

Tony jerked away from Noel. "Huh?"

Dave and Jonny snorted.

Tony's face reddened. He grabbed Noel's hand and walked over to join them. "Hey," he said, stopping beside Tracey.

"Hey." Tracey grinned broadly at her friend. "Let's go find Millicent's stone."

"You know where it is?" he asked.

She nodded and led her friends into the maze. She pointed out the crow sitting on top of the hedge.

"A crow? That's supposed to be bad luck," Noel said.

"Unless they like you," Tracey murmured.

Laura caught on quickly. "You said the picture on the stone was a bird?"

"I think Millicent loved them. That crow's pretty special. Come on." The crow hopped from the top of one hedge to the next, looking back and croaking at them. "Follow the crow, I guess," she told her friends.

The crow led them deep inside the maze. Tracey and her friends stayed quiet as they followed along behind it. The air grew colder as they traveled inward and a mulchy scent hung heavy in the air. As they walked Tracy told them about the entries in Millicent's diary.

"So, Stephanie gave Millicent a maze?" Sarah asked.

Tracey nodded. "Yeah, in the memory Grandma showed me, I saw them racing each other through the maze. Millicent really seemed to love it." She also remembered Millicent's collapse and Stephanie's terror at losing her friend. She had experienced that same terror seeing Kylie lying so still in front of her. Thank goodness they'd saved her.

"Where do you think the Serpent's Kiss went?" Laura asked. The crow led them around turn after turn, left, right, left and left again, moving them further and deeper into the maze.

Tracey shrugged. "I'm just glad it's gone." She slipped her hand into her pocket and brushed her fingers over the missing stone. It was cool to her touch and smooth, almost slippery. She didn't know why she didn't tell her friends she had it. So many people had tried to get the power from this stone. People had been hurt, nearly killed. It was safer that no one knew where it was.

"If we do find Millicent's stone, then what?" Jonny asked filling the silence.

Tracey turned right at the next T-intersection. Up ahead the crow hopped along the hedge looking back occasionally to make sure they were still following. They went right again then turned immediately left.

"Start looking for the next one," Tony said.

"Do we have any clues about it?" Dave asked. "I don't know about you, but I just want to sleep for a week. Can't we take a break?"

"Dave's got a point," Laura said.

Dave grinned broadly and pointed to his own chest. Tony snorted.

"We have to keep going," Jonny said.

Jilly nodded. "Jonny is correct. We must ensure Timothy cannot get his hands on the other stones. Without knowing where the Serpent's Kiss is, Timothy could be out there already searching. We cannot let him get to them first."

Tracey opened her mouth and then closed it again.

Dave halted. They all stopped to look back at him. "But we have two, nearly three stones. Timothy only has his own. Even if he finds the other two that's only three stones out of six. He can't come back with only three stones. Not enough magic, am I right? So we've already won. As long as Jilly and Tracey hold their stones, we've won."

Tracey walked forward until she stood right in front of him. "Three stones still hold a lot of magic, Dave. Timothy can still hurt a lot of people. We actually need to stop him. Stop him from influencing anyone he possesses." Her hand clenched around the stone in her pocket. "We have to find them all."

"Whoa, chill Tracey. We will. We'll find them." Jonny said throwing up his hands. Her friends were all staring at her.

"Sorry. I guess I'm pretty tired too," she told them. The crow landed on the hedge beside her and squawked loudly. "Let's keep moving, otherwise it'll be dark before we get out of here." She waved at the crow and it took off again. Tracey led her friends deep into the maze until at last they reached a dead end.

"Well, now what?" Jonny asked.

"I remember this. From the Vision in the amplifier. Hang on." Tracey pressed her hands against the far wall. In the Vision she had been sucked into the hedge. Nothing happened. She leaned in and felt something flat and hard, like wood. She pushed. There was a loud click and the whole hedge wall swung inward on creaky hinges that probably hadn't been opened since Millicent's last trip in here.

They stepped into a round empty clearing surrounded by hedges. "Wait." Tracey spun in a circle. "This isn't right. I remember a statue right in the middle. A baby angel."

"There's nothing here," Dave said. He walked the perimeter. "There's no other exit. We must be right in the middle of the maze. What do we do now? Why did the crow bring us here?"

"Tracey, do you feel that?" Sarah asked. She held up her hand as if pressing on an invisible wall."

"Magic," Noel and Tony said together.

Tracey sensed it too. Old magic. She peered back at the manor house rising high above the maze walls. "Inside the house was Stephanie's domain. But out here, this was Millicent's place. This was where she felt free." The Butterfly Stone warmed against Tracey's skin. From the corner of her eye, she spied Jilly's hand drift over the Tiger's Eye and knew she felt it too. "There's a settled spell here." Tracey closed her eyes and let her magic out to fill her body. She called on the Butterfly Stone, and her body buzzed with bright, shining, silver power. Suddenly she knew what to do, almost as if Millicent had whispered into her ear. "Hold my hands."

Jilly took one hand, Sarah took the other. Jilly stretched for Tony. Noel locked onto Tony's other side. Dave grabbed hold of Noel and Sarah, closing the circle of Mage-kind. "Show us what is hidden," Tracey whispered and the air blurred. Laura gasped. She and Jonny stepped back, watching the magic dance like dust motes in the sunlight. The glowing particles spun faster and faster until a shape appeared. It was the angel statue from the Vision. It held an arrow pointed at the ground.

At the base of the statue was a skeleton in a tattered blue dress. The crow swooped and landed on the ground. It hopped closer to the skeleton and cawed sadly.

"Oh," Sarah gasped.

"That's Millicent," Tracey whispered. If she released the hands of her fellow Mage-kind she knew the remains would disappear, never to be seen again.

"She died," Laura said. "Out here all alone. How sad."

The Butterfly Stone grew warm and burned, pulsing with a bright silver light. The Tiger's Eye on Jilly's chest glowed crimson, and Tracey's pocket vibrated. "Let me try something," Tracey said. She remembered the spell her uncle cast back in the bell tower. He had used pink powder as a catalyst. She didn't have any, but she knew who would. "Jonny, can you throw your powder bomb into the air?"

"How did you know I kept … fine." He pulled the small magic infused bomb from his pocket and launched it into the air. Tracey focused her magic and exploded it mid-flight, muttering the word mash Uncle Donny had used. Glittery blue powder floated down over the clearing, swirling around in the breeze.

"Millicent, show us your final moments," Tracey whispered and sent her magic into the powder.

It probably shouldn't have worked. But with the amount of magic flowing between the teens and Tracey's remembered spell, it did. The clearing grew blindingly bright, and when the light died away a woman in glittering blue strode into the clearing. A violet-blue stone pulsed around her neck. She panted as if she had been running.

"She can't breathe," Sarah said.

Tracey's sister was right. Millicent's chest heaved as she struggled to get enough air. She stumbled and fell at the base of the statue, staring up at the manor house above the maze walls. A voice traveled to their ears. Weak, yet full of emotion. Anger. "The fire cleanses the darkness and destroys evil," Millicent said to the manor house. Her breath caught again and she wheezed.

"Can you see … " Tracey whispered.

"Yes," Laura said, her voice full of awe and sadness.

Tracey wished she could help but they could only watch as Millicent's breathing grew more labored. The ghostly woman began to shake. Her head knocked against the stone plinth several times and after a dull crack she stopped moving. The crow let out a mournful croak and flapped its wings. The ghostly woman faded and her body became the skeleton once more.

"She was all alone when she died," Jilly said, releasing Tracey's hand to wipe under her eyes. As the circle of magic broke, they separated and stared, sad and silent, at the bones of the tragic woman.

"Why is she still here?" Dave asked.

"Because we broke her spell—the one that kept this place hidden," Tracey told them.

The crow hopped onto the skeleton and tugged at a silver chain. It pulled a deep blue, heart-shaped stone out of Millicent's ribcage.

"Whoa, wait, don't—" Tracey said, but the crow flapped straight to Jonny and dropped the stone on his head.

He caught it with both hands. "Ouch!"

Tracey smiled. "I think it just chose you as its protector, Jonny."

"But I'm not Mage-kind," he stuttered. His hands closed tight around the stone.

"I don't think that matters, Jonny," Laura said. "Remember, Officer Jameson wasn't Mage-kind."

"I believe you are a protector, Jonny." Jilly offered him a small smile. "Being a protector is not about being Mage-kind but whether you are loyal and true. Your heart makes you a protector, Jonny. Not magic."

Jonny held up the stone. "Aw man, I can't wear a stone shaped like a heart. What will everyone say—what will my brothers say?"

The friends laughed. "They won't even notice," Laura said.

"Besides with your sense of style, you could just tell them it's the next big internet thing. They'll believe it," Tracey said.

"I think it's very manly, Jonny," Sarah said, grinning wildly.

The deep blue heart had tiny pink flecks inside, and the picture of a crow etched into it. Jonny scratched at the crow. "It looks scratched but it's more like it's burned on."

Tracey clapped a hand on his shoulder. "Welcome to the stone club, Jonny."

"Does this mean I'll get possessed by Millicent?" he asked, white teeth pressing on his lower lip.

"Who knows? I guess we'll soon find out," she told him.

"Try and put it down," Jilly suggested.

Jonny dropped the stone on the ground and walked away a few steps. When nothing happened, he shrugged. "Guess it doesn't lock onto someone who's not Mage-kind." He picked up the Crow's Heart and pulled the chain over his head, tucking the stone under his shirt.

Dave scoffed. "Ha! Heart necklace."

Jonny lifted his head proudly. "Hells, yeah! Chosen one, right here." He pranced around the perimeter of the clearing, holding his hands up cheering like he had just won a boxing match.

Tracey and her friends laughed. "You have to keep it a secret," Sarah reminded him.

"Sarah's right. Plenty of people are after the stones. We can't let anyone know Jonny is holding one. We can't put him at risk," Tracey said. "Without magic, he can't protect himself the way we can."

"Eventually, whoever has Timothy's stone will come after us for the ones we have. We must be prepared," Jilly said.

They all nodded. Tracey pulled her hand away from her pocket. "Right. We should probably … no, I guess we can't tell anyone about Millicent's body. They'll know we have her stone. What should we do? We can't leave her here."

"We should bury her. There must be a gardener's shed nearby," Jonny said, glancing at Noel to confirm.

Jilly held up one finger. "We should hold a Mage-kind funeral."

Tony and Noel nodded. "That would work," Noel said.

"I've never been to one before," Tracey said. "My grandmothers are both alive and my grandfathers were Norms. They were buried the Norm way."

"It's pretty simple," Noel said. "Everyone form a circle around Millicent." The teens clasped hands and Noel called for their magic. Outside the Mage-kind circle, Jonny and Laura bowed their heads.

"We pass this life into the shadows of time," Noel said loudly. His voice was older, deeper, filled with mystery and sadness. "She was lost and alone, but now she is surrounded by friends. She is welcomed into your embrace with love and sorrow."

Their magic swelled and a bright orange glow settled over the skeleton. It shone brighter as Noel spoke. "Take her into your light. Take her home to where she will be loved forevermore." The light grew impossibly bright and when it faded Millicent was gone.

The crow squawked and took flight. They watched it glide away until its black wings formed a silhouette in the late afternoon sky. "You're not alone anymore," Tracey whispered to the wind and wiped away her tears.

For I am not mad. I am magic...

34

Prince Henry met them at the airport gate to say goodbye. Their flight home was due to depart in less than an hour, but it felt as though they had been at the airport for half a day. They sat sprawled across the lounge talking softly, and waited for their boarding call. Tracey was reading Millicent's journal. Knowing what she knew now, each passage seemed more tragic. She glanced up at Prince Henry's "*hello*" and wanted to hug him as soon as she saw him. His face was covered in rough stubble, and his skin looked dry and pasty. There were heavy shadows beneath his eyes. He stood with his hands in the pockets of his casual suit—no necktie—and looked them over.

"I didn't think we'd see you again before we left," Tracey said after the group welcomed him back.

"Tracey, can I speak to you for a moment?"

"Sure." She shoved the journal into her bag and pushed it closer to Sarah. Tracey waved at her mom and grandmother and wandered down the concourse with the famous actor. A buzz of magic electrified the air around them. Tracey assumed Prince Henry had cast some sort of glamour spell to avoid catching undue attention. There was a shiny new Mage-kind identification bracelet around his wrist. "How are you doing?" she asked.

"It's been a tough week."

"I'm sorry everyone found out."

They wandered toward the large windows overlooking the taxiway and stared out at a plane pulling up to the jetway. Tracey wasn't sure where to start. "What will happen to Agent Malden?"

"He's—ah—taking a forced leave of absence while they investigate his actions."

"He's not in trouble?"

"Oh he is. But who knows how it will end up, he has many friends on the council. He'll have to deal with what he did and come to terms with why he did it. It's a hard road to forgiveness."

"I forgave him."

"Not from you, Tracey. He needs to find it in himself. I hope he pulls through."

"It's sad."

"It is." Prince Henry stared down at his feet. "How could you forgive him? I'm not sure I would have been so magnanimous."

"He loved Agent Striker. I think love is really hard for a lot of people if it gets cut off too soon. It can go bad and rot from the inside out," she said, thinking of Timothy. "I think if you don't love yourself first it can really mess things up. Agent Striker was his partner—his one true love, and she died right in front of him. He was angry because he couldn't save her, and in his desperation to make things right his reasoning was clouded. It's not really his fault—or it *is*, but he's full of pain right now. He can't see the truth yet."

"That's a very mature way to look at it, Tracey."

"Yeah well, I can't fix him. I've been reading more of Millicent's journal." She snorted when he did a double take. "Yeah, I found it. Sorry I didn't tell you. Anyway, Millicent was alone for a really long time. When Stephanie wanted to be her friend she latched on so hard, she was willing to ignore all the bad things that happened around her because she didn't want to lose her new family. Timothy claimed to love Stephanie, but he was hurting her, and Stephanie … well, I'm not really sure who she loved."

Tracey's thoughts turned to Damian. His smile, his laugh, his warm lips. She thought about Tony and Noel too. Tony's red gaze and forced smile told her how pained he was to be leaving. He had been glued to his phone ever since they drove away. "So, what happens now?"

"You'll get a new handler."

Tracey glanced up. "Not you?"

Prince Henry shook his head. "Now that everyone knows I'm Mage-kind, my usefulness as an undercover agent has ended."

"Did they fire you?"

"No, but they've taken me off field work for a while. Until the media circus dies down. I don't know how long that's going to be."

"Oh." Tracey flipped her phone between her hands. "So we get someone new?"

"Yes. But she's an old school friend of mine. I trust her completely. You'll like her."

"Your friend?"

"Yes. I can't wait to introduce you actually. She's flying into Milton Falls next week."

"Okay," Tracey said. She would have to be okay about it. There wasn't anything else she could do. "Will the council curse us again? Our sentence still stands, doesn't it? We can't use our magic?"

"Your mom, grandmother, the council, and M-force are still discussing all of that. I don't know what the result will be. Given you know how to break the curse, I'm not sure it would do any good to reimpose the sentence."

She snorted. "What about your movie? Are you going to finish it?"

"Yeah. They're rebuilding the set, so we're on official hiatus. Fortunate, because after I introduce you to my friend, I have to go home. My mother has sent for me."

Tracey grimaced. "Oh, oh." The queen had called him home. If she was anything like Tracey's mom when she was mad, Prince Henry was going to have a lot of explaining to do.

"She's not happy about all the publicity."

"I'll bet."

"You can still email or call me whenever you need."

"I'm really sorry everyone found out you're Mage-kind."

He hummed. "I guess all of our lives have changed since you found the Butterfly Stone," he said.

"Yeah."

Prince Henry turned around. "Take care, Tracey. I'll keep looking, but since you were unable to find Millicent's stone with the Butterfly Stone's magic, I'm not sure I will be able to. And now that we've lost Timothy's stone—at this stage that's the more dangerous one out there. Our top priority is to find it."

Tracey didn't tell him they had found Millicent's stone. Agent Malden's betrayal made her afraid to trust anyone. "I hope you find them." Tracey's hand slipped back into her pocket. "At least Kylie is safe."

"There is that. Take care of your friends, Tracey. I'll be in touch next week."

Prince Henry walked away down the concourse. Tracey waited until he disappeared into the crowd. When he was out of sight, she pulled the Serpent's Kiss out of her pocket. The stone was the blackest of blacks. A rich, blood-red snake swirled down the center and depending on the angle she imagined she could see a pair of snake eyes. She pulled the chain over her head. As the stones touched, the Serpent's Kiss and the Butterfly Stone screamed.

Tracey opened her eyes in a dark place—a black worse than night. There was no moon or stars or even lamplight to break the nothingness. A shadowy man appeared in front of her, glowing red from within. A man she recognized.

Timothy's face creased in a grin.

"Hello Tracey."

About the Author

Laurie Bell is a former teacher who has worked with children of all ages in the literary sphere. She is a science fiction aficionado who is regularly featured by publications such as the Antipodean Science Fiction E-Magazine.

Laurie maintains an active blog of science fiction, fantasy, and flash fiction pieces, and serves as a volunteer in her local theatre company.

Discover more about Laurie Bell at:

www.solothefirst.wordpress.com

A Thank You from the Author

Covid in Australia is/was a crazy time. I wrote the Crow's Heart during one of the many lockdowns in Melbourne and edited it during several more. It was hard to concentrate, hard to be motivated, and hard to finish what I'd started, but I persevered and here we are. Tracey and her journey kept me going. To anyone who finds it hard to pick up a pen, it is worth it. There have been times where I have stared at a page and wondered, "What on earth am I doing?" Despite my doubts and imposter syndrome, I kept writing because I needed to tell Tracey's story. I'd like to thank the following people who helped make the Crow's Heart what it is.

Linh, the last few years have been crazy! I've loved our motivating talks, regular catch ups, and writing sprints. Talking to someone going through their own writing journey (though a different journey) helped me to realize that we are not alone in our writing bubbles—no matter how isolated and lonely it may seem at times. Writing is what we do and it is who we are. Your creativity astounds me and humbles me. I love your books and your art and your passion. Thank you for your advice and friendship. May we one day end up on the same desk signing books together!

To the **#Auswrites** crew—you get me. You keep me inspired with your words of wisdom and motivating calls to arms. I have found so many new writer friends on this thread and so many amazingly talented Aussie writers. I love the support, well wishes, and monthly prompt ideas. **#readmoreaussiebooks #Auswrites**

Australian Book Lovers!! Thank you for your support and for your incredible website and podcast. Veronica and Darren, you are amazing. Thank you for everything that you do.

If you haven't visited this website yet, why not? It is a font of information. If you didn't know about this website—I forgive you but get onto it immediately! Visit **www.australianbooklovers.com** to find some incredible reads, podcasts, and interviews. Aussie authors are the best! Love **@australianbooks**.

Carolyn and Edmund (and of course, Linh) for your CP & Beta-ery goodness! Every time I receive an email from you, my writing becomes better. You are all fabulous. Thank you for your valuable time. Keep on keeping on. I can't wait to read more of your words soon.

Martha and Frank — thank you for entering and donating to the 2020 Australian Bushfire Relief **#AuthorsForFireys** twitter campaign! It took a little while but here we are!

Mum and Dad, who keep reading and bugging me to find out what happens next. *Shhhhhhh, spoilers.* Wait until you see what happens next. Thank you for all your support! I love you both.

Nana. I love you. And I miss him too.

For all the kids I taught in the few short years I was a teacher — you will always inspire me. And to Elise and Taylah … you absolute stars, keep reading!

To all the readers who have contacted me online to tell me about reading *The Stones of Power,* and for those who share their reviews and photos and well wishes, I love hearing from you. I hope you love *The Crow's Heart* as much as I do. Do what makes you happy and sod anyone who tells you that you can't do something. If trying something makes you scared, try it anyway. You CAN do anything. You can BE anything.

Hayley and Stefanie (BFFs forever and always).

Lauren Lynne, THANK YOU.

The Wyvern's Peak Publishing team: D.C. McGannon, Michael McGannon, and Holly McGannon — thank you for believing in this series and in Tracey's journey. Thank you for jumping onto the merry-go-round once more with me. Without you, this series would not exist in its current form! I really appreciate you all.

James Gatherum-Goss and the Team at Dymocks Knox City in

Victoria, Australia. Thank you for all your support. To see my books on your shelves is a dream come true. Thank you for supporting local authors. Readers ... get out there and support your local bookshops and booksellers! They are truly awesome people.

Oh, and to Libby, Brigitte, Elise, Lisa, Jen, Kathy, Luneah, Stefanie, Hayley, Justine, Blair, Amber, Anthony, Cathy, Brian, and Berny — sorry for making you wait so long.

Gerry. I love you.

Thank you!

Please consider leaving a review on your favourite bookish websites.

Another stone is coming ...

For this and other exciting titles, visit:

www.WyvernsPeak.com

www.twitter.com/WyvernsPeak
www.facebook.com/WyvernsPeak

Sign up for our newsletter, get free stuff, and be the first to know when new books from your favorite Wyvern's Peak authors are released.

Follow Laurie Bell on Twitter

@LaurienotLori

Like Laurie on Facebook

www.facebook.com/WriterLaurieBell

Visit her website at

www.solothefirst.wordpress.com